Toric's Dagger

BY JAMIE EDMUNDSON

THE WEAPON TAKERS SAGA
TORIC'S DAGGER
BOLIVAR'S SWORD
THE JALAKH BOW
THE GIANTS' SPEAR

BOOK ONE OF
THE WEAPON TAKERS SAGA

TORIC'S
DAGGER

JAMIE
EDMUNDSON

Rarn
Publishing

Toric's Dagger
Book One of The Weapon Takers Saga
Copyright © 2017 by Jamie Edmundson. All rights reserved.
First Edition: 2017

ISBN 978-1-912221-00-4

Author website jamieedmundson.com

Cover: Streetlight Graphics

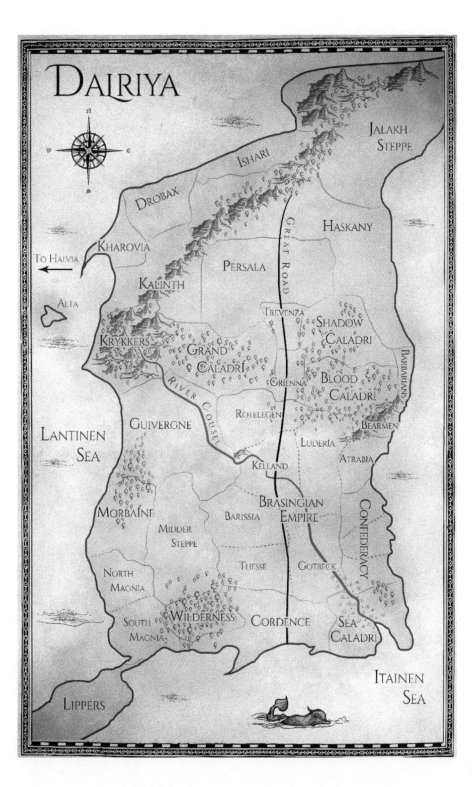

Dramatis Personae

South Magnians

Soren, a wizard

Belwynn, Soren's sister

Herin, a mercenary

Clarin, Herin's brother

Farred, a nobleman of Middian descent

Gyrmund, Farred's friend, an explorer

Edgar, Prince of South Magnia

Leofwin, Edgar's bodyguard

Brictwin, Edgar's bodyguard

Ulf, an apprentice smith

Bareva, Ulf's wife

Wulfgar, high-priest of Toric

Otha of Rystham, magnate, Wulfgar's brother

Ealdnoth, Edgar's court wizard

Wilchard, Edgar's chief steward

Oslac, Mayor of Halsham

Harbyrt the Fat, Marshal of the North

Kenward, a sheriff

Aescmar, a magnate

Burstan, a captain in the army

Hallaf, an outlaw

North Magnians

Elana, a priestess of Madria

Cerdda, Prince of North Magnia

Mette, Cerdda's mother

Ashere, Cerdda's younger brother

Sherlin, an earl

Middians
Brock, a tribal chief
Frayne, a tribal chief

Cordentines
Vincente the Fox, a merchant
Loris, a reeve in Vincente's town
Fulvio, a guard in the employ of Vincente
Glanna, King of Cordence
Rosmont, a Cordentine ambassador

Barissians
Dirk, a priest of Toric

Emeric, Duke of Barissia
Gervase Salvinus, a mercenary leader
Orlin, Emeric's chamberlain
Urval, Orlin's servant
Curtis, a soldier
Dom, a soldier
Bernard Hat, an innkeeper

Kellish
Moneva, a mercenary

Baldwin, Duke of Kelland, Emperor of Brasingia
Hannelore, Empress of Brasingia
Walter, Baldwin's younger brother, Marshal of the Empire
Rainer, Baldwin's chamberlain
Decker, Archbishop of Kelland
Gustav the Hawk, Archmage of the Empire
Ancel, a priest

Other Brasingians

Arne, Duke of Luderia

Ellard, Duke of Rotelegen

Coen, Duke of Thesse

Theodoric, a linen merchant from Thesse

Trevor, a Luderian woodsman

Guivergnais

Nicolas, King of Guivergne

Bastien, Duke of Morbaine

Russell, Bastien's man

Haskans

Shira, Queen of Haskany

Koren, Shira's uncle

Persaleians

Pentas, a wizard

Mark, King of Persala

Krykkers

Kaved, a mercenary

Rabigar, an exile

Caladri

Tibor, King of the Blood Caladri

Lorant, Prince of the Blood Caladri

Hajna, Princess of the Blood Caladri

Szabolcs, a wise man

Gyuri, a carriage driver

Marika, a carriage attendant

Dora, a carriage attendant

Emese, a carriage attendant

Vida, a carriage attendant
Joska, a carriage attendant
Elek, a carriage attendant

Odon, elder of the Grand Caladri
Agoston, elder of the Grand Caladri
Dorottya, elder of the Grand Caladri
Kelemen, a regional governor
Ignac, a wizard

Dorjan, King of the Shadow Caladri

Isharites

Erkindrix, Lord of Ishari
Arioc, King of Haskany
Siavash, High Priest of Ishari
Nexodore, a wizard with a death mask
Ardashir, a member of the Council of Seven
Tirano, a wizard, serving Emeric of Barissia

I

THREE CORPSES

*T*YPICAL, BELWYNN SAID, looking up as the sun disappeared behind thick clouds and the temperature dropped. *Why did we have to do the walking through the heat of the afternoon?*

Soren didn't turn to look at Belwynn. The twins always spoke in their heads when they were alone. It had become second nature to them ever since childhood. Instead, he squinted up at the sky.

It's going to rain soon. You wouldn't have wanted to walk through that.

Belwynn came close to making an irritable retort, but controlled herself. Was that a spot of rain? They walked on a bit. A drop landed on her cheek.

That was the trouble with her brother. He was always right.

As they approached the outskirts of the town, the spots of rain turned into a steady drizzle.

For all the wealth that's supposedly here, commented Belwynn, *I see a lot of poverty.*

Small wooden huts with sunken floors were scattered about in an irregular pattern. They looked soaked through already, as if they hadn't dried out from the last shower. Pitiful wisps of smoke could be seen emerging from the thatched roofs. They all had their doors open, and Belwynn peered in as she walked past. Babies crying. Women sewing. One woman was brewing beer, the pungent smell of hops emanating from the house. There were no men around — they presumably worked in town. Most of the houses had animals and small garden plots outside, as if the owners couldn't decide between living like peasants or like townsfolk. Some kids played outside in the rain, splashing through the mud. They got an earful from a tough-looking matron for running through her garden. But, in truth, it was impossible to tell where the mud ended and the garden began.

They continued into the centre of Vincente's town, where the homes were more substantial. The people they passed looked them up and down suspiciously. They were strangers, so it was to be expected. But Belwynn sensed more tension here than was normal. People who were out seemed keen to get on with their business and get in. Not just because of the rain. There was no chatting or laughter, like back home in Magnia.

Arriving in the market square, Soren looked around, squinting up at the shop signs.

Is that it? asked Belwynn, pointing over to an inn on the opposite side of the square. *The Three Tuns,* she added, reading the faded lettering on the sign; it bore a picture of three wooden casks, the kind that held wine. The front of the inn wasn't much to look at: old planks of wood that would soon need replacing, no windows, a narrow entrance.

Yes, that's it, agreed Soren, and led them over.

Belwynn had never mentioned it, but she was sure her brother's eyesight was deteriorating. Too many late nights reading old manuscripts had taken their toll.

It didn't look much on the outside, but inside, the *Three Tuns* was a substantial building, with a large open plan hall downstairs and rooms for guests on the top floor. It wasn't busy, though. A few groups of travellers had arranged themselves near the fire, and the smell of roasted meat set Belwynn's stomach rumbling. Soren was peering in that direction, but Belwynn was already looking into the shadowy, mostly empty recesses of the hall.

Sure enough, a figure emerged from a secluded table and headed towards them. He was tall and muscular, with dark hair and eyes above a sneering mouth.

'Took you long enough to get here,' Herin spat out.

He led them away from the inviting fire to his isolated table.

He sat down, fingers drumming on the table top. Belwynn and Soren joined him, shrugging off their packs.

'I've already ordered food,' he said in an accusatory tone.

Belwynn knew him well enough by now to ignore his rudeness.

'Clarin's here?' she asked.

'In the privy,' Herin replied. 'I swear, all he does is eat and shit.'

'Why don't you go over the plan?' asked Soren, in the tight voice he used when he was annoyed.

'There is a treasure room in the upstairs part of the building,' Herin began, keeping his voice down and looking around the inn for eavesdroppers. 'It holds chests full of coin and other valuables. There is a lock on the door that requires keys held by three different people, including one by Vincente himself. But we've got Soren to bypass that. So the main problem is neutralising the guards outside the room without drawing attention, then getting out quickly, and without being seen.'

'And we have help with that?' asked Soren.

'Hey!' came a booming voice from across the hall.

Striding over came Clarin, Herin's younger brother. Younger, but bigger. He was only slightly taller than Herin, but he had a massive chest, tree-trunk legs, and bulging arms. He had a mop of sandy hair and an altogether friendlier expression on his face.

'Good to see you both!' he exclaimed as he arrived at the table.

Belwynn and Soren both stood up to each receive a massive bear hug.

'Keep the noise down, you great idiot!' demanded Herin in a hissed whisper.

But it was water off a duck's back to Clarin, who took a seat with a beaming smile on his face.

'Journey reasonable, was it?' he asked them.

'Yes, no complaints,' replied Belwynn.

Soren raised an eyebrow at that.

'I was asking about the help we'll get inside Vincente's house,' said her brother, attempting to return to business.

'Two sellswords in there will help us,' explained Herin. 'We each get a one-sixth share.'

'How trustworthy are they?'

Herin shrugged. 'How trustworthy is anyone?'

'Without the philosophy?' requested Soren testily.

'They want their share of the money, of course; that makes them motivated. If something went wrong, would they turn on us to save their skins? Most definitely.'

'Wonderful,' said Belwynn drily. 'Who are they? What do they look like?'

'That doesn't matter. I've agreed to keep their identities secret; in case anything goes wrong.'

'Secret!?' fumed Belwynn, her voice threatening to climb louder than a conspiratorial whisper. 'So we don't know who's on our side in there? Do you know?' she demanded, turning to Clarin.

'Sure, I've known them—'

Clarin stopped speaking, too late, when he saw his brother staring at him.

'Do you?' Belwynn demanded of Soren.

'No, I don't. Belwynn,' he began, in his *let's be reasonable* voice.

3

'*Belwynn* what? Why does no-one think—' she continued, only to be stopped by the arrival of a barmaid at the table with the food.

They sat in stony silence as their food and cutlery were laid out. A huge bowl of stew wafted its flavours temptingly while they waited.

'Look.' Herin restarted the conversation when they were alone again. 'That's the demand that's been made, and I'm going to stick to it. Belwynn, your job is to keep everyone's attention downstairs. Clarin will be near you at all times. Soren and I will go upstairs as soon as we get the chance. Keep in contact with each other through your—' He waved a hand, unable to find the word.

Evil touch? Belwynn suggested, privately, to Soren.

It was Herin's most ambitious plan yet, relying on a number of individuals to carry out a very dangerous but apparently lucrative robbery.

'Who is this guy, anyway?' she asked, changing the subject. 'Why are we stealing his money?'

'Vincente the Fox, he's known as,' Herin explained, pausing as his brother began serving the stew, spooning it into the four bowls provided. 'Trader, smuggler, racketeer, pirate, robber...the list goes on. This little town is controlled by him, but he has a network up and down Dalriya. A very powerful man, above the law in Cordence. He and a few men like him are the ones running the show in this land.'

Herin looked straight at Belwynn. 'Don't feel sorry for this guy. He's intimidated and murdered his way to that gold over there.'

'And slaved,' said Clarin, dipping a huge hunk of bread into his stew. 'I've heard he's done that, too.'

'Alright, I get the picture. When do we go?'

'We eat,' said Herin, 'we make our preparations, then we go. Time to put your dress on. You did bring one, right?'

'Yes,' she replied, nodding at her pack.

Herin looked at her critically. 'Did you bring some cosmetics? You look half-drowned.'

'Oh, charming! You can shove this little adventure up your arse if you like, Herin.'

Herin and Belwynn stared across the table at each other. Belwynn turned to her brother, who seemed to find something so interesting about his food that he couldn't look up.

'This stew is great,' said Clarin, wiping the last bits in the bowl up with another chunk of bread. 'Anyone mind if I have seconds?'

Belwynn followed the others as they exited the Three Tuns and made their way through Vincente's town.

The sun had almost conceded defeat for another day, and the fading light gave the streets a more menacing feel to them, empty of people and eerily quiet.

Herin led them at a fast pace, flitting from one street to the next, keen not to be seen. Belwynn soon lost track of their whereabouts and resigned herself to just keeping up with the others.

Herin led them to a dark, narrow alleyway, the kind of place you would think twice about walking down, even in the middle of the day. At the end of the alley Herin crouched down, and they joined him in the same position.

Belwynn took care to keep the hem of her dress from trailing on the ground.

The rain was getting heavier now, and Herin brushed a hand through his wet hair in an irritated gesture, though Belwynn knew him well enough to know that he loved all this cloak and dagger stuff. He pointed ahead and slightly to the left. The end of their alley intersected at a right angle with a much broader, main thoroughfare. Herin was gesturing at a big townhouse which dominated the area.

The front of the house was stone-built with giant wooden doors. It was tall with a flat roof and crenellations facing the street. The left hand side of the house had a second storey built on it. Half a dozen armed men stood outside, mostly trying to shelter from the rain in the lee provided by the house wall.

'Always five or six at the front, at all times of day and night. At the back there are grounds that descend to a stream. Inside, more paid men and various retainers, friends and family, probably averaging thirty armed men at any one time altogether. Only other exit is the window that's on the top floor. That's how we're getting out.'

Herin was really speaking to Soren. Belwynn and Clarin were the ones who got told what to do. Herin and Soren were the planners.

'There's no other buildings nearby or in town where he has people based?' asked Soren.

'No.'

'Very well. Let's do it.'

Belwynn's insides churned as they approached the house. She had faith in Herin and Clarin, and most of all in Soren; but still she knew that what they were doing was very dangerous and could go horribly wrong.

The guards outside the house were huddled around a game of dice, but quickly stood when they saw them approaching. Both Herin and Clarin wore armour and carried long swords, sheathed in scabbards at their belts. The guards outnumbered them, but the two men were an intimidating sight, and Belwynn could see them touching their own weapons, checking they were near to hand should the need arise. Emboldened, they moved forward as a group, meeting them a few yards from the door of the house.

'What business have you here?' one of them demanded—a heavy-set man with an unruly beard that dominated his face so much that Belwynn couldn't tell his age.

'Evening,' said Herin calmly, resting his dark eyes on the bearded guard. 'We are come to Vincente's town to introduce him to Lady Melyta, a singer from Magnia,' he said, gesturing at Belwynn.

Belwynn did a small curtsy, while looking into the distance, as if making eye contact with men such as these was beneath her.

'Hmm. It's late for that, isn't it? They've already had their dinner inside.'

'We are somewhat late, yes. We have travelled from Magnia, our homeland, where Lady Melyta is known as the best minstrel in the land. She plays for all the lords there, and she is currently on her way to sing at King Glanna's court, at his request. I think your lord would not want to turn her away,' said Herin.

The guard with the beard looked them over suspiciously. He turned to one of his comrades, who shrugged.

'Fulvio,' he said, turning to one of the men, 'go ask for Loris, will you?'

Fulvio nodded and walked back over to the door. He banged three times on the door with his fist.

The remaining guards stood with Belwynn and the others, staring at them in silence.

'What are you, then?' asked the guard with the beard. 'Bodyguards or something?'

One of the big doors to the house opened, and Fulvio began speaking to someone in the doorway.

'That's right. It can be dangerous making long journeys these days.'

'Indeed it can. Just the two of you?'

'Only needs two of us,' interjected Clarin flatly, and Belwynn could see the hint of fear in the men's eyes at his sheer physical presence.

The bearded guard nodded.

'No horses? Walk all the way from Magnia, did you?'

'I'll ask the questions now!' came a voice from the doorway. 'Over here!'

The guards reluctantly gave way, allowing Belwynn and the others to approach the door. A balding man with sharp features peered out at them, screwing his face up at the rain that threatened to wet him.

'I'm Loris, the reeve of this town. A bard, I understand?' he said, quickly and directly, addressing Belwynn.

'The best in the business,' she replied haughtily.

'With two bodyguards,' added Loris. He looked Herin and Clarin up and down, nodding to himself.

'Your transport?'

'We have taken accommodation at the Three Tuns,' said Herin. 'Our coach is there.'

'And who's this?' Loris nodded in Soren's direction.

'This is Edward, the Lady Melyta's brother. I'm sure you see the resemblance?' replied Herin. 'Unfortunately, the gods decided to take away his sense when he was a small child. But the lady still meets her family obligations and takes him everywhere with her.'

Soren grinned and bobbed his head a few times.

Oh, very convincing, Belwynn said to him.

Soren ignored her.

'I see,' said Loris, 'yes, very unfortunate.'

He didn't make much of an effort to sound sympathetic. He looked them over one last time.

Belwynn could see his brain ticking over. As a group they were young, wealthy looking; unlikely to be difficult. Two soldiers, a woman, and her dependent brother didn't amount to much of a threat, either. If Vincente could afford to have guards posted outside his house, he doubtless had many more armed men inside.

'All right,' he said, 'come in.'

Loris backed away from the door and gestured them in.

They had made it into the house.

The door was shut closed and locked behind them; Belwynn just managed to catch a glimpse of the guards still standing outside, looking rather sorry for themselves.

They found themselves inside a porch area, all stone-built, where one guard was stationed on door duty. It seemed to Belwynn like a nicer job than being outside; he even had his own chair tucked away in the corner. Ahead, she could hear the noise of what sounded like a busy hall.

'I will take you to meet Vincente,' said Loris, leading them on through the porch door. They entered a passageway with four doors leading off it, two on each side, and a spiral stone staircase at the end which led upstairs. Belwynn tried to get her bearings. She could smell the kitchens from behind the first door on the left. Loris took them in the opposite direction; through the first door on the right, into the main hall.

It was busy, with more people inside than the inn where they had dined. A large fire burned in the centre of the room. Around it, in a rough square shape, were tables and benches, which may have been organised more neatly before the dinner but were now arranged in a disorderly fashion all over the place. Dinner was over, but drinking wasn't, and the room smelt strongly of alcohol. Some guests were holding mugs of ale; others were drinking wine, with barrels liberally spread among the tables. There must have been at least fifty people in the room, several of whom were armed men, but women and children were also present, as well as a few busy-looking servants. It was noisy, too, with men shouting at each other across the table or over to someone on the other end of the hall. If this was an ordinary night at Vincente's house, thought Belwynn, he must be a wealthy man, ranking alongside the most powerful barons back in Magnia.

Once a few people had noticed their arrival, the hall quietened somewhat. Vincente's guests studied Belwynn and the others.

'Is that your new wife, Loris?' a woman shouted out from one of the tables, to much amusement. Belwynn got a brief glimpse of her: jet black hair with leather clothing and a short sword attached to her belt. Belwynn gave a little smile at the joke, while taking a look at her potential audience. The faces were more interested than anything else, and certainly not hostile.

Loris scowled at the perpetrator, but carried on with his route, around the tables towards the dais at the far end of the hall. He held out a hand for them to wait and approached the dais alone.

There was only a very small table on the dais, where seven men had been quietly talking. Loris was talking to the one in the middle, presumably Vincente. He stood out in purple hose and a long purple jacket. He had grey hair, but a youthful face, and he was tall and lithe-looking.

His henchmen came in all shapes and sizes. At one end of the table was an absolute giant of a man, bigger even than Clarin, with oversized everything: head, hands, feet. At the other was a Krykker, the mountain race who had toughened, armour-like skin on their torsos. They rarely visited human lands, and Belwynn was surprised to see one in this place. The only Krykker she knew, back home in Magnia, was Rabigar the bladesmith. She knew him to be an exile, and wondered whether the same was true of this man. On Vincente's right was an older man with wrinkled, yellow skin, smoking a pipe, while between him and the giant was a small, wiry young man with a thin wispy moustache who looked to Belwynn like he was not yet out of his teens.

What an odd bunch, she commented to Soren.

Maybe Vincente promotes on merit, rather than looks, he observed.

Vincente looked over to Belwynn and beckoned her over with a slight hand gesture. She approached the dais. Some of the men grinned at her, perhaps hoping that she would find the situation intimidating; but she wasn't some country bumpkin to be impressed by a short dais with a merchant sitting on it, however wealthy he was.

'I am told you are on your way to the court of my dear friend, Glanna,' Vincente began, as if he were on first-name terms with the king of Cordence. Maybe he was. His voice was controlled and precise, but bore an unmistakeable Cordentine accent, stressing each and every vowel.

'I am due there tomorrow, Lord Vincente,' lied Belwynn easily. 'I was advised that this was the most important stop on the way. Your house is beautiful,' she added.

So easy, thought Belwynn, as Vincente visibly puffed up with self-importance, a smile playing on his face. He was no lord, but merchants are the same the world over, she thought: aspiring to be accepted into the ruling class. The idea that a royal guest should visit him first was enough to win him over and remove any doubts or uncomfortable questions from his mind; even if some of his colleagues, like the young man with the moustache, still looked suspicious.

'Well, we would be delighted if you would sing for us, Lady...?'

'Melyta.'

9

'Of course. Such a beautiful name.'

The Krykker smirked at that comment behind Vincente's back.

'You would want to sing up here, as your stage?'

'Indeed.'

'Then we will finish our business here and leave it for you. Loris will ensure you have anything else you need. And I insist that you stay the night here at my house, not at the inn. The accommodation there is reasonable, but isn't to a high enough standard. Loris, you will make the arrangements?'

The Krykker's smirk got even bigger. Meanwhile, Loris was nodding in agreement at his instructions.

Belwynn turned to the reeve. 'Well, I would like a drink for my throat,' she said demurely, coughing a little as the smoke from the pipe-smoker blew in her direction.

'Antonio, you oaf!' Vincente scolded the old man, slapping him on the arm several times. 'You have no manners!'

'A thousand apologies, Vincente.'

'Why are you apologising to *me*?' he demanded, raising his voice for the whole hall to hear.

'I beg your pardon, my lady,' said the old man, sounding quite contrite, his face drooping in apparent sorrow.

Everything alright? asked Soren, from his place to the side of the dais.

Yes. It's going well, replied Belwynn.

***

Soren had seen it before, of course; many times. But it still filled him with pride.

When his sister sang, the world stood still.

Standing on the dais, alone, she commanded the attention of everyone in the hall. Soren looked around at the transfixed faces which, moments ago, had been chatting and arguing, shouting and bragging; now they were deathly silent. Strong men, with their bulging muscles and weapons at their belts, now looked wide eyed and childlike. Their women had tears in their eyes. Their children, who had been driving them crazy moments ago with their constant foolery, sat cross-legged and angelic.

The plan was working. Soren turned to Herin, who was standing next to him. 'Time to go?' he asked.

Herin was pulled out of his own reverie and locked eyes with Soren.

'Yes,' he whispered. 'Follow me.'

Soren turned to go.

'Wait,' hissed Herin from the side of his mouth, looking at the stage again.

'What is it?' murmured Soren after a few nervous seconds.

'Nothing. I thought I saw one of Vincente's thugs...looking straight at us. But he's watching Belwynn now. Come on.'

They shuffled off, backing out to the door from which they had entered the hall earlier. The people around them barely noticed them passing as they focused on Belwynn's performance. One or two moved out of the way for them, but didn't divert their attention to notice who was leaving and where they were going.

We're going, he said to Belwynn, in case she hadn't noticed.

He gave her one last look, noting Clarin's reassuring presence by the side of the dais, before exiting into the passageway.

It was empty, but they were aware that there was a guard in the porch area, and they moved quickly and quietly towards the spiral staircase at the other end of the passage. Soren followed Herin up the stairs to the top floor of Vincente's house, where the treasure room was located.

Herin paused at the top to look around before emerging onto an upstairs passage, which ran directly above the downstairs one. When Soren joined him, he had a quick look around for himself. The upper storey of the house was much smaller than the lower. There was nothing to his left, above the hall, except an exterior stone wall. There were three doors leading off to the right of the passage.

'This way,' whispered Herin, and they began creeping down the hall. 'Vincente's private quarters,' he added, indicating the first door on the right.

They moved on to the second door.

'Let's hope our friends have done their work,' Herin said, before slowly turning the handle.

Gingerly, Herin pulled the door open. It was dark inside, with no light source. But slowly Soren's eyes adjusted, and he could make out a small antechamber.

There was another door to the left. Placed at intervals along the outside wall were three chairs—each with a corpse sitting in it.

'Come on,' said Herin, ushering Soren into the room.

Soren looked at the nearest body, that of a guard, slumped backwards in the chair. His throat had been cut, and black congealed blood had collected in a pool on the floor. He forced himself to look at the other two victims—two more guards, with similar injuries. It was a disturbing sight, made worse by the silence and darkness of the room.

'Did they have to kill them?'

Herin shrugged. 'Probably.'

Herin looked around the room and found an empty sconce on the wall.

'Shit. No-one mentioned how dark it was in here. We're not gonna be able to see anything.'

Soren took a length of candle from his inside pocket and cupped both hands around it. He found that they were shaking. He concentrated, gained focus, calling on heat to materialise from his hands onto the wick of the candle. The wick caught flame, and he moved over to the sconce, placing the candle inside.

The small light from the candle created eerie shadows on the walls. Soren had to force himself to ignore the three corpses who shared their confined space, illuminated by the flickering flame. He wasn't a religious man, but it was hard not to imagine that the spirits of the murdered men were in there with them.

He turned his attention to the door to the treasure room. As described, it had three separate locks on it, each with its own keyhole. He grabbed the handle and gave the door a yank, just in case. It was solidly locked in place.

Kneeling, Soren flattened his hands against the wood, concentrating, trying to search for the metal mechanism inside.

'Well?' said Herin. 'Can you do it?'

'I think so. I'll need a bit of time. Guard the door while I give it my attention.'

'Fine,' said Herin. He moved to draw his sword, and then, thinking better of it, pulled out a seax which had been strapped horizontally to his belt.

'No room to swing a sword in here,' he said by way of explanation, handling the weapon; in size, it was somewhere between a knife and a sword, with a wickedly sharp edge. Picking his spot, he went down on one knee facing the door. If anyone did bumble into the room, they were going to get a nasty surprise.

Returning to his work, Soren located the highest lock and formed a connection between the metal mechanism and his hands, through the wood of the door. Wriggling his hands up and down, he was able to raise the internal pins while also pulling the bolt to the right. He opened the lock, resulting in a loud click. Herin looked over.

'One down,' said Soren.

The next two worked along the same principles, and Soren was able to pull the bolt after a bit of trial and error. Standing up, he pushed open the door. Herin joined him with the candle he had retrieved from the sconce, and they peered in.

They had done it. Three large chests sat along the opposite wall, with various artefacts made of gold, silver, crystal and the like lay scattered on the floor. It was a very rich man's treasure hoard.

Herin and Soren looked at each other, smiling in jubilation at their success.

Herin rushed in and lifted the lid of the nearest chest, and Soren peered over his shoulder. It was full, mainly with coins: Cordentine florins, the distinctive wide, thin discs of gold; but also plenty of Imperial thalers, silver Persaleian denarii, and lots more, from all over Dalriya.

'I knew it,' said Herin, dipping a hand into the coins. 'I knew we could do it. This is a massive haul.'

'I know,' said Soren, 'but we're not done yet. We need to move.'

'Right,' agreed Herin, 'we prioritise. First, we get this chest into Vincente's room. Then the next two. Anything else really valuable, but otherwise we leave it.'

Herin and Soren grabbed one end of the chest each and carried it out of the treasure room and back into the adjoining chamber, where its three corpse guards still sat in silence. It weighed a tonne, and Soren was glad when Herin signalled to put it down.

Herin peered round the door into the passageway.

'Clear.'

Hefting it up again, they manhandled it out of the room into the passageway, Herin walking backwards towards the stairs, Soren facing forwards.

There were footsteps on the stairs. Quick footsteps.

Before he could react, Soren saw a face come into view. It was a young man's face, thin, with a wispy moustache, making his features rat like. Soren recognised him as one of the henchmen who had been sitting on the dais when Belwynn was introduced to Vincente. They were in trouble.

Unless—

'Herin,' he murmured, dropping his end of the chest and nodding towards the stairs.

The man had stopped.

'What are you doing?' he demanded in a loud voice.

Herin turned around. Lightning quick, he pulled the seax from his belt and threw it at the target. But the man was too quick, diving back down the stairs as the weapon clattered harmlessly against the stonework.

'Shit,' said Herin.

Soren could hear the man shouting as he descended back down the stairs.

Belwynn, he spoke to his sister, sending his thoughts down to the hall where she was still performing. *Belwynn, get out of there! Now!*

II

THE SMELL OF FAILURE

*B*ELWYNN, GET OUT OF THERE! *Now!*
      Belwynn stopped singing immediately. She took a few steps backwards on the dais. She gestured to Clarin for help.

Her audience in the hall murmured, as if slowly awakening from a dream. She could hear shouting outside the hall. Things had stopped going well.

Belwynn looked around, desperately trying to work out where to go. She had no idea. This wasn't supposed to happen. Clarin was heading towards her, but he was being so slow!

Behind him, a woman marched onto the dais, dressed all in black with black hair pulled back from her face. She walked directly towards Belwynn, who recognised her as the woman who had shouted out when they had entered the hall.

'I think we need to get out of here,' said the woman urgently.

The door of the hall crashed open, and one of Vincente's followers, the teenager with the moustache, tumbled in.

'They're stealing the treasure!' he shouted.

A few moments ago, one could have heard a pin drop. Now, the hall erupted in noise. Men shouted orders at each other. Some rushed out of the hall towards the stairs. Others turned to the dais, pointing fingers at Belwynn and Clarin.

'Yes, Moneva! Get us out of here,' said Clarin quickly, speaking to the woman.

The woman Clarin had called Moneva ran past Belwynn towards the back of the dais, where a small set of stairs took her upwards. Clarin gave Belwynn a gentle push to follow on. She must be one of the sellswords Herin had said was working with them, Belwynn surmised. She hadn't been expecting a woman.

Looking behind her, Belwynn gasped as a group of men approached the dais. Clarin drew his sword, causing them to pause, before he again pushed her towards the back of the dais.

Moneva's escape route took them up the stairs into a large, dimly-lit, and musty smelling room. It was a storeroom, with a stack of timber in one corner, a harness for a cart and horse lying in another. Big fabric sacks were lined up against all the walls.

An exit way to the room lay ahead and to the right, which was where the little light in the room was coming from. As Belwynn looked in that direction an armed man emerged, perhaps a guard to an alternative exit to the house.

'What's going on, Moneva?' he asked, walking towards them.

'Someone's tried to break into the treasure room.'

The guard's eyes widened in surprise.

'Who are they?' he asked, indicating Clarin and Belwynn.

With no warning, Moneva launched a kick in between the man's legs. It connected home with a crunch and the guard doubled over in agony. Clarin was quickly on to him, bringing his knee up and smashing it under the man's chin. Belwynn heard an unpleasant crack from the man's jawbone. Clarin loomed over him, fist raised.

'Clarin, enough!' demanded Belwynn.

Clarin looked up and headed towards the exit to the room, but Moneva reached out and grabbed him.

'No, we'll get trapped that way. Follow me.'

Moneva drew them instead in the opposite direction, deeper into the storeroom. Taking a right, she took them into a smaller chamber.

The latrines. A bad smell. And a dead end.

'What—' began Belwynn.

'Hush,' said Moneva.

Voices. Unsurprisingly, a group of men had now followed them up the steps from the dais and into the storeroom. They must have found the injured guard on the floor.

Moneva pointed at the wooden bench of latrines.

'When I say so,' she whispered, 'help me pull off the wooden board. Underneath are holes which go outside. We can lower ourselves down.'

'Into a dung-heap!' hissed Belwynn.

Moneva looked at her. 'You got a better option, princess?'

Belwynn knew the woman was right. If they didn't get out of here quickly they would be in big trouble. She held her hands up. 'Fine.'

They positioned themselves along the bench. When Moneva gave the word, they pulled up the whole plank of wood easily, lowering it to the floor, exposing a stone slab with four holes in it. Just big enough to fit through.

'Who's there?' came a voice from the storeroom.

Belwynn looked from Moneva to Clarin. They had seconds to act before they were discovered.

Clarin sheathed his sword, unbuckled his scabbard from his belt, and threw it down one of the holes. He placed each hand on either side of the hole and hoisted himself inside. It was a tight fit for him. He let go, shoving his arms in the air because they wouldn't fit by his sides, and half-slid, half-fell down the hole. Belwynn was convinced she heard an unpleasant squelch as he landed at the bottom.

'Get in,' hissed Moneva.

Belwynn sat on the stone shelf and dangled her feet down the hole. She looked down, and a wave of stench hit her, making her heave.

'I can't,' she began, but she didn't have a chance to finish the sentence— Moneva grabbed her waist and forced her over the hole before shoving her down.

Belwynn slid down the rough stone work and then into empty space—before she landed in a sea of excrement.

The momentum of the drop pushed her onto her knees, and she tilted forwards, arms outstretched, into the muck. It splattered up her chest and onto her face. Big hands grabbed at her, and she was unceremoniously hauled out of the pit and onto wet grass. Clarin stood next to her, equally caked in filth.

A few seconds later and there was a huge squelch as Moneva landed in the dirt. As Belwynn got to her feet, Clarin helped the other woman out.

They stood there a little while, eyeing each other up and down and wrinkling their noses.

'We haven't been introduced,' said Belwynn, holding out a hand. 'Belwynn.'

Moneva looked at the proffered hand, caked as it was in other people's excrement, then looked at her own hand, which wasn't much better.

'Moneva,' she said, clasping hands. 'Pleased to meet you.'

**

Soren winced at the sound of Herin dragging the chest towards the door of the first room they had passed on the corridor. Herin had described it as Vincente's private chamber. Soren bent down and grabbed the other side of the chest, and they carried it into the room before letting it fall to the floor.

Soren wasn't surprised to see that Vincente's room was richly furnished: decorative rugs lay on the floor and ornate tapestries lined the walls. In the centre of the room was a large bed with a canopy over it. There was an adjoining bathroom where he and his family could wash and make their toilet in private.

Soren was surprised, however, to see people in the room.

In the doorway of the bathroom sat a woman. Her hands were tied behind her back and a cloth gag had been tied over her mouth. Vincente's wife, perhaps, or maybe a servant who had been in the wrong place at the wrong time. At the far end of the room was an open window. By the window was a Krykker man, pulling at a length of sheet he had dangled out of the window. The other end had been tied to one of the legs of the bed.

Soren recognised him as one of Vincente's henchmen who had a place on the high table down in the hall.

'What's happening?' said the Krykker by way of greeting, giving his roll of sheets another yank. 'It'll hold my weight, so it should hold yours too.'

'Soren, this is Kaved,' said Herin quickly.

Soren nodded at Kaved in greeting.

'They're onto us,' continued Herin. 'We've got to get out of here now.'

'What!?' said Kaved, clearly disappointed. 'With only one chest?'

'Better one chest and our lives than all three and dead,' said Soren. 'Is there anything we can use to hold this door shut? The bed's being used to hold the rope.'

Soren and Herin both heard a noise and turned to each other. It was the sound of many men roaring as they ran up the stairs of the house.

'Quick! They're here!' shouted Herin, the unusual sound of panic in his voice.

'I'll hold the door for as long as I can,' said Soren.

He backed away from the door somewhat, and concentrated on building a barrier around it.

The defence spell was the first one he had ever been taught. His first teacher, Ealdnoth, had made him practise it hour after hour. 'The first thing a wizard needs to learn,' Ealdnoth had told him, 'is to defend himself against the many people who want him dead.' Soren had learned how to block a punch, then a sword strike. When he had mastered that, Ealdnoth would test his defences against a magical attack. He would probe and attack until Soren didn't have the energy to hold him off any longer. Eventually, he became so proficient that it was Ealdnoth who had to give up.

While he built his barrier, Herin shoved his weight against the door. Kaved joined them and grabbed the chest.

Soren could hear a crowd out in the passageway. There were lots of them.

'You go, Kaved,' shouted Herin.

Just then the door gave a lurch as someone tried to barge their way in. Herin forced it closed.

'How am I supposed to get down carrying this?' demanded the Krykker.

An axe head chopped through the door, narrowly missing Herin's head. He sprang back into the room.

'Just chuck it out!' he screamed at Kaved.

The axe was pulled back, and a chunk of the door came with it. Faces peered through the door at them.

'Kaved!'

It was Vincente's voice screaming through the door.

'You treacherous dog! I will gut you for this! What have you done with my wife?'

Soren continued to focus on the doorway, constructing a barrier that was strong enough to hold off Vincente and his men. He heard a grunt from behind him, and then a crash, as Kaved hurled the chest out of the window.

The door swung open, revealing a mass of angry-looking men struggling to get in. Vincente's giant henchman waved an axe in Soren's direction.

'Soren?' asked Herin, brandishing his sword.

'I've got it. You go.'

Herin rushed to the window and began climbing out, following Kaved.

The men at the door tried to barge into the room, but Soren held them out, an invisible but powerful force blocking the whole door frame. They shoved and pushed at it, hitting it with weapons.

'A wizard!' one of them shouted, pointing at Soren. 'There's a wizard in there!'

'Soren!' shouted Herin from outside the window. 'Come on!'

Soren turned around and made for the window.

Suddenly he went sprawling forwards. Vincente's wife had stuck out a leg and tripped him as he went past. His concentration on the door was completely broken, and he heard shouts as the group of men tumbled through it.

Not daring to look back, Soren picked himself up and sprinted for the window as he sensed someone behind him.

19

He hurled himself out.

He felt a hand grab at the back of his cloak, but his pursuer couldn't hold on. Instead, Soren was falling head first out of the window. In desperation, he stuck his hands forward and tried to create an upwards force that would cushion his fall.

He landed on the ground, and everything went black.

***

Moneva led them around the back of Vincente's house to the side. According to Herin's plan, this was where the others were supposed to have left the building, with the treasure, via the upstairs window.

It was now completely dark outside and still raining. Belwynn couldn't see where they were going and felt sure they were going to get caught any second.

Soren? Soren!

No response.

'He's not replying!' she whispered to Clarin for the third time. The warrior held out his hands in a helpless expression.

Moneva gave a shout, drawing a dagger from her belt. Belwynn made out the form of one of Vincente's men ahead: the Krykker with the smirk.

'Gods, Kaved! I nearly cut your throat!' Moneva hissed.

Kaved snorted. 'You nearly tried.'

So, the Krykker was the second of Herin's insiders.

'Where's my brother?' she demanded of him.

Kaved looked her over and jabbed a thumb back over his shoulder. Looking, Belwynn could see Herin coming their way, her brother's body slumped over his shoulder.

'What happened?' she demanded.

'He fell out the window,' Herin said, lifting Soren off and passing him on to Clarin to carry.

'He's well enough. I think. But we haven't got time now; they'll be following us.'

'The treasure?' asked Moneva.

'Disaster,' said Kaved, heading away from the house into the grounds at the back and indicating that they should follow him.

'We picked up a few coins from one of the chests that I had to throw out of the window. That's it.'

Belwynn saw Moneva roll her eyes and begin to say something, but she controlled herself, biting her tongue.

'Over here!' A shout came from behind them.

'Get on with it,' said Kaved, picking up the pace as the grounds sloped gently downhill.

Belwynn could hear the jingle of metal armour and weapons coming from behind them, seemingly on the trail of Herin and the others.

'Where are we going?' she asked.

Kaved didn't reply, but instead sprinted forwards towards a stream that flowed by quietly and appeared to mark the boundary of Vincente's house.

Pulling out a small hand-axe, he hacked at the moorings of a large raft that was half hidden behind a tree.

'Don't worry, Kaved's part of the plan will still work,' said the Krykker in a sarcastic voice. 'Get on.'

Kaved and Herin held the raft steady as Clarin walked on gingerly, gently lowering Soren onto its deck. Belwynn and Moneva followed on, trying to spread their weight so that it didn't tip. From somewhere Kaved now had a long pole, which he used to push them away from the bank.

'Shit,' said Herin.

A group of about a dozen armed men were running down the slope towards them.

'Faster!' said Moneva.

'I can't go faster!' responded Kaved angrily. 'We're on a raft, not a racehorse!'

He shoved the pole down onto the bed of the stream and pushed them away a little farther.

When the men reached the bank, Kaved had succeeded in nudging them out into the middle of the stream, too far out to be reached by a sword or spear. Some of the men tentatively put their feet into the stream, seeing if they could follow on foot.

Others arrived and crowded around the bank, shouting insults. One of them held a bow and reached for an arrow, ready to nock it and shoot. If he did, he could aim at virtually point-blank range.

'Archer!' shouted Belwynn.

As she did so, there was a movement on the other side of the raft, and a knife left Moneva's outstretched hand, burying itself in the neck of the archer.

Those men in the water froze, suddenly wary of their exposed position.

Meanwhile, Vincente had pushed himself to the bank.

'Get them!' he yelled at his men, gesturing angrily. 'You've given yourselves a death sentence for this!' he yelled towards the raft as it picked up a bit of speed in the middle of the stream and began to float away. 'You've made one hell of a mistake tonight!'

'Oh, fuck off!' Kaved shouted back at him. 'We didn't get hardly any of your money, anyway!'

Vincente's men were being herded into the stream, some making more of an effort than others. The eager ones were crossing the stream and threatened to reach the opposite bank before the raft did. Kaved pushed them closer to the bank, and Clarin was able to grab hold of an overhanging tree branch, pulling the raft in and then holding it steady as the others clambered out. Herin grabbed Soren under the arms and dragged him onto the bank. Clarin got himself off and picked up the wizard.

Soren murmured something unintelligible.

'Looks like he might be waking up,' the big man commented.

'I hope so,' said Belwynn, peering at her brother. There seemed to be a bit more colour in his face. 'What happened to him, Herin?'

'He held the door closed while we escaped. Then he jumped out of the window for some reason. But he cast a spell that cushioned his fall. It didn't look like he hurt anything.'

'Hit the ground in slow motion, sort of,' added Kaved, sounding slightly in awe of what he had seen.

'He probably used too much magic, too quickly,' explained Belwynn. 'It's happened before. It knocks him out for a while.'

'Well, we better keep moving,' said Kaved. 'Just a little way up here.'

They marched up the riverbank, away from Vincente's town, for a few hundred metres. It was pitch black now, and no-one had a light, but Kaved seemed to know where he was going.

Before Belwynn realised it was there, they had stopped by a cart, complete with two horses attached to it.

'Wow,' said Moneva drily, 'someone's been busy.'

'Yes,' said Kaved, climbing into the driver's seat, 'complete with provisions and enough space to hold three chests full of gold. Looks like all we're taking away is the six of us.'

'We got some of it,' said Herin moodily, helping his brother to lift Soren into the back of the cart. 'It'll cover our expenses.'

'Will it cover the loss of my lucrative wages?' asked Moneva pointedly.

Herin turned towards her. 'Just get in, will—'

He stopped speaking and wrinkled his nose. He looked at Moneva as if seeing her for the first time, then across at Clarin and Belwynn. He put a hand over his nose.

'What the fuck happened to you?'

III

INTRUDERS

T HE SUN SET THE WORLD alight that morning: brilliant orange shafts touching the sky, spreading along the horizon and driving down to the land.

My land, thought Farred, as he let his mount walk along for a while at its own pace, content to survey the world around him.

To his left, Gyrmund seemed content to ride in companionable silence too. The early morning was surely the best part of the day: everything to look forward to, and it was when the land here looked the most beautiful. The rolling grassland stretched on for miles in every direction, seemingly unending. The mist of the previous night still hung over the grass, as if the gods had decided to sprinkle Dalriya with fairy dust.

'Do you miss it?' he asked Gyrmund.

'What?'

'Walsted. The land here. The place where you grew up. I would find it hard to leave for as long as you have.'

'It's beautiful,' agreed Gyrmund, looking around. 'But so are other places. Just in different ways.'

Farred nodded. He would like to see other parts of the world too. But he also appreciated what he had here.

'Don't you ever get bored?' asked Gyrmund.

'Bored of what?'

'I don't know. I know you've got responsibilities here. But bored of the same routine. Doing the same things, at the same time...'

'Maybe. Though in some ways I've appreciated having some structure over the last few years, since Father died. But I know what you mean. I think I'm ready for a new challenge now.'

They rode on in silence again. It got Farred to thinking.

They had been inseparable as youths, raised as brothers after the death of Gyrmund's family. Farred had thought it would stay that way forever. It hadn't crossed his mind that it wouldn't. But now he was able to see the differences between them. Farred's parents had owned the estate here at Walsted. His family had done so for generations, since the Middians of these parts had agreed to bend the knee to the Kings of Magnia and their tribal lands were divided up. Gyrmund's parents, on the other hand, had rented their land and worked for Farred's family. That difference hadn't meant anything to Farred when he was a boy, but maybe it had to Gyrmund. And, of course, the two of them had wanted different things from the friendship at one point. But it still seemed strange that Farred, now, was the only one who called this place home. To Gyrmund, Walsted was still a refuge, a place he could stay if he needed to rest up or get some free lodging and dinners. But it was no longer his home.

'Time to stretch these boys' legs a bit?' asked Gyrmund.

'Come on then, Gamhard,' Farred called out to his mount, nudging him into a trot.

They were heading west, away from the sunrise, to where the plains of Farred's estate ended and became a wood of hills and hollow. Much of Plunder Wood was also owned by Farred, used for hunting game and to fetch timber. Beyond the woods was South Magnia proper, where the soil was deep and they farmed crops more so than animals.

After a while Gyrmund pushed his mount into a gallop and Farred let Gamhard join in. They raced along the open land, troubled neither by lake or stream, the ground dry from days of sunshine.

The woods became visible ahead. They headed for a wooden hunting lodge that Farred's father had built when they were youngsters. Here they could see to their horses and sort out which supplies they wanted to take into the woods by foot. Deer were the quarry today, and both men carried long hunting bows. Gyrmund had always been the slightly better marksman, taking the skill more seriously. Farred preferred spear and sword.

Once ready, they followed a well-worn track which took them deep into the trees. Midges buzzed around them, and Farred had to wave them away from his face. He was happy to let Gyrmund take the lead, and eventually they moved off the track and into the heart of the woods, where the going was tougher.

'We'll try up here,' said Gyrmund, pointing up a heavily wooded hill, his breathing heavy. 'We're more likely to find a buck and less likely to run into does.'

It was the birthing season, when does were avoided. They would either be ready to give birth or already have young fawns with them. Killing the mother would mean the fawns would die, too, and that was wasteful.

They settled in place under a tree which afforded a good view of the surrounding terrain.

After a horse ride and a woodland trek, Farred was hungry. He opened his sack and began to lay out the food they had brought. Bread, cheese and cold chicken had been wrapped up for them by the cook. They had also picked some blackberries on the way up. Gyrmund produced two flasks of ale from his sack, passing one over to Farred.

'Cheers,' they said, clinking their flasks together.

'You look after me well, Farred,' said Gyrmund, slicing the cheese with a knife and placing a slab on his bread. 'Thank you.'

'It does me good to get out like this. If you weren't here I'd be working all day.' Farred leaned back against the trunk of the tree and relaxed. 'I honestly don't mind if we don't see a single deer today.'

'You work hard, Farred. Your estate is in good order. Where do your ambitions lie next, though?'

'Ambitions? Well, I wanted to establish myself as a landowner after Father died. I think I've done that, now. If I want more, I'll need to make links with the crown.'

'Prince Edgar? Met him yet?'

'Yes, a couple of times. He actually passed through Walsted last year, first time he's crossed Plunder Wood.'

'And? What did you make of him?'

'We got on well. He's our age. Seems like a good man.'

'A good man? He won't last, then.'

'Maybe. But I hear that Cerdda of North Magnia has a similar character. Could be an outbreak of common sense amongst our rulers.'

'First time in a few generations if there is, but I suppose Magnia is due. No good for you, though, Farred. If you want to get in with the Prince, you'll need a war to fight in.'

'What about you?' asked Farred, changing the subject. 'No doubt you've got some ideas about where you're going to explore next. You've done virtually all of northern Dalriya now, haven't you?'

Gyrmund's eyes narrowed and he held up a hand for silence. 'I hear something.'

He moved onto his front and crawled off to the edge of their hill, peering down. He flattened himself down and turned back to Farred. 'You're going to need to see this. Just be careful.'

Farred did as suggested and moved carefully over to Gyrmund's location, staying low and using his elbows to pull himself along.

Gyrmund pointed down the hill and to the left. Farred had been expecting an animal. Instead, a troop of mounted figures was passing through the woods. His woods.

They were moving through quite difficult terrain and went slowly, so it was easy to take a look at them. There were no real distinguishing items, but they were all well armed. Some wore armour, and others didn't, though it looked like the latter group were carrying it on their mounts instead, which was understandable on a day like this. They were moving east to west and passed their location on the hill, no more than about two hundred yards away. Farred counted them.

'Twenty-one?'

'Yes.'

'Well armed. Lightly provisioned. Anything else?'

'Pretty sure they're from the Empire.'

'The Empire? So they've journeyed across the Steppe? And now through my lands, unannounced and on into Magnia? Who are they?'

'Don't know,' said Gyrmund, sitting up as the force moved out of sight. 'But that's our hunting trip over, I guess.'

'Yes. I'll have to follow them. I don't like it.'

'I know. I'm trying to think of a harmless explanation for it, but I can't.'

'Should I go back and raise a force?'

Gyrmund smiled. 'No way. An hour's ride back to Walsted, an hour at the least to gather people up and kit them out, another hour to get back here. They'll be long gone. We go back for our horses and follow them. Just you and me.'

'You're coming?'

Gyrmund looked offended. 'Of course!'

Farred smiled, relieved to have Gyrmund with him. He was the best tracker in these lands, and Farred knew he wouldn't lose his quarry.

'Come on,' said Gyrmund, eager to get going.

They packed their things into their sacks, slung them over their shoulders, and set off down the hill, moving with far more urgency than they had on the way up.

'Tell you one thing though, Farred. This might turn out to be the perfect way to impress your Prince Edgar.'

IV

TORIC'S DAGGER

THE MIDDAY SUN BEAT DOWN as the three riders entered the settlement of Ecgworth. Edgar, riding slightly ahead of his two companions, lifted his hand to shield his eyes as he peered ahead. He could make out the walls of the temple in the distance.

He had been riding for over an hour now, in chain mail. The summer sun had made the journey uncomfortable, and he had long since broken into a sweat.

He travelled along a dirt track, passing neat and orderly fields to his left and right. The wheat and barley already stood tall, shifting gently when a breeze tugged at them. Insects flew in and out, some filling the air with a buzzing or clicking noise. It had been a good summer so far, warm, but with enough rain as well. Ecgworth was a well-run estate, and it looked like the monks would be well supplied for the winter.

The peasants were busy at work in the meadow, hacking down the grass with sickles to make hay. It was a family affair; the children tasked with spreading out the grass so that it could bake dry in the sun. A few of them looked up as Edgar rode past, but they soon returned to their work. Visitors to the temple were not rare. If any of them recognised their prince, they showed no sign of it.

The track arrived from the west and joined on to the main road, heading north, which took Edgar into the centre of Ecgworth. He now rode past the homes of its inhabitants, simple wooden houses, but well-maintained.

The temple complex dominated the rest of the settlement. It was a large, rectangular site with a central location.

As he approached, Edgar could see the modest earthworks, on top of which the walls, made from thick planks of wood, had been driven in and tied together. In time of war, the walls could be manned, and the inhabitants of Ecgworth, and most of their livestock, sheltered behind them.

Edgar had visited the temple a number of times. It was an adequate defence, but could do little to stop a serious force from gaining entry. Edgar had asked for improvements to be made, and he was annoyed to see that nothing had been done.

The road took Edgar to the southern gate of the walls. Ecgworth was located in a flat plain, and the site of the temple gave little benefit in natural height. The priests had tried to compensate for this by digging a ditch around the site and using the excavated earth to create a raised surface on which to build. Nonetheless, when the prince stood in his stirrups, he could almost peer over the top of the wall.

Edgar's two bodyguards joined him at the gate. Leofwin had served Edgar for the last four years and had served his father before him. His nephew, Brictwin, was a few years younger than Edgar, and was learning the job from his uncle. Wordlessly, Leofwin drew his sword from its scabbard and banged on the gate three times with the pommel.

Edgar could hear movement on the other side of the gate, but there was no reply. Leofwin rolled his eyes at the delay, and began banging again. After another few seconds, he was rewarded with a voice.

'Who is there?'

'Prince Edgar demands entry,' boomed Leofwin with authority.

'Oh,' came the voice, before a head popped up above the wall. The guard was a young man who looked a little nervous at having to talk to Edgar directly. 'Please wait a moment, Your Highness. I will fetch Lord Wulfgar right away.'

Edgar nodded, and then the head disappeared again. He heard the noise of the gatekeeper jumping down from the wall and scurrying off in the opposite direction.

Wulfgar was High-Priest of the Temple of Toric. Edgar's father had given him the position, though not entirely out of choice. As well as being the leader of one of the richest religious communities in the kingdom, he came from a very powerful family: his older brother, Otha of Rystham, was one of the wealthiest landholders of South Magnia. Edgar knew both men well, and did not particularly like either of them. They were both arrogant and greedy, but their position of power meant that they had to be tolerated.

It was not long before Wulfgar came marching over to greet them.

'Get the gates open,' he demanded, in a voice used to authority.

The gate was slowly swung open, revealing Wulfgar, standing with his hands on his hips. To one side of him stood a small group of priests, simple brown robes belted at the waist. Although slightly red and out of breath, Wulfgar did not betray any other signs that he might be unsettled by Edgar's unannounced visit. He was a self-confident man, roughly the same age as Edgar's father would

30

have been. He was broad-shouldered and, despite being the high-priest, was dressed in the fine tunic and hose of a nobleman.

'How was your journey, Your Highness?' he asked Edgar as the prince and his bodyguards dismounted.

'It was fine. A little warm,' replied Edgar.

'Good, good,' said Wulfgar, walking over and clasping hands. 'Dirk, see to the horses, will you? If you'll follow me, my Prince?'

Wulfgar led them over to his hall, which had been built on the eastern side of the temple site. It was a typical single-storey nobleman's hall, similar to the one that Edgar had left that morning.

On their way they passed the temple itself. Beyond its entrance chamber, the main building was circular, with a domed roof. It was originally built some time ago, but its wooden exterior must have been replaced many times since then. It was decorated in a pleasing style. A large carving of Toric's sign of the sun faced them on the curving main chamber. Elsewhere were the buildings necessary for a settlement of this size to function: a stable, a smithy, a granary to store the food.

Edgar followed Wulfgar into the hall. A fire, located against one wall, created a welcoming, smoky environment. Two long tables with benches stretched along the centre of the hall, demonstrating Wulfgar's ability to feed a sizeable number of followers. Wulfgar could also afford to decorate his hall well. Tapestries covered all of the walls. The largest showed the rays of Toric's sun hitting the earth and giving life to the land, producing cereal crops, fruits and vegetables, animals and men.

Wulfgar gestured over to the top table. Edgar nodded to Leofwin. It was to be a private conversation. While Leofwin and Brictwin gravitated towards the fire, Edgar and Wulfgar sat down together.

'There was an attack on your temple,' began Edgar.

Until now, the prince had given his host no clues as to the purpose of his visit. For his part, Wulfgar had not shown the least bit of surprise or curiosity at Edgar's arrival. Now, however, with the cards seemingly about to be laid on the table, he could not help leaning forward and stroking his beard in a much more animated manner. He seemed to consider his response carefully.

'You may have received a somewhat exaggerated report, Your Highness. The night before last a rabble appeared outside the main gates. They demanded entry, but in all honesty seemed confused about their reasons. We dispersed them easily enough.' Wulfgar sat back in his chair. 'There was no bloodshed,' he added, in a reassuring manner.

Edgar suppressed a smile. It was common, in his experience, for priests to exaggerate threats to themselves, in an attempt to extract more funds. It was much rarer to hear one dismissing a threat.

'I have also heard that you have taken a prisoner?'

Wulfgar looked a little uncomfortable. 'Yes, Your Highness…a woman, possessed by some evil spirit, somehow made it past our gates and tried to steal Toric's Dagger from us. She was caught inside the temple itself! This group from the other night related to her in some way—amongst other demands, they wanted her released.'

Edgar nodded, thinking over Wulfgar's words. The high priest had tried to hide the fact that he had the prisoner, but he was probably not lying outright.

'Look,' continued Wulfgar, 'maybe you've had a complaint from some of these madmen, and perhaps you feel it's necessary to come here and find things out for yourself. But I can assure you that the matter has been dealt with. She has already been judged according to the laws of our community and has been condemned to death. I'm sure I do not need to remind you that, in all matters relating to Toric's Temple, the crown has ceded jurisdiction to me.'

Edgar suddenly didn't like the way the conversation was going. Wulfgar was puffing his chest out and jutting his chin forwards. He was trying to pre-empt any interference from Edgar in the woman's case, but the prince was not to be brushed aside so easily.

'I am aware of your rights, Wulfgar, and I fully support your decision. I would, however, like to see the woman before the sentence is carried out.'

For a moment the priest allowed a flash of anger to show on his face, but he soon controlled himself.

'The funny thing is, Your Highness, the woman says that she has already met you once before. She has, in fact, been demanding to speak to you, although I have explained to her that it is not in your power to overturn the decision.'

Elana was her name. She had come to Edgar's court about two weeks before, and he had spoken to her briefly.

Before then, rumours had already reached the prince of a priestess with unique powers who had been healing people across his kingdom. However, she had not come to court to heal, but to persuade people of some great threat to Dalriya.

Edgar remembered that she claimed the Dagger of Toric was somehow vital in averting this threat. She was certainly persuasive in her own way, and although she spoke passionately, she also spoke calmly, and was not, in his opinion, completely mad.

But she had no real evidence to support her claims, and Edgar had explained that, in such circumstances, he was not about to entrust the most holy relic in Magnia into her keeping. When, as Wulfgar had suspected, some of her followers brought her case to him yesterday, it was easy for Edgar to put two and two together and work out that she had decided to take matters into her own hands.

Wulfgar was right: the law said that Elana was his to try and to punish. So Edgar avoided that subject and pursued his request.

'That is correct,' Edgar confirmed in response to the priest. 'She has been at court once before. I would like to speak with her again, however. Where is she being held?'

Wulfgar did not answer the question immediately. He glanced over at the two bodyguards who had taken up residence by his fire. Edgar followed his eyes, and could barely believe that Wulfgar was considering resisting his request. He tried to control his anger. He had calculated that he could get what he wanted today with a casual personal visit and without creating a fuss.

If he wanted to, Wulfgar could refuse his prince's request or even have him ejected. Edgar would then ensure that he faced the consequences, but by that stage, people would begin to ask difficult questions about his interest in the matter.

To his relief, Wulfgar relented and ordered one of the priests in the hall to fetch Elana.

After what seemed an unduly long amount of time, in which the prince and priest sat in uncomfortable silence, Elana was brought into the hall.

Edgar found her to be just as striking as the first time they had met. He had seen women who were more beautiful. But she had strong features and an intensity which drew attention to her. Her pale skin and blonde, almost white, hair gave her an ethereal look.

As she was led to the table where Edgar awaited her, he noticed red marks around her wrists, which Wulfgar must have had tied. Still, that was likely the full extent of her injuries. Female prisoners could suffer much worse elsewhere.

Elana's eyes connected with Edgar's, and she nodded towards him, as if she had been expecting his presence. Considering her situation, she looked remarkably calm.

Wulfgar gestured to where she should sit and she did so, still without speaking.

'Elana,' began the prince, 'you are aware of the sentence passed on you?'

'Yes, my lord.'

'*Your Highness*,' corrected Wulfgar.

'Well...what is your defence?'

Elana looked at him quizzically, as if she were trying to work out the meaning of the question.

'She has already been tried in the relevant court, Your Highness,' interjected Wulfgar.

'I am aware of that,' responded Edgar roughly. He now returned his attention to Elana, who was beginning to annoy him just as much as the priest. Despite the fact that the prince had obviously travelled all this way to intervene in some way in her case, the condemned woman was acting as if the idea of making an appeal to him was somehow unnecessary. Edgar had begun to suspect that Elana was one of those pious people who expected their god to save them from trouble without doing anything much about it themselves— and in his experience, such people usually didn't survive for very long.

To his relief, she spoke up.

'My defence is that this kingdom, and every other in the land, are under threat from Ishari, and that to fight this threat I need the dagger of the Lippers. This man—' Elana gestured to Wulfgar '—doesn't want me to have it, because he thinks he owns it. Meanwhile, Ishari's power grows stronger, while I stay locked up in his dungeon. The weapon isn't even yours to give. It was stolen from the Lippers, who were chosen as its guardians, and who would have relinquished it to me.'

Although Elana was now putting forward her case, the bizarre nature of the argument did not help. Wulfgar put a forefinger to the side of his head and twisted it. Edgar tried to continue.

'It is true that Toric's Dagger was won from the Lippers by King Osbert of Magnia some generations ago, but it has been well preserved and honoured ever since, and as its guardians, neither Wulfgar nor I are prepared to hand it over to just anyone who claims it.'

Wulfgar nodded in solemn agreement, but Elana disagreed.

'The powers which have been granted to me by Madria, the true Goddess of Dalriya, are a sign from her that what I say is true and that the weapon should be entrusted into my keeping.'

'Blasphemy!' fumed Wulfgar. 'You would take Toric's holy weapon and use it for the evil designs of your false god!'

Edgar heard raised voices from outside the hall. It sounded like they were about to be interrupted, and if he didn't steer this his way now, the chance would be lost.

'Some of what you say may be true,' he began, holding up a hand for silence as Wulfgar started to object.

'I have heard that you do possess healing powers, and it is possible that they do derive from your goddess. That is why I have decided that your claims should be investigated. If my kingdom is under threat, then I am duty bound to defend it. Meanwhile, the Dagger remains here.'

At Edgar's last sentence, Wulfgar swung round to confront him as it slowly dawned on him what the prince was saying.

'This woman is not leaving my temple. She has been condemned to death and I will not withdraw my sentence.'

'The sentence stands. I have already told you that I support your decision. However, this woman may well be aware of a threat to my kingdom, and may even be able to help in its defence. In these circumstances the sentence will have to be postponed. As soon as I am satisfied that there is no threat, I will personally return her to you.'

The High-Priest did not have a ready response to this, and Edgar felt a little self-satisfied with his argument. Of course, Wulfgar knew that if he allowed Elana to slip out of his control the chances of her being returned were slim, but he could hardly accuse his prince of bad faith.

'Prince Edgar, I recognise that you are acting to protect our kingdom—your motives I can only commend—but I fear that this witch has somehow used her magic on you and is leading you astray. She has broken into one of our kingdom's temples in an attempt to steal our most precious treasure. She is devious and dangerous and I fear that I cannot in good conscience allow her to escape when Toric himself has instructed that she should be killed as soon as possible.'

Before Edgar had time to respond, the doors of the hall were thrown open, and the noise outside, of which he had been vaguely aware, burst into the room.

Several of Wulfgar's priests, weapons drawn, burst into the hall and towards the table where he was sitting. Leofwin and Brictwin moved over to the same area, but the priests had come to find the hall's owner.

As he drew closer, the man in the lead began shouting at Wulfgar. 'My lord, intruders have broken through the main gate, and now they're in the temple. At first, we thought they were the prince's men, but—'

'How many?' cut in Wulfgar harshly. He didn't wait for a response, but grabbed an axe from someone and led the priests back towards the doors. Everyone in the hall followed the high-priest's cue, arming themselves and streaming out of the hall.

Edgar and his two bodyguards followed them out.

The prince quickly surveyed the scene in the courtyard. Several bodies lay by the eastern gate, where the defenders must have put up some kind of resistance. The conflict had then moved to the temple, from which they could now hear shouting. The speed of the initial attack seemed to have taken the defenders by surprise.

'There are about a score of them, all on horseback,' one of the priests was informing Wulfgar.

'Follow me,' ordered the High-Priest. 'We'll trap them in the temple.'

Leofwin grabbed Edgar's wrist. 'My lord, I don't think you should put yourself in danger here.'

Edgar stopped and looked at Wulfgar's followers, who were earnestly listening to his barked instructions. There were barely a dozen of them, and though they might find reinforcements at the temple, they were in a weak position.

No-one seemed to know who the enemy were, but the fact that they were all on horseback indicated that they were probably well-trained and well-armed warriors, as did the ease with which they had breached Wulfgar's defences.

The Prince turned back to his bodyguard. 'They need our help.'

Leofwin looked at Edgar for a moment then simply nodded, though his disapproval was evident. 'Look to the Prince at all times,' he instructed his nephew, as the three men jogged over to catch up with Wulfgar's band.

The High-Priest turned around to look at his Prince, but said nothing.

'Is this all the fighters you have?' Edgar hissed at him, gesturing at the armed priests with him.

Wulfgar seemed taken aback by the question. 'Yes…there are some in the Temple, but we've lost those men at the gates,' he said, indicating the men who had already fallen.

Twenty fighters. That was all Wulfgar had to protect the Temple. He had spent too much on tapestries and feasting, and not enough on soldiers. But now was not the time to get into that argument.

They had barely walked a few more yards when Wulfgar's plan to catch the enemy in the Temple fell through. At first a handful, then all of the raiders emerged. Upon seeing Wulfgar's force, they quickly mounted their horses. All of them wore armour and carried weapons.

The High-Priest's march came to a halt as his men realized that they were faced by an enemy that was superior in every way.

The horsemen slowly trotted forwards. Edgar exchanged glances with Leofwin: Wulfgar's priests looked nervous and were liable to run if the enemy charged them. If they did run, they would be cut down and dispersed by the horsemen with ease.

The Prince pushed his way to the front. 'Form a semicircle behind me,' he ordered.

The priests looked to their leader, who looked relieved that someone else was taking charge of a situation that was getting more desperate by the second.

'Do as your prince commands,' Wulfgar growled, and took a position by Edgar's left side. Leofwin and Brictwin stood on Edgar's right side, while the priests took up position behind and to the flanks. They seemed a little more confident now that their prince had arranged them into a formation and that they were no longer at the front. Some of the more belligerent ones even shouted insults and curses at the approaching cavalry.

One of the attackers rode some yards ahead of the others, and Edgar assumed that this was the leader. He didn't wear any identifying symbols to betray who he was or where he was from. As he gradually drew closer, the prince could make out a moustache, and he could tell that he rode his horse naturally. The animal was powerful and expensive-looking.

He stopped some fifty yards from the defenders, and Edgar could see that he was being examined by his opponent in the same way that he was analysing him. He held the man's stare and hoped that he was at least making his foe think twice about attacking. In truth, the numbers and manoeuvrability of the enemy made Edgar's position pretty hopeless.

At first, the Prince had almost subconsciously assumed that these invaders were from North Magnia, the breakaway kingdom to the north with which his own kingdom had been at war for over a generation. Although there had been an official peace for some years now, small raids were not unheard of.

But as the rest of the riders drew up next to their leader and listened to his instructions, Edgar began to doubt this origin. For a start, he had lieutenants on the Northern border who should have intercepted a force like this before it had travelled so far south. The location suggested that these attackers came from the east, and this seemed to be confirmed by an examination of the enemy. Many wore moustaches with a shaved chin, a fashion in the Empire. Magnians tended either to be clean-shaven, like Edgar himself, or full-bearded, like Wulfgar.

Edgar's thoughts were interrupted by decisive action from the enemy. The horsemen trotted towards them and gradually picked up speed until they were charging at them, weapons drawn and ready.

'Brace yourselves,' ordered the Prince as his subjects prepared to face the onslaught.

The horsemen were advancing at a rapid rate and it looked as if they were planning to smash into Edgar's line without stopping. He felt sure that the horses would refuse to do so, but they kept coming. Then, in a perfectly executed manoeuvre, just as the Prince prepared for contact, the horsemen at the front pulled away to the sides and continued harmlessly past the Magnians. The rest of the horsemen followed, swerving either to the left or the right in the same way as their comrades.

Just as the last of the riders galloped past, Brictwin ran out from his position next to Leofwin to challenge the enemy. Acting with great speed, he took a swing at the last of the riders passing by.

This warrior did not look as experienced a rider as some of the others; he seemed to panic at Brictwin's approach and made a wild swing at Edgar's bodyguard, which failed to connect and left him off balance. Brictwin, meanwhile, managed to land a blow on the rider's leg. For a moment it looked as if the rider might regain his balance, but the speed at which he was travelling was too fast, and he tumbled off his mount onto the ground, while the horse galloped on.

Edgar did not join his bodyguard but turned around, fearing that the horsemen would themselves swing around and come at his position from the rear. He was surprised to see them keep the same course towards the eastern

38

gate. Some of the horsemen closest to the fallen rider did stop once they noticed that he was missing, and spied Brictwin, who was standing apart from the rest of the Magnians in a vulnerable position.

'Ho!' went the shout, and those at the front of the cavalry force, already out of the gate, stopped and turned around. Space was made for the leader to trot back to the front. It looked like they were readying to attack, to either avenge or to rescue their fallen comrade.

There was a bit of time to act as the enemy pulled their horses around, trying to get back into formation.

'Into the temple?' asked Edgar, thinking they might be better able to hold off a cavalry force there.

'Aye,' said Leofwin, sounding unhappy with the idea, but there was nothing else.

'Wait!' said the bodyguard, pointing to the north side of the complex.

Two men, each armed with bows, had taken up position on the inside of the northern complex wall and had already loosed an arrow each. The dark skin and long hair of the archers indicated that they were Middians.

Pulling back their strings, they aimed a second time at the mounted attackers. One arrow missed its target, but the other hit home, tearing into the flesh of one of the horses. The horse bucked up in pain, dislodging its rider, who managed to twist away and to the side as he fell, with a great thump, onto the floor.

Edgar studied their leader again; he was flanked now by two hostile groups, Edgar's force and the two archers. And the two archers were busy nocking another arrow to their bows.

The downed rider picked himself up, and, linking arms with one of his comrades, managed to clamber up behind him on his horse.

'We go!' Edgar clearly heard the leader shout as he wheeled his horse back towards the gates and moved off at pace.

The accent confirmed Edgar's suspicions: he was from the Empire.

The two archers tracked the departing riders with their bows, but didn't loose any more arrows.

When they were sure that they had gone, they unstrung their weapons and walked over. As they approached, Edgar thought he recognised one of them.

'It's...Farred, isn't it?' he asked, frowning at the man. He knew him as a nobleman from the plains to the east of the kingdom, but he couldn't understand what he was doing here.

Jamie Edmundson

'That's right, Your Highness,' said the man, going to one knee.

'Up, up,' insisted Edgar and gave the man a hug. 'You have my thanks.'

'They came here through my lands,' explained Farred. 'We happened to be out hunting and saw them cutting through Plunder Wood. We followed them here.'

'I'm grateful that you did,' said Edgar, looking at the second man, who he didn't recognise.

'This is my friend, Gyrmund,' said Farred. 'He's the one who hit the horse.'

This one didn't bend the knee, but offered his hand instead. Edgar was happy to take it.

'That was a fine shot.'

They all stood around for a while, letting their heart rates get back to something like normal.

'I guess they're gone,' said Edgar.

'They've got what they came for,' muttered Wulfgar darkly.

Relief began to flood over Edgar as the immediate threat disappeared. He felt like he hadn't taken a breath since he'd first seen the enemy. The priests, too, were beginning to feel the euphoria of surviving a battle, shouting out praise to Toric.

Leofwin, meanwhile, was marching over to his nephew. He was not happy. He looked down at the body of the fallen rider over whom Brictwin was standing and, kneeling, felt for a pulse.

'Alive, but unconscious,' he called over to Edgar. He stood and glared at the young bodyguard.

'You've let me down today, Brictwin. You deserted your prince, whom you are sworn to protect. I even told you to look to the Prince before the fight. Even these priests managed to hold their position,' he said, waving his sword at Wulfgar's followers in a dismissive way. He spat on the floor. 'You nearly brought the enemy back upon us.'

Edgar had heard enough of the conversation and walked over to join Wulfgar, who was making his way to the Temple. Farred and Gyrmund came with them. He felt sorry for Brictwin, who had shown bravery and skill in his first real armed encounter; but, ultimately, Leofwin was right. Edgar needed his bodyguards to stay close at all times. Brictwin's youthful rush of blood to the head might have got them all killed.

By the time that Edgar and Wulfgar had reached the Temple, the two bodyguards had re-joined their prince. The six men entered the building.

Unlike the priests at the main gates of the temple complex, the priests inside the temple itself seemed to have failed to put up a united resistance against the intruders. A few bodies lay in random places, neither moving nor making a sound, while their blood leaked onto the floor of their holy temple.

The sight was a gruesome one: the floor and walls were red and sticky in places, and it seemed as if every piece of furniture in the sparsely-decorated entrance chamber had been smashed or shoved over. Edgar told Brictwin to go back outside and prevent any of the other priests from entering the temple for now. Wulfgar and Leofwin checked the bodies of Toric's priests for life signs, but all of them had passed away within their god's temple.

Wulfgar, looking sombre, led them into the circular central chamber, the most sacred area of the Temple. Toric's Dagger was always kept in a chest on a table near the far wall, only removed for religious ceremonies.

Wulfgar and Edgar shared the same expression. They dreaded what they would find, and at the same time knew that their fears would be realised.

As they got closer, they saw a body slumped against the table.

'Anrik!' called Wulfgar as he recognised the priest. He knelt beside the body.

Leofwin walked over and studied the body, feeling for the pulse.

'He's dead,' said Edgar's bodyguard. He held up an arm by the wrist. The hand was a bloody mess of flesh. The fingers and the thumb had been chopped off in a clumsy fashion, leaving stubs of differing lengths.

Wulfgar gasped in horror.

'They tortured him,' said Leofwin, 'then ran him through with a sword.'

'Why would they torture him?' asked Gyrmund.

'I don't know,' said Wulfgar, looking up, distress on his face. 'The dagger is always kept in the chest. It isn't hard to find.'

Edgar marched over to the chest. The lid was up, the dagger gone.

'Maybe they killed him in case he could identify them?'

Wulfgar shrugged, but said nothing. It was a tired, hopeless movement.

The six men left the devastation of the Temple and returned to the main courtyard, where the priests and other inhabitants had congregated in the aftermath of the attack. They all talked for a short while, making guesses about the origins of the perpetrators.

Eventually Wulfgar ordered one of his men to begin the grisly clean-up operation in the Temple.

Edgar noticed Elana kneeling on the ground, apart from the main crowd. She was tending to an injured priest, who had presumably been stationed at the gate. She was cleaning his wound and talking in a reassuring voice.

It seemed like an age had passed since they had been arguing with Wulfgar in the High-Priest's hall, but it must have been no more than half an hour ago. It occurred to Edgar that, in the confusion, it would have been quite easy for Elana to have escaped from her captors—but, as before, she seemed oblivious to any danger.

'Are you well?' asked Edgar. It was a stupid question, but the adrenaline still racing around his body made him speak before thinking.

Elana turned and smiled in his direction. She pressed down on the forearm of the priest she was attending to with both hands. Was Edgar witnessing a healing miracle? It was difficult to say, since the arm was already bandaged. Elana wiped her hands on a scrap of cloth and stood up.

'I think we should be leaving, Your Highness,' interjected Leofwin.

Edgar nodded, recognising that they were all still in immediate danger. He marched over to Wulfgar. The High-Priest was surrounded by his followers, all asking him for direction in the wake of this disaster. Edgar noted that he was not quite so full of himself any more.

'Wulfgar,' he began, putting as much authority into his voice as possible. 'I need to return to my household now in order to deal with this invasion. I no longer have the time to argue with you. Both you and Elana will accompany me.'

Wulfgar stared blankly at his prince for a moment and then nodded his head in acceptance.

V

LEAVING

BELWYNN WAS NOW ITCHING to get moving. For every extra minute they wasted in discussion, the Brasingians were getting farther and farther away.

It wasn't Edgar's fault. He had responsibilities to keep everyone happy, and Belwynn felt lucky that she was not tied down in such a way. Still, the Prince had not been without luck himself today.

The rider had arrived at Edgar's estate of Bidcote about midday, informing his household that a small band of soldiers from the Empire had entered Magnia. Everyone who could use a weapon had set out for Ecgworth, fearing that Edgar had been killed or captured. But they had met the Prince and his small entourage about halfway to the Temple of Toric and accompanied him back to the relative safety of Bidcote. He was fortunate that the raiders at the Temple had not recognised him, or they would doubtless have taken the time to capture him as well as the damned knife, earning themselves a prince's ransom.

When he got back, Edgar immediately sent out messengers to raise troops as quickly as possible. There were never more than about forty men in the royal household at any one time, and, with news from the east still patchy, it was possible that the raid on the Temple was a precursor to a large-scale invasion.

In these circumstances, the prince's first priority was to raise an army to defend his kingdom. At the same time, he was making plans to retrieve the dagger, and it was here that Edgar was encountering problems.

He had been fortunate that Belwynn and Soren had arrived back in Magnia at this very time, since they, along with Herin and Clarin, were the obvious choice for this kind of operation.

She and Soren were cousins of Edgar's on his mother's side, and, while they were welcome at his court, their presence was a rare occurrence these days. They had experience of the Empire, they would not be required to stay with Edgar and the army, and they had a couple of acquaintances who could prove to be very useful. Most importantly for Edgar, they were family, and could be trusted.

The same could not be said for most other people in the room.

The Prince had decided to hold the meeting in his bedroom at the back of his hall to lend some privacy to the discussion. Although it was a big room, it was still packed. Loyal officers like Wilchard were here, but so were half a dozen noblemen plus other court hangers-on, all of whom expected to have a say. Some were perched on the bed with the Prince; others had been found chairs; still others stood.

Belwynn looked over to Clarin, who was slouched against the wall, no longer attempting to feign his boredom at the interminable proceedings. As soon as it had become clear that their group of four would form the backbone of the party sent to retrieve the dagger, Herin had ridden off to recruit his friends Kaved and Moneva and to pick up any vital provisions from the town. The question was, who else would be dumped on them?

Belwynn forced herself to turn back to the conversation. Wulfgar, the High-Priest, seemed to have brought all of his brethren who had not been slaughtered that morning with him. The man's colossal arrogance may have been dented on his arrival, but when he realized that his brother, Otha of Rystham, was in attendance as well, it had made a full recovery. The two men were trying to muscle in on the mission by turning it into some kind of religious pilgrimage. Edgar was dead set against their involvement. Yet he seemed to be supportive of another priest—the mystic named Elana—who was insisting that she come along.

Amongst the others present who were trying to get a word in edgeways was a nobleman named Farred. Belwynn had never met him before; he had apparently only recently inherited his father's estate, which lay on the border with the Midder Steppe. It was through these estates that the robbers had passed on their way to the Temple. He and his friend Gyrmund had made a crucial intervention in the confrontation at the Temple. They seemed to be sure that the robbers would be heading south-east, giving them the option of slipping back into the Empire via Cordence or the Wilderness.

Farred had suggested that his peers on the border would have been alerted by now and raised their forces, whereas news of the invasion was unlikely to have reached the south. It was a longer route back to the Empire, but probably the safest for the Brasingians.

Otha of Rystham, meanwhile, seemed oblivious to such concerns, but very intent on pressing his brother's claims for religious leadership on the issue.

'What I do not understand, Your Highness, is why you seem to give so much credence to what this heretic says—' Otha waved a hand in Elana's direction— 'yet you would deny the Church of Toric any say in our plans to restore His Holy Dagger.'

Otha was living dangerously, almost accusing his prince of heresy. Belwynn could tell that Edgar was reaching the end of his tether, but he had to tread carefully; he could not be seen to support a convicted criminal over the Church of Toric. Otha was skilled and experienced in high politics, and he usually got what he wanted. He had almost caught the young Prince in his trap— so the interruption of the conversation by the arrival of Soren and Ealdnoth was an obvious disappointment.

Belwynn's brother and Edgar's court wizard had been interrogating the Brasingian prisoner who had been knocked from his horse by Brictwin. Many in the hall greeted their return with clumsily concealed distaste. Most people connected to Edgar's household had, by now, come to terms with his patronage of wizards, but they still had difficulty with certain innovations they had ushered in. One of these was the use of their powers in questioning prisoners. Otha and his like favoured the traditional methods, which usually involved an assortment of sharp instruments and clamps, perhaps the use of fire, but always a lot of screaming and mess. The fact that Ealdnoth and Soren were able to get better results in less time, and with less unpleasantness, left them feeling dissatisfied, and even a little cheated.

'Well?' asked Edgar.

'We have a name,' answered Ealdnoth. 'Their leader is called Gervase Salvinus.'

Ealdnoth was interrupted by a whistle from Clarin.

'You know this man, Clarin?' enquired the Prince.

'Know him? Sure. Not really personal, you understand, but Herin and me fought under him a few years back now, and he was making a name for himself even then.'

'Making himself a name as what?'

'As a mercenary leader.'

Clarin began to regale the room with one of his war stories. It amused Belwynn to watch. No-one really wanted to hear it, but Clarin was such an intimidating figure that most people nodded along enthusiastically whenever his eyes met theirs.

Has anything been decided? asked Soren.

Not really. Wulfgar and Otha are still arguing with Edgar. It looks like we're going to be bringing some bloody priests with us. Are you alright after dealing with that prisoner?

Soren looked back to full health after the damage he had sustained from his fall from the window of Vincente's house. He had recovered consciousness on the journey back to Magnia in the back of Kaved's cart, though had remained groggy and weak the whole time. Belwynn hadn't wanted him to use his magic again so soon afterwards. There had been many times when Soren had pushed the use of his powers too far and blacked out as a result. Most of the time it had fallen to Belwynn to look after him until he recovered. But it hadn't happened for a long time now, since he had improved his mastery of his powers and understood his limits.

I'm fine, he said, *no lasting effects. Ealdnoth did most of it anyway.*

Ealdnoth had been Soren's first tutor in wizard-craft, and they still had something of a father-son relationship. Belwynn could well imagine Ealdnoth taking charge, even though her brother had now surpassed him in power.

Soren turned his attention back to the Prince as the conversation in the centre of the hall began to come back to the matter in hand.

'So who do you think he could be working for?' Edgar was asking Clarin.

Clarin shrugged his shoulders. 'It could be anyone—anyone with enough money, that is. Salvinus's services won't come cheap.'

'Did the prisoner know who was paying?' the Prince asked Ealdnoth.

The wizard shook his head. 'He's a new recruit; he doesn't know anything about the operation. He seemed pretty sure that they were going to head back to the Empire, though.'

'Right. I think we have wasted enough time already,' said Edgar, rising from his seat on the bed to emphasise the point. 'I've decided that Soren will lead the attempt to recover the dagger. Belwynn and Clarin are going with him, and hopefully Clarin's brother Herin will be able to join up with them later with some extra help.'

Edgar paused, and then turned to face Wulfgar and Otha.

'I have also decided that a representative from Toric's community should accompany them, that He may bless the enterprise. Wulfgar, I give you the choice as to whom.'

Wulfgar screwed up his face as he thought about Edgar's offer. Belwynn doubted whether the High-Priest really wanted many of his brethren to go on this expedition; he had already lost a good number of his priests today, and there was every chance that whoever accompanied them would not come back. He needed all the help he could get to rebuild his ravaged community.

Eventually, he nodded his consent. 'I have a volunteer, Your Highness, an initiate named Dirk who recently came to us from the Empire. He is healthy and able to defend himself. He may be of help to your cousins.'

Wulfgar pointed to the priest he had nominated. Belwynn looked him over: he was unremarkable, thin and shorter than average height.

I can't see him being much help, she informed her brother.

Soren grinned at the comment. *Who knows?*

The prince was speaking again. 'I have come to an agreement with Elana. I feel that her powers will be of help to you, Soren, and she is as desperate as anyone here to recover the dagger from the Brasingians. I have therefore agreed that she will accompany you, on the condition that, when the mission is over, whether it be a success or a failure, she returns to the custody of the Church of Toric in order that her sentence be carried out.'

Otha and Wulfgar cried out in protest, but Edgar was in no mood for further debate.

'I want you to leave right now,' he told the twins.

#

Once the decisions had been made, things moved quickly, and it was only minutes later that they found themselves in the courtyard of Edgar's hall, horses saddled and provisions prepared.

'If you recover the dagger there will be handsome individual rewards for everyone who took part,' Edgar announced. 'In the meantime, I am giving Soren enough money to cover any expenses which may occur.'

Edgar led Belwynn and Soren over to one side and handed the wizard a bag of money.

'There's Imperial thalers there as well. Use it all if you must. It is the dagger that is important. Losing the dagger is not going to help my situation here in Magnia, and I have had to cross Rystham today. There may even be an army headed this way, though I doubt it. It looks like this Gervase Salvinus had a specific mission here.'

'Your Highness, I am sorry to intrude.'

It was Farred, who had company.

'What is it, Farred?' asked Edgar.

Jamie Edmundson

'You will recall my friend, Gyrmund. He is well travelled around Dalriya and would like to offer his skills to help your cousins. I can vouch for his honesty.'

'Well,' said Edgar, 'that's very good of you, Gyrmund. I thank you. Soren, what do you think?'

'What can you do?' Belwynn asked the man bluntly.

'I know my way through the Wilderness, which is where I would guess the Brasingians are heading. I tracked them here, and I can pick up their trail again with no difficulty. I am an expert with the longbow,' he said, patting the weapon which was slung across his back, 'and I can fight.'

Well? Belwynn asked her brother.

I don't see why not, he replied.

'It sounds like you might be useful,' Belwynn told the man. 'We could do with your help.' She turned back to Edgar. 'We should make a move now.'

The Prince nodded and pulled Farred aside to speak with Ealdnoth.

Gyrmund and the twins mounted their horses and trotted over to where the other members of the party waited. Clarin was having a conversation with the monk, Dirk, though Toric only knew about what. Elana waited to one side, in silence.

As Soren and Clarin led the party of six out of the courtyard, Gyrmund said a quick farewell to Farred.

Belwynn drew up with the two priests.

'I want you two to know,' she told them, 'if you fall behind, we leave you. I'm not going to let either of you put the rest of us in danger.'

***

Horseshoes. Hammer and nails. Pokers. Plough blades. Locks and keys. Cartwheels. Files and chisels. All very good. All very well and good, and Ulf could do a wonderful job of making all of those. But armour? Spears and war-axes? No. Swords? Really fine swords, works of art that could be passed down the generations? No-one was ordering those anymore, and Rabigar had had enough.

Peace had come to Magnia at last. It was an idea that was disputed, of course. He still heard dire warnings about the North Magnians. Prince Cerdda and his brother were plotting this or that attack. People needed an enemy to talk about,

48

to scare each other about. But blade-smiths were always the first to know when peace had come. People stopped buying weapons.

Bang. Bang. Bang. Ulf was working hard as usual, powerful shoulders hammering away at the anvil.

'How's it going?' Rabigar shouted.

Ulf stopped. 'What?'

'Do you need a hand? Quite a few orders in, I see.'

'Nah, nothing that would interest you, master. You have a rest.'

'Oh. Right then.'

Bang. Bang. Bang.

He was a good boy, Ulf. Or young man now. Hard worker. Respectful. Grateful. But by the gods, did he piss Rabigar off when he treated him like a hoary relic. He headed for the exit from the forge.

'Master Rabigar?'

Bareva, Ulf's wife. She came waddling into the forge, her pregnant belly now much more of a hindrance than it had been a few weeks ago. She was a big woman, not that much smaller than Ulf, and it had taken a while for the baby in her belly to show.

'There you are. Customer asking for you.'

'Right you are. Thank you, Bareva. You can tell 'em to come in.'

Asking for me, thought Rabigar. *Dare I hope?*

A tall, powerfully-built man strode into the forge as if he owned the place.

'Herin? Good to see you.'

'Rabigar,' said Herin, clasping hands and shouting over the noise of Ulf's hammering. 'It's been a while, hasn't it? Boy, she's looking big now, isn't she?' he asked, nodding in the direction of Bareva, who had left the forge.

'Aye. Parents like that, baby's gonna be a monster, isn't it? Well, I'm hoping you've got a job for me.'

'Business slow?'

'Nah. *Business* isn't slow. Our lad,' he said, indicating Ulf over at the anvil, 'is very busy. Just nothing in the way of blade-work.'

'Good. Well, I had a very special favour to ask, and sounds like you might be willing to help me out.'

'Go on.'

'You won't have heard what's gone on at Toric's Temple?'

'Nope.'

'Attacked this morning by twenty-odd soldiers, from the Empire. Broke in and took Toric's Dagger. Worst part about it, I guess, is that Edgar was there when it happened. He's alright, though.'

Rabigar whistled at the news. 'Wait a minute. You're not asking me to make a new Dagger, are you? I mean, I know I'm good, but...'

Herin laughed.

'No. I'm leading the rescue mission for it, though. I need to set off as soon as possible and we need some emergency supplies.'

'Weapons?'

'Yes; only two. One, for a friend—a knife with a sharp point. She likes to throw it.'

'Does she now? Got a nice balanced one she can have.'

'Thought you might. Two, for me. I lost my seax.'

'Careless.'

'Well, let's just say a little adventure down in Cordence went a bit wrong. Thing is, I really need a replacement by the end of the day. Can you do it?'

'I can do it, Herin. But it will be a day-crafted seax, not a week crafted one like the last.'

'A day-crafted one by you is still as good as a week-crafted one from anyone else. I can pay you double. Our little adventure in Cordence wasn't entirely a loss, though we seem to have somewhat less than I thought we might.'

'You can pay me normal rates. I'll enjoy doing it. Might well be the last one I make here.'

'Last one? Are you serious?'

'Yeah, I think so. Time for me to move on. When I first came to Magnia I was recruited personally by Prince Edric. The south was pretty desperate at that point, and I was needed to ensure that the army was at least properly armed. He turned things around and they fought themselves to a draw and a sort of peace. I've got nothing against Edgar, but he'll never appreciate me in the same way as his father. For him, I've always been here; he's known no different. Anyway, I'm a weapons-maker, Herin, and there's no great call for it here anymore. But there's plenty of demand for it elsewhere. I've had offers.'

'I'm not surprised you've had offers to go elsewhere. And I'm sure you'd get paid a lot more, too.'

'That's right and money's important. It's important to everyone, of course. But when you're a Krykker living with humans you really need it. No real family, no real ties. Someone decides they don't like you around anymore, you have to be able to leave everything behind, fast. I know, it's happened to me more than once.'

Rabigar looked around at his forge.

'Plus, the boy, Ulf. Young man, I should say. He's more than ready to take this place over now. He's starting a family, needs the money. The timing's right.'

Herin looked thoughtful. 'Where will you go? Empire?'

'I've had offers. The agents of Duke Emeric have come calling.'

'I bet they have. Plenty of soldiers to arm in Barissia.'

'I don't know, though. Sentimental, you might think. But I like to think I'm arming the good men.'

Herin shrugged. 'The good men. In my experience the good men are the ones asking for their plough to be fixed, not the ones asking for a hundred spears. But I'm not pretending to be the best person to judge. I'm just thinking, Rabigar. You're handy with a weapon yourself. I can tell.'

'Of course. When I was younger I was as fearsome as they come.'

'Then come with us. Edgar is offering a reward to all who take part. Looks like we're heading towards the Empire. You could stay there, or move on somewhere else if it doesn't feel right.'

Rabigar puffed his cheeks out. Tomorrow. After all the years working in this forge, just to up and leave tomorrow, leave it all behind? That would be a hasty decision. But why did it sound so tempting?

'I don't know, Herin. You haven't given me much warning.'

'I know, I haven't. Not for the sword, either. Tell you what, Rabigar. Make me one last weapon. And while you're making it, think it over. Sleep on it, if I've left you any time for sleep. When I come to collect it first thing in the morning, you can leave with me, or not. How does that sound?'

Rabigar nodded, pursing his lips as he thought through the offer. 'I'll think on it, Herin. Thanks for the offer. I'll think on it and let you know tomorrow.'

VI

A MIRACLE

S O FAR SO GOOD, considered Belwynn.
  As Gyrmund had claimed, it hadn't taken long to pick up the trail again, and he had the party travelling at a pace that ate up the miles without exhausting the horses. These were roads and paths familiar not only to Gyrmund, but to Belwynn, Soren and Clarin also, and they felt confident that they would make ground on the Brasingians, who would have been less familiar with the territory.

This part of Magnia was prime arable farming land, and they passed through one well-organised village after another, well-tended fields that promised a good harvest. All the farming folk of Magnia followed the same seasonal routine. Belwynn knew it well. Their father had owned a number of estates, and Soren still had one of them, a village called Beckford. Belwynn had lived there by herself for a year and, without much else to do, had got involved in the day-to-day running of the estate: organising the labour, maintaining and upgrading the equipment, trying to improve yields. This time of year, early summer, was hay-making season, a big job which would require the whole village. The crop fields just had to be looked after and weeded until harvest time in late summer.

When they passed anyone, on the roads or in a village, one of them would offer a quick greeting and ask what they knew of the Brasingians who had passed through. Many had seen them, and the collective opinion of South Magnia appeared to be that they were about five hours ahead.

As for the two priests, they didn't say a word, to each other or to anyone else. Belwynn was used to riding, but she noticed that Elana, in particular, was already showing signs of being saddle-sore. The priestess did not complain, however, and seemed eager to keep up the pace of the pursuit.

As they progressed, they came upon the first patches of woodland which would thicken and become the Wilderness.

The group stopped only once during the day to rest, but as the daylight began to fade, Soren called a halt to the chase.

'We have to give Herin a chance to catch up to us. There is little point in risking one of the horses in this light. It will give us a bit of time to make a decent camp-site.'

'Very well,' said Gyrmund, 'let me pick out a good spot, then.'

As everyone began to make a camp a few metres from the road, Belwynn walked over to speak to Gyrmund, who was building a shelter for the night while the others fetched firewood and other materials.

'How far away do you think we are?'

'About five hours still. They're travelling just as fast as we are; they're not stupid. As soon as they've left Magnia they'll begin to feel safe.'

'Do you think we can catch them up?'

'That depends,' he said with a grunt, shoving a log up against the tree trunk he had picked out for the camp. 'They're not making their route obvious; they could be heading to Cordence or the Wilderness. We'll find that out in the morning. I think Salvinus will choose the Wilderness. A large force wouldn't be able to follow them there without stirring up the vossi. He could be relying on that to avoid an army coming after them.'

'The vossi. I've never seen one. Don't wish to, either.'

'I've had a few encounters,' said Gyrmund, now stacking branches against one side of the log to make a walled shelter. Belwynn began to help. 'They're strange. Not what you might expect. Usually, they don't attack unless they feel threatened. But if they do, it's an all-out attack that doesn't stop. With a group our size, they're likely to just leave us alone.'

'That makes me feel a bit better. I was trying to think from their perspective. Whoever planned this, that is. If they choose to go to Cordence, there's always the possibility that the Cordentines will interfere on the side of Edgar somehow. If they get through the Wilderness, they're home.'

'True. I hope you're right.'

'Why? We don't want to go into the Wilderness, do we?'

'Yes, we do. If they choose Cordence, we're still five hours behind them. If they choose the Wilderness I can catch them up.'

'You're pretty sure of yourself.'

Gyrmund shrugged, a hint of a smile on his face. 'I've been through the Wilderness a number of times. Not many other people have. If one of those Brasingians knows the place too, fair enough. But it's not very likely.'

'If no-one else would want to go in there, why have you?'

'To test myself,' he said, his half-smile turning into a grin.

'To test yourself,' she repeated sarcastically. 'What kind of a crazy person would do that?'

He laughed, holding out his hand.

'Gyrmund. Pleased to meet you.'

Belwynn shook hands, shaking her head as she did.

Elana and Dirk came back to the camp with an armful of sticks each, which they dropped down by the proposed site of the fire. Following behind came Soren, who had collected some stones for the fire pit.

'Gyrmund reckons that we're about five hours behind,' Belwynn explained to the others. 'If we enter the Wilderness tomorrow morning Herin won't be able to catch us up.'

'He'll catch up,' answered Clarin, barging into camp with a clump of green branches he had chopped off. When ready, he would add them to Gyrmund's structure to create a bit of waterproofing and insulation. The fact that Clarin never seemed to experience anxiety of any kind annoyed Belwynn, who often found herself worrying twice as hard about things to make up for it.

'Well, he's *your* brother,' she said.

Clarin just chuckled. As he and Gyrmund finished off the shelter, the others gathered round to get the fire ready.

'So... Dirk. Wulfgar said that you were from the Empire—whereabouts, exactly?' asked Belwynn, trying to start a conversation.

'I'm from Barissia. A town called Magen, near Coldeberg.'

'What made you come to Magnia and join the Temple of Toric?' probed Belwynn.

'Serving Toric is the highest honour one can have,' Dirk replied, jutting his chin out somewhat.

Belwynn noticed Elana frowning at that comment, but the priestess said nothing.

'I am under His direction,' Dirk continued. 'He has chosen me to return the Dagger to its rightful place.'

It wasn't really a satisfactory explanation, as far as Belwynn was concerned, and she sensed that Dirk wasn't too comfortable with the questioning. Whether he had something to hide or whether he was a private person, it wasn't easy to say. She supposed that being a Brasingian may not have made him too popular back at the Temple, and he was perhaps a bit nervous on that score.

'How about you, Elana? Where are you from?'

'Kirtsea. It's a fishing village, just north of the border in North Magnia.'

Belwynn nodded. 'I've heard of it, never been there. Nice place?'

'It's beautiful.'

'Do you have family there?'

'Yes. I've had to give up a lot to serve Madria. I hope that one day I can go back.'

Another cryptic response, thought Belwynn. *Maybe that's just priests.*

'Where is your home?' asked Elana.

Belwynn thought about it. *Our home?*

'Soren owns an estate called Beckford, right in the middle of South Magnia.'

'We both own it,' said Soren.

'By Magnian law, *he* owns it,' she said to Elana. 'Still, I've certainly spent more time there than him. Our father was a nobleman with lands all over Magnia once. But Beckford is all that's left of them.'

'What happened?' asked the priestess.

Belwynn sighed. She looked at Soren, who shrugged his acceptance.

'Our mother was killed when we were ten. A raid from North Magnia on one of our houses. My father was away, fighting in the war.'

Belwynn's voice faltered a little. She still got emotional telling the story.

'The village had already been raided once, and my mother went back to help the people. She'd brought them seeds, animals, and equipment so they could start up again and feed themselves. But the raiders came back. They killed everyone, took everything and left. They could have got a ransom for my mother. My father would have paid anything, but they just killed her. He never recovered. When the war ended he just drank. He got into debt and sold off half his lands and kept on drinking. He died five years after our mother. We sold off the rest of his lands to pay off his debts, but he had more debts than he did property by then. Prince Edric had to help us. He was our uncle, you see. He let us keep Beckford. So, anyway, that's our home now, I guess. I lived there for a year. Soren's never been back. Not much of a home, really.'

'I'm sorry,' said Elana. 'It must have been difficult for you to lose your parents like that.'

'It was, I guess. But we weren't alone. We've always had each other.'

Gyrmund and Clarin came to join them.

'Well,' Belwynn said, deciding to change the subject, 'things are likely to heat up tomorrow, especially if we're heading for the Wilderness. Gyrmund, I don't imagine that everyone here is entirely familiar with it. Perhaps you should tell us what we're letting ourselves in for.'

'The Wilderness is dense. If that is where the Brasingians have gone, we'll have to leave our horses behind at some point. There are tracks, but unless you know what you're looking for, it's easy to get lost. Then you've got the inhabitants. There are the vossi, primitive but potentially very aggressive. If they think we're a threat to their territory, they will come after us and they won't give up until we're all dead. There are humans living there as well, but not in big numbers and unlikely to take us on, especially if your friends arrive. Outlaws are able to make a life for themselves on the edges of the forest. If you want to survive in there, you've got to be fit, quick, and silent.'

'What do the vossi look like?' asked Elana.

'About five feet tall. Their skin is brown and hard, tough like leather. They're fast and persistent. Hopefully we won't meet any of them at all, but...' Gyrmund let his sentence hang there, emphasising that, once they entered the Wilderness, the course of events would be out of their control.

'Sounds fun,' suggested Clarin.

It didn't look like anyone agreed with the big warrior, but equally no-one looked like they wanted to argue the point.

'Well,' said Soren, 'we'd better try to get some rest. Might be the last night we get a peaceful sleep for some time.'

'I'll take first watch tonight,' added Clarin. 'Always pays to play safe. Now, come on, Gyrmund, are you gonna get this fire lit? I'm starving.'

It had been a mild summer's night, and Belwynn hadn't been asked to keep watch, but she still felt as though she hadn't slept. Gyrmund got them all up at a ridiculously early hour and got them moving again at the crack of dawn, despite Belwynn's complaints that they had to wait for Herin and the others anyway. Soren left a written message for Herin under a rock at the camp site, explaining the route they were likely to take. Clarin shook his head at the scrawly lines he left on the paper, as if the purpose of reading and writing was beyond him, which perhaps it was.

Clarin's alternative form of communication was to cut a slash into the bark of the tree they had slept under. To Belwynn, this could have meant anything or nothing, but the big man nodded to himself with satisfaction, as if he had solved some weighty problem.

They rode all morning, eating while on the move, stopping once only for a toilet break. The roads of Magnia became tracks on which they had to ride single file. The Magnian villages which they had passed so regularly yesterday became less frequent as the rich farmland increasingly gave way to woodland. Settlements became smaller, isolated hamlets which had been cut out of the forest, or the odd wooden shack that blended into the trees from which it had been built. The people here were warier, alarmed at a second group of riders passing through so soon after the Brasingian soldiers. But they were communicative enough to say in which direction they had gone, and that was all that mattered.

Belwynn's excitement from yesterday had not reappeared today, and she slumped in her saddle, trying to keep her eyes open. No-one else seemed to be in the mood for talking either; Gyrmund was focused on the terrain ahead, and the two priests were trailing behind, their thoughts concealed.

In the end, just to help her stay awake, she asked Clarin to recount one of his war stories. It did little good, since Clarin tended to dwell on marches and formations and long, involved anecdotes about people she'd never met, his voice becoming a background drone which threatened to send her to sleep at least as much as complete silence would have done.

By mid-afternoon they were in the no-man's land between the state of Magnia and the lawless Wilderness. Officials could draw lines on maps, subdividing the world into neat parcels, but there was no neat border here. This was territory over which Prince Edgar couldn't offer his protection, and was therefore a land of bandits and outlaws.

Gyrmund had stopped to gather them together.

'I've detoured a bit from the route they took. In the next clearing is effectively the last outpost of civilisation around here: Hallaf's Home. Hallaf and his extended family are all outlaws, but he can be reasoned with if he can see a profit to be made. This is the last place we can leave the horses in safety, other than just abandoning them in the Wilderness, which is presumably what Salvinus has done.'

Belwynn patted her horse.

'Well, there's no way we're doing that. But won't that give them an edge in terms of speed?'

'Not really. Either way, we're walking from here on in. The Wilderness is rocky and treacherous; a horse will break a leg before too long in there, and that causes unwanted attention.'

'Let me handle the negotiations,' said Soren. 'Clarin, just look scary and don't speak.'

'Righto, boss.'

They guided their horses downhill through the trees until they saw the roofs of Hallaf's Home below them.

As they got closer, Belwynn got a clearer look at the settlement. She had never seen anything quite like it. Each building was constructed from a variety of the timber materials that surrounded them. They had their choice of tree around here: tall, thin birch grew alongside sprawling ash; mighty oaks shared the land with squat maples. In addition, each building had a completely different design. There was a sunken hut with four wings, laid out in the shape of a cross. There was a U-shaped construction with a garden in the open courtyard. A tall, thin building, which from the outside looked as if it must have had at least four storeys, had a spiral staircase on the outside, leading to the roof. At the far end was a huge building which most closely resembled a warehouse and was the size of all the others put together. There were almost a dozen of these oddities in all. It looked to Belwynn like everyone had taken part in a building competition. And that they had all got steaming drunk beforehand.

There was no central courtyard or anywhere to head to, so Gyrmund stopped outside the U-shaped house and dismounted. The others followed suit. Belwynn could see how stiffly Elana moved as she tried to dismount, and she gave her a hand down.

'Sore legs?' asked Belwynn.

'I've never ridden so much in my life,' said Elana.

The priestess rubbed at her hamstrings and her lower back. She eased up and stretched, visibly looser.

'Magical powers?' asked Belwynn.

'Healing powers.'

Belwynn wasn't about to be converted by watching someone stretch their back out.

'Mmm. Excuse me if I'm sceptical.'

She looked around her. Slowly, and silently, the residents of Hallaf's Home emerged. Some from their homes, some from the forest around them. Adult males for the most part, teenagers through to older men. Many clutched axes, no doubt ready to use them as weapons if necessary, but not in a threatening manner. Not yet, anyway.

A few children came out as well, followed by one older woman with straggly, matted grey hair and eyes that wandered about independently of one another.

The men all had the same kind of look to them, so it was easy to believe they were mostly related in some way. They had big, powerful shoulders, slightly hunched forwards; prominent brows and foreheads, with big bushy beards covering the rest of their faces. No-one in Hallaf's Home seemed to worry too much about their appearance, with worn and mismatched clothing the norm, where there was any. Most of the men went bare chested; their body hair was apparently all they needed to keep them warm.

Hold me back, Belwynn said to Soren, unable to resist. *I think I've finally found a flock of suitors.*

The people of Hallaf's Home gathered around the house, not too close, saying nothing, neither to Belwynn's group nor to each other. *Perhaps they're mute,* thought Belwynn.

Then the door of the U- shaped house opened, and an elderly man appeared and slowly walked towards them. He was grey and balding on top, with a straggly grey beard. As he approached them, Belwynn saw that he had a patch of raw, red, mottled skin on his face, centred around the left side of his forehead and spreading outwards in an irregular pattern, down to his cheek and the top of his nose. It was an infection of some kind which was eating into the man's face, stopping the wounds from healing over. And whatever little creatures were doing it, they were really messy eaters.

'Hallaf,' said Gyrmund, nodding in greeting. 'I am Gyrmund. I have visited with you before, you may remember.'

'Yeffin, reckon y'hav,' said the old man. His dialect, if that was the issue, made his words virtually unintelligible.

'This is Soren,' Gyrmund explained.

'Greetings, Hallaf,' Soren began. 'We are heading into the Wilderness and have come to sell you our six horses. As you can see, they are all healthy and strong.'

Hallaf shuffled over and made a show of inspecting each one, though it was clear as day that they were all fine horses in excellent condition.

'Yeffin,' he muttered, presumably in confirmation.

Belwynn raised her eyebrows at Clarin, and he just shrugged back, equally bemused.

'Here is my offer,' continued Soren. 'You will pay us only sixty crowns for the horses—'

'Yeffin!' screeched the old woman, shooting one arm up into the air in apparent celebration.

'But,' continued Soren, giving the woman a stern look, which made her lower her arm again, 'you will keep them in as good a condition as you have received them, for half a year. Should we return at any time in that period, we are entitled to buy them back from you, at a total cost of one hundred and eighty crowns. If we do not return before half a year has passed, they are yours to do with as you please. Do you understand my terms?'

'Aye, yeffin I do,' said old Hallaf, and he spat onto his palm before holding it out to Soren.

Belwynn could see Soren look from the wet palm to the sticky red face.

'That won't be necessary,' he informed Hallaf. 'One more thing that you all should know—' Soren addressed the whole community formally, raising his voice. 'I am a spell-caster, and I wreak dire vengeance on anyone who doesn't uphold their side of a bargain.'

Soren held out one hand, concentrating. Hallaf's people watched.

Then, his hand burst into flame, orange and yellow light flickering. With a twist of his wrist the flame went out. His hand was unharmed.

The old woman let out a blood-curdling scream, while the men who had gathered around took a step or two back, suitably intimidated, it seemed. All except one of the children, who politely clapped.

Gyrmund turned and looked up the hill they had come down.

'Anyone hear that?'

Belwynn listened. She couldn't hear anything, and neither could anyone else.

'Riders,' he said, sounding sure.

That was enough for Clarin, who drew his sword and moved to face the threat. Gyrmund strung his bow. Hallaf's people followed suit, handling axes and clubs and looking in that direction.

Then Belwynn heard it—horses coming their way at quite a pace, faster than they had come down. Then they burst into view atop the hill, slowing as their mounts picked their way down through the trees.

'Herin!' called Clarin, waving up at his brother.

The old woman gave another blood curdling scream, for no apparent reason.

There were three other riders with him: Kaved and Moneva, their new recruits from Vincente's town, and a second Krykker. At first, Belwynn assumed it was a friend of Kaved's—then she recognised him.

'Is that Rabigar? The smith from Bidcote?' she asked Soren out loud.

Soren peered up. His eyesight wasn't as sharp as hers after his years squinting at books in bad light.

'Yes, it is,' he agreed as they approached. 'Looks like he's brought half his merchandise with him, as well.'

Indeed, Belwynn could see various weapons poking out of their saddlebags. She knew that Herin had a silver tongue, but she was surprised to see he'd persuaded Rabigar to come along. Still, she had little doubt that he was a resourceful man to have along.

The arrivals immediately brought a new energy and volume to Hallaf's Home.

'More women!' exclaimed Kaved as he approached, leering unpleasantly at Belwynn and Elana.

'I've been trying to understand why he thinks anyone would be interested in an ugly, lecherous, foul-smelling Krykker for over a day now, but I'm still none the wiser,' Moneva said, smoothly sliding from her mount to the ground. 'No offence, Rabigar.'

Rabigar rolled his eyes, as if he had had enough already. 'I must be mad to have agreed to this,' he said, without much humour in his voice.

Unlike Moneva, he struggled to dismount, dropping to the ground with a clank.

Herin was already down, clasping arms with his brother.

'Did you get my directions?' Clarin asked.

'Yes, and each time I saw one, I thought to myself, 'more pissing about'. I thought you lot would have made better time than this!'

'Did you get my note?' asked Soren, looking a bit put out.

'Erm, yes. I had a read of it while we were following Clarin's directions.'

Clarin gave a self-satisfied smile.

'At least we treated our horses well. Look at these poor creatures!' said Belwynn.

Each of the four horses was in a lather and blowing hard.

'We're in a rush, aren't we?' demanded Herin. 'What's the story here?'

'I've just sold our horses to Hallaf, here,' explained Soren, gesturing to the old man who was looking on with interest.

'Ours too!' Herin said, barging over to Hallaf. 'How much are we getting?'

'We want you to buy these at the same price,' explained Soren. 'That makes it one hundred crowns for the ten horses.'

'Nah, nuffin doin' on that,' replied Hallaf. 'Sixty for the ten, it be.'

'Nuffin!' shouted the old woman in support.

'We're offering ten prime horses for a hundred crowns and he's saying no!' demanded Herin. 'Fine, we'll leave and take the lot with us.'

Herin made a play of walking off with his horse, which soon changed Hallaf's mind. The old man was getting a bargain, and everyone knew it.

'Eh, eh, not too fast,' he got out, panicking that he might lose the whole deal. 'Money's coming. Hallaf's good as his word.'

Hallaf went back in to his house and, after some time, re-emerged with a bag of money. When Gyrmund checked it, he was some crowns short of the hundred, and he was sent back in to get the right amount.

'What in hell are we doing messing about with these inbreds?' demanded Herin, chafing to get moving. They had all unloaded their packs from the horses and were standing about, ready to go. 'We're losing time here!'

'Shhh!' hissed Belwynn. She really didn't want to get into a fight with Hallaf's sons, who were still standing around, weapons in hand.

Eventually the old man re-emerged and handed over the money.

'Right, let's get moving,' said Herin.

'One more thing, before we go,' said Elana.

She approached Hallaf.

'You have helped us today, Hallaf. The Goddess Madria would bestow a blessing on you, to ease your suffering.'

The priestess reached out to the old man. He took a step back at first but, looking at her curiously, allowed her to place both hands on his face. Belwynn cringed at the thought of touching those weeping injuries.

Elana held her hands in position for some time, and then withdrew them.

There was an obvious visible difference. The redness was gone, as if the infection had been drawn out. The damage to the skin was still visible, but it looked like an old wound that would scar over, and heal.

Elana stepped away.

Hallaf blinked with wide eyes, touching his hands to his face as if he couldn't believe what had happened. The men of the settlement, presumably many of whom were his sons, walked over to him, equally astounded, peering and prodding at the old man. The old woman tottered over, squinting up at him. She drew in a breath, and Belwynn thought that she was going to let out another scream, but instead a tight breath escaped from her throat and that was it.

'Thanking you, lady. Thanking you,' said Hallaf, his voice wavering and tears in his eyes.

It was a moving sight. Toric only knew how much irritation and suffering the man had endured. His family was gathered around him, clearly happy for the father of their community.

Elana held up her hands.

'Please. Thank Madria; *she* healed you. I am just her channel.'

She turned around and returned to the group.

'Still sceptical, Belwynn?' she asked.

Elana had a funny expression on her face, like a young girl's *I told you so*. It made Belwynn smile.

'That was really impressive, Elana,' said Soren.

'Yep, you don't see that every day,' added Moneva.

'Well,' said Elana, 'as I said, Madria has given me these powers.'

'Good for Madria,' snapped Herin. 'But are we going to leave now?'

'Yeffin,' said Belwynn.

'What?' demanded Herin, as everyone started to leave Hallaf's Home, Gyrmund in the lead. 'What the hell does that mean?'

Clarin slapped his brother on the back, chuckling. 'Herin, you had to be there.'

VII

CREATURES THAT COME OUT AT NIGHT

THEY TRAVELLED ON FOOT in a south-easterly direction to reconnect them to the route taken by the Brasingians, and it didn't take long to find it. The trail they had left was now so obvious that Belwynn could have followed it by herself. Twenty horsemen in single file had thrashed through the forest floor, churning the ground and ripping plants, not to mention horse dung here and there. After a while there were footprints as well as hoof prints, meaning they had decided to stop riding and walk their mounts. This was hardly surprising; it was difficult terrain now.

The trees closed in on them and blocked the sunlight, making it much cooler. Thorns, sprouting from the forest floor, scratched them and got stuck in clothing. The ground underfoot was uneven and sloped up and down, tiring out Belwynn's thigh muscles as she pushed up and straining her ankles as she manoeuvred down. She was fearful of turning an ankle, but Gyrmund kept up a severe pace as he tried to make up time on his quarry. He knew which direction they were going in, and would take them on a shorter or easier route when possible to make up time, always keeping in touch with the trail they had left. As he went he gave warnings about this or that hazard, and they got passed down the line. Other than that, there was no talking—just the sound of breathing from the exertion.

It didn't help that, thanks to Rabigar, they had become a walking weapons arsenal. Belwynn presumed that he and Herin had organised the weapons for everyone, and she had no doubt they might be needed, but in this environment they made the going even tougher.

Belwynn had a light sword that allowed her to swing and thrust without losing balance. She was no fighter, but she had sparred plenty of times with Clarin and Herin, who had taught her the basics. Herin's sword was much bigger; he used it two-handed and liked to fight with speed. He also carried a seax in his belt and had a bow, coloured black with charcoal. His brother Clarin preferred to use sword and shield. His size and power, however, meant that he could use a sword that was almost the same weight as Herin's with only one arm. Rabigar was the other member of the group who favoured fighting with a sword and shield. Kaved had a sword and hand axe. Both Krykkers wore metal armour on their arms and legs, complementing the hard scales that grew on their torsos. Moneva wore a short sword on each hip. Gyrmund carried sword and bow. Dirk carried a mace, a favourite weapon of the Order of Toric. Soren and Elana carried no visible weapons and were not expected to fight.

They looked the part, and there were some very experienced fighters in the group. But they had never fought as a unit, and Belwynn knew that they would struggle to face up to Salvinus and his twenty veterans. In that situation, they'd have to hope that Soren could tip the odds in their favour.

Gyrmund called a halt, and Belwynn peered forwards from her position in the line. It looked like they had come to a clearing, and Gyrmund seemed to be looking around, perhaps fearful of an ambush. Signalling for them to stay where they were, he moved into the clearing, studying the ground, walking a circuit around it. He walked off into the trees on the other side for a small distance, then came back again, gesturing for everyone to enter the clearing.

'We'll have a brief rest here,' he said.

'Thank the gods,' said Moneva, dumping her pack on the ground. 'I hate this place. Why did you bring me here?' she asked Herin accusingly.

'It'll do you good to get some fresh air,' he suggested. 'How are we doing then, Gyrmund?'

Their guide made a face. 'I don't like it. This is where our friends said goodbye to their horses. Vossi tracks come from that direction, to the east. They came here and took the horses, but they were handed over to them.'

'Handed over?' asked Soren.

'I mean that both groups were here at the same time. The vossi didn't arrive later. It can't have been an accident; it all looks pre-arranged. Which is worrying.'

'Why?' demanded Herin.

'If Salvinus has an arrangement with a vossi tribe, they could be hostile towards us.'

'What would the vossi do with the horses?' asked Belwynn.

Gyrmund shrugged. 'Eat them, probably. Or sacrifice them.'

'Sacrifice, then eat them,' said Soren.

'Better than riding on the fucking things,' said Kaved.

'Could they have a vossi guide?' asked Rabigar.

Gyrmund shrugged. 'It's possible. I've never heard of vossi doing that before.'

'Any good news?' asked Moneva petulantly.

'Well, they spent some time here, maybe waiting for the rendezvous. We've made up a bit of time on them now. We're three to four hours behind, I would say. They set off in that direction, to the north-east; as we would expect, they're heading for the Empire. They'll be spending the night in the Wilderness. We need to move on a bit more and then find somewhere to make camp ourselves.'

Gyrmund kept them going in the half-light, keen to use his knowledge of the terrain to keep moving after the Brasingians had most likely stopped for the day.

By the time he decided to call a halt, Belwynn was exhausted. All she wanted to do was set her blankets out and go straight to sleep, and most of the others seemed set on the same idea. However, as she got ready, she realised how hungry she was, and she lay there, exhausted, watching Gyrmund and the others get a fire going and then put some pans on it. Eventually, he handed out bowls of stew, and she sat up, spooning the hot food into her mouth with her fingers as quickly as she could.

'Now this is good stuff!' Clarin congratulated Gyrmund. Even Dirk mumbled an appreciation.

'So, Elana. That was some impressive magic you used earlier,' said Soren. 'How long have you been able to do that?'

'For a few months now. I wouldn't call it magic, though.'

'A few months?' he repeated.

Belwynn understood what her brother was thinking. He had studied and practised for years, to the point of obsession, to develop his powers. And she had learned to do that in a few months?

'Not magic?' asked Belwynn, intrigued.

'I'm not a wizard, like your brother. I am a vessel; my powers were given to me by Madria. I think it is very different.'

Belwynn nodded. She was still finding it difficult to get her head round the idea of the goddess in all of that.

'And Rabigar. What made you leave Bidcote and your smithy for this?' asked Soren.

The Krykker thought about the question. 'For this?' he said, gesturing at the Wilderness around them with a wry smile, 'I have no idea. But I have been an exile from my homeland for many years now, Soren. When you are told that you cannot have something, it makes you want it all the more, am I right?'

'Oh, yes,' said Kaved, grinning. 'When a girl says no, for instance?'

Rabigar looked at Kaved with distaste. Belwynn had been too preoccupied to notice before, but even though they were both Krykkers, their relationship seemed strained.

'I've travelled around the lands of Dalriya for many years now, and when I find a place which lets me live in peace, I settle down. After a while, however, I realise how unhappy I am, and that I do not truly have a home. So I pack up and move on again. The smithy is in good hands; my apprentice Ulf has taken it over. Prince Edgar has been very kind to me, but I do not think I shall be returning to Magnia.'

'Perhaps you felt moved to leave because you have been chosen, Rabigar,' said Elana in a soft voice. 'Perhaps we have all been chosen, in our own ways, and given a purpose.'

'We Krykker are a practical people, lady. We do not think in such mysterious ways.'

'That is not to say they are not true,' answered the priestess.

'Ha,' barked Kaved. 'Good luck converting Rabigar Din to your religion, sweetheart.'

'What does Din mean?' asked Belwynn. She had only ever heard Rabigar addressed by his first name.

Kaved looked at Rabigar, who didn't look happy.

'You better tell 'em now you've said it,' said the Krykker bladesmith darkly.

'It's not a bad name,' answered Kaved. 'Krykkers have their hierarchies to maintain, and the number of letters in your name denotes your status. Din is a peasant's name. When Rabigar was exiled he was also stripped of his status—his old name is gone, and when speaking of him we are supposed to use the name 'Din'. Those of us with some sympathy call him Rabigar Din.'

Rabigar had been a familiar figure to Belwynn while growing up. Everyone knew about the Krykker bladesmith. They knew he was an exile. And they knew never to ask him why. Kaved was getting very close to the subject, and Belwynn felt uncomfortable and intrigued at the same time.

'I don't suppose you've told anyone about the reasons for your exile?' Kaved asked Rabigar, grinning.

'No,' said Rabigar.

He wasn't smiling, and the atmosphere was becoming strained. Kaved, however, seemed unconcerned. 'Well, don't worry. Your secret's safe with me.'

'You have the advantage over me,' said Rabigar slowly. 'I don't know what you've done.'

'I do, don't I?' replied Kaved, a smirk still playing on his face.

'What about you, Kaved?' asked Belwynn, trying to turn the conversation around. 'Were you given a peasant's name?'

'Oh, no such excitement for me. I'm from simple warrior stock. No, my reasons for leaving weren't so special. You could say I have a problem with authority. I prefer to make my own decisions.'

'I'll drink to that,' said Herin.

The tension around the fire eased somewhat, and people began bedding down for the night after an exhausting day. Belwynn knew that she would sleep immediately.

'We'll have to keep a watch, tonight,' said Gyrmund. 'It's vital. I'll go first.'

Belwynn cringed at the idea of staying awake alone during the night in this place. She closed her eyes and hoped that the men would do it, feeling guilty as she did.

'No, you've worked hard today and we'll need you to be alert tomorrow,' said Rabigar. 'You sleep through. I'll take first watch.'

'Wake me next,' offered Clarin. 'I'll wake up the loudest snorer.'

Not me, thought Belwynn, relaxing a little.

'Are there creatures in here, that come out at night?' asked Moneva after a pause.

'Most of the creatures in the Wilderness are nocturnal,' said Gyrmund. 'You've got all your usual rodents—'

'Wait,' interrupted Moneva. 'Please, forget I asked. I don't want to know. I really don't want to know.'

Belwynn was woken by Soren crouching over her.

We've got visitors, he explained.

Belwynn immediately got up and began to pick up her possessions. She didn't need to be told that these 'visitors' were not going to be friendly. *Where are they?* she asked her brother.

Herin says there is a group heading straight this way from the north—he doesn't know how many, but they're close.

Everyone was up and ready to leave. Gyrmund silently beckoned them to follow him in an easterly direction, while Herin and Clarin brought up the rear. The group were kept to a slow pace by the need for silence and the fact that it was still dark. Soon, however, they heard screams coming from the direction of their night's camp.

'Vossi!' shouted Gyrmund. 'We're going to have to run for it!'

More and more screams came from behind them, and Belwynn felt sick in her stomach as she realised what the numbers of vossi on their trail must be.

There's got to be a whole tribe of them out there! she said to Soren as they tried to keep up with Gyrmund.

Before her brother could reply, however, Belwynn tripped over a snag in the forest floor and hurtled face-first into the ground. Soren stopped to pick her up, but by the time the twins were on the move again, Herin and Clarin had caught up with them and urged them on faster.

Belwynn looked behind her and immediately wished she hadn't.

The vossi were plainly visible in the distance. The trees seemed to be crawling with them in every direction as they gave chase, screaming at each other, or maybe at their quarry. They all had the same brown, bark-like skin and were running at full pelt towards them. She could make out small weapons glinting in the dark, spears and daggers, weapons that didn't slow down their pursuit, unlike the swords and shields that her companions carried. Belwynn's quick glance was enough to tell her that the vossi were gaining on them, and she smiled bitterly as she realised that the tables had been turned on them—the hunters were now the hunted. Gyrmund was taking them in the opposite direction of Salvinus. In an instant, their plans had disappeared.

The pace of the chase now began to take its toll on the Magnians as they became tired and ragged. Elana was finding it difficult to keep up and was being helped along by Rabigar. Belwynn's lungs felt like they were going to burst, but fear kept her moving. She heard whistling sounds from behind them and turned to see vossi missiles hurtling towards them. Thankfully, they were falling short of their target, for now.

After heading in a north-easterly direction for some time, Gyrmund tried to change tack and take them north-west. There were vossi there, however, and a shower of missiles forced him to return to his original course.

Herin ran up to speak to Gyrmund. 'We've got to do something!' he shouted. 'We're going to end up trapped or walk straight into an ambush!'

'I know. I'm working on it.'

'Well, hurry up! We haven't got much longer,' demanded Herin. 'I'm going to buy you some time,' he said, and returned to his position at the back with his brother.

Belwynn looked back as Herin shouted in Clarin's ear. The two brothers stopped running and took shelter behind a large tree.

As Clarin hefted his shield off his back, Herin grabbed his longbow and took an arrow from his quiver. Drawing the string back to his chest, he released the bolt at the nearest vossi. It managed to dive out of the way, but Herin was already releasing his second arrow at another of the vossi, and this one struck its target full in the chest. The brothers' move succeeded in temporarily halting the chasing pack, who stopped to fire their own missiles. Clarin, however, was ready for this, and used his shield to protect both himself and his brother from the long range attacks. Herin was able to release a few more shots at the enemy, but their position became increasingly precarious as more vossi came into view every second.

Meanwhile, the others had stopped once they had gained a safe distance, and Belwynn watched with increasing foreboding. Kaved must have been doing the same; he now ran back in the direction of the brothers. Belwynn turned to look at Soren, but he was in deep conversation with Gyrmund and Rabigar, while the others were, like her, desperately trying to catch their breath.

The number of missiles raining down on the brothers was now unmanageable, and Clarin was slowly retreating, holding the shield in front of him to stop the darts, spears, knives and other weapons hitting flesh, moving from one clump of trees to the next. At the same time, the vossi had become bolder, and a number of them charged at the brothers, both of whom drew their swords. The longer reach of the brothers allowed them to swing their weapons and connect with the vossi enemy. Herin leapt back out of reach of the retaliatory blows, while Clarin used his shield to further effect and stopped any of the vossi breaching his defence.

Kaved had now reached the conflict after running at full speed towards them. 'Run!' he shouted at the brothers as he let his charge carry him into the vossi, sword and axe both twirling about him.

'Move it!' shouted Gyrmund, seeing Herin's stand fall apart. Belwynn forced herself to turn away from what was happening behind them and followed Gyrmund's lead. He was taking them in the same north-easterly direction as before. Her left ankle sent jolts of pain around her body every time she put her weight on it, and she realised that she must have damaged it in her earlier fall. The adrenaline of the chase had masked the pain until now, but she was determined not to slow everyone else down and pressed on. Their brief rest had allowed a number of vossi who had been running parallel to the group to almost catch up with them, and they were forced to head due east as more vossi missiles clattered into the trees around them.

Belwynn looked behind her and was relieved to see the figures of Herin, Clarin, and Kaved all sprinting in her direction, followed by the vossi, who now looked even more terrifying as they screamed out their challenges, intent on taking revenge for their fallen tribesmen.

Ahead of her, Gyrmund seemed to be looking around frantically as he led the group on, as if trying to find a landmark amidst the endless backdrop of forest. He must have spotted what he was looking for, as he whirled round to speak to the rest of the group.

'Soren is going to cast a spell of protection over us so that the vossi can't reach us. He can only keep it going for a short while, so follow me closely and don't stop for anything. We're heading for a bridge.'

Herin and the others had caught up and heard the last half of Gyrmund's message, but there was no time for questions as he turned back and headed north-west at running pace.

Belwynn let out a whimper as she forced herself to start running again. Clarin must have overheard, as he gripped her under the arm and ran next to her, taking some of the weight off her ankle. 'I'm in the wars too,' he confided, and nodded down at his right leg, where a vossi dart was protruding from his thigh.

Belwynn would have asked after his injury, but she no longer had the breath for speech. Gyrmund's route was now leading them into the chasing vossi, who were already dispatching their missiles at him. Soren's magic was working, however, as the missiles which came into contact with his invisible barrier bounced off it. Belwynn knew how much concentration and effort was required to keep the barrier effective and was relieved to see that Moneva had guessed as much and was leading her brother through the maze of trees and other obstacles.

Gyrmund reached the waiting vossi, and he and Rabigar began slicing into the creatures. The vossi were unable to break through the barrier, but they seemed quite able to send their weapons the other way. When Kaved moved up and joined in with the free hacking, the uneven nature of the contest forced the vossi to retreat out of the way, and Gyrmund was able to lead them on.

Belwynn sighed with relief as they were able to begin moving again. They were now surrounded by the vossi on every side, pressing in on them, trying to find a weakness in Soren's defences. She could see their faces quite clearly, painted with red dye, all scarred brown skin and dark eyes staring at her. They were sending killing blows straight for her, and only Soren's magic was stopping them from connecting. She felt panic rise within her and looked over at her brother, knowing that soon his powers would fade and they would be doomed, chopped to pieces here in the middle of this horrible forest. She wanted to communicate with him and ask how long he could carry on, but knew that it would just be a distraction for him.

When would they get to this damned bridge? The only thing keeping Belwynn sane was Clarin's tight grip on her, guiding her along and lending her his strength and confidence.

Then, suddenly, they were upon the bridge. It was a rickety looking thing, made of rope and wood, and Belwynn seriously wondered whether it was safe to cross. She did not for a moment, however, think of not attempting it—such was her desperation to leave their pursuers behind. Some of the vossi tried to prevent their passage, but Herin moved forward to attack along with the two Krykkers, and they were soon dispersed. The vossi were now totally disorganised—their quarry had turned back in on them and they had lost their shape, along with a number of their warriors. They continued to scream at each other, but none of them seemed able to take charge of the situation.

Meanwhile, Gyrmund began to lead the party across the river. Elana balked at stepping onto the bridge and stared down at the fast-moving current of the river below. Dirk, however, grabbed her by the wrists with a look of wild panic on his face and dragged her onto the structure. Clarin shoved Belwynn forward behind the priestess as he and his brother brought up the rear.

By the time Belwynn reached the other side of the bridge, Kaved and Rabigar were already cutting the rope and chopping the planks of wood which kept the bridge secured to their side of the riverbank. She leapt off the end of the bridge without looking back and ran to where the others had taken cover behind a copse of trees a few yards away.

The vossi were still shooting at them across the river, and Soren maintained his spell, the strain evident on his face. Belwynn peeked through the trees to see the two brothers and the two Krykkers sprinting away from the riverside in their direction. The bridge which had saved their lives was now floating on top of the water, and on the other side of the river the vossi screamed in frustration as those who had tried to follow the group across the bridge pulled themselves out of the water.

Belwynn pulled back and, letting out a sigh of relief, leaned over to speak to her twin. 'You can stop now Soren. We're safe.'

VIII

THE STAND

A S THE GROUP STOPPED to catch their breath and their bearings, Elana began to tend to the injured parties. She slid the dart out from Clarin's thigh and inspected the wound.

'It's poisoned,' she informed the warrior matter-of-factly.

Clarin frowned, the closest he came to showing any signs of concern. 'Will it be alright?' he asked.

'Yes,' replied the priestess confidently, and forced a finger into the hole made by the dart, wiggling it around inside. She then held her hand over the wound for some time, letting her healing powers flow into Clarin's leg.

'I wish I'd been hit by a dart,' leered Herin, leaning over to inspect Elana's handiwork.

'And not in the leg, either,' joined in Kaved.

Belwynn couldn't appreciate their banter so soon after their near-death experience. Her body was still shaking uncontrollably, and she just hoped that no-one else would notice.

Elana left Herin to bandage up his brother's thigh and walked over to where Belwynn was sitting next to Soren.

She distrusted the priestess. Soren was tired after his exertions, but he would recover, and Belwynn knew best how to look after him. After all, she had been looking after him since before she could remember. It wouldn't hurt to have Elana look at her own ankle, however, and she would be able to examine the priestess's claims of healing powers at the same time.

'Soren is fine,' Belwynn informed her, 'he just needs to rest.'

Elana nodded in acceptance. 'Shall I look at your ankle, then? I noticed you hobbling.'

'Yes, please, Elana.'

The priestess knelt in front of Belwynn and took hold of her left foot, resting it in her lap. The ankle was throbbing. Belwynn doubted whether she would be able to walk on it for some time, and feared holding back the rest of the group.

Elana began to massage the ankle. At first, Belwynn had to grit her teeth in pain, but gradually she felt her muscles relaxing and the ankle becoming more flexible. As Elana's hands pressed into the ankle, she could feel a sensation of warmth entering ligament and muscle, restoring the damaged tissue. When she was satisfied that her work was done, Elana bandaged up the ankle, giving it support without putting too much pressure on the injury.

Belwynn had to admit, to herself, that the priestess had done a good job.

'Are you able to walk?' asked Gyrmund, putting the question to Soren and Belwynn.

'They need to rest,' Elana answered for them.

'We've got to move,' he replied. 'Those vossi are of the red-face tribe. It wouldn't surprise me if they have made a deal with Salvinus—and even if they haven't, they'll still be after us, and they know exactly where we are. We've got to put some distance in now or it will be too late.'

Belwynn was well aware of the situation they were in. 'I can walk,' she said. She looked over at her brother, who gave her a nod, apparently too tired to speak. 'Soren can, too, but he'll need some help.'

Help was forthcoming, as Clarin and Herin put Soren's arms over their shoulders and grabbed him around the waist. He barely had to carry any of his own weight—just concentrate on putting one foot in front of the other. Gyrmund and Rabigar led the party off, while Kaved guarded the rear. Belwynn stayed close to her brother, anxious for him, yet relieved that both were now able to keep up with the hard pace that was being set.

Gyrmund tried to put as much distance between the group and the broken bridge as possible, but it wasn't long before the vossi reappeared. They were moving in small clusters of two or three, spreading out across the Wilderness, renewing their hunt. One call would soon bring the red-face tribe back on their trail. Whenever Gyrmund heard them approaching—for it always seemed to be Gyrmund who heard them first—he directed everyone to the nearest hiding place to the side of the track. He would then slither off to investigate and return when the vossi had moved on.

As time went by, the vossi came more and more regularly, halting the group's progress. Gyrmund began to leave the others in a secure place for a few minutes while he scouted the area up ahead.

On one such occasion, while Belwynn was taking the opportunity to make Soren and herself eat something, Herin spotted a group of three vossi heading their way. A whispered warning spread through the group and swords and knives were drawn in anticipation of conflict. The three vossi were threading their way through the thick foliage of the forest, apparently talking to each other in their high-pitched language. It looked like they had found their tracks.

The vossi continued to move towards them. Herin and the others were confident enough of dealing with them should the group be spotted, but the real danger was that the calls of these three scouts would bring the whole red-face tribe down on them again. Herin began swearing at the absent Gyrmund, but he was not going to save them from this situation.

Moneva interrupted the warrior's list of hissed expletives. 'We're going to have to deal with them before they spot us.'

Herin seemed to be musing over their options, but eventually nodded his agreement.

'The rest of you stay here for the time being. Moneva, you swing round to their right and I'll take the left.'

Herin drew his seax and began crawling off in the direction of the vossi. Moneva reached down to her right calf where she had a knife of her own attached to her leather trousers. As she unsheathed it, Belwynn noticed it was an unusually thin weapon which ended in an extremely sharp point.

Herin and Moneva soon slid out of sight. As Belwynn concentrated on their movements, she noted that neither was quite as quiet or mobile as Gyrmund in these conditions.

As the seconds went by, Belwynn and the others found themselves straining their eyes and ears, trying to fathom out where the two of them were. The three vossi continued to make their way towards them in a roundabout direction, and Belwynn almost found herself feeling sorry for the enemy that had almost scared her witless earlier in the day, knowing that they were totally oblivious to the fact that two trained killers were at this very minute stalking them in the undergrowth.

It happened so suddenly that Belwynn almost shouted out loud with shock. As the vossi continued to make their search of the area, two black blurs of movement erupted upwards from the undergrowth on either side and darted towards them. Moneva attacked a split second before Herin did. From Belwynn's point of view, it looked as if she didn't even make contact with her first victim. Before the corpse began to tumble to the floor, she reversed the swing of her first strike and drove the sharp point of the blade into the throat of the second vossi, who had not been able to react to the speed of the attack. Herin, meanwhile, had approached from the opposite angle and grabbed the mouth of the third vossi from behind, ensuring that no noises escaped from his victim as he deliberately and carefully slit its throat. As the bodies of the vossi fell to the ground, so too did those of the killers. Within a matter of seconds, it was over, and the forest returned to peace, as if the deadly spectacle had never happened, but had been some figment of Belwynn's imagination.

It was some time before Gyrmund returned, and his extended absences always worried Belwynn, knowing as she did that it would be much easier for him to slip away alone than with nine other people. Thoughts of escape seemed to be far from his mind, however. 'I've found the trail,' he whispered, perhaps by way of explaining his long absence.

Belwynn had pushed Salvinus to the back of her mind since the flight from the vossi, almost giving up on them rediscovering the trail. Gyrmund, on the other hand, had obviously kept his mind firmly on his quarry, leading them all not only away from the chasing vossi but back towards the Brasingians. Belwynn noted that surprise registered across the faces of many of the others, an involuntary admission that, like her, they had little idea of which part of the Wilderness they were in now, and were reliant on his expertise.

Herin, on the other hand, was not the kind of person to admit such a weakness. 'How far behind are we now?', he demanded.

If Gyrmund detected any hostility in Herin's voice, he chose to ignore it. 'We're about four hours behind.' He paused for a moment. 'If we want to follow them we're going to lay ourselves open to the vossi again. I'm sure that they know that we're after Salvinus and they're taking special care to look in this area.'

Although spoken as a statement, Gyrmund was really asking them a question: were they prepared to risk the vossi again in order to catch up with the Brasingians?

Belwynn wasn't sure if she *was* prepared to risk the vossi again, and turned to look at her brother.

Soren stared straight ahead. 'Take us to the trail, Gyrmund.'

As Gyrmund once again led the group through the forest, their spirits began to rise. Belwynn was no exception and was sure that, like her, the others felt glad to have regained a measure of control over the situation they were in. They were no longer simply running away from the vossi but were taking steps to recover the ground they had lost.

The person they had to thank was a rather enigmatic man. He had joined the group almost as an afterthought, but was now one of its most important members. The challenge of catching up with Salvinus seemed to have evolved into something of a personal test of Gyrmund's abilities, and he accepted the addition of the vossi into the melting pot with grim fortitude.

Belwynn moved up to the front of the line, where Gyrmund was keeping the group some feet away from the main track in an effort to hide them from the vossi scouts. "How are we doing?" she enquired.

Belwynn studied Gyrmund's face as his eyes glanced towards her to acknowledge the question and then quickly returned to the forest scene, looking to the side, up in the trees and then ahead as he tried to make out forms in the shadows of a rocky outcrop. The man was in a constant state of vigilance, but it wasn't a strained or worried state; it seemed to be his natural way of doing things.

His eyes returned to Belwynn's. 'Not too bad.' He smiled grimly. 'It seems as though I underestimated this Salvinus. He's managed to stay pretty much the same distance ahead of me since we left Bidcote.'

Bidcote, thought Belwynn. It seemed like an age since they had parted company with Edgar, but it had only been two days. 'Why did you decide to come with us, Gyrmund? Did Farred ask you to?'

'No. I make my own decisions. Farred is just a friend of mine.'

'How did you meet him?'

'We grew up together.'

'So, why did you decide to go on *this* expedition?' Belwynn persisted.

'Toric's balls, you like your questions, don't you?' Gyrmund admonished with a frown. He shrugged. 'I'm the best tracker around. I was the best person for the job, and the way things turned out, you wouldn't have had a chance without me.'

Belwynn decided to let his arrogance pass, given that what he had said seemed to be the truth. 'But you knew more than everyone how dangerous it would be. It's hardly worth the risk of a bit of coinage or favour from Edgar to you.'

Gyrmund looked at her, as if it was for the first time. 'I'm not interested in Edgar's favour. As for the risk—look, you may be a cousin of Edgar's, but that doesn't mean that you, a woman, have to go charging into the Wilderness after twenty-odd soldiers, does it? The risk is why most of us are here, and why we decided to keep up the chase with the Brasingians. To test ourselves. If we just cared about the money, I'm sure there are easier and safer ways to earn it.'

There was something in Gyrmund's words that disappointed her, though they were perhaps true enough. As they waited to get moving again, Belwynn thought about it, looking around at her companions. The risk, the challenge, the adventure. This was why Gyrmund was here, why Herin was here, even why Clarin and no doubt most of the others were, too. There were far easier and less life-threatening ways to earn money for people with their skill set than this chase through the Wilderness, that was for sure. Herin and Clarin could be highly rewarded by any number of ambitious noblemen or wealthy merchants for doing very little from one week to the next but drink their host's wine and abuse his servants. Instead, they chose to put themselves in danger, to test themselves and hone their skills.

For Soren and herself, though, the danger had never been the attraction. It was the chance to put things right in a world where most things seemed to be wrong. Toric's Dagger didn't mean that much to her personally. But it was a symbol to their people, an ancient relic, which had been plundered by a bunch of mercenaries. It hadn't been stolen on a whim, either; it had been taken in a carefully-conceived operation. The whole business felt threatening, even sinister.

Maybe she was just naive. Maybe right and wrong didn't come into it that much. And then there had been the attempted robbery of Vincente a few days ago. Sure, he probably wasn't a very nice man. Yes, they needed the money. Badly. But since when had her brother use his powers simply to rob people? It seemed like, without her noticing, they had got a bit lost; aimless. Belwynn was beginning to think she had had enough of putting herself in these situations.

Gyrmund made a flapping motion with his hand, trying to get everyone to crouch down in the undergrowth, but it was already too late. To their left, on the other side of the track they were following, he had spotted a couple of vossi. Unfortunately, the vossi had spotted them as well. Hardly surprising, thought Belwynn, with all ten of them trudging through the forest. At first the two vossi looked shocked and a little afraid at coming upon the enemy, but soon began screaming their find so that the noise carried through the Wilderness.

Gyrmund swore under his breath. He replaced his bow over his left shoulder, which he had presumably unfastened to silence their discoverers. Sure enough, the calls of the two vossi were being answered by the others of their tribe, and the forest around them erupted into high-pitched noise, which seemed to Belwynn to come from all directions.

'We're gonna have to move!' shouted Gyrmund, not waiting to see if people followed but running on ahead.

He took them down a bank and onto a new track, perhaps one made by the vossi or the animals of the Wilderness. Gyrmund's jog seemed to be as natural to him as walking, as if he could keep it up for hours without losing breath. For Belwynn to go at the same speed, however, sapped her energy and burnt her lungs. The two vossi made no attempt to interfere with their getaway, apparently content to wait for reinforcements. This didn't stop Herin from firing an arrow in their direction, which crashed harmlessly into the trunk of a tree. This aggression brought renewed screaming from the vossi, which only served to put Herin in a fouler mood than before.

They continued to run along the winding forest track as the red-face vossi behind them began to organise their chase. Before long they started to run into vossi searching parties of two or three, but these did not try to tackle them alone, preferring to wait for reinforcements. They had obviously learned to fear Herin, Clarin, and the others as a result of the confrontation before the bridge and were not prepared to risk joining the other vossi who had fallen under the Magnians' blades.

Soon, however, Belwynn could look behind them and see a large chasing pack of vossi, screaming and letting off the odd dart or stone in her direction. Elana began to fall behind, and Belwynn could hear her fighting for breath as her body tried to pump enough air into her lungs to keep her moving. Ahead, the stronger members of the group were beginning to separate from the slower runners. They had to stop, however, when six vossi emerged from the trees to the left to block their path on the track.

The danger was obvious: if they did not get past, and quickly, they would be caught by the vossi behind them.

Gyrmund and the others drew their weapons and charged the vossi. Fortunately, it was over in seconds. First one, then two, then all the vossi broke away and ran back to the safety of the trees. One lay dying on the ground, and a couple of the others had received injuries, but none of Belwynn's companions had been hurt.

The brief melee had wasted valuable time, however. Gyrmund was searching the surrounding terrain, a look of anxiety plainly visible on his face.

What's he looking for? Belwynn asked her brother.

Somewhere to make a stand, came the reply. *We can't outrun them.*

A feeling of dread came over Belwynn, since it was plain that they couldn't outfight them, either. There were too many of them.

Soren grabbed her wrist. 'We're off!' he shouted.

Gyrmund had apparently made his decision and was taking them in the very direction from which the six vossi had attacked them. Flanked by Clarin and Herin, he made his way from the track into the forest. The vossi backed away, albeit screaming their defiance. Gyrmund pointed towards a mound, barely a hundred yards away, as he was talking to the two brothers. As Belwynn followed on, she could make out Herin nodding his agreement at Gyrmund's proposition. Everyone began to make a dash for the point of defence. The vossi were now within missile range of the group and their eagerness made them discharge whatever long range weapons they had. Now that they were back in the forest proper, the trees gave them enough cover, and the group made it to the mound without injury.

Once there, Herin began shouting instructions to everyone for the defence of the mound.

The south-east side of the mound, facing the oncoming vossi, was dominated by two large oak trees. The central point of defence was between the two trees, and here Herin positioned himself, Clarin, and Gyrmund. Clarin, whose large shield would be able to defend himself from missile attack, stood in the centre. Herin and Gyrmund stood either side of him, able to use the trees as shelter if necessary, with a good view of all the approaching vossi, in order to use their longbows to best effect. On the other side of Gyrmund's tree, to his right, Herin had positioned Moneva, and next to her was Kaved. His job was to prevent the vossi coming from the flank. Such a task was more than difficult considering the numbers of the enemy. To Herin's left stood Dirk, waiting in the shadows of the tree, and next to him was Rabigar, who had been given the same job as Kaved. Herin had asked Belwynn, Soren, and Elana to stand behind this line of seven, further up the mound, and to intervene wherever they were needed.

The mound was situated in a small clearing in the forest, and as the vossi approached they stopped short of entering the clearing, preferring to gather in the trees beyond it. Now that Belwynn and the others had stopped running and decided to make a stand, the vossi seemed more agitated than ever, but they looked more confused than aggressive.

Why are they acting so strange? Belwynn asked Soren, using their telepathic link to keep the question private.

I think we might have stumbled onto one of their burial mounds. They seem nervous about coming closer, although it looks like they're beginning to overcome any doubts.

Some of the vossi leaders had now appeared on the scene and were screaming orders at their soldiers, but the whole approach to the mound seemed very disorganised. Still, they were in no rush, thought Belwynn, and it was her companions who would feel the nerves more as time went by and the ranks of the vossi continued to swell.

Individual vossi were now running into the clearing and approaching the mound, screaming their defiance before backing away again. Herin and the others kept to their positions as the bizarre antics of the vossi continued. One of the braver vossi exposed his genitals to those present on the mound before returning to the safety of the trees on the outskirts of the clearing, to the apparent congratulations of his comrades. The success of this exploit provoked a spate of similar gestures and taunts amongst the vossi.

What are they doing now? asked Belwynn, unsure whether to be intimidated or amused.

I don't know, replied Soren, sounding equally bewildered. *They might be trying to provoke us into attacking them, but surely, they don't think we're that stupid.*

The vossi tactics were now challenged by Herin who, evidently getting bored with the impasse, fired an arrow straight at one of the demonstrating vossi, which struck it full in the chest; the creature keeled over dead in the middle of the clearing. Herin quickly grabbed another bolt and pulled back the string of his bow, threatening to repeat the attack. This gesture caused the clearing to empty again as the vossi retreated to the treeline.

The screaming amongst the vossi now resumed, and soon large numbers were being pushed forwards towards the mound. A barrage of missiles descended upon the defenders as they were forced to take cover behind the two oak trees. Belwynn, Soren, and Elana knelt as stray stones hurtled in their direction. Clarin also knelt and, rather than using one of the trees as cover, he placed his whole body behind his shield. This seemed to invite attack, and the vast majority of missiles were now raining down on the large warrior as the vossi sought to penetrate his defence. However, the vossi had used many of their long-range weapons already this day, and they did not seem to have either the amount of ammunition or the skill to succeed in getting past Clarin's shield.

Herin and Gyrmund now began to shoot back at the vossi, each shielded by one of the trees. They were increasingly able to pick off their targets without putting themselves in too much danger. Herin had an upright style, pulling the string to his chest and looking around before he let go. Gyrmund pulled his string all the way back to his ear, carefully aiming the flight of his arrow so that he was as accurate and deadly as possible.

It wasn't long before the vossi leaders realised that the missile contest wasn't getting them anywhere and screamed new orders to their troops. The vossi stopped shooting altogether, and a short period of silence followed, interrupted by the hard *twang* of Herin and Gyrmund's bow strings as they continued to take advantage of the sitting targets.

Then, one by one, the vossi began to scream their defiance to those on the mound until every single warrior joined in the chorus.

'Prepare yourselves,' shouted Herin above the cacophony.

As the words left his mouth, the vossi charged. It was a disorganised mess, since many of them didn't seem sure which part of the mound they should be attacking, but it was a frightening sight nonetheless. Herin and Gyrmund had a few seconds to release their last arrows before discarding their bows and drawing their swords.

The vossi reached the centre of the mound first. Once they were only a few yards away, Clarin led a counter-charge into the enemy. Shouting twice as loudly as any of the vossi, he used his shield as a battering weapon, shoving it into the vossi at face height and then bringing his sword over his shoulder in a high arc so that it crashed down into his chosen victim with such force that it almost cleaved it in two. Herin and Gyrmund followed his move, slashing into the vossi with speed and strength while retaining enough manoeuvrability to dodge the returned blows. The vossi who had reached the mound first now looked like they regretted it, but the ranks behind them pushed them onwards, forcing the three defenders to back away to their original places in between the two great oaks. This was no bad thing, as the vossi were no longer able to outflank Herin or Gyrmund, but had to come at them face on.

In the meantime, more of the vossi had reached the two sides of the mound. To Belwynn's right, Moneva was parrying and defending her position on the other side of Gyrmund's oak tree, while Kaved was hacking and slashing at the vossi with sufficient aggression to keep them at bay. Belwynn turned her attention to the left, where the vossi were just reaching Rabigar and Dirk. As the first vossi approached, Dirk took an enormous back-swing with his mace and aimed a blow. The weapon connected powerfully with the face of its target, leaving the vossi in a crumpled heap on the floor, its head lolling at a strange angle away from the rest of its body. Unfortunately, the force of Dirk's blow was so powerful that it pitched him forwards, and, as the next vossi came towards him, he didn't have enough time to pull back the mace to defend himself from the blow.

The vossi thrust a wicked looking blade towards Dirk's midriff and the best the priest could do was to twist his body away and try to avoid the impact. He was unable to escape the blow, however, as the vossi lunged forward and stabbed into his side.

The blade penetrated deeply, before the vossi withdrew the weapon, leaving a deep gash pouring with blood. Dirk staggered backwards, then collapsed to the ground. As the vossi stood to full height, the blade of Rabigar's sword sliced into its neck, killing it immediately. The Krykker proceeded to swing his weapon in deadly circles, forcing the other vossi to back away as he inched forwards to stand over Dirk's body.

Belwynn rushed forward to help and grabbed Dirk under the arms, trying to hoist him further up the mound. She was soon joined by Soren and Elana, and between them they pulled the priest away to relative safety.

Elana began tending to Dirk, but it was clear to Belwynn that he was in a bad way. *Can't you use your defence spell again?* she pleaded to her brother as she watched Rabigar slowly being forced backwards by the vossi. The vossi had found themselves a weakness in the mound's defences, and although they rightly feared Rabigar's whirring blade, they also knew it was only a matter of time before they pulled him down.

I'll use it if I have to, Soren replied, *but it will run out eventually and then I'll have nothing left.*

'Then think of something!' Belwynn screamed aloud at her brother, before drawing her sword and rushing down the mound to help Rabigar. Belwynn immediately regretted her words: she shouldn't have handed all the responsibility over to Soren. They were all in this mess together, and shouting at each other wasn't going to help—only cause panic. There was no time to apologise, however, as Belwynn gingerly entered the melee, prodding and then thrusting at the vossi, causing them to back off a little and giving Rabigar some time and space to regain a measure of control over the situation.

There was little the Krykker could do against such numbers, however, and Belwynn soon realised that one false move could result in a death blow from the vossi. As they swung and shoved their weapons towards her Belwynn was forced to retreat up the mound, and Rabigar went with her, standing shoulder to shoulder. It seemed painfully obvious to Belwynn that the vossi could easily move round the bottom of the mound and climb it from the other side, thereby surrounding the nine remaining defenders, but right now the vossi seemed too intent on striking at the nearest enemy to consider that.

As she was forced to give more ground, Belwynn took a quick look around. She was now almost above Herin's position on the mound and the vossi would soon be able to attack him from the side. Belwynn realised that such an attack would spell the end of Herin's defensive ring, and she resolved to stand her ground and not give the vossi a further inch. Another quick look behind her and she saw that Kaved and Moneva were also being forced to give ground to the vossi, though they were not yet in quite so perilous a position. As she turned back, Belwynn was quick enough to see that one of the vossi had decided to end the deadlock.

It charged straight up the mound, heading for Belwynn. The whole attack lasted seconds, but for Belwynn it happened in slow motion: he vossi leapt towards her, spear held in front and aimed for her heart. Belwynn's body seemed to react to the threat independently of her mind, primeval instinct taking over. Gripping the sword so that it angled downwards towards the tip, just as Clarin had made her grip it time after time until it was second nature, Belwynn took a stride with her left leg down the slope and knelt on her right knee whilst, in the same movement, extending her sword forwards. The vossi's spear passed harmlessly overhead, while its charge propelled it onto her blade, the sword slipping easily into its guts. Its momentum nearly knocked her over, but she had the strength to keep her kneeling position, shoving the creature onto the ground in front of her, its weapon dropping from its lifeless hand.

Belwynn wrenched at her own blade, which had become embedded deep into her attacker. It came free, bringing with it the stinking entrails of the slain vossi, but not quickly enough.

One of the vossi had followed up the attack and now dove towards Belwynn, its face contorted into a vicious snarl. Belwynn thought it must be too far away to reach her, but as it threw itself to the ground the vossi stabbed a knife into her foot.

The impact and pain of the injury threw her into a state of shock. It felt as though the knife had torn right through her foot and impaled her onto the

85

mound. Belwynn looked up into the eyes of the vossi, its hand still gripping the handle of the knife with all its might.

Suddenly, from the corner of her right eye, Belwynn detected movement. Her stomach contracted with fear, but she forced herself to turn her head around to face what she expected to be her killer. Instead all Belwynn saw was a blur streaking past her.

She followed its direction and saw Herin slamming his sword downwards into the prostrate vossi, then clashing one-handed with another vossi while his other hand felt at her foot. Herin removed the knife and then danced backwards, grabbing her around the chest and hurling her further up the mound. She looked up to see Clarin retreating up the mound towards her as he covered Herin's move. This in turn forced Gyrmund to do the same, and as Belwynn scrambled backwards everyone seemed to follow her, forming a tighter and tighter semi-circle.

Then, behind her, Belwynn heard an almighty scream, the scream of a vossi, yet so loud it didn't seem possible that it could belong to a single voice. Belwynn didn't feel like she could face any more, but she turned around and looked up to the centre of the mound where Soren was.

Or, at least, where Soren had been.

Soren, Elana and Dirk had now been replaced by a swirling distortion of light, a gaseous substance which seemed to be taking shape whilst emitting the enormous sound.

The shadowy form slowly came to resemble a face, vossi-like in its features, but with burning green eyes and a mouth that, as it opened and closed, let out a scream that must have been heard throughout the Wilderness. Belwynn could now make out what must be words in the vossi language, and she turned around to see what effect the apparition was having on their enemies.

The vossi had stopped their attack on the defenders and were staring up at the face, worry lines creasing their faces, occasional exchanged glances or words passing between them. Clarin and the others looked unsure how to react, nervously looking over their shoulders but keeping an eye on the vossi in case their attention was drawn back to the fight. The vossi were now in a state of confusion, but their leaders began to rally their soldiers, shouting in their faces, hitting them and forcing them to renew their advance on the mound.

Just as this seemed to be working, the noise from behind Belwynn got louder, so loud that it hurt her ears, and she was forced to drop her sword and cover them with her hands. The vossi began to do the same and started to back away from the mound.

Then, a beam of light seemed to shine out from the apparition on the mound and strike the vossi warrior standing closest to Clarin.

For a moment the figure of the vossi was lit up like a beacon, and then flames erupted from his clothing. The vossi struggled in the flames, writhing in agony, and Belwynn caught the smell of burning flesh in her nostrils. Those surrounding the vossi torch, a look of terror in their eyes, turned and ran from the sight. For a moment they met some resistance from their leaders, desperately trying to stop the rout, before every vossi warrior turned their back on the mound and ran, in every direction, into the forest.

As floods of relief overcame Belwynn she turned around once more to look up at the mound. The image of the vossi face before her was now dissolving, and behind it she could make out the figure of Soren.

He was stood facing her, arms outstretched, veins standing out, eyes rolling up into his head in convulsion with a visible streak of blood running from his nostrils.

As the last vestiges of the image disappeared, the convulsions stopped, and he collapsed onto the ground.

IX

AFFLICTIONS

BELWYNN GAVE HER FOOT ONE final look, marvelling at the scarred tissue that, moments before, had been a gaping wound. She shoved her shoe back on. Elana had dealt with all the injuries. She looked exhausted from the healing she had carried out. But two problems remained.

'They shouldn't be moved,' Elana informed Herin in a tired voice. 'It could cause permanent damage.'

Herin grimaced. Both Soren and Dirk lay unconscious. Soren had not woken since he had collapsed on the ground after the vossi had fled. Dirk had been awake at first, but in agony, crying out in pain: mostly unintelligible, mixed in with pleas for help. He asked for help from the gods, from his mother but, interestingly, not from Toric. After Elana had treated him, he had grown calmer and fallen asleep. Belwynn would have been quite happy to risk Dirk's health, since the priest had been of little help so far, and she knew that Herin was thinking the same thing. The vossi had gone, but no-one knew if or when they would return.

Belwynn's own injury was not too serious, though it would still give pain every time she put any weight on it. None of the others had sustained any serious injuries, but they were all itching to get moving away from the bloody mound. The fact that Soren, who had probably just saved everyone's lives, was now seriously ill, kept them from departing the scene.

'We're going to have to build stretchers,' said Rabigar. 'We'll be able to move them a fair distance before nightfall. Then we can decide what to do in the morning.'

'Agreed,' said Belwynn quickly. She looked around at the group, but no-one disagreed with the plan, even if they wanted to.

'Well, now that's settled,' said Kaved, 'we'd better get a move on.'

The group wasted no more time as Rabigar and Kaved began hacking off adequately-sized branches from the trees around the mound. Belwynn and Moneva picked up branches lying around the forest floor and collected those obtained by the Krykkers, bringing them to the centre of the mound, where

Herin, Clarin and Gyrmund set about lashing them together to make platforms strong enough to carry the weight of the two men.

They worked quickly, and before long they were gingerly lifting the wizard and the priest onto the stretchers.

'How ill do you think he is?' Belwynn asked Elana.

The priestess pursed her lips. 'I don't know. His affliction seems to be more of the mind than of the body, and the powers that Madria has bestowed on me are not as effective in healing it.'

Belwynn nodded. 'I think the magic that he used on the mound was too great for him to control; he put too much into it. What with the magic he used to get us to the river as well...I don't think he had any energy left.'

'*I've* never seen anything like that before,' said Kaved, with apparent sincerity in his voice. 'I didn't think people could do that...'

Belwynn guessed that was the closest the Krykker ever came to saying *thank you,* and she smiled in recognition. The truth was, she hadn't seen Soren do anything like that before, either. It was a different kind of magic, different from what he had learned from Ealdnoth. It was witch magic.

Gyrmund led the group off in a north-easterly direction while Herin and Clarin carried Soren's stretcher and Rabigar and Kaved carried Dirk. It was very slow going, especially because everyone was so exhausted from the combat on the mound. The adrenaline from the fight had left Belwynn's body, and she felt empty and drained. By nightfall, however, they had covered enough ground to feel that they were a safe distance from the bloody scene, and with very little conversation tried to make themselves comfortable on the forest floor. Belwynn lay next to her brother's prone body, still breathing, but dead to the world.

Eventually she fell asleep.

*****

Prince Edgar was sitting in his tent with Ealdnoth, his court wizard, and his two bodyguards, Leofwin and Brictwin. They were awaiting the arrival of Wilchard, Edgar's chief steward, with the Cordentine ambassador.

The wait gave Edgar time to contemplate his plans. It had been two days since the attack on Toric's Temple, and he had been busy. The potential threat to the kingdom had led Edgar to raise an army, and he had issued orders to all those in the land who had a duty to provide their prince with soldiers. Not all of those who had been ordered to had as yet provided men, and this meant that Edgar would be able to issue fines or even confiscate the land of those who had failed in their duty. In any event, a threat had not materialised, but Edgar knew that it was a foolish ruler who, once he had an army at his disposal, did nothing with it.

The complication associated with raising an army was that all the grand magnates of South Magnia were there as well, keen to show off the soldiers under their command, eating the army rations at an alarming rate and drinking too much. The inevitable result of such a volatile mixture was arrogant confrontation.

Edgar was aware that, with no enemy, he could not hold the army together for long. Men such as Otha of Rystham were already letting their suspicions about Edgar's motives be known. So far, he had spun them along with some vague pronouncements about the robbers of Toric's Dagger having possibly come from North Magnia. Mention of the kingdom's bitter enemies had been enough to keep his nobles relatively happy with their prince. The army had marched northwards all day yesterday, albeit at a leisurely pace, and Edgar had let the rumours of a confrontation with North Magnia grow. Aware that he was playing a delicate game, the Prince of South Magnia was not yet ready to show his hand.

Wilchard and Rosmont, the Cordentine ambassador, were shown into the tent by the guards outside. King Glanna of Cordence was a wealthy man and could afford to have a number of permanent ambassadors in his employ. Their job was to spread Cordentine influence throughout Dalriya and stick their nose into other people's business, reporting all they heard back to the Cordentine court. South Magnia was not considered important enough to have its own ambassador; instead, Rosmont's remit was to cover all the lands of south-west Dalriya. Edgar felt that he was at court quite often enough.

Wilchard bowed to Edgar. 'Your Highness, Lord Rosmont of Cordence.'

'Please sit down, gentlemen,' said Edgar, nodding to some seats prepared for the meeting. Wilchard was about the same age as Edgar, an old childhood friend, and now an adviser who usually participated in such meetings.

'Your Highness,' began Rosmont, bowing low. Rosmont began his usual speech, which involved a formal greeting from King Glanna and incorporated a brief history of all the special links and mutual treaties between the two countries.

Edgar maintained a fixed smile throughout the proceedings as the ambassador listed what King Glanna believed to be the Prince's most special virtues.

'Please send King Glanna my best wishes,' replied Edgar when, at last, Rosmont had finished.

Rosmont bowed low in acknowledgement. 'I understand you have another ambassador at court, from the newly independent provinces of Trevenza and Grienna?', he enquired, sounding all innocence.

'Yes, a man arrived late last night, but I have yet to speak to him,' answered Edgar.

'Ah,' came the reply. Rosmont was obviously doubtful of this, but in truth, the ambassador, whom Edgar understood to be a high-ranking cleric of Grienna, had been so tired from his speedy journey that he had been allowed to rest and was due to speak with Edgar after this meeting with Rosmont. The two provinces had only just claimed independence from Persala, and were now desperately sending envoys across Dalriya in the hope that other states would acknowledge this independence and lend some legitimacy to the move. King Mark of Persala would, of course, treat any such acknowledgement as an attack on his sovereignty.

'I was sorry to hear about the loss of your national treasure the other day,' said Rosmont, moving on to a new subject, 'and shocked to hear that you were threatened yourself?'

'Yes, a shocking business all round.'

'And the direction your army is going would indicate that you believe North Magnian agents were behind it?'

Edgar knew that Rosmont would be all over these events, but he wasn't about to give him anything here, either. 'Nobody should jump to conclusions over this incident,' he said sternly. 'I have sent my own agents after the robbers to retrieve our treasure. It wouldn't be politic to say anything else at this time.'

Rosmont quickly accepted that no information was forthcoming on this subject and moved on to another, namely rights over the Wilderness. Mention of the place made Edgar think of Soren, Belwynn, and the others. In the past days he had put the loss of Toric's Dagger to the back of his mind and relied on his cousins to retrieve it. He hoped they were doing well.

'...King Glanna feels that such an arrangement,' Rosmont was saying, 'can only be beneficial to both parties.'

The Cordentines seemed to be proposing that a formal division of the Wilderness between themselves and South Magnia should take place. At the moment, while those kingdoms that bordered the Wilderness laid token claims over it, in practice the place was a law unto itself, and no-one's authority extended very far into the forest. King Glanna was always trying to win rights and ownership over places, whether by trade treaties or secret understandings, but Edgar could see little advantage in a treaty of ownership with the Cordentines when neither side had any authority over the place they were carving up.

'And what thought has King Glanna given to the Empire's view of such an arrangement?' asked Wilchard.

'King Glanna's view is that Emperor Baldwin will have little interest in the destiny of the Wilderness, particularly if he is drawn into confrontation with Persala.' Rosmont's eyebrows always raised to the corners of his face when dealing in intrigue, and now was no exception. The Cordentines expected a confrontation between Brasingia and Persala over the provinces of Trevenza and Grienna, and while their attentions were turned they could lay claim to the lion's share of the Wilderness; maybe even begin the difficult process of bringing it under the authority of the Cordentine crown.

Edgar nodded in understanding. 'What you say is interesting, Lord Rosmont. You will understand, of course, if I discuss your offer with my ministers first.'

'Of course,' came the smooth reply.

'If we are now finished,' said Wilchard to Rosmont, 'I will escort you out.'

With a deep bow and a few words of gratitude, the Cordentine ambassador was led out of the tent. Edgar rolled his eyes in relief. 'What did you make of that?' he asked Ealdnoth.

'I don't like it,' the wizard replied. 'We offend Brasingia while Cordence makes a move on the Wilderness. Glanna's soldiers are free, while most of ours will still be tied up defending the northern border. Cordence will have a perfect excuse for building up a large army near our border, and we can hardly object if we have signed a treaty agreeing to it all.'

Edgar had to agree. 'Knowing wily King Glanna, I don't intend signing up to anything with him that isn't in our obvious interest, because it will doubtless be in his. But if he's thinking of making a move on the Wilderness, what's to stop him swallowing it up whole?'

'We could probably frustrate his plans enough to make it too difficult to be worth his while. Plus, if Baldwin doesn't like it, he'll face the wrath of the Empire on his own and may lose some of his beloved trade deals there; I'm sure the threat of that would stop him dead in his tracks.'

Edgar grinned at his adviser. Ealdnoth was not the most powerful of wizards: he admitted himself that Soren had more natural talent, but he was clever and experienced, and was worth as much to Edgar as an adviser as he was to him as a user of magic. Edgar would reject Rosmont's offer, though it would perhaps not hurt to string him along for a while first.

Wilchard returned to the tent and immediately agreed with Edgar and Ealdnoth's assessment.

'Can you give me an update on what we know about developments in the north before we meet the Griennese ambassador?' Edgar asked his steward.

'The balance of power there is shifting firmly towards Haskany. Since he took power, Arioc has won huge swathes of territory from the old Persaleian Empire. As you know, last year it looked like the whole of Persala would collapse when the old Emperor Conrad was deposed by a coalition of generals, led by Mark. However, by rejecting the old title of Emperor, hardly fitting anymore, and by overhauling the army, the new King has secured his position in the country. Mark still has enemies within the country—after all, he seized the throne by force; in the trading provinces of Trevenza and Grienna the people object to paying high taxes to defend what they see as other people's land. Short-sighted of course, but there you go. It looks like they've decided now is the time to make a break.'

'How do you think Brasingia will react?' asked Edgar.

'Persala has always been an enemy, and if the Empire supports the two provinces with enough force, Mark doesn't have the resources to take on Baldwin—not with Arioc waiting in the wings to swallow him up. Baldwin is not a hasty man and may decide to wait to see how the rebellion develops. He may even have some sympathy with Mark. No doubt he has been weighing up his options.'

If the two provinces were to succeed in their bid for independence, they would need the military support of Baldwin of Brasingia. Edgar realised that the Emperor may have already promised this in an attempt to destabilise his neighbour. Either way, the real momentum in this crisis was going to come from Brasingia, not Magnia.

When the envoy was ushered in, he promised a certain sum of money and beneficial trading rights in Grienna and Trevenza in exchange for Edgar's recognition of the two provinces as states outside the jurisdiction of Persala. Edgar's decision was unlikely to alter the balance much either way, but he decided that he would have to let the envoy leave empty-handed. There was no reason to become involved in the conflict, and it was far wiser to wait on Baldwin of Brasingia's response before he came down on either side.

Events in the north were becoming a concern to the Prince of South Magnia, however, and he talked about them with Wilchard and Ealdnoth long after the envoy had left. If war was coming to Dalriya, he had to make sure that South Magnia was in a strong enough position to defend itself.

The orders to raise camp had to be given long in advance because of the cumbersome nature of Edgar's army. It seemed to take an age for orders to pass down the chain of command, and the majority of the Prince's troops were not professional soldiers, but men who only sporadically became warriors when asked to do so by their liege lords.

Despite this, the main part of the morning was still left when the army of South Magnia resumed its progress northwards. The soldiers would often be greeted by the folk who lived in the villages and farmsteads through which they passed: some simply gawped at the sight, others offered food or drink. All of them were desperate to know where they were going.

As Edgar rode along, never far from his dutiful bodyguards Leofwin and Brictwin, he heard many a soldier claim that the Prince had decided to invade his northern neighbour, a claim which he noted was greeted with mixed enthusiasm. While some of his countrymen might delight in taking the old enemy to task, many realised that war meant hardship and taxes, especially for those who dwelt nearest the enemy border.

It was before midday when Farred arrived. Edgar was eager to hear all his news but decided that it would do better to travel a little farther and stop for lunch, when he could sit with Farred, Ealdnoth, and Wilchard to discuss his plans for the day.

After another hour's journey they came to a suitable location on the outskirts of a sizeable northern town called Halsham. Because of its size and location, Halsham was an important strategic settlement to the princes of South Magnia. Edgar's father, Edric, had encouraged its growth, giving it certain rights to trade and self-governance, and in return the town councillors committed themselves to provide resources to the crown, particularly in times of war. One of the most important of these was providing supplies to the royal army, and Edgar now demanded that the town of Halsham feed his troops while he met with his advisers.

Since Farred's arrival a few days ago, Edgar had developed an immediate liking to the man. He gave his opinions with honesty and intelligence, and he was not afraid of action or of doing things a little differently. Edgar had decided he would be the perfect man to undertake a special mission to the court of Edgar's neighbour, Prince Cerdda of North Magnia.

Cerdda and Edgar shared many problems, stemming from the separation of Magnia into two states after years of civil war. Edgar's father, Edric, had become the leader of one side in the war. He had agreed a peace with his enemy, Bradda, whereby Magnia was divided in half. Neither Edric nor Bradda would claim the title of king, but instead be known as princes of the South and North. When Edgar and Cerdda inherited their father's positions, the peace had held.

The biggest danger to both Edgar and Cerdda was from their own nobility, and it was with this in mind that Edgar had sent Farred to meet with Cerdda. In the borders, both princes were dependent on their followers to defend their territory, and this dependency had long been taken advantage of.

The individual who offered the biggest threat to Edgar was Harbyrt the Fat, Marshal of the Northern Marches. Harbyrt owned vast stretches of land on the northern border and had many men in his power. Few in the region could stand up to him, and those that tried would more than often end up dead, their lands confiscated by Harbyrt as he used his military powers to brand them a traitor. The problem for Edgar was that he could do little to curtail Harbyrt because of the ever-present threat of war with North Magnia. Harbyrt would have little compunction in transferring his allegiance to Cerdda, which would give the North Magnians a big advantage in terms of territory and military strength.

Edgar had thus been forced to accept several indignities from Harbyrt the Fat. He had once sent a trusted friend to the region to act as royal sheriff in an attempt to impose his will on the region. Harbyrt had continually frustrated his efforts, and, as the conflict became violent, Edgar had been forced to withdraw his sheriff and replace him with one who could work with Harbyrt.

The problem had become more sinister in the last year; Harbyrt had married his son to the daughter of Earl Sherlin of North Magnia, who held similar powers to Harbyrt. These men, who were supposed to be enemies, had developed a powerful alliance and were now strong enough to ignore their notional superiors. Harbyrt had sent no soldiers for Edgar's army, despite being one of the richest barons in the land. While men like Otha of Rystham might frustrate Edgar, Harbyrt the Fat had come close to rejecting his authority, and Edgar had long resolved to deal with him. With an army at his disposal, Edgar saw an opportunity to put Harbyrt in his place. He had sent Farred to Cerdda to explain the army's proximity to the border and gain his support for the plan. What Edgar didn't want was for the North Magnians to react aggressively to the move and set back the already-difficult relations he had with them. Since Farred was descended from Middian tribesmen, with no history of enmity with North Magnia, Edgar had chosen him to act as something of a neutral go-between.

'How did they react?' asked Edgar as they sat down to eat.

Farred grinned. 'Positively, Your Highness. However, Prince Cerdda did insist on changing your plans slightly.'

Edgar raised his eyebrows, but allowed Farred to tell his story.

'As you had hoped, Cerdda is equally as frustrated with Earl Sherlin as you are with Harbyrt. The alliance between the two has made Sherlin a rival power to Cerdda within the country—some men apparently give their loyalty to the Earl above the Prince. There are even rumours within North Magnia that the two magnates intend to formally unite their lands and declare themselves independent of both South and North Magnia, effectively creating a separate state.'

'They wouldn't do that,' interjected Wilchard. 'They are in a perfect situation now. Subjects in theory, independent in practice. If they tried to go their own way, they would have to fight for what they already own.'

Farred shrugged. 'No doubt that is true, but arrogant men such as these soon tire of even the pretence of subordination. Either way, this is the background on which Cerdda reacted to my visit, and he was eager to join in the fun. As we speak, he is now raising his own army, and intends to enter the lands of Earl Sherlin whilst we move north to meet Harbyrt. He is using the presence of our army as his reason for the action. He intends to deal with Sherlin, and says he would be only too happy to offer any assistance with cutting Harbyrt the Fat down to size.'

Edgar smiled. His plan seemed to be working. Ealdnoth, however, did not look so pleased.

'Do we know that we can trust Cerdda?' asked the wizard. 'And even if his intentions *are* the same as ours, the presence of two armies, both of which are under the impression that they are there to fight each other, is asking for trouble. Events can soon spiral out of our control.'

'I believe we can trust Cerdda.' answered Farred. 'One problem, however, might be his younger brother, Ashere. He seemed hostile to any agreement with South Magnia.'

Edgar nodded. 'By all accounts Ashere has never forgiven his brother for failing to attack me when I was at my most vulnerable, just after my father died. He may try to sabotage the plans; it would be all too easy to lead an attack on our troops and provoke a retaliation. However, I must trust that Cerdda can keep his brother in check. The opportunity we have here is too great to pass up. My magnates would never allow me to move against one of them: it would be an infringement on their power. This way, before they know it they will have taken part in a show of strength against Harbyrt the Fat that will weaken his position severely. If Cerdda does the same with Sherlin, we will have stopped a potential threat to my sovereignty in its tracks and improved relations with our neighbours. There are risks involved in this, but the potential benefits are worth it. I don't intend to spend the rest of my reign circumscribed by men like Harbyrt the Fat.'

When Wilchard advised Edgar's generals that Cerdda was raising an army in North Magnia their support for the campaign was renewed, and the whole army began to prepare itself for battle. Edgar took the opportunity to visit with the mayor of Halsham, a landowner and trader named Oslac, at his impressive town-house. Oslac had recently been elected mayor by the council of Halsham for the third year running, and Edgar had worked with him in the past. Halsham was a proud town which resisted the influence of Harbyrt the Fat in its affairs, and Edgar had done his best in the past to give Oslac sufficient powers to continue this resistance. When the Prince confided to the mayor his plans for Harbyrt, Oslac was only too pleased to offer whatever help he could.

Edgar's problem was that Prince Cerdda had asked for two days to raise a sufficient force to carry out their plan. Edgar's own nobility wanted to press on now, before the North Magnians could prepare for their arrival. In addition to this, Edgar did not want to arouse the suspicions of Harbyrt the Fat, who had not sent any message to his prince, despite Edgar's proximity to the northern border. As Marshal of the North, Harbyrt was expected to be a leader of any northern campaign, but so far he had not been involved in any way. Edgar wanted to keep it this way. It would be more difficult to suddenly turn on Harbyrt if the Marshal and his soldiers had been part of the royal army for a few days.

Edgar had hoped that he would be able to march his army straight to the heartlands of Harbyrt's estate and punish him before anyone had realised what was happening, but while Cerdda's involvement might result in a more complete victory, it also complicated the picture. What Edgar needed to do was freeze time in South Magnia for a day or two, so that his troops and Harbyrt's stayed apart, while in North Magnia Cerdda got his own force together. He had decided that Oslac and his town residence might be able to help him do just that.

X

UNDER THE INFLUENCE

B ELWYNN STOOD, EXHAUSTED, taking in the town of Vitugia. It was a small border-trading town, situated in Cordence but close to the Empire and the Midder Steppe. Goods bought and sold here might be sent north up the Great Road or taken south to the long Cordentine coast, where they could be transported by ship.

Back in Cordence, then. It was a week now since their brief trip to Vincente's town, and Vitugia had a similar feel to it. A few big houses for the rich, and lots of very poor ones. A rather mean-looking inn, where Herin was negotiating their accommodation. Although Magnia and Cordence shared a border, they were very different countries. Belwynn knew that history had played its part in this. Magnians were proud that they represented the only humans of Dalriya to have resisted the Persaleian Empire at its height. Cordence, on the other hand, and despite the distance between them, had been the most loyal of Persaleian provinces. Whereas the Brasingians had fought bitter wars to overthrow Persaleian rule, Cordence had never rebelled—just drifted into independence when it found itself geographically cut off from its mother. The Great Road still connected Cordence and Persala in a very real way, and the Cordentines were a nation of traders, always keen to get the best deal and get one over on their neighbours. Magnians, on the other hand, were a nation of farmers, and, to Belwynn's mind, had more of a sense of community. That was why Magnian inns were friendly and welcoming, and Cordentine inns were mean and penny-pinching.

Herin poked his head around the door and made a small signal with his forefinger that everyone could come in. Belwynn hobbled after him, eager to get inside The Grape and Goat and spend the night under a roof for the first time in days.

It had been a long day, dragging Soren and Dirk through the undergrowth of the Wilderness, but they had not been troubled by the vossi, and eventually Gyrmund had led them out of the forest and into Cordence. Everyone's spirits were raised by leaving the place, especially Moneva's. She became positively gregarious, speaking in full sentences again, rather than the series of grunts and swear words she had deployed over the last few days. While Belwynn was glad to have left the Wilderness, she was not in the mood for chat, and it had fallen to Gyrmund to entertain Moneva, which he didn't seem to object to.

He had established that Gervase Salvinus and his mercenaries had passed this way in order to connect with the Great Road, and by offering the chance of sleeping at an inn this night he had persuaded everyone to keep going at a fair pace. Dirk made a speedy recovery from what had seemed, yesterday, to be a fatal wound, and they had been able to discard one of the stretchers. Soren, however, remained unconscious, though sometimes he could be heard to mutter some incoherent speech out loud before returning to silence.

Herin had organised rooms for everyone, and Belwynn was grateful that he had arranged for her to share with Soren. Elana came in to check on him before retiring to her own room, but the priestess seemed unable to help. Belwynn knew that Soren had exhausted his powers back in the Wilderness, and she knew, too, that her brother might not recover from the expenditure.

Belwynn heard a knock on the door and realised that she must have fallen asleep. After checking on Soren, she opened the door to Moneva.

'We've arranged for us all to have some supper,' she said. 'The landlord is putting it out now. No change?' she enquired, nodding over to where Soren lay.

Belwynn shook her head in response. Moneva waited as Belwynn splashed some water on her face to wake herself up. They had only known each other for a few days, but they already had the easy familiarity that comes with travelling together and sharing danger.

Belwynn felt guilty for having gone to sleep and allowing everyone else to organise the food and accommodation. She went over to Soren and took the money which Prince Edgar had given them for their expenses from her brother's inside pocket. With Soren unconscious, she had to take charge of the situation. Edgar had entrusted the retrieval of the dagger to them, and so far, they had failed him.

Belwynn and Moneva went down to the main part of the inn and joined the others in a welcome hot meal. Belwynn immediately noticed that most of her companions had begun drinking, and they continued to do so throughout the meal. She could understand their desire to celebrate escaping with their lives. The inn was very busy with the arrival of the group of ten from the Wilderness, and the landlord apologised that he didn't have as much food available as he wished. The soup was watery, and the inn lived up to half of its name by providing goat as part of the main meal. It was stringy and tough to eat, and Belwynn haggled down the price of the nine meals because of it. The fact that Clarin, Herin, and the others all wore their weapons to the meal no doubt helped, and the landlord seemed very keen not to upset his guests. Belwynn was happy that he seemed to be a man who asked very few questions so long as he was paid promptly, which she made sure he was.

The food and drink lifted the mood of the nine companions even further, and Belwynn was persuaded by Clarin to try some of the wines available. Everyone was keen to indulge themselves after the threats they had all faced in the Wilderness, and Belwynn was surprised to see Dirk knocking back his fair share of drink, especially so soon after his injury. Elana, too, seemed to want to make the effort to join in with the group, though she drank only a little watered-down wine and took it in turns with Belwynn to check on Soren. Soon Belwynn found herself laughing at the antics of Herin and Kaved despite herself, and also found herself warming to her new companions. Their time in the Wilderness had brought them closer together.

After a while Herin and Kaved seemed eager to leave the inn to find amusement elsewhere. 'When you get a close brush with death like that—' Kaved seemed to be addressing everyone in the inn—'you realise what's really important in life...and that's why I intend to couple with as many women as possible tonight.'

'And my investigations this afternoon—' if anything Herin was louder— 'established that Vitugia is not quite as dull as first meets the eye.'

Belwynn realised that the two of them had spent their free time looking for prostitutes and had obviously struck lucky. 'Why is it that after any crisis men find the need to sow their seeds? Believe me, if you two had perished in the Wilderness, mankind and... Krykkerkind... would have managed quite well without you.'

'Perhaps someone's feeling a little bit jealous?' leered Kaved.

'No human woman is going to sleep with you, Kaved,' Moneva joined in. 'You should stick to your own species.'

'I think they will,' answered the Krykker, producing a few gold coins from his pockets and waving them at Moneva. 'And I've found that one must take companionship wherever one finds it.'

'Who else is coming?' asked Herin. 'Clarin?'

Clarin glanced sideways at Belwynn, stared into his drink and shook his head. 'Looks like he's got other plans for tonight,' Kaved smirked.

Belwynn felt her cheeks flush red with embarrassment and stood up sharply. The speed with which she got up made her feel dizzy and made her realise how much she had been drinking.

'I'm going to check on Soren,' she declared, and left the table without looking at anyone. As she made her way to her room she berated herself for going red, and berated Clarin for looking in her direction that way. She had known for a long time that Clarin was interested in her, but he didn't need to make it so obvious to everyone else. She was sure that he had slept with plenty of whores in the past and didn't see why he had to stop himself tonight on her account.

Belwynn entered the room and went straight for the window, which she opened, and then gulped in some night air to cool herself down. She then went over to where Soren lay and took his hands in hers.

Oh, Soren, hurry up and get better. I need you, Belwynn said.

Belwynn.

Belwynn heard her brother's reply, but there was no movement from Soren's body.

Soren, are you awake? Soren!

There was no reply this time, but Belwynn had heard her brother's voice, and to her that meant he was getting better. She lay next to him for a while in the hope he might wake, but he didn't stir again.

Belwynn knew that Soren wouldn't have approved of the drinking downstairs. She remembered the fights he used to have with their father. Father would sit alone until late into the night, drinking and brooding. 'There was nothing I could have done,' he would always say, sometimes repeating the words over and over. Belwynn would agree with him. She hated that he blamed himself. He seemed to be asking for forgiveness from someone. From his children or from himself? From his dead wife? Soren would shout at him, and their father would shout back, calling Soren sinful and wicked for his dabbling in magic.

'There was nothing I could have done,' their father would say, until one night Soren shouted back, 'I will become so powerful that I can stop it! I'll be able to stop things like that ever happening again!'

'Get out!' her father had roared at him. Soren had gone and never come back.

Belwynn returned downstairs to tell everyone that Soren had spoken to her. It was now a lot quieter after the departure of Herin and Kaved. Gyrmund and

Moneva were talking to each other, slightly apart from the rest of the group. From the corner of her vision Belwynn saw Dirk stumbling over from the bar in their direction. As he approached them he sank down on his knees in front of the priestess.

Dirk pulled up his shirt and showed Elana the scar where the vossi blade had punctured his body.

'You have saved my life by a miracle of healing,' he solemnly pronounced to the priestess. Despite being obviously under the influence of alcohol, Dirk was speaking quite clearly.

'I didn't save your life, Dirk. It was Madria, Goddess of this land, who healed your wound.'

Dirk nodded at this statement in acknowledgement, his head bent slightly forward, in deference to Elana, or Madria, or both. 'Yes. Madria has blessed me in a way I have never felt before. By saving my life she has asked that I now devote it to her. This is why I have decided to renounce my allegiance to Toric and turn to the one true goddess. Elana, I submit my soul to Madria's keeping, and ask that I become your disciple.'

'This is what Madria wishes,' replied Elana. 'Dirk of Magen, you shall be my first disciple.'

Elana touched Dirk's forehead and then raised him to his feet.

Belwynn caught eyes with Clarin, who looked as surprised about the episode as she felt. She felt that something significant had just happened, and was reminded that Elana had led an attack on the Temple of Toric to get the dagger for herself.

This softly-spoken priestess had an agenda all her own with regards to its recapture. Now she seemed to have converted a priest of Toric to her own cause.

Belwynn resolved to keep an eye on the life-giving priestess of Madria.

Belwynn's morning was filled with joy because, when she woke, Soren was already awake and sitting up in bed. He was still weak, but strong enough to resume the journey north. In fact, Soren looked in better shape than some of his companions that morning—many of whom were now paying for the excesses of the night before. Herin, Clarin and Kaved had spent the early hours of the morning finding ten suitable horses for the journey along the Great Road into the Empire. They had been forced to pay above the odds, but Belwynn and Soren were grateful for their efforts and only too happy to pay over a large portion of Edgar's money in order that they renew their chase of Salvinus' mercenaries on horseback. When Belwynn tried to express her thanks, however, her companions responded with a strange series of grunts, which was apparently the only form of communication they were capable of for the rest of the morning.

Dirk, too, seemed to be suffering from a hangover, as he rode next to Elana with slit eyes and a pale, slightly grey complexion. Sometimes keeping the horse in the right direction would prove too much, and he would veer off the track into the grassy verge by the side before awkwardly returning to the group. The whole episode between them from the previous night seemed even stranger this morning, as if it had been a dream.

Elana was involved in a running argument with Kaved. 'Well, surely,' the Krykker was saying, 'if your great goddess 'Madigar' can heal up this man's wound—' Kaved gestured in Dirk's direction— 'she can cure me of a bloody hangover!'

Elana finally lost her patience. '*Madria* certainly does not respond to foul language. But that is not the point. Maybe I could rid you of it...but I think it is a good lesson for you not to indulge in excessive drinking in the future.'

'A lesson!?', exploded Kaved, and then wished he hadn't, grabbing each side of his head with his hands as if it would split open without being held together.

'Well, you're both making me feel a lot worse,' interjected Herin. 'Let's have some peace for a while.'

Kaved muttered something under his breath about suffering in silence, but kept relatively quiet.

Belwynn and Moneva, on the other hand, were in high spirits, and took great delight in increasing the irritability of their comrades by reminding them that they had brought it all upon themselves. Gyrmund and Rabigar rode with Soren at the front and soon connected the group onto the Great Road.

The Great Road had been built by the Persaleian Empire at the height of its power. It led from their northernmost territories in Haskany all the way south in a straight line to Cordence. It was a demonstration of power, a way of transporting armies and supplies from one region to another with great speed, and a boost to pan-Dalriya trading and communications. It remained, for many, the greatest achievement of human civilization, and now confirmed the place of the Brasingian Empire as the dominant power in Dalriya, since almost half of the Great Road lay within its boundaries. Most travelling from north to south now took place via the Road rather than by sea, and it passed right through the capital of the Empire, Essenberg.

The group had decided that Gervase Salvinus had most probably headed back to his own power-base in the duchy of Barissia. There were many travellers on the Great Road, but none of those questioned were able to confirm whether or not their decision was sound.

The Road was the border between the two southernmost duchies of the Empire—Thesse to the west and Gotbeck to the east—the latter ruled over by an archbishop rather than a duke. The plan was to continue north along the Great Road and then take the Barissian Road west into the duchy, heading for its capital, Coldeberg, where they were sure to get some information on the whereabouts of Salvinus.

Many of the group were eager to question Soren about the events on the mound in the Wilderness, in particular his apparition which scared off the vossi tribesmen.

'What exactly was the image you conjured up?' asked Moneva.

'When the vossi were reluctant to approach us at first, it made me realise that we had stumbled onto a vossi burial ground. The vision I created was one of their gods, Riktu, who is lord of the vossi underworld. I made him berate them for making war on his sacred site. He eventually persuaded them to leave.'

'Well, I think we all owe you one,' she replied.

'I used to think that all wizards were con-artists,' interjected Kaved, 'but you're different. Where does that kind of power come from?'

'I have always had magic within me, Kaved. The Caladri have long used and accepted magic, while the Isharites control powerful yet terrible sorcery. For my part, I have been blessed with some power which I had to learn how to use and control. I've spent my time learning from masters of the craft, just the same as you have spent yours learning how to fight and to use your weapons in battle.'

'I find it interesting, Soren,' said Rabigar, 'how you distinguish yourself from the likes of Elana. It is obvious to us all that you both have special, extraordinary powers at your disposal. Elana freely admits that her powers come from a superhuman being, her goddess Madria, yet you say your powers all come from within. We Krykkers have long held the belief that there can be no such distinction. Whether you know it or not, your powers have been given to you by spirits not of this world, in just the same way as Elana's. I do not agree with allowing interference into our world from unknown forces outside it, however well-meaning your intentions. It is dangerous.'

Kaved made one of his smirks at this statement. 'All that rather depends on what you call extraordinary powers, does it not, Rabigar?' he asked enigmatically.

Rabigar shrugged the question off.

'Well, it is certainly dangerous,' Soren replied to Rabigar. 'You have all witnessed that. As for the powers coming from outside forces, that is very far from the truth. They come at a considerable cost to myself.'

Rabigar didn't reply, and the group rode on in silence for some time.

Elana insisted that, for Soren's sake, it would be best if they had a brief rest for lunch, but they were all soon back in the saddle again. The nature of the Great Road meant that they were eating up the miles, and Gyrmund suggested that they might even make it to Barissia by the end of the day.

It was mid-afternoon when the group came upon the lone rider sat on his horse by the side of the road. Up to now travellers on the Great Road had done their best to politely avoid coming into contact with the strange mixture of heavily-armed men, women and Krykkers. Belwynn could sense them speculating about what business she and her companions were up to, but it seemed that none of them really wanted to find out. Merchants would do their best to avoid looking anyone in the eye, and noble retinues, using the Great Road to travel from one estate to the next, would grudgingly allow them space on it.

As Gyrmund and Rabigar approached the stranger, it seemed that, contrary to previous experience, this man was actually *waiting* for them to arrive. He had a stunning appearance, jet black hair down to the nape of his neck, a black silk cloak which reached to his knees, and the most expensive-looking stallion Belwynn had ever seen.

What really drew attention, however, were his eyes. They were red.

Belwynn had never seen anything like it. Deep red eyes, as if they were on fire, and they were looking at the approaching group with an unreadable expression. Belwynn sensed power in this man. She looked back to his cloak, the hems of which were decorated with runic inscriptions.

He's a wizard, Belwynn almost hissed to Soren, as if, by thinking too loudly, Red-Eyes would hear it.

Yes. A powerful one. We're going to have to be very careful here.

'Well met, friend,' Gyrmund greeted him nonchalantly, as if he had already met a number of red-eyed travellers on the road that day. It was a neutral

106

welcome, except for the fact that Herin, Clarin and Kaved had all ridden from the back of the line to the front, hands stroking the inches of air separating them from the hilts of their weapons.

The man smiled, a friendly smile, revealing white, polished teeth. 'Well met, friends,' he began, his voice strong, resonant and confident. 'I saw you approaching and wondered if I might accompany you along the road for a short while. I fear it can be dangerous to travel on one's own these days.'

The words raised Belwynn's concerns higher. It seemed that little in this world could provide much of a danger to this man.

'We travel alone,' said Herin coldly, not fearing to stare into those red eyes for signs of dissent.

Before the stranger could respond, however, Soren contradicted Herin's decision. 'I think in this case we could make an exception, Herin. It will not cost us anything to travel with an extra companion for a short time.'

Herin looked at Soren. Belwynn knew that her brother was probably the only person that Herin might allow to overrule him. With a raised eyebrow, he conceded to his wishes.

'If you think so, Soren,' he said.

'You are all most gracious,' said Red-Eyes, inclining his head, as if he were oblivious to any undercurrent of tension in the group. 'My name is Pentas. I am pleased to meet you all.'

Soren introduced himself and his companions, using their real names, which raised further eyebrows, but no comment from the rest of the group. 'Where are you headed?' he enquired of Pentas.

'To Persala,' he replied, 'I felt that I must return to my home there, because of all the recent troubles.'

'What troubles are those?' asked Belwynn. 'I'm afraid we've heard little of events to the north in recent days.'

Pentas nodded, though Belwynn thought he looked a little surprised. 'Well then, I must report to you that Trevenza and Grienna have broken away from Persala in a pact of independence. I fear that war must be inevitable. Of course, such a situation will be of more concern to myself than to a Magnian.'

Belwynn knew that her accent was unmistakably Magnian, but she had travelled enough to know that Pentas's was not strong enough to place, and so she reserved judgement on whether he was Persaleian or not.

'And where are you headed, friends?' Pentas asked.

It was an awkward question, since they didn't want to tell this stranger exactly what they were up to. Herin looked about to tell the wizard to stuff his questions, but instead turned to Soren.

'Coldeberg,' replied Soren.

Herin frowned, unable to understand why Soren was deferring to this man, but he kept his mouth shut.

'Interesting,' replied Pentas. 'I thought you would be heading south, back to Magnia.'

He looked at Dirk as he said this, red eyes fixed on the priest. Dirk looked troubled under that glare and turned to Elana for support.

'No,' she replied. 'We are heading north.'

Pentas now turned his gaze on Elana, but the priestess looked straight back at him without wavering. He nodded.

'Very well. It is very kind to let me ride with you as far as Coldeberg.'

What was that about? Belwynn asked Soren.

Not sure, he replied.

Soren still looked tired from his exertions in the Wilderness, and Belwynn suspected he was hiding the extent of the damage done. She had to ask another question of her brother, however.

Why did you let him ride with us?

I don't think we had much of a choice in the matter, Soren replied.

You mean he's a more powerful wizard than you?

You could say that.

Soren sounded down, almost bitter; Belwynn decided to leave it at that.

The group continued their journey north, and Pentas did not hinder the speed of their progress, but rode along comfortably in the middle of the group, as if he were out on a ride with friends. He behaved as if he were blissfully unaware of the nervous looks that some of the others gave him, but Belwynn knew it was an act and kept her eyes on him.

It was early evening when Gyrmund turned around to advise the group that they would shortly be turning off the Great Road onto the Barissian Road, which led directly to the capital, Coldeberg. He was quickly advised to face ahead again, however, by a hissed whisper from Rabigar.

In front of them was the second lone mounted figure they had come across that day. Belwynn was unsure where he had come from; suddenly, he was sitting there, ahead of them, in the middle of the road. Pentas had been an arresting sight, but this newcomer managed to trump it. His mount and his clothes were just as expensive, but instead of the red eyes, he wore a mask which covered his whole face.

It was a death mask, a human skull stripped of flesh and skin, seemingly frozen in a contorted howl of pain.

It sent shivers down Belwynn's spine, and she could sense from behind the empty eye sockets the malevolent presence of the wearer, studying them.

The figure nudged his horse and trotted slowly towards them. Belwynn felt the saliva in her mouth dry up as Herin, Clarin and Kaved once more moved from the back of the group to the front to face the danger.

'Give me the dagger,' demanded the skull in a rasping voice, as if the figure behind the mask was indeed a corpse, raised from the dead and given the power of speech.

In response Herin and the others drew their weapons and spread across the road in a fan shape, readying themselves for an attack. The mask stopped his advance and waited, as if daring them to try anything.

'Be careful,' warned Soren in a tense voice.

Belwynn could see a scabbarded sword at the right thigh of the figure, but it had not made any attempt to reach for it. As she had with Pentas, Belwynn could sense the power emanating from the creature in the mask.

Just as she thought of the red-eyed wizard, he trotted his horse past her and towards the confrontation. Clarin and Gyrmund turned around in surprise but allowed him to move between them and out onto the road to face the waiting threat.

Belwynn's mind was racing. She wanted to shout out that they didn't have the dagger, but no-one else had offered that information, so she decided that it was best to keep her mouth shut.

'You,' said the masked figure as Pentas approached, in a voice filled with hostility and disdain. 'You would do best to stay out of my way, Pentas.'

'I got here first, Nexodore. You're too late. The dagger is now my responsibility.'

Nexodore cackled at Pentas's front, but there was no humour in the laugh. 'These matters will never be your responsibility, Pentas. I will not think twice about casting you down if you stand between me and my duties.'

'Then there is nothing left to say,' answered Pentas.

His voice was firm and betrayed no emotion. For a moment Belwynn wondered whether anyone in this world would dare do anything even to displease this red-eyed man, whose presence was so powerful. She half expected this Nexodore to turn around and ride back from where he came, but both men sat still, facing each other across a few feet of road.   Belwynn felt a buzzing sensation in her head which grew and grew by the second as the hairs on her body began to stand on edge.

They're testing each other out, trying to find a gap in each other's defences, said Soren.

What can you do? asked Belwynn.

Nothing.

Belwynn looked around at her companions and saw that they, too, were feeling the side effects of this magical duel. Even the horses whinnied nervously.

Then, suddenly, wave upon wave of power surged from the two figures. Belwynn turned back to look at the two wizards and nearly wretched with the effort as the magical forces at work surged into her body. They were still sitting perfectly still, in the same position, but for some reason Belwynn felt that it was Nexodore doing the attacking.

Then, from the corner of her eye, Belwynn noticed a flash of metal. Herin's drawn sword seemed to be sucked from his grasp, and the weapon flew straight towards a point between Pentas's shoulder blades. Just as the blade was about to sink into the wizard's back, its flight was halted in mid-air, and it clattered harmlessly to the ground.

Pentas had stopped an attack, but his concentration, it seemed, had been affected. Almost as soon as Herin's sword hit the ground Pentas's horse collapsed. It seemed to Belwynn as if the stallion suffered some kind of internal haemorrhage. With a sudden jolt, it spasmed and then its legs gave way, causing Pentas to topple forward off his mount. Nexodore held his hand above his head, ready to finish off his defenceless opponent, when an arrow whistled past his head.

Instead of sending the spell to Pentas, he quickly adjusted, and the power was instead directed at Herin, who had tried to make up for the embarrassment of losing his sword by taking out the wizard himself. Herin was hurled from his mount by the power of the blast, shooting into the air for a few feet before crashing to earth.

Pentas had been given the precious recovery time he needed, however, and he slammed his palms onto the Great Road. There was a deafening, tearing sound of rock on rock, and then the ground between the two wizards opened up. Pentas had created a crack along the road, allowing hot steam to billow forth from the fissure. Now it was the turn of Nexodore's mount to lose its footing, and both horse and rider tumbled into the widening hole which Pentas had rent in the earth.

Pentas had no time to gloat, however, as the ground beneath him also gave way, and he was dragged into his own trap, followed by the carcass of his horse. Clarin, who had moved forward after his brother had been attacked, was now forced to quickly backtrack to avoid joining the two wizards. The whole group quickly moved away to safety, Gyrmund grabbing the reins of Herin's horse to pull it away as well.

The cracking of the ground ceased, though it continued to smoulder.

As the others went over to check on Herin, Soren and Belwynn went to look at the hole. Soren gingerly peered down, but shook his head. Belwynn looked for herself, but could see no trace of any of the bodies which had been sucked in, surely to their deaths. The fissure stank of rotten eggs, and they reluctantly walked away.

Herin was a little dazed, but had no serious injuries. He did, however, get upset when Clarin ruefully informed him that his sword had joined the two wizards in their deep grave.

'Don't tell me I've lost another one!' he groaned.

'Well, what was all that about?' asked Kaved, and everyone looked to Soren for an answer.

The wizard, however, shrugged his shoulders. 'I can't tell you much. Nexodore is a name I know, a man of great power who serves Erkindrix of Ishari. I don't know the name Pentas...but what I do know is that we've just been involved with two of the most powerful wizards of Dalriya. For both of them to come looking for us, personally...I don't know. I don't know what's going on. But any wizard of real power in Dalriya will have heard what went on here; the expenditure of magical power was incredible, and if these two came looking for us, then anyone else will now know exactly where we are as well. I suggest we get as far away from here as possible, as quickly as we can.'

'Well, I'm not going to argue with that,' said Gyrmund. 'We might not make it to Coldeberg before nightfall, but I'm all for giving it a try.'

XI

A CROWN AND A HAT

THEY DIDN'T MAKE IT to Coldeberg, instead spending the night outdoors. Everyone agreed that it was safest to keep a low profile and avoid possible detection.

Belwynn was tired, but couldn't get to sleep. Night noises sounded like they could be people out in the dark, looking for them. When she did finally drift off, she dreamed of being chased by a man with red eyes. When he caught her, he turned into a skeleton and dragged her underground, to the land of the dead.

Belwynn awoke the next morning feeling little better for the few hours of sleep. Gyrmund and the others had taken shifts keeping watch through the night, but nothing had happened. Everyone was still on edge, however. Just as in the Wilderness, the group felt as if they had now somehow become the hunted rather than the hunters. It was clear that they had become involved with the dark powers of Ishari, yet no-one could put their finger on how or why. They hoped to find answers in Coldeberg, both to the whereabouts of the dagger and to the reasons why it had been stolen. Everyone was aware that, once Ishari took an interest in you, it did not let go.

Coldeberg was situated in the middle of the duchy of Barissia, and it would take most of the morning for the group to get there, though the Barissian Road took the traveller straight to the city.

'What is the city like? I've never been,' Belwynn asked, to no-one in particular.

'Bigger than anything in Magnia,' Herin replied, 'but not the same size as Essenberg.'

'It's long been the administrative capital of the Dukes of Barissia,' explained Soren, 'and it gets substantial local trade and internal trade within the Empire. But it's not a great trading city, because it's located away from the Great Road.'

'No real reason for traders to go there rather than Essenberg,' added Herin. 'It gets a few from the Steppe, selling cattle; some from Guivergne who come down by river. But a lot of the Middian tribes aren't that keen on Barissians, not after Emeric's wars there.'

'Can't blame them, either,' added Clarin.

Belwynn knew that the two brothers had fought for Emeric as mercenaries a few years back, and that they had bitter memories of it.

'Barissia's farming country,' said Moneva, sounding dismissive in a way that Belwynn didn't much appreciate. 'Wealthy enough, but a bit insular.'

No-one was really selling the place, and as they approached the city along the Barissian Road, Belwynn picked up on an uneasy atmosphere. They were greeted with stares and whispers more than she had expected—far more than they had received on the Great Road.

Furthermore, there seemed to be more than the normal number of soldiers on the road. They all wore the livery of the dukes of Barissia, the charging boar, and the group encountered many bands of soldiers, all on their way somewhere with varying degrees of urgency. They were almost always challenged for their business by these soldiers, and they soon learned that the best answer was that they were on their way to Coldeberg to enlist with the army. Since everyone seemed to be either in the army or on their way to join, they were greeted with much less suspicion.

Coldeberg was built on a hill, so that the northern part of the city became visible from the road first. As they got closer, the southern half of the city came into view, the whole place enclosed by steep, grey stone walls.

They arrived at the main gate, where city guards were questioning those who came in or out, meaning that there was something of a wait until they got to the front of the queue. Flags had been positioned, one each side of the gate. One had the charging boar of the dukes of Barissia, the other a large golden crown on a red background.

When it came to their turn, the guard on their side of the road looked them over, frowning, not quite sure what he had in front of him.

'We're here to join the army,' stated Kaved, as if it was a momentous occasion that required a fanfare.

The guard looked a little underwhelmed. 'You all together?' he asked. He was smartly done out, and it looked like he was expected to do a thorough job of monitoring the traffic coming in to the city.

'Not really,' replied Kaved. 'Us two are,' he said, indicating himself and Rabigar, 'and we hooked up with these poor souls on the road,' he finished, indicating everyone else.

'I'm not sure that the army has Krykkers.'

'It does now,' said Kaved, so mean-looking and full of confidence that the guard quickly moved on.

'Are all of you joining the army?' he asked, looking doubtfully at Belwynn, Elana and Moneva. It wasn't unusual for women to accompany their menfolk in the army life, whether married or not. Indeed, they were very useful when it came to the myriad jobs that needed doing to keep an army on its feet. It was much less common for women to be employed as soldiers, though it did happen.

Moneva scowled, fingering the two swords at her hips.

'You saying I can't?' she demanded.

'I always travel with my wife,' explained Herin, grabbing Belwynn by the waist. 'I can't leave her behind. We're too in love.'

Belwynn silently fumed as Herin pulled her in close, feeling self-conscious and trying not to blush, knowing that inside Herin was laughing his head off.

'Where do we sign up, anyway?' he asked the guard.

'Up at the castle,' said the guard, looking at them all with a certain distaste before waving them through into the city.

'You can get your hands off now,' said Belwynn irritably.

'Of course,' Herin agreed mildly, with a smirk on his face. 'Just trying to make us look convincing.'

Dirk knew the city well and he suggested that they try to find rooms at The Boot and Saddle, a large inn in the north-west quarter of the city that was hospitable to foreigners. He considered it to be one of the best places for keeping a low profile. Once through the gates, the Barissian Road they had arrived on became the main street of the city, running east to west.

Immediately to their right sat Coldeberg Cathedral, home of the Bishop of Coldeberg, who had the exclusive right to worship all the Brasingian gods. But on their way, they passed several other temples to specific gods. Sibylla, goddess of health and prosperity, was popular with townspeople. Gerhold, lord of war and friendship, was favoured by soldiers. There was a smaller temple for followers of Toric, the Magnian sun god. It had perhaps been established by Magnians who had moved to Barissia at some time.

Many smaller streets ran off the Barissian Road, where specialist traders sold their wares. Tanners, metalworkers, cloth-workers, grocers, bakers, more and more. Dirk informed her that the market was in the downtown part of Coldeberg, to the south.

Towering over everything, though, was Coldeberg Castle. Located at the highest point of the city, the northern city walls doubled as the castle's outer wall, and the structure then sprawled down towards the Barissian Road in an irregular hexagonal shape with six large towers and a massive gatehouse. Its looming presence made it clear that the dukes of Barissia were in charge of the city and made it feel like they were watching everything that was going on.

The streets were busy. Most of the people here weren't residents of Coldeberg, but had come in from the surrounding villages to buy goods they couldn't get at home and perhaps to sell their own. A conspicuous presence on the streets were the groups of mercenaries who had been recruited by Duke Emeric. They hung out in small groups, watching everyone else at work while they lounged around, drinking and playing cards, moving from one inn to the other, arguing with each other or passers-by or shopkeepers. They added an unpleasant ingredient to the city's atmosphere, and Belwynn was pleased to be with Clarin, Herin and the others, whose physical presence and grim expressions ensured that they were given a wide berth.

Dirk took them almost as far as the western gate of Coldeberg before turning right and taking them up some twisting, narrow streets. Then they were there, in the courtyard of the Boot and Saddle.

It was a large, well-maintained building with a sizeable stable where they left their horses.

'The landlord goes by the name of Bernard Hat, on account of his large collection of hats,' explained Dirk with a straight face as they made their way into the establishment.

It was busy inside. According to Dirk, this was the most cosmopolitan of the inns in Coldeberg, and Belwynn noticed a few individuals and groups of foreigners, especially Middian tribesmen, whose dark skin and long, tied-back hair made them very distinctive. Mercenaries and soldiers dominated the clientele, however—drinking early in the day and creating a loud and rowdy atmosphere. They had to squeeze past tables and through knots of drinkers to make it to the bar.

'You must be Bernard,' said Moneva to a man serving behind the bar. He was wearing a green beret, tastefully decorated with two feathers. 'I love your hat!'

Bernard beamed at the compliment, and was an attentive host, getting their orders in quickly and making sure that he found them seats.

'Theodoric!' he exclaimed to a man occupying a table with only one companion. 'I've brought you some interesting conversation while you have your lunch!'

'Ah! Sit down, grab a chair, that's right,' said Theodoric welcomingly. Bernard made sure that his guests were all seated before rushing off back to the bar.

As they waited, Herin struck up a conversation with Theodoric, a lean man who introduced himself as a linen merchant from the duchy of Thesse.

'I'm waiting on a final sale, and then I'm back home,' he said, perhaps by way of explanation as to why he was sitting in the inn at midday already a little worse for wear. He was sitting with what Belwynn assumed to be his assistant, a large man about the size of Clarin, who was gawping at a spider in the corner of the inn, apparently oblivious to the conversation going on around him. Belwynn also assumed that Theodoric paid his assistant criminal wages, that his assistant probably did not know or care, and that both were fairly happy with the arrangement, except that Theodoric naturally craved a bit of conversation from time to time.

'Has business been bad?' enquired Herin.

'Business is never bad if you have a brain in your skull,' answered Theodoric, and proceeded to flap his forefinger in thin air a few inches from his ear, which everyone understood to be an attempt to tap the part of his anatomy he had been referring to. 'I'll tell you this, though.' Theodoric's voice lowered to what he believed to be a conspiratorial whisper, 'when I come back, I won't be bringing linen.'

There followed an uncomfortable pause, until Herin realised he was supposed to respond. 'What *will* you be bringing?' he reluctantly asked.

'Weapons. Swords, armour, bows, arrows. They're all cheap in Thesse, nobody wants 'em there, you see. But here in Coldeberg, of course, demand is sky high.'

Herin made a face at Rabigar, who was listening attentively.

'Why is that?' Herin asked.

Theodoric frowned at Herin, tried to focus on him but then gave up. 'Are you new here or something?'

'Yes.'

'Oh. Oh, well then, you haven't heard.'

Another uncomfortable pause. 'No.'

'It's been going on for a few days now, you know, rumours at first, but then you get the more official announcements, until the day before yesterday there was a formal ceremony in Coldeberg Cathedral. A duke isn't good enough for Barissia anymore, oh no, if us Thessians have a duke, then these Barissians can't possibly settle for a mere duke themselves, can they? So Duke Emeric is now no more—long live King Emeric! Unbelievable! These Barissians.' Theodoric shook his head at the Barissians. 'Of course, you know what this means now, don't you?'

Herin and the others shared astonished looks at the news. Theodoric, however, was still expecting an answer, so Herin shrugged his shoulders at him.

Theodoric shook his head again, this time at Herin's apparent slowness. 'It means war! When Emperor Baldwin hears about this he's going to march his army straight at these Barissians. That's why there's all these soldiers around and that's why demand for weapons is so high. These Barissians are preparing for war! Unbelievable!'

Herin had a foul expression on his face and proceeded to interrogate Theodoric about the best place in the city to pick up a quality sword to replace the one he had lost. Everyone else, meanwhile, huddled together to discuss the news.

'I don't like this,' said Soren. 'Gervase Salvinus, a Barissian, steals Toric's Dagger. Emeric of Barissia declares himself king. And behind it all I see Ishari at work. I don't know how yet, but it's all linked together somehow. We need to spend this afternoon gathering information.' Soren looked at Dirk. 'What do you know of Emeric?'

Dirk shrugged. 'Arrogant, ambitious...but not stupid. He wouldn't attempt anything like this without knowing that he had support from someone else. I guess that Ishari and Haskany are the most likely candidates.'

'Pentas mentioned trouble in Persala,' Belwynn reminded everyone. 'This could extend beyond the Empire.'

Soren nodded. 'Right. I suggest we go about our business in ones and twos so that we attract as little attention as possible and meet back here this evening. I've got something I need to do on my own.'

Belwynn felt a little taken aback by the abrupt statement, but chose not to pry. 'I've got something I need to get as well. Clarin? Will you come with me?'

'Sure,' replied the huge warrior.

'Well, we need rations getting...Moneva and I will do that,' volunteered Gyrmund, but if Moneva was surprised by the announcement, she didn't show it.

'I'll go with Herin to get his sword,' said Kaved.

'Right,' began Soren, 'if you three don't need anything, it might be best for you to stay put and look after our gear. The more of us who go out there, the more chance we have of finding trouble.'

Soren's implied message was that a Krykker and the two founding members of a strange new religious sect might attract more trouble than was average.

'Well, I'd like to get some clothes, and I might be able to get in touch with some contacts in the city,' replied Dirk. 'I don't mind picking up anything for anyone else, though.'

With that agreed, eight of the group made their way into the streets of Coldeberg, leaving Rabigar and Elana behind at The Boot and Saddle.

XII

TRIMMING THE FAT

EDGAR SAT ON OSLAC OF HALSHAM'S bed, awaiting news. A messenger from Cerdda of North Magnia had arrived at the town, and was currently meeting with Wilchard before the news was brought to Edgar.

Edgar, of course, had been ill since yesterday morning. Officially ill, that is. Unofficially, he was feeling great.

To buy himself and Cerdda time, Edgar had decided to suddenly fall ill. Oslac, at whose house Edgar was staying, rushed to find Ealdnoth. Ealdnoth immediately diagnosed the illness. It was a rare illness that no-one else had heard of before, it had a long and unpronounceable name, and worst of all, it was extremely contagious.

Rumours flew around the camp, many suggesting foul play on the part of the North Magnians. The campaign was halted in its tracks just as conflict with the old enemy seemed imminent. Edgar was confined to his room; only Ealdnoth and his two bodyguards daring to stay with him. Leofwin and Brictwin took turns in keeping guard outside the room; the other sleeping with their prince in the room. The loyalty of the two men was commended by many, though the commending was carried out at a healthy distance. Edgar's room was given a wide berth. Many sympathised with Oslac over the disruption caused to his house and the fact that Edgar had dined with him and his young family the night prior to the illness taking hold. Many gave Oslac and his family a wide berth, too.

Ealdnoth let it be known that Edgar had asked for Wilchard to take charge of the army during his illness. For some reason, Wilchard had never been so popular. Many a grand nobleman of South Magnia took time from their busy schedule to speak personally to Wilchard, to praise him on the fine job he had done for his prince over recent years and to remark on how well he handled the onerous duties of managing the army. They even confided to him their own fears for Prince Edgar's health, and what might befall the kingdom should he tragically succumb to his terrible illness. Edgar had no heirs, and there was no obvious successor to the throne. Many a grand nobleman gave Wilchard their own opinions as to who would be best placed to take over the leadership of the kingdom in such a grave situation. Wilchard listened politely and passed on everything he heard to Edgar. Edgar wondered if he should be ill more often.

All in all, the ruse had worked very well. Harbyrt the Fat had doubtless heard about the fate of his prince. He and his following had still not joined up with the royal army. Edgar knew that Harbyrt's scheming mind would be working overtime. If Edgar did die now, it would be the perfect opportunity for him to declare his independence. South Magnia would be in chaos and there would be no one to stand in his way.

Of course, what Harbyrt didn't know was that Edgar was feeling fine and biding his time until he was ready to confront his wayward vassal in person.

There was a knock at the door. Brictwin stood up from his prone position on the floor, where he had been catching up on some sleep, and Edgar shouted for his visitors to enter. Leofwin opened the door from the outside, let in Wilchard and Ealdnoth, and closed it again.

'Take a seat,' said Edgar, motioning to Oslac's bed, upon which his councillors duly perched.

'Important developments,' began Wilchard with little preamble. 'Last night Ashere, Prince Cerdda's younger brother, led a surprise attack on Earl Sherlin. Apparently, it came completely out of the blue and was a complete success. Sherlin was captured, and before his men knew anything about it, Ashere had delivered him up to his brother to stand trial on charges of treason. Cerdda has raised a small army and is currently located just a few miles north of the border. He sends apologies for not advising you of Ashere's attack, but because it was a risky venture, he preferred to wait on its result and then report to us on the current situation. He advises you to strike at Harbyrt soon. There is probably a fair chance that he knows nothing of these events yet.'

Edgar had to stand up with excitement. 'Yes. We move now and we move fast. Wilchard, I'm suddenly feeling a lot better, and feel good enough to resume command of the army. We leave within the hour. If anyone feels that their men cannot be mobilised before then, they will have to stay at Halsham.'

As it turned out, with a little grumbling aside, all of Edgar's commanders had their troops ready on time. His recovery was seen by many as a sign of Toric's blessing on the campaign. The story was that Edgar wished to link up with Harbyrt to share information and combine forces before pushing into North Magnia. More than one lord openly complained about the lack of any action from Harbyrt so far. Edgar agreed that his Marshal had a number of questions to answer and was happy to see that he was likely to enjoy some support from his nobility in bringing the man to task.

It was only a few miles from Halsham to Harbyrt's castle at Granstow, the largest of half a dozen strongholds in the northern marches which were in his keeping.

It was mid-afternoon by the time it came into view, however. Well-positioned on a hill overlooking the surrounding territory, Granstow was one of the largest border castles which had been built during the years of civil war. Nonetheless, it was designed to be effective rather than grand-looking. The regular garrison would only be about fifty strong, though that in itself was a considerable expense on food and wages. It could hold considerably more people when necessary. The central keep, perched high on an earth mound, was stone-built, but the rest of the fortifications were constructed from wood from the local area. It couldn't hold out against a determined army forever, but that wasn't the point. Granstow was part of a network of fortifications along the border to deter raiders from North Magnia. Should they be faced with a full-scale invasion, the garrisons' job was to disrupt the enemy and hold out until relieved.

Edgar decided to pitch his army's camp a mile away from the castle. It left something of a no-man's land between the two forces. The prince wanted Harbyrt to be the one to cross it.

It was some time before a messenger from Harbyrt arrived. The messenger turned out to be Kenward, officially royal sheriff of the region, but in reality, securely in Harbyrt's pocket. He was a man about the age Edgar's father would have been: bushy, grey hair topping a large-featured, flat face that Edgar didn't like very much. Kenward was taken to Edgar's tent to talk with the Prince.

'Greetings, Your Highness,' began Kenward, 'we did not expect your visit, I am afraid, but arrangements have been made at the castle for your entourage to stay.'

'You did not expect my visit, Kenward?' enquired Edgar in a quiet voice, yet it's tone hinted of anger and contempt. 'In time of war with the Northerners I would hope my marshal and sheriff would expect to be involved a little.'

Kenward inclined his head at the prince's response but offered no apology. 'Of course, both Marshal Harbyrt and myself have been busy, stockpiling and garrisoning our strongholds and raising our soldiers. I am merely explaining that we did not receive notice of your plans to march the army here...in fact, the last message we received was that Your Highness was gravely ill.'

Edgar didn't like the sheriff's words, demeanour, or his tone of voice, and felt like smashing a gauntleted fist into his face, but he controlled his emotions. After all, this man wasn't the target today. 'Yes, well, I thank you for asking after my health, Sheriff. I am in fact fully recovered and feel no need to impose on Harbyrt at Granstow when I can spend the night here amongst my soldiers. I would, however, very much like to speak with Harbyrt regarding the forthcoming campaign, and would be grateful if you could fetch him for me.'

'Of course, Your Highness,' replied Kenward, doing his best to hide his discomfort. 'Do you intend to strike at the enemy tomorrow, sire?'

'You will understand, Kenward, if I keep my plans to myself and my trusted councillors for the time being. It would be a blow if they were to find their way into enemy hands.'

'Of course, Your Highness,' repeated the sheriff, before bowing and leaving the tent.

Satisfied with his strategy, Edgar called a meeting of the Royal Council. The Council was a vague body of advisers to the Prince, selected by Edgar himself from those in attendance on him. Since many of the most powerful men in the kingdom were present with their retinues in the army, it was difficult for Edgar to keep the council manageable in size without putting people's noses out of joint. Thus, along with loyal supporters like Wilchard, Ealdnoth and Farred, this meeting also involved men whom Edgar had been obliged to invite. Otha of Rystham, probably Edgar's wealthiest vassal, was there along with his brother Wulfgar, High Priest of Toric. Aescmar, the bulk of whose lands were held by the Magnian coast in order that he co-ordinate the kingdom's naval defences, was also present. He was a man who kept himself to himself, happy not to interfere with Edgar's plans if Edgar did not interfere with his. He seemed to take his responsibilities seriously, though, and Edgar had no quarrel with him.

Harbyrt took his time to get from his castle to the camp. No doubt his lack of haste was a reminder to his Prince that he would not be treated like a wayward lackey. The facts of the matter were, however, that the Marshal could offer little resistance to Edgar when he had the kingdom's army with him, and wasting time now just served to irritate his peers, who were also waiting for him to arrive before the Council started.

When Harbyrt eventually did arrive with a small entourage, he was immediately taken to the royal tent. Edgar had ordered that no refreshments were to be offered beforehand in the hope that Harbyrt would arrive in a foul mood. The man was no fool, however, and when Leofwin and Brictwin stepped aside to let him manoeuvre his bulk inside, he immediately bowed to his Prince and clasped hands with the others present, as if nothing was amiss. Farred's face was the only one he did not recognise, and when introduced, he made a jest about Steppe tribesmen attending Royal Council in an obvious attempt to reduce the standing of someone he correctly guessed to be a royal loyalist. The dangers of councils, as Edgar and his father before him had found out, was the tendency of the nobility to stick together as a group to defend their own rights and privileges, and to see the prince as something of a threat to these.

'I have called this meeting,' began Edgar, 'in order that we discuss our plans for the next phase of this campaign.'

Wilchard, on cue, was the first to respond to this announcement. 'First I feel I must speak my mind on some aspects of the campaign so far. It is my opinion that, in the grave situation in which we find ourselves, the support of Harbyrt as Marshal of the North has been totally inadequate.'

'How dare *you* pass judgement on *me*?' Harbyrt stared around the tent in incredulity, looking for support, his face and neck mottled with red blotches as his anger boiled over. 'You're nothing but an upstart royal boot polisher, you piece of fungus!' Harbyrt roared at the chief steward, spittle shooting in Wilchard's direction.

Edgar surveyed the assembly. Normally, Harbyrt's bluster would have been enough to see off the attack from Wilchard. Wilchard was not from a great noble family, and many of those present did resent the power he wielded in the kingdom, whereas Harbyrt was one of them, and therefore should be defended at all costs. These were not normal times, however. This was time of war, and self-survival was of vital importance. Wilchard had shown himself to be an able commander; he oversaw the army logistics and had made sure it was fed and well supplied. He had kept the peace in an army which seemed to have as many officers as soldiers with a mixture of discipline and diplomacy. Harbyrt, on the other hand, a man who was supposed to be a key leader in times of war, had not figured at all, and was resented for this. Edgar's Council, therefore, was not sure who to side with and looked to their Prince for a decision.

'I think we should hear Wilchard out, Harbyrt, and then you may defend yourself.'

Harbyrt looked around the tent again, but found that he had no overwhelming support as he had hoped. On all previous occasions when Edgar had tried to corner his marshal like this, Harbyrt had simply walked away, retreating to his northern power base and daring Edgar to do something about it—which, of course, he couldn't. Now, however, as much as he no doubt wanted to walk out, Edgar had an army with him. That changed the dynamics more than a little.

Wilchard, then, was allowed to continue. 'Four days ago, Prince Edgar sent out orders that every magnate should raise his quota of troops because the kingdom's most precious treasure, the Dagger of Toric, had been stolen, and it was feared that an invasion would follow,' began Wilchard slyly, making sure that he mentioned the dagger in order to get Wulfgar on side. 'Since that time, we have heard nothing from Harbyrt, despite two further attempts at communication. We have all done our best to keep this army going, and when we approached the Magnian border the least I expected was information on the situation in the borderlands and confirmation that your forces and strongholds were ready. I would have expected you to join up with the royal army long before now.'

Wilchard's words were greeted with the odd murmur of approval from around the Council, but Harbyrt was ready with his comeback.

'Your words display a totally unjustified lack of faith in me, steward. My soldiers have been working for days on preparing the kingdom's northern defences for sieges, a task which may prove to be vitally important. I have sent scouts across the border to keep an eye on enemy activity to make sure that the royal army could approach in complete safety. Why would I join up with you when we need a force here on the border, ready to react to the enemy should they make an incursion before the royal army approaches? While you have been camped out in Halsham, it is my forces who have been working tirelessly for the kingdom. I didn't expect gratitude, but all I have found is accusation!'

'Nobody is accusing you of anything less than total commitment to the kingdom, Harbyrt,' began Otha of Rystham, slithering into the argument. 'We are all grateful to have you working so tirelessly for us all. Perhaps all this really boils down to is the lack of...communication on your part, simply to reassure us that all was well in the north.'

'Well, perhaps I could have spared some time to keep you better informed,' Harbyrt conceded gruffly. 'If you all feel that I have failed in that regard, please accept my apologies.'

Otha had succeeded in taking the fire out of a confrontation which Edgar had hoped to stoke up. He was not going to let his chance slip away, however.

'Apologies are all very well, Harbyrt, but I need to be totally confident that the administration of my northern provinces is being handled correctly. Your recent conduct has only added to feelings of unease which I already held. It is my opinion that authority in the northern marches needs to be re-organised.'

'What do you mean, *re-organised?*' barked Harbyrt, as the red blotches returned to ruin his complexion.

'Since my father's time, responsibilities in the north have been shouldered by just one man. I think that after this campaign is over it will be the perfect opportunity for me to take a fresh look at arrangements here and share out some of this responsibility.'

Harbyrt's temper boiled over again. 'You can't get rid of me, Edgar. I have rights in this kingdom. My lands aren't yours to give away.'

Edgar quickly responded before Otha of Rystham gave a sermon on the laws of the kingdom. 'Harbyrt, I do not intend to take any of your own lands from you, and I still intend for you to be one of my leading magnates in the region. I simply require other leaders as well. Yesterday I was gravely ill, and that led me to think about what the consequences would be if you were to take ill in a similar way. If I had other lieutenants in the region, my peace of mind would be far greater. As for lands, a large proportion of those which you control are royal lands, given to you by virtue of your title as marshal. I intend to redistribute some of those...perhaps amongst some of your fellow councillors here.'

That was the clincher. A number of Edgar's magnates had looked slightly unhappy about this public curtailment of Harbyrt the Fat's power, even though it was generally understood to be in the kingdom's interests, simply because, if he could do it to Harbyrt, what was to stop him from doing it to them? The possibility of some of the lands being shared out now meant that many in the room seemed to be on board with the idea of re-organising things in the north. *Of course*, they muttered to one another, *you had to feel a bit for Harbyrt, but really, he did have it coming, and it was in the interests of the kingdom. The* kingdom *had to be put first.*

Harbyrt was ordered to stay with the army. The Council agreed that the army's current position, just a few miles from the border, was basically sound. The camp was now tobe fortified with a ditch and wall of stakes.

Edgar took personal control over Granstow Castle. Ealdnoth's suggestion that they should send a messenger to Cerdda of North Magnia was unanimously agreed with. After all, if they could get to the bottom of this conflict and end it without going to war, it really would be much better. Edgar knew that the thought of all those lucrative northern estates being pillaged by North Magnians had nothing whatsoever to do with this sudden desire for peace. A messenger was sent immediately, and Edgar's army entrenched its position while it waited for a reply.

The South Magnian request for peace talks was answered promptly. Ten North Magnians, including Prince Cerdda himself, were making their way to the giant ash tree in Adingley, a well-known meeting place for the people of the area for generations, and now conveniently located near the Magnian border. Edgar decided that he too would travel there himself. As well as Leofwin and Brictwin, he chose as his companions Ealdnoth, as Chancellor; Farred, who had already met with Cerdda, though that meeting was always to be kept a secret; Wulfgar, as the leading prelate of the kingdom, and the high-ranking noblemen Otha of Rystham and Aescmar. Finally, Edgar thought it might be wise to take Harbyrt the Fat and Kenward his sheriff, just to make sure that no mischief was caused while he was away.

Wilchard was left in charge of the army and Edgar's party made their way to the prearranged spot.

Harbyrt seemed to have been struck dumb by the sudden turn of events he had experienced this day, but Edgar hoped that he wasn't plotting his revenge. It seemed that the Marshal had not yet heard about the arrest of Earl Sherlin in North Magnia, and Edgar had chosen not to mention it. If revenge was on his mind, he would soon find out that he no longer had the resources at his disposal to mount a challenge to Edgar's authority.

They arrived at Adingley in good time and Edgar was relieved to see that Cerdda was already there with nine companions, waiting by the ash tree. While the hostilities between the two kingdoms had been a pretence, meetings such as these were always dangerous, since it was the perfect opportunity to isolate an enemy with a few followers and ambush them.

Cerdda, however, had come in good faith. This was the first time that the two princes had met. Cerdda, unlike most Magnians, was dark-haired with amber-coloured skin. Edgar remembered his father telling him that all of Bradda's three children had got their dark looks from their mother, Mette, whom Edric used to say was the most beautiful woman of her generation.

The two clasped hands and introduced each other to their companions. Cerdda's brother Ashere had come as well. He was almost a mirror image of his older brother, except for his more youthful looks, and the fact that he smiled a lot less.

Edgar suggested that the two of them talk alone for a while, leaving their followers to enjoy a few bottles of wine which Otha of Rystham had provided.

'I see you've brought Harbyrt with you,' began Cerdda once they were out of earshot.

'Yes. I have reduced his power in the north, but he will still have a significant estate. I did not want to totally humiliate him and force him into a rebellion.'

Cerdda pursed his lips. 'Edgar...yesterday Ashere intercepted a letter which was intended to reach Earl Sherlin.' Cerdda produced a piece of parchment from inside his tunic and handed it over to Edgar. 'The bearer of the letter was captured: one of Harbyrt's men, named Torlin.'

Edgar shrugged to indicate that he did not know the man.

'Sherlin admitted to the conspiracy, admittedly under some duress.'

Edgar scanned the few lines of scrawled writing.

'Greetings, brother. The time may be at hand to bring our plans to fruition. The fox cub has fallen seriously ill. Prepare and wait for further news. Patience now may soon be rewarded.'

Edgar had no doubt that he was the fox cub referred to, a choice of words which galled him. Harbyrt's seal was not on the letter, so there was no definite proof that it was his. It was quite possible that Cerdda's zealous brother, Ashere, had composed it himself. Edgar, however, had no doubts that Harbyrt and Sherlin had conspired along those lines, and he was quite prepared to use the letter as evidence.

'Where is Sherlin now?' he asked the Prince of North Magnia.

'Dead. He was executed this morning. The man was too dangerous to leave alive. It is difficult to say how many people in my kingdom were embroiled in his treacheries. Suffice to say that my enquiries have suggested more names than I had expected.'

Cerdda spoke with some bitterness, for which Edgar did not blame him. 'You had no choice, Cerdda, and from this letter it seems that I have none either. Know that you have my support should anyone try to avenge Sherlin's death.'

Cerdda nodded in thanks. 'I do not pretend that I have received no positives from these events—an important one being your friendship, Edgar. I had a grin on my face for hours after Farred left. I have enjoyed our little intrigue. Your father was always honourable towards me, and you have been, too. Magnia has spent a generation embroiled in internal jealousies...it is high time we took steps to retrieve our standing in Dalriya.'

Edgar smiled. 'Your feelings match with my own, Cerdda. On the subject of Dalriya, Farred told you of the theft of Toric's Dagger?'

Cerdda nodded gravely. 'He did. Is there any more news?'

Edgar shrugged. 'I sent a group to follow the Brasingian robbers. At the least I hope they will be able to tell me where it is and who has it. I have heard nothing so far, however.'

Cerdda gestured towards Ealdnoth. 'Is that man your wizard?'

Edgar nodded. He knew that Cerdda did not have a wizard himself; many rulers of Dalriya considered them to be a dangerous, untrustworthy sect, and had anyone who possessed such skills killed. 'He is one of my most trusted advisers, Cerdda. And very useful. You should get yourself one.'

Cerdda smiled. 'Maybe.'

'Well...perhaps we should join the rest of them...we *have* agreed to peace, haven't we?'

Cerdda grinned. 'I suppose so. I must admit, however, that the first war of my reign has not been quite how I imagined it would be.'

'Mmm... you expected more fighting, perhaps?'

'A bit more, yes.'

The two princes strolled over to their followers and announced that peace had indeed been agreed. Both sides showed genuine relief and felt able to relax into some more unrestrained drinking.

Edgar took an opportunity to pull Otha of Rystham to one side.

'What do you make of the peace, Otha?'

'Good news, of course. It would appear that the North Magnians were not involved in the theft of Toric's Dagger, then?' enquired the magnate pointedly. Otha wasn't stupid. No doubt he had suspicions about the game Edgar had been playing. But Edgar was still one step ahead.

'Not entirely. We may never know, but it is quite possible that Earl Sherlin of North Magnia was involved.'

'Sherlin? Really?'

'Yes. I'm sure it won't have escaped your attention, Otha, that Harbyrt and Sherlin have grown close recently.'

'Well...Harbyrt's son married Sherlin's daughter...'

'Without my permission. I have long had suspicions, Otha, and it seems that Prince Cerdda has, too. Sherlin was executed this morning.'

'What!?' gasped Otha.

Edgar put a finger to his lips. 'For treason,' he murmured. Now Edgar produced the piece of parchment from his tunic. 'This was picked up by the North Magnians, apparently in the possession of one of Harbyrt's men, on the way to be delivered to Sherlin.'

Otha perused the document. His expression was grim. 'There's no evidence that Harbyrt issued this.' The words were Otha's, but they lacked his usual conviction.

'No conclusive evidence, perhaps. I cannot claim to be surprised by its contents, however. Harbyrt has shown a total absence of loyalty since I came to the throne. I cannot tolerate the situation any longer. I need your support, Otha. Emotions will run high if I execute my own marshal. I need you and Wulfgar to publicly support my decision, and, united, we can stifle any opposition.'

Otha looked as if he were in physical pain. 'This is a difficult situation, Edgar. We cannot legally deprive Harbyrt of life or land without a fair trial. I cannot be seen to endorse the denial of a lord his rights.'

'He cannot be allowed to live, Otha. As for his lands, however, there is no evidence of his son's participation in the plot, and I intend to let him inherit his father's estate when he comes of age. In the meantime, the estate must be administered on his behalf, and I see you as the perfect choice for this. You can fill the vacuum of power in the north caused by Harbyrt's removal and lend some stability to the region. What do you say?'

Otha was being offered a fortune. For the next few years he would have control of the resources, revenues and men from Harbyrt's lands. With this addition to the lands he already held, it would make him unquestionably the greatest noble of Magnia.

Otha looked over to where Harbyrt was standing uncomfortably with Kenward, the sheriff. 'He has to go. I will support you, Edgar.'

Edgar had judged correctly. Harbyrt's fate was now sealed. He was just about to offer Otha his thanks when the sound of a horse riding at full gallop caught his attention.

It was a single rider, who pulled up by the ash tree where everyone was congregating. Edgar and Otha walked over to see what was happening.

The rider jumped off his horse and bowed to Cerdda. 'Your Highness, I bring news from the north. Her Royal Highness your mother instructed that I should find you and relay it immediately.'

'Of course. You can tell us all unless it is of a private nature.'

'My lords, there are early reports of an invasion of Persala by King Arioc of Haskany. It took place yesterday and they say that the capital, Baserno, has fallen to him.'

There were gasps all round and Cerdda let out a whistle. 'If Baserno has fallen then the whole kingdom may be lost. What of Mark?'

'It is unclear whether the king is dead or alive, captured or escaped. I believe there have been conflicting reports.'

Edgar felt like he was in shock. Persala was the great founding state of mankind; history had begun with its rise to greatness. Magnians defined themselves in relation to Persala, being the only people of Dalriya to successfully resist the Empire at its height. In more recent times, Persala had lost its dominance to Brasingia, and was not even the strongest power in the north any more, as province after province had been torn away. But for it to be conquered in one day? It was difficult to come to terms with.

Cerdda caught Edgar's eye and interrupted his thinking.

'Well, my friend, it looks like we may have a busy time ahead of us.'

Edgar could only nod in agreement.

XIII

THE BOAR STRIKES

'TWO THALERS PER ARROW!' exclaimed Gyrmund, genuinely shocked at the charge.

The fletcher, on the other hand, maintained his disturbingly cool composure and smiled back. Gyrmund was sure that he could even detect a hint of pity in the man's face. He turned around to Moneva for support, but his companion did not seem particularly interested in the price of arrows.

'Seventy-five marks for forty,' stated Gyrmund, in a voice that suggested he would not take no for an answer.

The fletcher let out a puff of air and then screwed up his nose as he considered the offer. Eventually, he nodded his consent, and Gyrmund left the man having spent twice as much as he had planned.

'This is ridiculous!' began Gyrmund as he and Moneva made their way back to The Boot and Saddle. 'Duke Emeric's army seems to be swallowing everything up. Arrows I can just about understand, but how much did we have to pay out for a bit of bread and cheese?' Gyrmund could feel himself getting hot.

'What's the matter with you, Gyrmund? I haven't seen you get this stressed before, and I think we've been through some worse experiences recently than getting overcharged! There's nothing we can do about it, so just forget it.'

'Well, it's this city. There's too many people milling around. I'll be glad when we get out of here.'

Moneva laughed. Gyrmund couldn't remember hearing her laugh before.

'What's so funny?'

'We're like chalk and cheese, you and me. I spent three miserable days in the Wilderness, sleeping on the forest floor, being permanently uncomfortable, getting chased by those creatures, seeing nothing but trees all day...while you seemed to be having a great time. Now, I'm back in Coldeberg, looking at the stores, looking at all the people and what they're up to, enjoying a bit of city life, and you're moaning about it and can't wait to leave!'

Gyrmund smiled. 'I didn't realise you had such a bad time back there.'

The conversation paused as they briefly separated to either side of the road to allow a horse and cart to pass by.

'So, you've been to Coldeberg before?'

'Yes. I spent some time here a few years ago. How about you?'

'I've passed through a few times.'

Moneva laughed again. Gyrmund didn't think he was being particularly funny and decided that Moneva must be genuinely happy to be here. 'So, you've got fond memories? What did you do here?'

'I worked for a merchant who was based here; in fact, he probably still is. He had interests all over the Empire and in Guivergne, so I travelled about a bit.'

'What did you do?'

Moneva sighed. 'Well, I spied on his rivals, I spied on his business partners. I sabotaged his rivals' plans, I sabotaged his partners' plans. It was good money, but in the end it got a bit boring. A bit too easy. In the end I was charging so much for the tiniest little things that even he decided I was too expensive.'

'So why did you take up this little assignment?' asked Gyrmund.

'Well, there's the money, of course. But really, I thought it would be interesting. I suppose I can't complain on that score.'

'Good answer,' said Gyrmund approvingly.

Moneva raised an eyebrow, but said nothing.

'So, how long have you known Herin?'

'Why do you ask?'

Gyrmund shrugged. 'Just asking.'

'I met Herin and Clarin while I was working here, as a matter of fact. They were fighting as mercenaries for Emeric in his war with the Black Horse tribe. He already had a sizeable army back then and the merchant I was working for managed to squeeze a tidy profit out of the whole affair. Herin and I made sure we did alright as well; the army structure was totally disorganised, and so it was quite easy for him to get his hands on provisions, which I could sell on. Since then I've bumped into them a couple of times. Last time was when I was working in Cordence. For another greedy merchant, as it happens. I'm wondering now whether I wish I hadn't bumped into them again.'

'Yes, I know what you mean. I wasn't quite expecting things to turn out as they have.'

Gyrmund and Moneva fell silent. They rounded a corner and found themselves back at the Boot and Saddle.

'Pretty quiet,' commented Moneva as they walked in.

Gyrmund looked around. There were no customers in the bar area and even the owner, Bernard Hat, was absent.

'Well, I'm going to put this food away and see if Rabigar is about. I expect they've booked rooms upstairs.'

Moneva nodded. 'I hope so; a bit of rest would do me the world of good. Be careful, though. It's eerily quiet around here.'

Gyrmund made his way behind the bar and into the kitchen at the back. There was no sign of any staff here, either. What was more, the room had been left in a mess, pots unwashed and food lying about. He looked around for somewhere to store the provisions he had bought. He heard footsteps behind him and turned, half expecting that Moneva had come to look for herself.

She hadn't.

Three soldiers had followed him around the bar and into the kitchen, weapons drawn. Gyrmund dropped his stuff and grabbed his sword. He made a move for the exit at the back of the kitchen. But as he approached the door, it burst open from outside, and three more soldiers entered the kitchen, trapping him.

'Drop it!' shouted one of them at Gyrmund, but he was not eager to part with his weapon so easily. He looked around the room: there was a window, but he had no chance of escaping through it in time. He was caught between the two groups of soldiers, and six blades were pointing towards him. They were all dressed in the uniform of Barissian soldiers.

'You are under arrest by royal order,' explained the man at the front of the first group. 'If you do not drop your weapon we will take you by force. I advise you not to take that option.'

The man spoke with confidence, and Gyrmund realised that he was in a no-win situation. It was better to submit to the soldiers than die pointlessly in the kitchen of this inn. If they wanted him dead, he would be. Gyrmund knew that Herin, Soren and the rest were now his best hope of staying alive. He dropped his sword and allowed the soldiers to take him.

Once his sword clattered to the floor the soldiers pounced, beating him to the floor and pulling his hands behind his back so that they could tie them together with rope.

'It would have been better for you if you'd died with some honour here,' whispered one of his assailants in his ear, and Gyrmund felt a sick feeling in his stomach. He berated himself for walking into a trap, for entering this damned city in the first place.

He thought of Moneva, which made him feel even worse. If it was better for Gyrmund to die now, then it was doubly true for her. He had no illusions about the standard treatment of female prisoners by soldiers in this part of the world.

Gyrmund was led out into the rear courtyard of the inn, where he was surprised to see another two dozen soldiers waiting. It was obvious that these soldiers had been lying in wait for them to arrive. His captors shoved him in front of the man who must be their leader. He wore no distinctive clothing but he was sat astride a powerful looking warhorse, emanating a sense of authority over the proceedings. Gyrmund noticed a scar running down the left side of his face, from ear to chin.

'Here's the man, General Salvinus,' said Gyrmund's captor with pride.

Salvinus? Gyrmund could hardly believe that the man they had been chasing was now sitting opposite him. His look of surprise was picked up by the rider, who smiled maliciously at him.

'Go and help them get the woman, then,' Salvinus shouted at his officer, and the men quickly hurried back to the inn. 'And be quiet! More of them could be coming at any minute!'

Salvinus turned his attention back to Gyrmund.

'You recognise my name, then?' he grinned.

Before Gyrmund had time to reply Salvinus had kicked out at him, his boot smashing into Gyrmund's chin and sending him crashing to the floor. Gyrmund landed badly on his back because of his tied hands, pain shooting up and down his spine. He turned back to his attacker, who was sliding off his horse to the cheers of his soldiers. He turned around at his men with a look of anger and put a gloved finger to his moustache, silencing the noise immediately.

Salvinus moved over to Gyrmund and crouched down next to him, so that they could talk quietly.

'So, you're the one who managed to track me through the Wilderness, eh?'

'Yes. You make it sound more difficult than it was, though.'

Salvinus smiled and produced a knife, which he proceeded to push against Gyrmund's throat, drawing blood.

'Do you have the dagger?'

Gyrmund looked up blankly, not comprehending the question. Surely Salvinus had the dagger—wasn't that the whole point? The question reminded him, though, of the sorcerer Nexodore, who had demanded the dagger from them on the Great Road. Something wasn't right, but he was at a loss to know what.

Gyrmund could see Salvinus's eyes studying his reaction, and he brought the knife away from Gyrmund with a look of half-hearted disappointment, as if he had been expecting Gyrmund would be unable to help.

Salvinus was interrupted by the return of his soldiers. Gyrmund turned around to look for Moneva but she wasn't with them. About a dozen soldiers were now reporting back to him, and he felt foolish for not noticing their presence in the inn. Hopefully Moneva had.

'What's the matter?'

'She's not there, general,' Salvinus was informed.

'What do you mean? I saw her go in with my own eyes, you idiot.'

Salvinus turned back to Gyrmund and replaced the knife at his throat. 'Where is she? I'll slit you open if you don't tell me. King Emeric wants you alive, but if you put up a struggle...what can I do?'

'I don't know where she went...we split up when we got inside.' Gyrmund felt some shame for blurting it out, but the man already knew that Moneva had gone inside the inn.

Salvinus waited a moment and then withdrew the knife a second time. 'I'm bored of talking to you,' he told Gyrmund. 'Curtis, search him, mount him up, and take him to the castle. We'll teach these foreign bastards not to interfere with the Kingdom of Barissia.'

Curtis stepped forwards and lifted Gyrmund onto a horse, shifting him around until he could sit upright. Salvinus, meanwhile, had returned his attention to the search for Moneva.

'I'm going in there myself and you lot are coming with me. She went in, she hasn't come out, so she's still bloody in there!' He turned around one last time to look at Gyrmund. 'Oh, I nearly forgot. Just to get you in the mood for your stay in the castle dungeons, you should look at the landlord of this inn. When I arrived, he decided that he would rather take sides with you than help me carry out the king's business. I loosened his tongue eventually, but I was still not satisfied with his loyalty.'

Curtis grabbed Gyrmund's reins and led him out of the yard entrance, escorted by three more soldiers.

There the Barissians had erected a stake, and when Gyrmund looked, he saw that placed on top of it was the decapitated head of Bernard Hat, still adorned with his green beret.

***

Belwynn had been enjoying her afternoon in Coldeberg. Clarin was easy company and she began to relax after the stresses and strains of recent days. As far as information gathering had gone, they had achieved little except to find that the name Gervase Salvinus was familiar to many in the city: he had been chosen by Emeric as the general of the army which was being raised in Barissia. While people in the city were overwhelmingly loyal to their new king, there did not seem to be much genuine enthusiasm for war. Like Belwynn herself, the citizens of Coldeberg did not seem to fully understand why Emeric had chosen to declare his duchy independent of the Empire.

Having asked several questions of the tight-lipped citizens, Belwynn and Clarin decided to head back to the Boot and Saddle. She was still worried about Soren. He seemed to have recovered physically from his ordeal in the Wilderness, but he was not himself, and had been eager to leave the inn on his own. Belwynn wanted to communicate with him but sensed that he wanted time alone.

She was slightly surprised, then, when he contacted her.

Belwynn, where are you? The tone seemed urgent.

We're just on our way back now.

Stop.

Belwynn sensed fear in her brother's thoughts and came to an abrupt halt. She grabbed Clarin's arm to make him stop as well.

'What is it?' asked the big warrior.

'It's Soren. Something's wrong.'

Clarin looked around them and placed his hand on the hilt of his sword, but seemed content to let Belwynn continue her private conversation.

Emeric's troops are swarming all over the Boot and Saddle. It's not safe there. I'm in an alleyway off Orchard Lane, two streets before the inn. Meet me there.

The instruction was simple enough, and Belwynn relayed it to Clarin, who grimaced but nodded his consent. Orchard Lane happened to be the next street on their right, and they entered it warily, on the lookout for soldiers. Belwynn spied Soren signalling from his alleyway and they quickly met up with him.

'What's happening?' Belwynn and Clarin asked the wizard in unison.

'I nearly walked straight in,' began Soren. 'I've been to the north-east of the city this afternoon, and I was returning to the inn via the back yard rather than the front.' Soren's face was grim, but Belwynn just wanted him to spit out the news. 'The head of Bernard Hat has been placed on a stake there. I tried to get a glimpse of what was going on without being seen and saw soldiers in the yard. I skirted round the edge of the inn and I'm pretty sure that they're inside as well. I think...I think they're waiting there for us to return. We left Rabigar and Elana in there...some of the others might have returned already.'

Belwynn swallowed hard. If Bernard Hat had been decapitated, what had been done to the others?

'Why do you think that they're after us, Soren?'

'Emeric is obviously linked to the dagger—'

'Yes, but how did they know where we were?' Belwynn was having trouble getting her head around this new turn of events. She looked at Clarin. Concern was plainly visible on his face, no doubt concern for Herin's whereabouts, but he was saying nothing. The three of them were used to working together in these situations. Soren did the thinking; Clarin would agree with his course of action.

'I think,' began Soren, responding to his sister's question, 'we've been betrayed. Someone's told Emeric of our whereabouts. Those soldiers seemed to know that if they waited in the inn we would be coming back.'

'I've just seen Dirk walk past,' interrupted Clarin, who had been keeping an eye on the top of the street.

'Dirk?' Soren sounded surprised. 'Go and grab him, Clarin.' The big warrior dutifully ran off back to the top of the street to stop Dirk from walking into the trap which had been set for them.

Belwynn watched Clarin go and then turned back to her brother.

'Betrayed? But who knew that we were all coming back now?'

Soren shrugged. 'No-one else did.'

'You mean you think it was one of us?'

'Most of us have had a chance to get in contact with Emeric's forces this afternoon if we'd wanted to.' Soren looked up at Clarin and Dirk who had turned into the street and were walking over. 'And here comes my prime suspect.'

It seemed to Belwynn that Clarin had taken Soren's instructions to grab Dirk quite literally. He still had a hand on the priest's shoulder, and the pair had the appearance of a wayward son and his father.

'What's going on?' asked Dirk.

'Where's the dagger, Dirk?' asked Soren.

Belwynn and Clarin shared confused glances but allowed Soren to continue without interruption.

'What do you mean?' began Dirk, but he looked into the wizard's eyes, boring into his own, and seemed to think better of continuing.

The priest put his hand inside his tunic, fumbled around a bit, and produced a knife. It had a jewel-encrusted hilt, a thin blade, and ended in a sharp needlepoint.

Toric's Dagger.

'I think you've got some explaining to do,' said Soren.

***

Gyrmund was taken directly to Coldeberg Castle. He was given no opportunity to escape, his attempts at conversation were met with a stony silence, and before he knew it he was being led through the keep into the main courtyard.

The castle was heavily defended. Gyrmund was shocked at the number of soldiers moving around the structure. His hopes of getting out of his situation alive were diminishing by the second. At first, he had castigated himself for allowing Salvinus to catch him so easily, but now he had come to terms with the fact. His thoughts had turned to escape. Gyrmund realised that his best hope lay with being rescued by the other Magnians. He just hoped that some of them had evaded Salvinus's trap.

Curtis shoved him off his horse. His hands still tied, Gyrmund fell badly off the beast. He twisted his body around to land as best he could, but his right shoulder took the impact and was snapped out of place. Gyrmund's back was already damaged from the confrontation with Salvinus at the inn, and as he landed pain lanced up and down his spine. He cried out in agony, leading to much amusement from the soldiers watching in the yard. Curtis yanked him to his feet. The pain in his shoulder didn't stop. He worried that it had been dislocated, but he refused to give the Barissians any more satisfaction by letting them know.

Curtis prodded him over to a doorway in the corner of the yard, and Gyrmund entered the castle proper. Curtis led him along a stone corridor, decorated thickly with tapestries on both walls, while behind him three other soldiers continued to guard his progress. He could not help but be impressed with the small part of the castle he was being shown. Both as a fortress and as a display of wealth and power, Coldeberg Castle came second to few. Certainly, thought Gyrmund, nothing in Magnia was a match.

In the Brasingian Empire, though, things were different. Impressive as Emeric's castle and army seemed to be, he was no match for Emperor Baldwin, and Gyrmund took some consolation from the joy he would feel when Baldwin burned the place to the ground. If he was still around when that happened.

Gyrmund's spirits dropped again, however, with the arrival of the moment he had been dreading. Turning the corner, Curtis took him past a couple of armed guards and began descending a stairwell. They were now headed for the dungeons, and a real feeling of dread passed over Gyrmund.

As they descended deeper into the bowels of the castle the air became stale and his feeling of confinement began, long before he was placed in the irons that he knew would be waiting for him. The descent, down the twisting staircase, was even longer than Gyrmund had anticipated. The journey ended though, and Gyrmund alighted from the last step into a stinking smell of sewage. Torches adorned the walls, but they did little to break through the underground gloom. The grimy, squalid bits of the dungeon which Gyrmund could make out made him think that was probably a blessing.

'Herman!' shouted Curtis into the murk.

The address was met with silence. Gyrmund looked at Curtis but he didn't seem moved to try again, so they waited. His shoulder throbbed with pain. He worried that if he had to stand for much longer, he would faint.

Eventually, Gyrmund could make out a shuffling sound, which was gradually getting closer. Gyrmund was now ready to meet with the deformed, brutish, stereotypical jailer he had been expecting. Such a figure duly emerged out of the darkness. Trailing a crippled leg behind him, the jailer gave Gyrmund a smile full of rotting teeth as he lumbered closer. He was a giant of a man with fists the size of a man's head. Two-thirds of his own head was purple, the skin twisted and uneven, as if it had been held in a pan of boiling water for a very long time. One eye was useless, a milky white colour in the midst of angry purple. This, however, did not seem to be Herman. Next to him was a small, thin man with a sharp nose and a thin, black moustache over sneering lips. While his purple-headed colleague seemed positively pleased to see Gyrmund, this man gave him a once-over with hostile, beady eyes.

'Follow me,' Herman ordered, turning around and retracing his steps down the dark corridor. His accomplice gave Gyrmund one last smile and shuffled along next to Herman. Curtis gave Gyrmund a sharp prod in the back to ensure that he followed after them and walked along behind. Obviously, he was going to fulfil his duties by ensuring that he didn't leave until Gyrmund was locked up in chains.

Gyrmund's eyes began to adjust to what little light there was, and he began to make out a door to a cell further up the corridor. It had an iron frame and vertical iron bars so that the jailers could look into the room. As they approached the door, Gyrmund could see a man sitting against the far wall, his arms and legs in manacles.

It was Herin. Their eyes met. Herin had a look of cold rage in his eyes. When he realised that it was Gyrmund a look of disappointment passed over his face. Gyrmund understood why; he represented one less potential rescuer.

Herman unlocked the door and Gyrmund was shoved into the cell. Sitting next to Herin was Elana. On the opposite wall was Rabigar. Both were in manacles, too.

Herman pointed to a place next to Rabigar. 'Over there.' Curtis violently pushed Gyrmund in that direction, causing him to crash against the wall and land awkwardly. He could not stop himself gasping out loud as his injured shoulder flared in pain.

'Get him ready, Greg,' ordered Herman.

The big jailer knelt, grinned at Gyrmund, and pulled him into position. Curtis moved closer and pointed the tip of his sword towards Gyrmund, discouraging a struggle. Greg put one shackle around Gyrmund's ankle, clasping it into place and then locking it, before repeating the process with the second ankle. Herin and the others watched on in silence. Greg then pulled out a knife and lumbered behind Gyrmund to cut his bonds. Curtis leaned closer and rested the end of his sword on Gyrmund's chest. Greg cut through the bonds, but immediately grabbed one wrist and placed it into a manacle. Once he had secured both arms he pulled back to admire his work. Curtis withdrew his sword.

'Have fun,' he advised Gyrmund, before, with a nod to Herman, he left the cell and made his way out of the dungeon.

140

A short period of silence followed. Herman was staring intently at him. Gyrmund felt panic begin to rise within him. He couldn't stand the idea of rotting away in this place. The threat of violence hung heavy in the air. He looked over to his fellow prisoners. While it felt wrong, he was relieved that he wasn't on his own. Herin and Rabigar had grim faces, but were not showing any fear; their expressions were more like anger. Elana was a picture of calm. She had no reason to be, but it made him feel a bit better.

A rasping noise made him turn his attention back to Herman. The jailer had withdrawn a knife of his own, a wicked looking instrument with a serrated edge. Still staring into his eyes, Herman walked slowly towards him and dropped down to rest on his haunches.

He slowly moved the knife up between Gyrmund's shackled legs until it rested against his manhood. The jailer still said nothing. Gyrmund didn't know how to respond, so he kept quiet, his eyes flicking down towards the knife and back up to look at the jailer.

Herman, eyes still boring into Gyrmund's, put pressure on the knife. The blade sliced through the leather of his trousers. Herman pushed the cold metal up against the inside of his thigh, then against his member. Terror welled up within him. but he resisted the urge to shout out and to struggle. He had to keep control. Silence obviously wasn't working. He forced himself to swallow, his mouth dry with fear.

'What do you want?' he asked, trying to keep his voice steady.

'I have been asked, by the King,' began Herman quietly, 'to discover the location of a certain weapon. I do not intend to fail him. I now have five prisoners. You and your prick are therefore dispensable to me. Tell me where it is or I cut it off.'

Gyrmund's mind raced to find the best answer. He had no doubt that he was dispensable to this man. Would he go through with his threat? Should Gyrmund pretend that he knew something? Pressure down below told him that the jailer wanted an answer now.

'I don't have it…I've never seen it and I don't know where it is. I didn't even know that one of us had it…'

Herman's expression didn't change, and the blade remained where it was. Seconds passed; they seemed like hours to Gyrmund.

Herman's hand moved. He withdrew the knife and stood up. Gyrmund let out a ragged breath of relief. The jailer looked around the cell.

'Maybe none of you know anything useful. Maybe you do—but I *will* find out either way. When I'm finished with you, you'll be telling me how many times you wet the bed as a child.'

His eyes found Rabigar. 'I'm going to start with this one,' he advised Greg. 'You should have stayed with your own kind, Krykker.'

Rabigar looked at Herman as if he were something unpleasant found on the bottom of his shoe. Greg lumbered over and detached Rabigar's chains from the wall. He held onto them as if they were puppet strings. 'Get up,' ordered Herman.

Suddenly, Rabigar sprang to life. Despite the chains weighing him down, he thrust himself towards the big jailer holding his chains. Greg was taken by surprise and was slow to react. As Rabigar dived into him, Gyrmund saw the Krykker snatch the knife which the giant had been using from his belt. Greg grabbed Rabigar by the hair and yanked the Krykker away with an iron grip. Rabigar slashed upwards at his arm and Greg howled in pain, letting go of the Krykker. However, with his other hand, the jailer yanked at Rabigar's chains, and the Krykker was pulled to the floor. Greg's booted foot slammed down on Rabigar's hand, effectively disarming him. Meanwhile, Herman jumped on top of the Krykker's back, wrapping one arm round his neck in a headlock and placing his own knife at Rabigar's throat.

'I should kill you now for trying that!' screamed the jailer hysterically. It was clear that he had got a fright.

Rabigar was breathing hard, down on all fours with one man on his back and the other holding his chains. Greg moaned in pain.

Herman smiled. 'To teach you a lesson for wounding Greg, you should be made to suffer as he has.'

In a deliberate movement, Herman withdrew the knife from Rabigar's throat, reversed the blade, and sent it into his eye.

Rabigar roared out in pain, and Gyrmund cried out in shock. The Krykker reared up and knocked the Barissian off his back. Greg, however, gave the chains another yank, and dragged the Krykker across the floor, towards the door of the cell. Rabigar clutched at his eye as he was dragged off down the corridor. Herman picked himself up. He bent over, wheezing. It looked like he had some kind of injury. Then Gyrmund realised that he wasn't injured—he was laughing: a silent, breathy noise that made Gyrmund feel sick. He slowly stood up and gave the cell and its prisoners a final look.

'I think the rest of you should reconsider,' he said, gesturing into the corridor. 'I've only just started with him.'

***

Belwynn stared down at Toric's Dagger.

She had seen it once before, when she and Soren had visited the Temple with her father. It had a fancy enough hilt, if you liked that kind of thing, but the blade itself didn't seem that special. There wasn't much of it—just a thin sliver of metal that ended in a thin point, for stabbing. Tiny runes had been inscribed onto the blade. It wasn't in a language she understood, and as she stared at them they began to swim and swirl around in front of her eyes. Belwynn drew her eyes away from the dagger and returned to the conversation at hand.

'...from the beginning, all of it, and make it quick,' her brother was ordering Dirk.

Dirk nodded his acceptance. 'I have been living here in Coldeberg for some years now. I am not a priest, I make my living by...well, mainly by thieving.' He spread his hands, as if to apologise. 'For a while now Emeric has been building up his power, hiring soldiers—he seems to have unlimited supplies of money from somewhere. A few weeks back the word was spread about to people like me that he wanted Toric's Dagger. There would be a reward of thirty thousand thalers, a small fortune. I wanted that money.' He shook his head, seemingly in disappointment at himself.

'I decided that the best way to gain access to the dagger was to become a priest of Toric. It took a while, but I was accepted, just about a week ago. I sneaked into the Temple during prayers and took it. It was pretty easy. I was planning my escape when Salvinus and his men broke in. Obviously, he was too late, and he never got the dagger. But everyone assumed that he had. The suspicion was totally off me. If I had left of my own accord, it might have awakened some suspicions. By volunteering to go with you, I could leave freely and get protection on the way back to Coldeberg, where I knew Salvinus would be heading.'

'You had it *all the time*?' Clarin blurted out. 'In the Wilderness, on the Great Road when that sorcerer attacked us—'

Words failed the big man and he grabbed Dirk by the throat.

'Leave him be,' snapped Soren.

Belwynn could tell that her brother was just as angry as she and Clarin were. That he had put them all in unnecessary danger was bad enough, but it was the fact that he had made fools of them all which rankled the most.

'So this afternoon,' Soren began. 'Why didn't you take the dagger straight to Emeric when you had the chance?'

Dirk had the gall to look affronted by the suggestion. 'I would never do that, not now. Now I understand why it is so important. Elana has explained it all to me.'

Something in that comment made Belwynn uneasy.

'Does Elana know that you've got the dagger?' she demanded.

'Yes,' replied Dirk meekly.

'Gods!' thundered Soren. 'Who else knows?'

'Just her and me…and now you three,' answered Dirk defensively.

Soren pushed his hand through his hair as he tried to take control of the situation in his mind. Belwynn felt the same way; her head was spinning. The attack on the inn, their friends captured. Dirk and the dagger. What should they do now? 'So what have you been doing today?' she asked the thief.

Dirk shifted his pack off his shoulder and opened it up. He shoved his hand inside and pulled out a white cloak. 'I bought this, so that I can look like a proper disciple of Madria,' he said, holding it up for Belwynn to see.

Soren groaned and rolled his eyes up in his head. 'You do realise that Elana has probably been captured by Emeric?' he demanded of Dirk.

The thief-turned-disciple looked shocked. 'What do you mean?'

Belwynn realised that they hadn't told Dirk about the situation. Soren, however, looked impatient to get moving.

'I'll fill you in as we go along. We need to establish what exactly has happened and, if necessary, think of some way to rescue the others. Meanwhile, I still think we've been betrayed, and you,' he said, pointing at Dirk, 'are still the most likely candidate, despite what you've said.'

He stared balefully at the Barissian, took a step towards him, and snatched the dagger from his hand.

'And I'm keeping hold of this.'

XIV

ARIELLA & TIVIAN

TIME HAD PASSED, JUST a few minutes maybe, but it seemed longer. Gyrmund had been sitting in silence with Herin and Elana, none of them knowing what to say after Rabigar had been dragged away.

Herin shifted his position. 'So, how did you get caught, Gyrmund?'

Gyrmund turned his thoughts away from Rabigar and the jailers. 'Moneva and I arrived back at the inn and they were waiting for us. They cornered me in the kitchen, but they couldn't find her, and hopefully they won't. Do you know it was Salvinus?'

Elana nodded. 'He came for Rabigar and I at the inn. He wanted to know where the rest of you had gone, but when we wouldn't tell him he sent us here.'

'What about you?' Gyrmund asked Herin. 'He said he had five of us. Is Kaved here?'

'Yes, they got us first. Kaved and I went into town, but then split up while I went to get a sword. I arranged to meet him later in the town square. When I got there, Salvinus himself was waiting for me, with half a dozen men. I had to give up my sword. I'd only just bought it,' Herin fumed, as if another lost sword was the worst that had happened. 'When I got here, Kaved was already in the cell. They took him for questioning. We haven't heard from him since.'

The sick feeling in Gyrmund's stomach returned. He felt like vomiting. Kaved, then Rabigar—who would be next?

Herin was chewing at his lips, studying him. 'Listen you two,' he began, 'Salvinus knew exactly where to find me. He knew to go to the inn; he knew to wait there for you and the others to come back. Someone's told him. If Gyrmund was with Moneva the whole time, I suppose that rules her out. It wasn't Soren or Belwynn or Clarin, I know that for a fact. But how else would he know where we were?'

Gyrmund thought about it. It did make sense. Salvinus seemed very well informed. 'Does that mean it was one of us? He may have had an informer at the Boot and Saddle.'

Herin shook his head. 'The thing is, only Kaved knew where to find me.'

Gyrmund had no reply to that. It was the first time he had seen Herin look unsure of himself. Maybe the Krykker had betrayed them. No doubt he would receive a substantial reward from the new king. Something was still troubling Gyrmund.

'What I don't understand is—why do they think that we have the damned dagger?'

***

Belwynn and Clarin turned the corner and hurried back to the alleyway. Time, they knew, was not on their side.

Clarin held the lute in his big hands, arms out in front of him. This was hardly a sight which made them look less conspicuous, but they had not been delayed in the city streets.

When they reached the alleyway, Soren and Dirk were waiting for them. Her brother's face looked grim. 'We've been waiting outside the inn, but no-one has turned up. I think we have to assume that all six have been captured. That means we have to go in after them.'

Clarin and Dirk nodded in agreement. Belwynn knew that this was a desperate move. At least the two men were committed to it. Clarin wanted to rescue his brother; Dirk was committed to saving Elana. Belwynn dipped into her pack and pulled out the robe she had chosen for Soren, throwing it over. He quickly shrugged it on over his clothes.

'Right, it's best that everyone leaves the talking to me where possible,' he began. 'We are likely to have to rely on Dirk to locate them. Our movements will be limited. Of course, it is more than likely that we will be recognised. We have to be ready to flee if necessary; it will do no good to the others if we are captured as well.' Soren paused before continuing. 'None of us knows why yet, but the dagger is important to them.' He pulled it out from one of the pockets in his cloak. 'We are going to be bringing it into the castle. I believe that it is better for Dirk to have it for now. He has a higher chance of escaping. If we fail and he escapes, he has agreed to return to Edgar and explain what happened.' Soren sighed. 'Any questions?'

'Yes,' said Belwynn. 'How can you trust him like this?'

'I have no other choices, Belwynn. If he was working for them, why would he still have it on him?'

It was a logical argument; she had come to the same conclusion herself. But that didn't mean she trusted the thief. Still, what else could they do?

'Alright, let's get on with it,' she conceded.

Belwynn stashed her sword in the shadows of the alleyway, just in case they had the chance to retrieve it.

Clarin, eager to get going, handed her the lute. He stroked the hilt of his sword and led them out of the alley.

Belwynn followed on, thinking over Soren's plan to get them inside Coldeberg Castle. The four of them were to pose as travelling entertainers: Belwynn a singer and musician, and Soren a conjurer. This was a variation on a routine they had done more than once, and the twins knew their parts. Belwynn had chosen herself a lovely dress and picked out a suitable robe for Soren which had stars embroidered onto it. Clarin was their bodyguard and Dirk a servant. Quality entertainers were usually allowed into the courts of rich noblemen. Since Emeric was now a king, Soren reckoned he would be even more likely to want to celebrate and provide entertainment for the lords and ladies of his new kingdom. Once they got inside, Dirk could peel off and explore the castle.

Clarin led them on the uphill journey towards the castle. As they crossed a street Belwynn could now see the building looming ahead.

On the other side a trio of soldiers walked by in the opposite direction. Belwynn's nerves began to jangle. Coldeberg was crawling with soldiers, and some of them would be out looking for her and her friends. Fortunately, the soldiers were laughing and joking between themselves and did not seem interested in them. It made her wonder, however, about her twin's rescue plan. There was a fair chance that they would be allowed entry. But once inside it would not be long before they were recognised by someone. They were asking to perform before Emeric himself, for Toric's sake! She knew that they would have to rely, again, on Soren's powers.

How are you, Soren' she asked, concerned about the idea. *How well recovered are you?*

I'll have to be honest with you, Belwynn, he replied, looking ahead rather than at her. *Since I woke up after the Wilderness, I've had nothing. I've lost my powers. I burned them out, or something, by overextending myself that day. I went to seek help this afternoon but found none. I'm sorry.*

Belwynn didn't know what to say. Her mind was already in bits, and now this? Everything she and her brother had worked for, vanished? And now when

147

they needed his magic the most, they were about to march into Coldeberg Castle without it? She tried to collect her thoughts and make a reply, but as she did they turned the corner and came upon the gatehouse.

This stone building controlled access into the rest of the castle. If it was under siege, the drawbridge would be up and the portcullis down. Now, however, two guards stood on the drawbridge to deny entry. As they approached the two young soldiers, Soren moved to the front. They held out their spears in warning.

'What business do you have here?' one of them called out.

Soren approached with an air of friendly confidence. 'Hello there! Well met, good soldiers of Barissia. I am Tivian the Magnificent, a conjurer of the very highest quality. And this,' he said, gesturing extravagantly towards Belwynn, 'this is the Lady Ariella, a minstrel with the sweetest voice in all of Dalriya. We have come here...'

'Sir!' interrupted one of the guardsmen, calling into the gatehouse.

After a few moments a portly, older man emerged from his quarters in the gatehouse. He looked the four of them up and down.

'Well met!' began Soren, and repeated his introductions, word for word, with the same enthusiasm. 'We have come here to help celebrate King Emeric's consecration as King of Barissia.'

The old soldier didn't seem as impressed as he should have been. He stroked at his moustache. 'Who are these two?' he demanded gruffly, gesturing at Clarin and Dirk.

'The big man is our bodyguard. It will not surprise a man of your experience to know that some of the roads we travel could be very dangerous if travelled alone. We have long found it necessary to secure the services of a hired man. In truth, it is a very great drain on our resources, but we have been left with little choice,' Soren explained, with a self-pitying simper.

'What about the other one?' pressed the soldier.

'Oh, he is nothing, nothing but our simple-minded servant.'

The old soldier stroked at his moustache again. 'Well, they have more than enough servants in the castle, and there is no need for a bodyguard here either.'

Soren put on a troubled expression. 'Oh no, we must have our men with us, we must!' He skipped forward towards the soldier and grabbed his hands. Belwynn could just make out a glint of metal as he pressed something into the hands of the soldier. 'Please allow them as well, sir!'

The old soldier pulled his hands away from Soren, but seemed to have a contented expression on his face. 'Well, alright then, but he'll have to hand in his weapon,' he said gesturing towards Clarin.

Clarin unbuckled his sword and handed it to the soldier.

'Dom!' shouted the captain into the gatehouse. Another soldier came hurrying out. He was young looking, with big, bushy eyebrows. 'Take these four to see Master Orlin. If he doesn't want them, escort them back out of the castle again.'

'Yes, sir!' exclaimed Dom. He waved them all to follow him and began marching across the drawbridge.

Belwynn and the others followed behind. The two soldiers on the drawbridge moved aside to let them pass.

They were in.

Dom led them into the outer bailey of the castle. They were now within the walls of Coldeberg Castle. As well as the gatehouse, the castle had six towers, between which ran the high walls. Since the castle was situated in the far northern corner of the city, half of the castle walls doubled up as the city walls as well. The bailey was open to the elements, with a few wooden buildings. Belwynn noticed a stable to their left and a training yard in the distance. The other half of the site was taken up by a large stone building, two storeys high. This would be where the residents lived and where Emeric had his hall.

Dom led them towards the entrance to the living quarters. A huge wooden door was open, guarded by a further two soldiers, wearing the livery of the Duke, now King, of Barissia.

'Are you really a conjurer?' asked the young soldier as they continued to make their way.

Soren raised an eyebrow, but stopped and grabbed a coin from inside his robe. He placed it on his thumb and then flicked it high into the air. As it came spinning down he clapped his hands. The coin had vanished. He took a step towards Dom and placed his hand behind the soldier's ear. When he withdrew his hand, he was holding the coin.

'That's amazing!' said the soldier, his thick eyebrows raised in wonder.

Soren took a small bow. 'Onwards?' he suggested.

Dom nodded and took them to the door. 'I'm taking them to see Master Orlin,' he told the two guards. They stepped aside.

149

Dom ushered the group through the door and into the stone structure. They entered a sizeable hallway. Candles set in finely-worked sconces and intricate tapestries lined the stone walls. On the wall to their left, a fire blazed. A number of people were warming themselves there. On the right hand and opposite walls were doors, leading to other parts of the castle.

'Orlin's chambers are upstairs,' Dom informed them, and led them to the corner of the hall where a set of stone steps led upwards. Next to them, steps led down, beneath the castle. These steps were guarded by another couple of soldiers. Belwynn exchanged glances with the others. The significance of that was lost on none of them.

They continued up the steps, which were thin and steep and circled upwards at a tight angle.

'Is Orlin the king's steward?' Belwynn asked the soldier as they reached the top of the stairs.

'He's the royal chamberlain. He runs the castle for the King. He oversees the entertainment for the court. He'll probably want to use you for the evening meal, when King Emeric feasts his lords.'

Once they reached the second-floor hallway, Dom led them through a door on the right and onto a corridor. They began to pass doors to rooms on the left and right, but the soldier led them on until they reached the last door at the end of the corridor. He banged on the heavy wooden door and it was promptly opened. A smallish, balding man with a hooked nose poked his head into the corridor.

'What do you want?' he demanded.

Dom did not seem taken aback by the rather unwelcoming response. 'I have escorted these travelling entertainers here who would like to perform for the King.'

'Hello there! Do I have the pleasure of addressing Master Orlin—' began Soren, but he was interrupted.

'No, you don't,' said the man at the door. 'I work for him, he's busy right now. But it's my job to sort out the riff-raff. What do you do?' he demanded.

'He does really great magic tricks!' Dom answered for Soren in an excited manner.

Orlin's man did not look impressed. 'Show me.'

Soren produced two coins. He showed the man that both hands were empty apart from the coins. With both coins in his left hand, he put the hand into a fist. He then used his right hand to take one of the coins from the fist and gave it to the man. Soren then opened his left hand again. The two coins were still there on his palm.

Dom gave a little clap. Orlin's man grunted, pocketing the coin. 'What about the others?' he asked, waving a hand at Belwynn, Clarin and Dirk.

'Well,' began Soren 'these two are mere servants, but this is my sister, Ariella. She has the sweetest singing voice in all of Dalriya!'

'Let's hear it, then.'

Belwynn cleared her throat. She decided to sing a well-known song from the Empire, which she thought would suit the audience. *The Fight for Freedom* was a song celebrating the end of Persaleian rule over the Brasingians.

Even after the first few words, Belwynn's singing began to have its usual effect. A gift, many people had told her. A singing voice she had been given, capable of melting the hearts of the coldest men of the land. The first line was enough to bring tears to Dom's eyes. After the first verse the other man had succumbed. His face had a look of wonderment on it, as if he was experiencing emotions he didn't think he had. Belwynn stopped after the first verse and chorus, but that was enough.

'Yes, well, I'm sure you'll do just fine,' mumbled Orlin's man, and fully opened the door to let them enter.

As they entered the room Dom called out a goodbye and, brushing a tear from his eye, made his way back down the corridor.

Belwynn and the others had entered an antechamber. It was a well-furnished room which led on to two further rooms, but their host gestured that they should sit and wait here. Belwynn sank down into a comfortable seat and the others did likewise.

'My name is Tivian the Magnificent,' said Soren. 'May I have the pleasure of your name?'

'Urval.'

There followed an uncomfortable silence, during which it seemed that even Tivian the Magnificent was lost for words. However, Urval eventually decided to break it.

'I will tell Master Orlin that you're here, but don't expect him to be hurried, he's a busy man.' Urval glanced over at Belwynn with a pained expression, as if he didn't want to be reminded of any emotions he might have felt from her song. 'I'll get you some drinks first,' he said.

'That is very gracious, sir,' responded Soren. 'However, there is no need to get this one a drink,' he said pointing at Dirk. 'While we like to have our bodyguard with us at all times—for my sister's protection, you understand—this one is little use to tell the truth. If you have a servant's quarters he would be best off there.'

'Yes, it's downstairs. He just has to say that I sent him. He'll be looked after alright down there.'

'Off you go, Skerit.'

Dirk got up and left the room.

***

Rabigar was lying face down on a table, his hands and ankles bound. He was vaguely aware of his torturers working on his back with a cutting instrument, as if they were trying to remove the scales from his flesh. They were talking, to each other or to him, he wasn't sure. The pain in his head was dominating all of his senses. It left him feeling nauseous.

The attack in the cell had left him blind and, he thought, dying. He couldn't scream or shout out. Herman and Greg could have done anything to him now; it would not register above the pain caused by his eye wound. Every now and again he would get a woozy sensation, as if he was about to faint. He fought against it, fearing that he would never regain consciousness if he lost it now.

He only dimly heard the knock on the door. His torturers exchanged words. The cutting of his back stopped. It went silent. He heard the door being opened. There was muffled shouting from behind him and then a sharp, piercing scream to his right. It went silent again. Rabigar concentrated on his hearing, trying to block out the pain so that he could try to understand what was going on.

Then someone spoke to him, a soft voice. 'Rabigar? Can you hear me?'

He hadn't been expecting a woman's voice.

He worked up some spit so that he could reply.

'Moneva?'

XV

A SONG FOR A KING

BELWYNN, SOREN AND CLARIN were sitting in Orlin's chambers, waiting.

Belwynn plucked nervously at the strings of the lute. She re-tuned the instrument until it sounded perfect, then adjusted it some more. Every few seconds one of them would look anxiously at the door. They hoped for the return of Dirk, that he had not betrayed them and that he had located their friends. They feared the return of Urval, that their subterfuge would have to continue and put them in greater danger.

Eventually they heard footsteps and the sound of voices approaching the door. Clarin stood up. The door swung open. It was Urval. He entered the room with another man.

'This is Master Orlin, chamberlain to King Emeric,' he announced gruffly.

Two more men hovered in the doorway. They had swords strapped to their waists. Clarin looked at Soren. Belwynn knew that, with a nod, Clarin would set on all four. But with no weapon himself, that would be a desperate move. Soren hesitated briefly but decided against it and stood up himself.

'Ah, Lord Orlin, a great pleasure to finally meet you,' he began, bowing his head towards the floor. 'I am Tivian the Magnificent. My sister, the Lady Ariella, and I have travelled a long way to entertain this great court.'

Orlin snorted. He was an older man, draped in expensive clothes. He had a long face, accentuated by a thin grey beard which ended in a slick point. His eyes were piercing blue and he studied each of them with the attitude of someone who was continually disappointed with the stupidity of those he encountered.

'I sincerely doubt that your sister is a lady, in which case you should not use the title.'

Tivian the Magnificent laughed nervously.

'It is not my habit to meet and greet every entertainer that passes through this castle. But when informing me of your arrival, my servant advised me that your sister was a very good singer. In the twenty or so years that he has worked for me, Urval has never been so fulsome in his praise. As a consequence, both myself and the King are interested to hear this voice.'

Orlin turned his gaze to Belwynn again.

'If the voice is as pretty as the vessel, it must be special indeed.'

Belwynn blushed and muttered a demure thank you.

'You will perform at this evening's banquet, in about two hours. But first, King Emeric has requested a private audience. This is a great honour I have arranged for you. Do not disappoint.'

No. Belwynn's heart dropped into her stomach. The plan had gone wrong already. They were going to be taken to see the very man who was hunting them down.

'Of course not,' enthused Soren, 'my heart is beating wildly with excitement.'

Orlin frowned at him. 'Most importantly, do not make the mistake of addressing him as a duke. It must be king. That would be more than your life is worth.'

Orlin turned around and left the room. The four men headed back down the corridor. Belwynn, Soren and Clarin followed behind.

At the end of the corridor they came to the stairs. Belwynn looked around, wishing that Dirk or even Herin would rush up to intervene. But no-one did. They continued towards their destination, Belwynn's sense of dread growing with each unavoidable footstep.

Instead of going down the stairs they went through a second door. This opened into an antechamber. Two armed soldiers watched them walk straight past. Urval opened a large wooden door and ushered everybody through.

Emeric's chamber was not large; his main hall would be downstairs somewhere. Belwynn had been expecting more people, but only two were waiting for them.

Sitting on a large chair at the end of the room, facing them, had to be Emeric. Belwynn had to admit that he carried himself like a king. He was not tall, but well-built, had mid-length jet black hair, which he pushed back, and a pale complexion. He was wearing leather and looked like he had just come back from, or was about to go, hunting.

Standing next to him was an unusual looking man. That was, he looked unusual at first sight, but on second sight Belwynn found it difficult to decide why. Certainly, he did not dress like a Brasingian nobleman. He wore a long fur cloak with inscriptions sewn into it around the edges. He did not carry a weapon.

154

He was clean shaven with very closely-cropped dark hair. It was his eyes, maybe. They were a dark, strange colour, close to violet, she thought. When Belwynn looked at his eyes they gave nothing away, no expression, no emotion.

Watch out for Emeric's friend, advised Soren. *I think he's an Isharite. He could be a wizard.*

'Your Majesty, the songstress Ariella, at your request,' introduced Orlin.

Belwynn curtseyed, and Soren gave a deep bow.

Emeric looked Belwynn over. 'Very nice. Who are these?' he asked, waving a hand at Soren and Clarin.

'Greetings...' began Soren, but he was cut off by Orlin.

'This is the brother, the conjurer. This is their guard.'

'Did I ask to see them?' The question was put innocently enough, but Belwynn could sense the steel underneath.

'No sire, you did not. My apologies. I will ask them to leave,' replied Orlin.

'No. They're here now. They may stay,' announced the king magnanimously.

At a prompt from Orlin, Urval moved over to the side of the chamber and grabbed a stool, which he carried towards Emeric. He deposited it about twelve feet away from the king. Orlin and Urval then moved over to stand by the wall on one side of the room. The king gestured for Belwynn to sit on the stool. Belwynn, carrying her lute with her, did so. She sat down, facing only Emeric and his friend. Meanwhile Soren, Clarin and the two soldiers were left to find standing positions along the second wall.

Choose a long one, advised Soren. *Try to keep it going until the others get here.*

If they get here, thought Belwynn. It did not seem as though Dirk had betrayed them and warned the Barissians of their presence, but that did not mean that he would or could locate and free the others. Unfortunately, that prospect appeared to be all they had. Emeric inclined his head towards her, indicating that she should begin.

With his dubious position as a newly crowned king in mind, Belwynn decided that it was best to steer clear of any songs connected to the Empire. She settled on the neutral song of *Celandine the Slave Queen*.

Celandine was a girl from the coast of Kalinth during the time of the Vismarian Onslaught. The local knight, Hector, had failed to defend his people and instead paid tribute to the Vismarians to stop their attacks. He took Celandine from her home and sold her into slavery to the rovers of Vismar. She became the slave of Bringar, a fierce warrior, who took her back to his home.

Over time, however, Bringar fell in love with Celandine, and made her his wife. To honour her, he returned to the shores of Kalinth with his war band. There he won a great victory over the Knights of Kalinth. Hector and many of his allies lay dead, and Bringar established a Vismarian kingdom there. Celandine returned to her homeland to be crowned queen.

Belwynn sang, playing the lute to support her voice. She used her voice to throw out patterns, to entice and entrance the listener and dominate their senses. She pulled them into the song so that all they were aware of was the music, the story, and her.

It did not take long for Emeric to lose himself in her voice. She could tell the signs by now. The eyes were the best guide. Emeric's became transfixed, focusing on some object in the distance, looking at her but through her at the same time. Frowns of concentration on his forehead eased away and his facial muscles relaxed. A light smile appeared on his lips.

Others soon followed: the two soldiers, Urval, even stern Lord Orlin.

But one man did not lose himself in Belwynn's song. The man from Ishari was indeed looking at her, but in a very different way from the others. His strange, violet eyes were staring into hers, as if he could see through into her mind and her soul. He made no facial gesture other than the stare, and once Belwynn noticed that, it became difficult to concentrate on anything else.

As Belwynn sang and strummed the closing notes of the song, the Isharite began clapping, making stilted, discordant noises.

'Very good,' he pronounced as he clapped, though his sneer said otherwise. This had the effect of waking the others from their reverie. Emeric flashed his companion a look of anger for making the sound, but it passed quickly. He shook his head, as if waking up from sleep. The other listeners did the same.

'Ariella, come here,' beckoned the King.

Belwynn placed the lute on the floor and stood up from her chair. She walked over to him. Emeric remained seated. The Isharite still stood beside him, watching her, his sneer not far from his lips.

'That was wonderful, Ariella,' Emeric declared in a quiet voice. He offered Belwynn the palm of his hand. She placed her own in it. Emeric raised her hand and gave it a kiss, lingering just a touch longer than politeness allowed. He gave her it back reluctantly. Emeric's eyes glanced over towards Soren. 'This conjurer,' he began, keeping his voice to little over a whisper, 'he is your brother, yes?'

'That is right, Your Majesty,' replied Belwynn.

156

'Ah…' Emeric looked pleased. 'You must stay at court for a while. Both of you, of course.' Emeric's eyes moved from hers to appraise her body, looking at her breasts, her hips, and her legs. There was no doubt why he wanted Belwynn to stay around.

Belwynn forced herself to continue with the routine. She had to hope that this would soon end. 'You are most generous, Your Majesty.'

From the corner of her eye Belwynn saw the Isharite smirking.

Emeric followed her gaze. 'Don't mind Tirano. He can be tiresome, but he has his uses.'

Emeric indicated that Belwynn should step to the side as he turned his attention to the small gathering in the chamber. 'I am well pleased with this performance. Ariella will be invited to sing more of her songs at supper tonight. Her brother will also perform,' he added. 'This song of Celandine has much to teach us. This Bringar of Vismar was not born a king, but he made himself one. Those men who cannot defend their people, men such as this Hector, will have their titles stripped away. Soon there will be many changes in Dalriya. We in Barissia are the ones who will rise to glory.'

Everybody in the chamber politely applauded Emeric's speech, including the Isharite, Tirano. Belwynn noted that he even nodded in agreement with the king's words.

Then the door opened. One of the soldiers from the antechamber outside had pushed it open, and he now leaned into the chamber.

'Kaved the Krykker,' he announced.

Before Belwynn could take in what was happening Kaved sauntered into the room. He took a few steps and then stopped dead. For a moment he stared at Belwynn, then at Soren and Clarin standing by the wall.

'What the fuck is happening here?' he demanded.

Then everything happened very fast.

Belwynn's head started swimming. Kaved was the traitor, and he was about to blow their cover.

'How dare you burst in here and speak to the King like that?' Orlin was demanding of the Krykker.

At the same time Kaved was speaking. 'That's them, you idiots! They're the ones with the dagger!'

Now it was time for Emeric and the others to look around in bewilderment.

Belwynn grabbed the opportunity. She leant down and grabbed the knife she had been concealing in her boot. Before he had time to react, she grabbed Emeric off his chair and put the knife to his throat. Tirano grabbed at the arm of the king as if to pull him away.

'Let go or he's dead!' screamed Belwynn, more hysterically than she had intended.

Tirano let go and backed off. The two soldiers along the wall had drawn their own swords and now faced her. Meanwhile, Kaved and the two guards from the chamber were closing in as well.

Belwynn pressed the knife edge into the king's neck, drawing blood. 'Tell them to stop or I'll do it!'

'Stop! She's got a knife,' shouted Emeric hoarsely.

'Do as the king says. No closer,' Tirano commanded Kaved and the soldiers.

The soldiers, even Kaved, did as they were asked, but still held their swords. Belwynn had bought them some time but they were outnumbered and the longer the face-off went on, the more likely the rest of the castle would hear. Her knife hand had begun to shake, causing Emeric to utter a fearful *careful* as it scratched against his throat.

What are we going to do? she asked Soren.

'Give it up, Belwynn,' shouted Kaved. 'They won't hurt you. They just want the dagger.'

'Shut up, traitor,' Clarin shouted back at him. 'Where's my brother?'

'Here I am,' came a shout from the door.

Belwynn peered over to the doorway. Standing in the entrance, sword in each hand, stood Herin. *Don't say he's betrayed us as well,* she thought.

He raised one sword so that it was pointing at Kaved's head. 'And now you pay for your treachery.'

Herin rushed into the room, throwing one sword to Clarin while lunging at the Krykker with the other. Kaved met his sword stroke and the clash of steel rang out in the room. Then, behind Herin, Belwynn saw Moneva enter the room.

'This way,' Moneva shouted over to them.

Belwynn tried to pull Emeric in the direction of the doors at the far end of the chamber. Her knife hand, however, was now shaking violently; she could no longer control it. She looked over at Tirano and saw him staring intently at her. He was using magic. Her hand began to jerk away from Emeric's neck, so that the knife was no longer pressed against him. The king took his chance. With one hand he grabbed Belwynn's wrist, pushing it away, and then smashed backwards with his other elbow. Emeric caught Belwynn in the face and she fell backwards, dropping the knife.

Belwynn landed sharply on her backside. Her nose throbbed and she felt dazed. She could hear shouting all around her and the clash of swords. Then arms grabbed at her, half dragging, half lifting her to her feet.

It was Soren. He was pulling her over to the doors. Herin was slashing wildly at Kaved and had pushed him backwards into the room, but the Krykker was resisting. Closer to the doors, Moneva was clashing swords with one of the guards; another lay on the floor, clutching his chest.

'This way,' came a shout, and there was Dirk, beckoning them out of the room. Belwynn and Soren passed through the doors and turned around to look for Clarin. The big warrior was walking backwards in their direction, fighting against Orlin's soldiers. Belwynn could see a body lying on the floor and thought at first that it was Emeric, but she could see him by his throne, along with Tirano and Orlin. She realised that the body must be that of Urval.

Then Emeric, Tirano and Orlin began moving towards Clarin, and Belwynn could see swords in their hands. 'Clarin, watch out!' she called. Dirk responded by running over to stand by Clarin, but they were too heavily outnumbered.

'Herin!' shouted Soren. 'We've got to go!'

Herin had pressed Kaved back and back but had not found an opening in his defence. He took a step back and looked around at the room. After a brief respite he pressed on at Kaved once more, but after three strokes he suddenly pulled backwards. In a fluid movement he spun around and moved on the soldier who was fighting Moneva, swinging at him from behind. The soldier never saw the blow coming as Herin's sword sliced into his neck. Moneva stepped over the body and, together with Herin, moved in to help out Clarin and Dirk.

Belwynn looked behind her, through the next set of doors towards the stairs. There was no-one there, but it was only a matter of time. 'Hurry up!' she shouted back into the room. They were moving towards the door but still facing outwards to defend against the Barissians.

'I'll come back for you,' Herin snarled at Kaved.

'You'll finish it now, unless you're craven,' Kaved barked back.

Moneva turned around and skipped through the door, past Belwynn and Soren. 'Follow me,' she called without stopping. Belwynn and Soren ran after her, and soon made it to the stairs. Moneva was already halfway down. Belwynn began descending down the thin and winding steps, Soren close behind, and Dirk behind him. At the bottom Belwynn arrived in the castle hallway where the fine tapestries hung, with the fire still blazing. Thankfully, nobody was standing around it any more. She wondered why and turned around to ask Moneva.

'We've dumped the bodies down the stairs,' she answered, before Belwynn got her words out.

'This way,' said Dirk.

Rather than attempt to leave via the bailey and through the gatehouse, Dirk took them through another door, roughly beneath the door to Emeric's chambers on the floor above. They ran behind him, down a long corridor with rooms on either side. The corridor ended in an opening into a room from where Belwynn could hear clanging noises and the occasional shout. Dirk ran straight in and she followed.

The room turned out to be the castle kitchens. There were a dozen people working there: kneading bread, filleting meat, boiling stew, washing and carrying pots, pans and utensils. When Dirk entered there were shouts and challenges. After he had waved a sword at them and Belwynn and the others entered the room, they piped down.

Dirk took a second to get his bearings and then moved to the far end of the room. He dropped his sword and began moving a huge set of shelves containing pots and pans, crockery, tubs of sauces and bags of flour and salt. A couple of plates fell off and smashed onto the floor. Soren rushed over to give him a hand and they shifted it out of the way. They had revealed an iron gate, which Belwynn hadn't even noticed behind the shelves. Soren pushed and pulled at the gate, but it was secured with a lock. They didn't have a key.

Dirk fumbled in his pockets and pulled out a slim piece of metal which ended in a short curvature. He inserted it into the lock and then wriggled it about inside. Meanwhile, Clarin and Herin had entered the kitchens, looking behind them for any potential pursuers. After a few moments Dirk gave it a full twist and pushed open the gate, which moved with a rusty screech. He rushed through and Soren followed behind him.

Belwynn went through after her twin into a small, round stone room. She briefly glanced up, and realised that she was in one of the castle towers. Two feet above them was a grate, forming a murder hole through which burning oil could be poured down onto attackers. It was more than likely that there were some guards in that room now. Dirk moved directly to a postern gate in the opposite

160

wall and jiggled his skeleton key in the lock before it clicked. They burst through the door and found themselves outside the city walls, on a long grassy slope leading downwards. Beyond they could see meadows and fields.

'Keep moving,' said Herin, 'get away from the walls!'

They ran down the slope, Belwynn's legs going so fast that she thought she would fall over. She turned back to see some guards lining the walls looking at them, but there didn't seem much they could do from up there. Then, a file of soldiers emptied out of the gate they had used and called out a challenge before pursuing them down the hill.

'Where are we going?' shouted Soren, his breath ragged already.

'Just keep going,' Moneva shouted back. 'With some luck Gyrmund will meet up with us. If not, this could be the briefest escape in history.'

They kept running away from the city. Belwynn's lungs were beginning to burn. She could see that, up ahead, there was farmland, and to the right a track led off in the direction of Kelland.

Then she heard the horses coming. How could they have got a mounted force here so quickly? She had to turn around and look.

A group of half a dozen horsemen were coming towards them from the west side of the city. She could see the lead soldier wore the livery of the dukes of Barissia.

Moneva turned around, too, and stopped running.

Belwynn took a second look. Rather than six horsemen, there were in fact only three of them, each one riding a mount and bringing a spare with them.

The man in the lead, wearing the soldier's uniform, was Gyrmund.

He drew up, gritting his teeth as if he was in pain, as Belwynn and Moneva ran towards him. Moneva climbed up onto the spare horse and held out a hand for Belwynn to climb on with her, since there weren't enough horses for one each.

Behind Gyrmund came Elana, not finding the task of riding and holding the reins of another horse quite so easy. Rabigar was even further back, there was something over his eye...no. On closer inspection, she saw that he had no eye any more, just a bloody socket where it had once been.

'What happened to Rabigar?' Belwynn blurted out.

Gyrmund screwed up his face, as if he was about to cry. 'They took his eye,' he said, almost choking on the words.

Belwynn physically flinched at the news. Clarin swore out loud. 'How is he?' Soren asked Elana.

'His eye is gone. I have done what I can for him.'

'Can't you fix it?' asked Belwynn.

'I can't grow back an eye,' responded Elana. 'He needs rest for his body to cope with the shock.'

'We can't give him rest,' said Soren. 'Not now.'

As Rabigar pulled up, Herin quickly clambered on in front of him and took the reins. Rabigar put his arms around Herin's waist and slumped forwards. Clarin and Soren took the remaining spares. The soldiers were only a couple of hundred yards behind them but it looked like they had already given up on the chase.

'Come on,' said Herin, 'we have to assume that they'll be sending a force after us. We can talk later.'

Moneva kicked their horse on and Belwynn was forced to hold on to her waist. Belwynn realised that they were on her own horse, the one that they had bought back in Vitugia. Gyrmund and the others had somehow gone back to the Boot and Saddle to collect them. There was a lot of explaining to be done at some point, but for now Belwynn was content to look back as Emeric's soldiers and castle receded into the distance.

They were still in danger, she knew, but nonetheless she felt a sense of relief at leaving the place behind. Belwynn thought that she would be quite happy if she never saw Coldeberg again.

XVI

THE IMPS

GYRMUND TOOK THEM ACROSS the open land north of Coldeberg onto a track that headed in a north-easterly direction and would take them to the Kellish border. It was certainly the shortest route out of Barissia. The track was narrow and uneven, not nearly as fast as travelling on the Barissian Road; but if they tried to cut east they would almost certainly run into Emeric's soldiers. Meanwhile, they had to assume that a force would be coming after them, and at a faster pace, given that many of them were sharing horses. Rabigar had his arms around Herin, his one eye closed and his face deathly pale, with a pained expression. He obviously needed to rest, but they simply couldn't afford to.

They passed through Barissian farming land, gently rolling terrain with fields of grass, crops and grazing animals, not unlike the Magnian lands Belwynn had grown up in. They were rich lands, but she knew all too well how much work the farming folk who lived here had to put in to keep them that way. She wondered what they thought about their duke spending all their taxes on mercenaries and threatening war with their neighbours. She knew from her own bitter experience what civil wars did to places like this.

'Look there!' shouted Clarin, pointing behind them. Belwynn could see that the land they had travelled across gradually declined and, on the horizon, from the direction of Coldeberg, was a large group of riders, perhaps two score in all.

'Can we get to the border in time?' Belwynn asked.

Gyrmund pulled a face. 'I don't think so.'

'Herin and I could hold them up for a bit,' suggested Clarin. But even he sounded doubtful.

'We'll carry on for now,' said Soren. 'Let's not do anything reckless until we know we have to.'

They moved on again, but that sick feeling had returned to Belwynn's stomach. The others were probably hoping that Soren could help get them out of the situation again. She knew he couldn't.

They rode on. Afternoon was turning into evening, but it was a fine summer's day and Belwynn knew that they wouldn't be saved by the drawing in of the night. It didn't seem like they would reach Kelland before the end of the day either. As each minute passed, things got a bit more desperate. When she looked back she saw that a smaller group of riders, about half a dozen, had detached itself from the main group and were gaining on them much faster. As soon as this front group caught up with them they would be forced to stop, and then the main group would be on them too.

Ahead, Gyrmund began to slow down.

'What is it?' shouted Herin.

'Soldiers.'

'Barissians?' Belwynn asked. 'How could they have got ahead of us?'

'Not sure who they are,' said Gyrmund.

They trotted forwards, unsure whether they were about to be trapped between two forces and if they should make a break for it across country.

Belwynn peered over Moneva's shoulder to take a look. There was a sizeable force of riders spread across the track and to either side of it, at least as many as the chasing Barissians, who were now catching up fast. This second force wasn't moving, however. They seemed content to watch.

Belwynn turned around. The leading group of six riders were very close now; she could make out their individual faces.

'We've got to do something!' she said.

'Let's risk it, then!' replied Moneva.

Moneva spurred her horse on towards the waiting group of soldiers.

'Moneva, wait!' shouted Gyrmund, but she ignored him.

Sitting at the front, a few feet ahead of his troops, seemed to be the leader of the small force. He was approaching middle age, had close-cropped black hair and stubble. Neither he nor his soldiers wore any identifiable markings—just simple-looking leather armour—but their weapons and their horses looked expensive enough.

'Who are you?' demanded Moneva.

It was a little too bold an opening for Belwynn's taste, and the man seemed to think so, too, as he reacted with a frown and a half smile.

'I am Walter, Marshal of the Empire,' he replied. 'And I was wondering who you might be, too.'

'Thank the gods!' declared Moneva and rode the short distance over towards him.

Some of Walter's troops moved forward, as if they saw Moneva as a threat, but he held up an arm and they stayed in position. Gyrmund and the others, hearing his reply, joined them. Meanwhile, the first six riders of the Barissians had pulled up, looking warily at Walter's war band themselves.

Walter? Isn't that Baldwin's brother? Belwynn asked Soren.

Yes, he replied. *We may have just been saved.*

'We've just escaped from Coldeberg,' said Moneva, apparently neither shy nor hesitant about explaining the situation to him. 'Those are Barissian soldiers after us. Did you know that Emeric has made himself king?'

'Yes, I had heard,' replied Walter, still finding something amusing about the encounter. 'That's kind of why I'm in the area.'

The rest of the Barissians had now caught up with the lead group, and they sat as their mounts drew breath, staring balefully at Belwynn and the rest of them. One of them trotted forwards from the group, stopping when he reached the halfway point between the two forces. He had a mean-looking scar from ear to chin and sat there, an air of confidence about him.

'Salvinus!' hissed Gyrmund.

This was the man they had been chasing? Belwynn felt almost pleased to finally put a face to the name.

'Have you come for a fight, Salvinus?' Herin shouted towards him. 'I'm ready for you, if so.'

Soren had to reach over a restraining hand to stop Herin moving forwards. Belwynn wondered if Herin would have been quite so full of machismo if he wasn't sitting with about fifty imperial soldiers. He probably would, she decided.

Salvinus ignored Herin's invitation.

'Walter,' he said, nodding at the marshal.

'Gervase,' came the reply.

Suddenly Belwynn was filled with doubt. They were on first name terms. Might they be allies?

'This group you've apprehended are escaped prisoners from Coldeberg. They tried to assassinate Emeric today. I am taking them back there.'

'Indeed, so they tell me. Why don't you tell me something, Gervase? Did they try to kill Duke Emeric or King Emeric?'

'King Emeric.'

165

'Indeed. That puts a rather different perspective on the situation.'

'I don't see what it has to do with it.'

'You don't see?' Walter's tone moved from genial to outraged in three words. 'You don't see how that makes him a traitor?'

For the first time Salvinus looked a bit disconcerted. He tried to shrug the issue away. 'A title is a title, to me. I know that Emeric meant no offence to Baldwin over it. He still recognises his authority as his liege lord and emperor.'

'A subject receives his title from the emperor. He doesn't presume to take one himself. We both know what Emeric has done, so don't play the innocent, Gervase.'

'Look,' said Gervase, still all reasonable. 'That business needs to be settled between Emeric and Baldwin. Fair enough. Our business here is about these prisoners. You're on Barissian soil; that can be overlooked. But you don't want to get personally involved in this, Walter. You don't want to make a personal enemy of Emeric. Believe me.'

'He doesn't want us,' said Soren. 'He wants something we have. I think Emperor Baldwin would be very interested in it.'

Walter raised an eyebrow at that. 'Thing is, Gervase, I'm on Imperial soil, and I'm Marshal of the Empire. Unless you want to make a fight of it, which I don't recommend, you'll have to run back to Emeric without your prisoners. And you can take him some personal advice from me. He better come crawling to Essenberg with an apology soon if he wants to keep his duchy.'

'This is very stupid, Walter,' said Gervase, at last flashing some anger of his own. 'We'll get what we want in the end. You don't know who you're dealing with.'

'Oh, you might be surprised about what I know,' responded the Marshal.

Gervase turned his horse around and left without another word.

He passed his men and carried on back down the track towards Coldeberg. Turning their mounts around, the rest of the Barissians followed him. Belwynn and the others watched them go until they were left alone with Walter and his soldiers.

'Thank you so much,' said Belwynn to him, meaning every word.

'Well, you're welcome. This has been an unexpected end to the day. But I should warn you, based on what I've just heard, the Emperor and his ministers will want to hear about this. If you were planning on going to Essenberg anyway, well that's just fine, and we can all stay friends. But if you had other plans, I have to tell you, they've been changed. You're coming with me to see my brother. Whether you like it or not.'

'It was Kaved,' said Moneva. 'He betrayed us to Salvinus.'

The inquisition had begun, then. And maybe the recriminations.

Yesterday Walter had taken them another two miles along the track to his camp, and most of them had collapsed into the beds he had provided for them without saying a word to each other. Belwynn certainly had. But now that they had slept and Walter had seen to it that they were provided with some army rations for breakfast, she got the feeling that the talking would start. Personally, Belwynn didn't have much appetite for either.

Everyone had taken up a seat around a dead fire as Walter's men broke up camp and prepared to set off for Essenberg. Herin was grim faced. Rabigar had been treated again by Elana, and she had cleaned the eye up a lot, so that it didn't look half as bad as yesterday. It still looked terrible, though. She wondered why they hadn't covered it with anything. But why should he? To make Belwynn feel better?

'How do you know?' asked Gyrmund.

'He came in as Belwynn was entertaining Emeric,' said Clarin, who recounted the brief adventures of Tivian and Ariella.

Gyrmund's eyes opened wide.

'Yes,' said Clarin with a chuckle, 'you missed out on some fun there, Gyrmund.'

'So Kaved's still alive, then?' Gyrmund asked.

'Yes,' said Herin, his voice steely, 'but I'll make sure he pays for what he's done.'

'Why did you bring him?' asked Rabigar. His voice sounded like he looked: injured, and hurt. 'I knew he couldn't be trusted...'

Belwynn felt desperately sorry for the Krykker, but she felt sorry for Herin, too. He could hardly look at Rabigar, but he made himself.

'I'm sorry, Rabigar. I swear to you: I'll make him pay. I'll get revenge.'

That was perhaps the first apology Belwynn had ever heard Herin make. She could tell that there was a part of him who wanted to turn around and head straight back to Coldeberg right now.

'Why did you ask me to come with you? Why didn't I say no and stay where I was?'

Rabigar sounded miserable. In mourning. Elana had apparently stopped the pain from his eye, but she couldn't heal the loss he was suffering. That would take time, but right now it was raw and there for all to see.

'I'm sorry,' repeated Herin, his mouth dry. 'What else can I say?'

There was a horrible silence. Eventually Soren filled it.

'So, you know what happened to us; our meeting with Emeric. What about the rest of you?'

'Moneva freed us,' began Gyrmund, 'she won't tell us how...'

Moneva shrugged. 'Getting into places without being seen is what I do. Carry on with the story.'

'Then Dirk found us,' continued Gyrmund. 'He told us you were upstairs and that he knew the way to a postern gate on the north side of the castle. We agreed that some of us needed to get out and pick up the horses or we'd never get far, even if we did make it out of the castle. We had to risk going back to the Boot and Saddle.'

True enough, considered Belwynn; without the horses they would almost certainly be dead by now. They would also have needed to get Rabigar out at that point. She shuddered to think what state he would have been in.

'He then saw this soldier he recognised,' said Gyrmund, handing this part of the story over to Dirk.

'Do you remember the soldier who took us to Orlin's rooms?' asked Dirk.

'Yes...Dom, wasn't it?' said Belwynn. 'A funny little chap.'

'Well,' said Dirk, 'Gyrmund had put on a soldier's uniform, so I told him to ask Dom to help him take some prisoners back to see Salvinus.'

A soldier's uniform taken from some dead soldier Moneva killed, no doubt, Belwynn said to Soren.

She got them out, didn't she? he replied.

'He was a very helpful fellow,' said Gyrmund. 'We walked straight out through the gatehouse entrance; Dom did all the talking for us. When we got to the Boot and Saddle we went straight for the stables. I don't know if Salvinus or his men were still there, in the building or out the back. Didn't seem like it. No-one came out to challenge us, anyway. We simply rode out and carried on through the West Gate.'

'What about Dom?' asked Belwynn. She was soft, she knew, but she didn't want them to have harmed him.

Gyrmund smiled and shook his head. 'We gathered up six of the horses. I told him that they were the prisoners' horses and that Salvinus would want to inspect them. When we rode off we left him standing there, a puzzled expression on his face.'

'Well, thanks for coming back for us,' said Belwynn.

'Yeah,' said Clarin, 'and at least we know we can trust Dirk now after the dagger thing.'

'What dagger thing?' asked Gyrmund, frowning.

Clarin shook his head. 'I clean forgot,' he said, 'most of you still don't know!'

'Don't know what?' said Herin through gritted teeth.

Belwynn suddenly had a bad feeling.

'Dirk had it all along!' said Clarin, seemingly oblivious that this might not go down too well.

'Hold on a minute,' said Herin, his voice getting loud, 'what do you mean he had it all along?'

The two brothers both looked at Dirk.

'I—I stole it from Toric's Temple before Salvinus got there. He never had it.'

Herin slowly stood up. 'You mean all this,' he said, waving his arms around, 'all this happened because they knew we had the dagger? You let us blunder into Coldeberg unprepared when you knew they would be after us?'

He began walking towards Dirk and slid his sword from its sheath as he did.

'Herin, that isn't getting us anywhere!' shouted Belwynn.

Clarin quickly shot up and moved between Dirk and his brother.

'Get out of my way, you idiot!'

'No, Herin.'

Herin pointed his sword at him.

'Get. Out. Of my fucking way.'

Clarin drew his own sword. 'You're not getting near him.'

It was said in a matter-of-fact way, but Belwynn had rarely heard Clarin deny his older brother anything. The two men stared at each other.

'This is ridiculous,' began Gyrmund.

'Shut the hell up,' Herin interrupted him.

'I told him not to tell anyone,' said Elana, quietly.

Everyone turned to look at her.

'You knew all along, too?' demanded Herin, still brandishing his sword.

'When Dirk told me, I wasn't sure if we could trust everyone. He has kept it out of the hands of Ishari. That's the most important thing.'

'But we were supposed to be taking the dagger back to Magnia,' said Soren. He looked angry himself now, just in a more controlled way than Herin. 'That was what the rest of us were trying to do. You weren't, though. Were you ever going to tell us you had it, I wonder? I don't see how you dare talk about trust.'

Elana nodded. 'Yes. I'm sorry. If you had found out that Dirk had the dagger, you would have insisted on taking it back to the Temple. It wasn't safe there. Ishari would have just come back for it.'

There was clearly something in what the priestess was saying, Belwynn had to admit.

'So where should the dagger go?' she asked Elana, intrigued.

'I don't know where, exactly, for sure,' began Elana apologetically.

'I'm not listening to any more of this,' said Herin. 'She's either got a screw loose or she's lying. If you were a man I'd have given you a smack in the teeth by now.'

Herin's temper tantrum was irritating Belwynn now, but she held her tongue.

'Madria doesn't tell me everything!' Elana tried to explain. 'She speaks to me in visions, in instinct. I know that Dirk should have the dagger. I know that we should be going to Essenberg, not back to Magnia. I don't understand everything that is happening, though.'

It sounded heartfelt enough, but it left everything totally in the dark nonetheless.

'What are we going to do?' asked Belwynn.

Everyone looked at each other; no-one seemed to have a quick answer. Soren puffed out his cheeks and let out a deep breath.

'It looks like we're going to Essenberg, anyway. It may not be a bad thing that the Emperor hears about all of this. After that...we'll have to wait and see.'

'In the meantime, are we trusting this little shit with the dagger?' demanded Herin, pointing his sword at Dirk.

'He hasn't behaved as if he's working for Ishari, Herin,' Soren said mildly. 'In fact, quite the opposite.'

'No, not at all,' responded Herin sarcastically. 'He's only robbed our nation's treasure and taken it to Coldeberg.'

'Well,' said Soren, losing patience, 'do you want it?'

'I don't particularly want the thing,' snarled Herin, taken aback a little, 'I just don't want him to have it a moment longer. You take it, Soren.'

'Shush,' said Moneva, flicking her eyes over to the side.

Belwynn looked over and saw Walter approaching. He and a few of his men were leading some horses over. Nine in all.

'Morning,' he said, looking around the group. That faint smile hovered at the corner of his mouth again. Had he heard any of their conversation? Belwynn wondered what he was thinking.

'I've brought over your mounts for the ride to Essenberg, plus three spares.'

He seemed to be the kind of person who never went anywhere without spares of anything. Belwynn guessed that probably made him a good general.

'We owe you thanks,' said Soren. 'Not only for the horses.'

'Well,' replied Walter, 'when we got word of Emeric's coronation, my brother sent me off to investigate and bring back intelligence. Potentially a dangerous mission. We're both lucky that one of my scouts spotted you when he did. You're my intelligence. So thank *you* for showing up when you did. Are you all ready to ride?' he asked, his eyes lingering over Rabigar and his damaged face.

'Aye,' said the Krykker. 'I think we've done enough blathering here.'

They had a full day's ride ahead of them to reach Essenberg. It was another clear day, and everyone seemed confident that they would be sleeping indoors tonight. Everyone seemed to have had enough talk for a while, and they mostly rode in silence, each lost in their own thoughts, and not necessarily the cheery ones. Herin brooded over Kaved's betrayal, and Clarin, who had stood up to his brother earlier, was unusually quiet. Rabigar was distant and withdrawn. Soren was dealing with his own inner demons over the loss of his magical powers since the fight in the Wilderness—an issue that he had kept from everybody except Belwynn. Dirk, who for now still kept Toric's Dagger in his possession, also looked troubled. Gyrmund and Moneva were perhaps the only exceptions, talking quietly to each other every now and again. No doubt Gyrmund felt some relief at no longer having to think about where they were going or worry about enemies behind or ahead. Walter was in charge today, and the marshal seemed happy enough to leave them alone as long as they didn't cause him trouble.

His soldiers knew their jobs, and everything was performed to military precision, as if they were in hostile territory rather than on the road back to their own base. The scouts rode out to survey the terrain in all directions. Walter himself stayed at the front of the line and was regularly reported to by the scouts. A rear-guard of ten soldiers ended the line, keeping Belwynn and her party in the middle. Protected—or contained, whichever way one wanted to look at it.

After a few hours they were well inside Kelland and Walter ordered his men to wear the uniform of the duchy, showing the eagle symbol of his own family. The track they had started on had now become a road. The villagers in this area sold their surplus crops in Essenberg, and the traffic heading into the city became steadily heavier. They passed small groups of farmers and merchants, who were expected to make way for the imperial army. Walter offered the odd greeting as he passed, but he was only interested in getting back to the capital, and his men left these travellers to their own business.

They made a brief stop for lunch and Belwynn took the chance to stretch her legs. Clarin joined her and they walked a few feet from the road in silence, stopping at a stone wall that kept in a herd of cattle, looking out over the Kellish countryside while the sun shone down directly overhead. It was a peaceful, idyllic little scene.

'Reminds me of Beckford,' said Belwynn.

That was where she had met Clarin and her brother. She had been living with Soren at the house of the marsh witch, Delyth. It was an awful place. It stank to high hell. There were no humans nearby; instead, the lizard men who infested the Gotbeck marshes were regular visitors, and the old hag, Delyth, acted as if she were their queen. Then, one day, Soren had sent her home. Told her not to contact him. Didn't tell her why, and she still didn't know to this day.

She returned to Magnia and lived by herself in Beckford for a year, waiting for him to return from his apprenticeship with Delyth. She busied herself with estate business. Herin and Clarin's father lived nearby, and she met them when they returned home to see him. Their father had been sick and died shortly after they returned. A neighbouring landowner had begun to give her unwanted attention and asked her to marry him, refusing to take no for an answer. The brothers scared him off for her, and they had become friends. Looking back, it seemed to her now not to have been such a bad period of her life, even though she had thought herself miserable at the time.

'Do you ever wonder where you'll end your days?' she asked the warrior.

Clarin looked over the farmland. 'Yes. Somewhere like this, I hope.'

She turned to him. 'Really? I didn't think you'd be the farming type.'

'Why not? When I'm too old for this nonsense,' he said, patting his scabbard, 'I'll need to settle down. Buy a piece of land, start a family. That's what most men want, isn't it?'

'Maybe,' said Belwynn. 'It's what most men tell themselves they want, perhaps. But look at you; Herin; Soren. After this, are you all going to club together and buy a farm? I don't see it.'

Clarin laughed. 'Yeah, that does seem kind of hard to picture. I can't see your brother on the farm. Or Herin, for that matter. I can picture myself there, though.'

Belwynn looked at him. Maybe he could. Maybe she could, too.

They looked out over the fields a while longer.

Footsteps coming towards them made them turn around. It was Walter. Coming to check on them? Belwynn wondered whether he was really interested in them or whether he was just being the good general, checking that all his pieces were in place, looking out for obstacles in the plan.

'Nice view, isn't it?' he asked, joining them to look over the wall.

'Very,' said Clarin.

'I hope it stays that way,' the Marshal commented.

'You mean if there is war with Emeric?' asked Belwynn. 'Do you think that's likely?'

'Likely? Let me put it this way. If it wasn't for the troubles in the north, we'd have been taking an army to Coldeberg, not fifty men.'

There was a pause.

'You haven't heard?' he asked, studying their faces.

Belwynn remembered the cryptic comments of the wizard with red eyes, Pentas, about Persala.

'Nothing concrete,' she said. 'We've been on the road a long time.'

'Right,' he said. 'Well, it's no secret. A few days ago, two states, Trevenza and Grienna, declared independence from Persala and made a request to join the Empire. We didn't commit to anything at the time. Then, just before I left Essenberg, we heard the news that a Haskan invasion of Persala had taken the capital, Baserno. The Persaleian army is destroyed.'

At first Belwynn assumed that Walter was joking, but he said it in such a matter of fact way. Persala was the great power in the north, even if it had lost control of the south of Dalriya some time ago. It had been a great power for hundreds of years. For it to lose its capital and its army in an instant didn't seem possible.

'Where does that leave your brother?' Belwynn asked.

'He's in a difficult situation. Does he allow the Haskans to take these two provinces and let Arioc's army reach the northern border of the Empire? If he stands up for them, he risks immediate war with Haskany.'

'And this is the moment that Emeric declares himself king,' added Clarin. 'Hardly a coincidence.'

'No, it can't be,' agreed Walter. 'Which is why anything you've learned about what's going on in Coldeberg will be very much appreciated by the Emperor.'

They rode on for the rest of the afternoon and early evening. Despite herself, Belwynn was excited about visiting Essenberg and meeting the Emperor. They had all gone to the city last year: she, Soren, Herin and Clarin. On one of their adventures working for a merchant. The job had been little more than a glorified shopping trip: taking some valuable jewellery there to be sold and bringing back the money, without losing either. Soren had disappeared one night on some mysterious mission, and she had gone drinking with Herin and Clarin. She had ended up in bed with Clarin at the end of the night. The next morning had been awkward. Neither of them had mentioned it since, and that was that.

Essenberg itself was considered by many people to be the greatest city in Dalriya, and, Belwynn reflected, had perhaps lost its biggest competition, now that Baserno had fallen to the Haskans.

Belwynn thought of Essenberg as a beating heart, with many arteries giving it life. The first to give it life must have been the river Cousel, since the city featured an island in the middle of the river, which made it an ideal crossing place. The Cousel ran from the Krykker Mountains down through Guivergne and the Empire and emptied into the sea where the southern Caladri lived. It was the biggest river on the continent and an important trading route as river barges passed up and down it, easily carrying heavy goods by water that would have been much more difficult to transport by land. Just as important now was the Great Road that passed through Essenberg. It was where north met south and where traders from all parts of the continent could meet and do business in safety, with the emperor's soldiers there to enforce the law. Essenberg also enjoyed a central location within the Empire itself, with roads from Coldeberg,

Witmar and Guslar all meeting there. In short, Essenberg's location made it almost destined for greatness.

Eventually they saw the walls of Essenberg ahead of them. Most of the buying and selling was done for the day, and there was no queue for entry as they reached the Coldeberg Gate. Walter's status meant that they were all waved through without challenge, and they passed into the city.

They were in the Market Quarter of the city, where the Great Road, the road to Coldeberg, and the road to Valennes in Guivergne all converged on the south side of the river. This part of the city had been given over to the merchants and farmers who brought their goods from all over Dalriya to sell. Most of the stalls were now empty, and the local farmers had left for their homes, but some citizens were still plying their trade. Hot food was on sale for those who needed their dinner, and Belwynn's stomach rumbled at the smells of fresh-baked bread and sizzling meats. Some stallholders, perhaps those who most needed the money or hadn't got rid of their produce, remained, shouting out their final offers. The crowds had died down, but the numbers were still healthy as people strolled along in pairs and small groups, enjoying the summer evening.

Their route took them straight to the heart of the market where, ahead of them, Albert's Bridge, a hugely impressive stone and concrete construction, spanned the river. It was wide enough for people to walk six abreast, and Belwynn could see that a number of vendors had taken up positions along the bridge, selling jewellery and trinkets to rich men's wives and girlfriends. To their left was Baldwin's Bridge, a military bridge that formed part of the circuit of the city walls and defended Essenberg from a potential attack downriver by the Guivergnais. It was reserved for use by the army rather than civilians and was linked to two towers that had been built either side of the river, so that defenders could move on and off the bridge with ease. Two catapults were stationed on the bridge, so that boats could be sunk before they reached the city.

Instead of going in this direction, Walter took them right onto the Great Road. This led them into the Army Quarter, where the Imperial Headquarters was located—colloquially known as the Imps. It had a large, rectangular site on the far side of the city, next to the river. This stretch of the river featured the First Bridge, made up of two separate bridges that each crossed from one side of the river bank to Margaret Island, in the middle of the Cousel. Elsewhere in this part of the city was the lion's share of the residential buildings, crammed in between the Great Road and the city walls.

Their route took them close to the First Bridge, so that Belwynn could see the trees on Margaret Island, before turning right to the Imps. The perimeter was marked out by wooden stakes but there were no defences and no guards. When Walter arrived, a few orders were barked out, and a group of boys came over to take the horses to the stables. Belwynn dismounted stiffly and handed over the reins to one of the boys, who she supposed were in training to become soldiers.

'Till!' Walter called over one of the boys. 'Take our guests to the dining hall and tell the cooks that I said they should be fed.'

Walter turned to them. 'I will see to it that you all get a bed for a night, too, in the barracks. It may not be the most comfortable accommodation, but it will be the best we can do at short notice. Then I'll have to go over and see Baldwin. You'll get an appointment some time tomorrow.'

'How safe are we here?' Elana asked him.

To Belwynn's mind the priestess was being unnecessarily fearful, and she shared a look with Soren. Herin was less subtle, rolling his eyes for all to see.

Elana picked up on the response. 'The Barissians could have people in the city now, could they not?'

'They do,' said Moneva. 'Emeric will have sent his followers to the Great Road as soon as we escaped. They'll be here by now.'

'Relax. You're in the middle of the Imps, surrounded by soldiers,' said Walter, waving his arms about him with a smile. Elana still looked less than convinced, and the marshal's face grew more serious. 'If I'm not around, ask any soldier for help. If the worst happens you can seek refuge at the castle. Or at the cathedral, with Archbishop Decker. He can be completely trusted. But listen—you'll be perfectly safe here.'

XVII

THREE COFFINS

'IT'S NOT SAFE HERE,' said Moneva.

They were in the dining hall of the Imps, where neat rows of benches and chairs were laid out and the soldiers garrisoned here got their three square meals. They had arrived too late for dinner and a grumbling cook had served out watery soup, dry bread and waxy cheese.

'The food's not that bad,' joked Clarin.

'How so?' Soren asked Moneva in a tired voice.

He sounded like Belwynn felt—ready for bed and not in the mood for paranoia.

'We were seen coming in through the Coldeberg Gate. Two men were sat down, chatting by the side of the road. One of them followed us into the market. A third man tailed us from there to here. He's probably watching the Imps now, or someone else is.'

That changed things somewhat.

'Barissians?' Soren asked Moneva.

'I presume so.'

'Why didn't you tell Walter?' asked Gyrmund.

Moneva shrugged. 'We all trust him now?'

'You were quick to trust him when the Barissians were after us,' pointed out Gyrmund.

'We were about to get killed!' retorted Moneva.

Belwynn looked around at everyone. Tired faces, struggling to think straight. They had all been through a lot in the last few days.

'We need to be careful,' said Soren. 'If this is true, we don't know how many of them there are. Emeric also had a wizard with him, called Tirano. It's possible he is here, too.'

'*If* it's true,' said Belwynn doubtfully.

'Why would Moneva make it up?' demanded Gyrmund heatedly.

'Whoa, no need to fight about it,' said Moneva. 'I understand if people want some proof. I'll take Herin with me and we'll find the spy watching us. Will that do?'

'Yes,' said Belwynn, feeling slightly ashamed. 'Sorry.'

'Don't be sorry. We all need to be careful.'

'We need to decide what to *do*,' said Herin impatiently.

'We could ask Walter's troops to post a guard,' suggested Soren.

Moneva made a face at that. 'Assuming they're Emeric's people and they're after the dagger, they'll want to come for it while they know where it is and while it's not under lock and key somewhere else. This could be their best chance. Most likely in the night while we're asleep. It could get dangerous here.'

'What do you suggest?' asked Soren.

'If it was up to me, I'd move out of here, so they don't know where we are anymore. It's safer.'

'What about this wizard, Soren?' asked Herin. 'Can you handle him?'

'No,' said Soren, looking around at everyone. 'No. It's time I come straight with you all. I haven't been able to use my powers since I lost consciousness in the Wilderness. I won't be any help here.'

There was an awkward silence after Soren's revelation.

'I'm sorry, Soren,' said Clarin. 'Will it come back?'

'Thanks. I hope so. But we need to focus on this now.'

'I think we should try to leave without being seen,' said Elana.

'Agreed,' said Gyrmund.

'Herin?' asked Soren.

Herin looked in two minds, which was unusual for him. 'Kaved might have come with them,' he said.

Belwynn hadn't considered that.

'We need to focus on our safety, Herin,' said Rabigar. 'We can get our revenge another time.'

'Okay,' said Herin, relenting. 'What now?'

'It's already getting dark, 'said Moneva. 'You and I are going to find out who, if anyone, is watching us. Ideally, eliminate them. Then get out of here.'

'Where to?'

'Margaret Island. It's not inhabited at night time.'

'Very well,' said Soren. 'Moneva knows Essenberg better than anyone else. We'll spend the night on the island. Then, in the morning, we need to make our way to the castle as soon as they open the gates.'

They had been allocated a barrack hut to themselves, and they stripped the beds of blankets so that they would be warm on the island, which might get chilly overnight.

So much for a sleep in a bed, complained Belwynn to Soren.

When Herin returned with Moneva, he swiped a flat hand across his neck, to indicate they had killed someone. No-one was keen to ask questions about it.

Instead, they made their way out of the Imps, Moneva leading them out the back way towards the river and then following it along towards the First Bridge. They travelled by moonlight. Moneva held up a hand for them to stop.

She peered towards the bridge and then hastily indicated that they move towards the river. Belwynn crept slowly towards the bank, fearful lest she trip over, then sunk down onto the ground. Everyone lay or crouched down and looked in the direction of the bridge.

Presently, they heard voices from that direction that got steadily louder, until a group of about a dozen came into view. It was an eerie feeling, watching them in the darkness. It made Belwynn wonder if anyone was out there watching them.

It was too dark to make out faces or to tell whether any of them were looking in their direction. They all looked like men, some clearly carrying weapons. They walked with purpose, not as if they were revellers who had been drinking all evening. A cold feeling clutched at Belwynn. Everything about them suggested that they were here for them, and they had nearly walked straight into them.

They waited by the bank as the group of men continued past. They could have been innocent men going back to their homes but they were heading in the direction of the main entrance to the Imps.

'We can't wait here all night,' hissed Herin.

'I'll take a look,' said Moneva.

She set off, moving along in a crouched position towards the bridge. Belwynn watched her peering around before she made her way onto the bridge. She disappeared from sight.

The seconds passed like hours. Had those men found the dead body of the spy, or found him missing? Had they gone to their hut and found *them* missing?

Belwynn looked back the way they had come, worried that they might be followed to the river.

Eventually Moneva returned and waved them forwards. They shuffled over towards the bridge, Belwynn looking nervously around in all directions.

'It's clear,' whispered Moneva.

Belwynn hoped she was right. They walked along the wooden First Bridge, which was only the width of two people. In the daytime, users of the bridge had to go single file so they could pass people coming the other way. Moneva set a fast pace so that they weren't out in the open for too long. She moved like a cat, making no noise, but the same couldn't be said for everyone else. Despite his efforts, Clarin clunked along like a giant learning to play the drums. Still, the sound of the Cousel flowing beneath them was surely loud enough to drown out the noise of their movement.

Then, they were off the bridge, onto the soil of Margaret Island.

Moneva didn't hesitate, taking them left into the trees that covered the north side of the island. Belwynn hoped she wasn't going to take them too far, since she was sure that at any moment she would walk into a hole or a tree.

Something ran off to her left.

'There are creatures here!' she exclaimed.

'Rabbits,' said Moneva.

'How did rabbits get here?' she whispered to Clarin.

'Hopped across the bridge?' he suggested.

Finally, they stopped at a grassy ridge with a decent view back to the bridge, but far enough away not to be seen.

'Is this it?' asked Herin.

'Yes,' said Moneva, 'I hope you like it,' she added sarcastically.

'Do you think those men we saw were Barissians?' asked Belwynn.

'Yes,' replied Moneva. 'Almost certainly sent to kill us. Sweet dreams.'

Belwynn took a long time to get any sleep. It felt strange on the island at night time and her mind refused to relax. Rabigar slept badly, and she heard him cry out more than once.

It seemed that as soon as she nodded off, everyone else had woken up and was ready to go. A sparkling white sunrise was blasting its way in between the trees on Margaret Island, and if she didn't have such a pounding headache, Belwynn thought she might have found it a beautiful sight.

The plan this morning was simple enough: head straight for Essenberg Castle and ask for admittance. The unknown was whether the Barissians would be waiting for them there, or along the way. Soren made it clear that if they couldn't get there safely they would have to leave the city without seeing the Emperor.

They left Margaret Island via the other bridge, arriving on the north bank of the Cousel. The bridge fed into a street which ran straight to the Witmar Gate and became the Witmar Road, taking travellers to the capital of Luderia. They were now in the Cathedral Quarter of Essenberg. Up ahead and slightly to their left, they could see the spire of the cathedral, the tallest building in the city. Not far to the left of the cathedral stood Essenberg Castle, which dominated the Castle Quarter of the city.

It was towards the castle that Moneva led the group. This was the part of the city where most of the more established shops were located, but the city was still waking up and the streets were nearly empty. As they got nearer to the castle they began to pass the houses of the wealthier citizens of Essenberg, keen to get locations close to the seat of power. Several them were in the process of being rebuilt or extended, testament to the period of prosperity they were enjoying.

They turned a corner and opposite them was the central square that held the castle. The building was an impressive piece of construction, and that was perhaps its main purpose. Whereas Coldeberg was stronger defensively, Essenberg Castle was more graceful. A square structure with four square towers on each corner, from whichever angle you looked at it, you saw clear geometric lines. Its walls were whitewashed so that it gleamed amid the dirt and muck of city life. The crenellations along the top looked almost too perfect, as if they had been made to make the castle look pretty rather than to be used for the dirty business of war. The eagle flag of Kelland fluttered in the breeze on the roof, but so too did the stag, symbol of the Brasingian Empire. Its seven antler tips represented each of the seven duchies and emphasised their unity. The emperor's castle spoke of truth and justice, ideas that, in their own way, were just as potent as the mercenaries Emeric had bought and the new crown he had on his head.

Belwynn felt an urge to get to the castle and meet with the Emperor. Moneva, however, didn't look so keen. She was peering into the square.

'There's a group of men sitting in the corner,' she said. 'Armed. Hard to say whose men they are, but they're not wearing uniforms.'

'How many?' asked Herin.

'Eight.'

'We could fight our way through them if necessary,' he suggested.

Moneva screwed up her face. 'Maybe, but there could be more of them in the streets off the square...'

'Someone's coming,' interjected Gyrmund sharply.

They turned to face the threat, what weapons they had appearing in hands.

A lone figure had detached itself from the shadows of a house and edged towards them. It was a young man, wearing the vestments of a priest. He stopped, eyeing up the group and their weapons. He seemed to be a bit unsure as to how to proceed.

'Hello. My name is Ancel,' he began. When he spoke he had a smooth, confident voice. 'I work for Archbishop Decker. He sent me to find you,' he said, glancing towards the square. 'He asked me to take you to the cathedral. It's not safe for you here.'

'Why not?' asked Soren. 'Doesn't the Emperor have control outside his own castle?'

'Orlin, Duke Emeric's chamberlain, is here in Essenberg. He arrived yesterday and went straight to the Emperor, asking him to apprehend a group of your description if you should arrive. There are other men from Barissia here as well. I don't know how many—some in groups, some alone.'

'What is your interest in this?' Soren responded.

'His Grace spoke with Marshal Walter about you. He wants to keep you safe.'

'Walter said we could trust the Archbishop, remember?' said Belwynn.

'But can we trust Walter?' asked Herin.

'The longer we stand around discussing it, the more conspicuous we get,' said Moneva impatiently.

'Alright,' said Herin irritably, 'back to the cathedral, then. I'm tired of all this skulking around.'

Ancel turned around and led them down a narrow street. If he was planning an ambush, this would be a perfect place, thought Belwynn. Instead, he turned right, and they could see the spire of the cathedral ahead of them.

'Don't turn around,' Moneva whispered harshly from the back. 'We're being followed. Two of them. They've probably watched the whole thing.'

'Two isn't enough,' said Clarin.

'It's enough to find out where we're going and get others,' replied Gyrmund.

'Don't worry,' said Ancel, turning behind him. 'We're nearly there.'

They picked up their pace but didn't run, moving along a street with residential housing on each side. They were now approaching the tall walls of the cathedral from its west side. Then, Belwynn noticed a small wooden door in the cathedral's west wall. Ancel made straight for the door. He rapped on it four times.

'It's Ancel.'

Glancing behind, Belwynn could see two men halfway up the street, looking in their direction.

The noise of sliding bolts came from behind the door, and it opened inwards. They dived through; the men had to bend down to get under the lintel. They found themselves in a small antechamber, just off the main nave of the cathedral. Another young priest waited until they were all through and then shut the door, slamming home a series of bolts.

Belwynn and the others wandered into the nave. The ceiling stretched high above them, decorated with holy images of the various gods worshipped in the city.

Great pillars separated the open space into areas where each god was isolated and could be worshipped by their followers. Lars the Creator held the world and the planets in the palms of his hands. Lady Alexia, the Protector, could be asked for help from those in need. Justus, God of Death and Justice, held a sword and scales, and could deliver his verdict on a supplicant's enemies. Sibylla, goddess of Health and Prosperity, might be called on by a young wife hoping to conceive, or an old man with money problems. Some visitors came to see one of the gods; some came to see several. But all visitors were equal, and all gods were equal. All prayed under one roof. All religious service was carried out under the watchful eye of the Brasingian Church, which had won a measure of control over the different sects in the Empire by establishing these united cathedrals in the major cities.

Ancel had not stopped to look around, but had marched on, into the nave and towards the rear of the cathedral. He turned around to wait for the others to catch up.

'The private chambers of the cathedral are behind here,' he said, pointing up at a large, red set of curtains. 'His Grace will be waiting for us,' he added.

Pulling aside a section of curtain, Ancel walked through, holding it up for the others to follow. Within a few yards the wide expanse of floor narrowed into something more like a corridor, with stone walls on either side where separate rooms had been built. As Ancel entered the corridor he was challenged by an older priest.

'Archbishop Decker asked me to bring these people to him as a matter of urgency,' explained Ancel.

The older priest frowned at Belwynn's group. 'You're not going in with those weapons,' he stated.

'We're not dropping our weapons,' retorted Herin. 'We don't even know why we've been brought here.'

The older priest's face looked aghast. 'You can't barge into the Archbishop's chamber armed like a bunch of killers!' he exclaimed.

A door further up the corridor on the right slowly opened. Everyone turned around. A third man, even older, now appeared, moving with small steps into the corridor. Belwynn noted he was at least seventy if he was a day.

'It's alright,' he said, his voice shaky with age. 'They are welcome to come in. Well done, Ancel.'

Archbishop Decker had a large, well-furnished chamber in the cathedral, as befit his rank. His official residence was by the river. Like most powerful men, suspected Belwynn, Decker knew he was better off closer to the centre of power. Here he was a short walk away from the court of the emperor.

Decker sat his guests down. He nodded over to Clarin.

'I was a soldier once,' he said in his reedy voice. 'A long time ago now. You might find that hard to believe.'

'A little,' said Herin, looking him up and down.

Decker smiled at that, showing what was left of his teeth.

'Ha, no doubt! I made the right decision, though. Here I am, three score and ten; another war is coming, and I'm set to outlive another generation of young men.'

'Fair enough, if your goal is simply to live as long as possible,' said Gyrmund.

Decker widened his arms, encompassing the cathedral. 'I've done a bit better than just live, wouldn't you say?'

Belwynn was regretting their decision to come here to bandy words with a half-dead archbishop.

Emeric's spies are probably bringing a troop of soldiers this way right now, she said to Soren. *If we had gone straight to the castle we could have got in there by now.*

'Anyway,' Decker continued, 'young men with swords don't listen to old bishops; there it is. I spoke with Walter about you and thought you might have something important to tell us all. But when he got back to the Imps, you had gone. Meanwhile, Master Orlin arrived straight from Barissia with who knows how many underlings, wanting you caught and handed over. At that point I *knew* that you were of importance and needed to be found. If you weren't already dead. And, here you are.'

The Archbishop stood up, taking the manoeuvre slow and steady.

'I think it's now time to show you all something,' he smiled, almost mischievously.

What now? A tour of the cathedral? Belwynn fretted.

Decker exited the chamber and turned right, taking the group further down the corridor. It ended in a circular shaped expanse of floor with a metal pole in the middle, which the archbishop headed for. Decker looked at his guests and beckoned Clarin over.

'Could you do the honours?' he asked, pointing at the stone floor.

Clarin frowned, but obligingly took a look at the floor. The big man's frown deepened and he knelt down by the pole. Finding a gap in the stone floor, he placed both hands in and pulled upwards, bringing a stone slab with him. He manoeuvred the slab away and carefully laid it down.

Belwynn couldn't help moving closer to take a look. The slab concealed a set of stone steps, which wound their way down into a cellar.

'The crypt of the Dukes of Kelland,' announced the Archbishop.

Picking on Clarin again, he gestured to the wall where a lighted torch was hanging.

'You may lead on, sir,' he said.

Clarin picked up the torch and began the descent, holding on to the pole as he twisted around the thin steps. As he disappeared from view, Decker followed behind. The archbishop went incredibly slowly, leaving Belwynn and the others standing around at the top.

Eventually, they made it down into the crypt. Clarin had used the torch to light a number of lanterns before hanging it up. Decker asked Herin to place the slab back over the top of the stairs. The lanterns cast an eerie, flickering light in the cold, humid crypt, picking out recesses in the rock and creating dark shadows. As Belwynn's eyes adjusted she saw that along the walls, to the left and right, were the rectangular stone coffins of the three previous Dukes of Kelland.

Each one had a carved likeness of the duke on the lid, looking sternly out from their rest, still grasping their favoured weapons in different poses with which to defend their territory. Their names had also been carved into the stone beneath their feet, so that Belwynn could read along: Manfred the Great gripped a great sword with both hands, laid along his chest and legs; Duke Bernard, Baldwin's father, held sword and shield in battle-readiness; Duke Albert had his sword buckled at his waist and his palms pressed together on his chest in prayer.

Belwynn brought her attention back to Archbishop Decker, still wondering why he had brought them down here. He was at the far end of the crypt with Clarin. He pointed to another gap in the wall, again big enough for Clarin to place both hands in. Clarin pulled, then pushed. Nothing happened.

'This way,' said Decker, using his hands to make a circular motion towards the right.

Instead of pushing away or pulling towards him, Clarin used his grip to push upwards on the wall. He briefly strained with the effort, and then the mechanism kicked in, a section of stone wall rolling away to the right like a wheel.

When the stone disc stopped moving, there was a gap in the wall big enough to walk through. It was dark, but Belwynn could make out a passageway.

'The underground route into the castle,' announced Archbishop Decker. 'Very useful over the years for the dukes to have a secret way in and out. And today, very useful for us.'

XVIII

AN AUDIENCE WITH THE EMPEROR

B ELWYNN LOOKED AT THE MIRROR again. She was about to meet the Emperor of Brasingia, and no amount of cosmetics or changes of hairstyle altered the fact that she looked a tired, haggard mess.

It had taken him a while, but Archbishop Decker had led them through the short tunnel from the crypt under Essenberg Cathedral to the wine cellar of Essenberg Castle.

He had immediately taken them to Baldwin's chamberlain, Rainer, who explained the situation to them more fully.

'The Emperor is due to meet with Orlin for a second time this morning. Before you start to worry, we already know, in a general way, the state of affairs in Barissia. For the time being it suits us to keep our knowledge of events in Barissia to ourselves. So, the Emperor meets with Orlin, agrees to hand you over if you are found, and Orlin leaves.' Rainer waved his hand, as if Orlin were a fly he was swatting away.

Rainer wanted to know the details of their time in Barissia. Soren gave him the bare bones, but demanded an audience with Baldwin himself. Rainer politely nodded.

'Yes, yes, the Emperor will want to speak to you today. He is also meeting with a Haskan envoy from King Arioc this morning. As I'm sure you'll be aware,' Rainer continued, forcing a smile, 'there is much to talk about there. So, I propose a meeting this afternoon. In the meantime, I can arrange a suite of apartments here in the castle for you to rest in. Not as spacious as would ordinarily be the case, but we have a lot of visitors in the castle at the moment.'

Soren and the others had agreed to the afternoon meeting. They also agreed that not everyone need go, so, as well as the twins, Herin, Gyrmund and Moneva were to come. Despite being related to a prince, being given a meeting with the Brasingian Emperor gave Belwynn a bit of a thrill. The afternoon slot also gave them time to get some rest and take stock of the situation.

As it was, Belwynn had fallen asleep, and had woken up with little time to get ready. Rainer had sent an aide, who told them to be ready to meet with Baldwin in twenty minutes.

The door opened.

'All well?' enquired Soren, taking a step into the room.

'I suppose so,' Belwynn replied, staring unhappily at her reflection.

Moneva, who had been sharing the room with Belwynn, got up off the bed and joined them. She took a brief look in the mirror herself, smoothing down her chin length jet-black hair in five seconds.

'I hate people like you,' said Belwynn grumpily.

Moneva smiled and gave her cheek a pinch.

'She looks beautiful, doesn't she, Soren?'

'For Toric's sake, haven't we got more important things to worry about?'

Moneva shook her head at him. 'A *yes* is what we were looking for.'

The others were waiting in the corridor, along with an aide sent by Rainer.

'We're ready,' said Soren. The aide wordlessly turned around and walked ahead, leading them to the great hall where Baldwin did his meeting.

'This guy's so full of himself he gets his servant's servant to collect us,' said Herin.

'You are going to behave, aren't you?' asked Belwynn.

Herin snorted in disgust at the question.

At the end of the corridor they went down a flight of stairs to ground level. Here they briefly went outside into a courtyard. There was some evidence of military preparations here. At the far wall Belwynn could see three wagons being loaded with food, weaponry and other provisions. The Kellish war machine was slowly rousing.

After a quick check that they were unarmed, Belwynn and her four companions were allowed into the hall by the two sentries. Although Baldwin toured around the Empire, he spent much of his time here, and the hall was designed to impress the visitor. Tapestries depicted the great events of imperial history. All four emperors were shown. Manfred the Great was shown as both a warrior and peacemaker, forging the Empire. Emperor Ludvig, Duke of Rotelegen, was a pious figure, uniting the disparate faiths in one church. Bernard was a defender against enemies abroad. Finally, Baldwin was an architect, building a new age of prosperity.

Four pillars stood in a rectangle shape in the centre of the hall, supporting the roof. It was big enough to hold dozens of people for feasts or formal ceremonies. Now, however, it held only twelve. At the far end of the hall there were two tables. Off to the side, the smaller one seated six bodyguards, bearing different liveries, all fully armed. At the larger, main table, a further six people stood up from where they had been seated at the far end as Belwynn and the others approached.

Welcoming them, Rainer stepped forward to do the introductions.

'His Imperial Majesty, Emperor Baldwin; His Grace Ellard, Duke of Rotelegen; His Grace Decker, Archbishop of Kelland; His Lordship Walter, Marshall of the Empire; His Lordship Gustav, Archmage of the Empire.'

Belwynn muttered a *my lord* after each name was announced and nodded in what she thought was the right direction.

Rainer began the other set of introductions, impressing Belwynn by remembering their names.

'Soren and Belwynn, cousins to Prince Edgar of South Magnia; Herin of South Magnia; Gyrmund of South Magnia; Moneva of…?' Rainer hadn't been told where Moneva was from.

Moneva's lips twitched in amusement.

'Of Dalriya,' she said.

Baldwin smiled. 'Quite right. None of our business. Though your accent sounds more than familiar. Sit down,' he said gruffly, gesturing at the opposite end of the table. 'That's the formalities over with. I want to keep this informal. I understand that you've already met a good number of our group already, one way or another.'

He spoke with the same trace of humour Walter did, as if they were all sharing a joke amongst themselves.

Belwynn and the others found a chair and everyone sat down. Feeling a bit more relaxed, Belwynn took another look at the Emperor close up. Baldwin was essentially an older version of Walter. He had a powerful build and a firm, strong face, surrounded by cropped, dark hair which also contained flecks of grey. He had more lines on his face than his brother, no doubt caused by the years of extra responsibility.

Belwynn briefly examined the other new faces. Duke Ellard was perhaps ten years older than the Emperor. He had a soldierly look to him, as if he were used to giving out orders, though he looked less than interested in Belwynn and her companions.

Gustav was a different kind of man. While tall, he was no soldier; his body had been left slim while he pursued his magical gifts. Soren had told Belwynn a bit about him over the years, though her twin had never met him. He was perhaps the most powerful human wizard in Dalriya. Born in the Empire, Baldwin had wanted Gustav's services at court. He eventually got them, but Gustav had come at a high price. Not only money and property, but an official title—Archmage of the Empire. This had brought the Emperor into trouble with the Church and others who despised magic as an abomination and objected to any official recognition. However, imperial recognition for Gustav had made the position of wizards in the Empire and its neighbours safer than they had been for generations.

'I should apologise,' began Walter, looking at each of them. 'Last night I should have brought you to the castle immediately. I didn't imagine that the Barissians would be so brazen as to send such a significant force into the city after you.'

'There's no need to apologise, my lord,' responded Soren. 'You weren't in full cognisance of the facts and, for that, we apologise. There are certain things we felt we needed to tell the Emperor to his face.'

'Well, I am all ears now,' said Baldwin. 'You have news from Barissia, perhaps very important, since Emeric seems desperate to get his hands on you. Rainer also tells me you bring news from Magnia.'

Before the meeting they had agreed on two things. Firstly, that Soren would do the talking, and secondly, that he would be completely honest. Baldwin and his advisers already knew much, and they needed the Emperor's support in their current situation. Hiding things from them could jeopardise that.

So, Soren began at the beginning, by giving an account of the attack on the Temple of Toric and Edgar's decision to send them to retrieve the dagger. He outlined the pursuit through the Wilderness, not hiding the fact that he was a wizard. He explained, as best he could, the encounter with Pentas and Nexodore on the Great Road. Naturally, this sparked an interest.

'Gustav?' Baldwin enquired, seeking elaboration.

Gustav had leaned forwards in his chair at Soren's description of the fight between the two wizards.

'I know the names. They are lieutenants of Erkindrix. I believe that both are on his Council of Seven, meaning that they answer to no-one but him. Arioc of Haskany is another member—that is the level we are talking about. Why they should fight each other is, therefore, beyond me. We could speculate that they both wanted to be the one to take this dagger to Erkindrix and win his favour. But the fact that they both became personally involved in this is remarkable. In that sense, it makes the dagger a bigger issue even than Emeric.'

Ellard snorted, a look of disgust on his face. 'A poxy dagger won't seem a bigger issue when Emeric decides to move his army.'

'Can I see it?' Gustav asked, ignoring the Duke.

Soren handed it over. Gustav peered at it, studying the writing. He traced his forefinger up the length of the blade and handed it back with a slightly disappointed look.

'Interesting. I'm not sure what to make of it. Where did the dagger come from originally?'

'In our country the legends say that the Magnians defeated the Lippers and took the dagger as spoils.'

'Nothing to do with Toric?'

'I think he was given the credit by the Church.'

'Have you held the weapon? Felt any kind of reaction from it?'

'No, I…' Soren seemed a bit unsure what to say. 'I have lost my powers. It happened when we were going through the Wilderness. I overextended my powers.'

Gustav's eyebrows rose slightly and a look of sympathy appeared on his face. 'I see. Perhaps you and I can talk about that later, Soren. I certainly felt nothing, anyway.'

Soren continued. He told them about Kaved's treachery in Coldeberg and Dirk's revelation that he had had the dagger all along. He finished the tale with the escape from Coldeberg and their recent adventures in Essenberg.

'Thank you for being so frank, Soren,' said Baldwin. 'I will repay you in a moment by updating you on recent developments here. You may wish to carry this news back to Edgar. First, I want to get the nature of Emeric's rebellion straight in my head. You say this wizard, Tirano, is from Ishari. In that case, Emeric could have given his allegiance to Ishari, and may be preparing a coordinating attack from the south.'

'That would be my guess,' said Walter. 'He's been recruiting every sellsword in the Empire for weeks now. I wouldn't be surprised if Arioc, or whoever, has offered him the Empire in return.'

'Possibly,' agreed Baldwin. 'All of this is confirmation of our suspicions that Emeric's actions are a bit more than opportunism, and he may not be easily bought off. I have received a letter from Coen, informing me that Prince Edgar is holding some kind of Conference of the South,' said Baldwin, changing the subject. 'When is it, Rainer?'

'Two days' time.'

'He aims to secure an agreement for the southern states of Dalriya to send us help. I am very grateful for this. I am sending an ambassador out today. I don't know whether you intend to return to Magnia now. But you are welcome to write a letter to Edgar yourselves if you wish. My ambassador will ensure that it is delivered.'

'Thank you,' said Belwynn. 'We will.'

'You have told me of events in the south, and so I will pass on what we know of events in the north. Walter?'

Walter nodded and unfurled a map of Dalriya on the table so that everyone could see.

'The threat from Ishari really only began about a year ago,' continued Baldwin. 'Everyone knows that they control the Drobax—potentially a fearsome threat, but they have been relatively quiet the last ten years. Three years ago Arioc took the throne of Haskany. King Harel died suddenly with no male heir. Arioc had a claim through marriage to a relative.'

Baldwin shrugged. 'It happens. Suddenly, Ishari was in a stronger position. We became worried, but not overly concerned. Haskany raised troops, but only to fight a long, drawn-out campaign against the Barbarians of the east coast. Kharovia allied itself to Ishari, probably out of fear of the Drobax. Last month they took the island of Alta from Vismar. These were small events. No, it was the fall of Persala that took us by surprise.

'We don't know what Erkindrix and Arioc's ultimate intentions are. But I couldn't let them take Trevenza and Grienna as well. That would put Arioc right on our border. So, yesterday, Trevenza and Grienna were both fully incorporated into the Empire. I've made my move. Will it make Haskany think twice about pushing further south? Or will they take it as a cause for war? The evidence now suggests that they've been planning for a war for a long time.'

'We've just had Arioc's envoy in before you,' said Ellard, becoming interested in this part of the conversation. 'They refuse to accept the status of the two provinces as belonging to the Empire. They claim them for themselves, as part of Persala. That doesn't sound like backing down to me.'

'If war comes—' Baldwin took over again, 'we are in real trouble. With Emeric's army they have us caught on two fronts. If I take an army north to fight Haskany, it leaves the Empire open for Emeric's army, and vice versa. That's why we're having to play it cagey—tolerate Orlin and the Barissians, despite the fact they've put soldiers onto the streets in my own city.'

He raised a fist, as if he was going to bang it onto the table, but controlled himself, gradually relaxing his hand.

'If Emeric had any sense of strategy he'd have sent his army to Essenberg already, but he's never had sense, thank the Gods. But it's not just the Empire,' the Emperor continued, sounding passionate. 'If the Empire falls, Guivergne, Cordence, even Magnia—they will all follow. We are heavily outnumbered, and allies are scarce. Our relations with Guivergne are not good. They will not lift a finger to help. Neither will the Confederacy. King Jonas of Kalinth is weak, too fearful of the Drobax to act. I send him a message of support against Ishari, and he wrote back to say that he has good relations with Erkindrix! There is no stomach for a fight there.

'What does that leave me?' said Baldwin, looking at the map of Dalriya, emotion creeping into his voice. 'The Krykkers. The Caladri. I have little contact with them and know nothing of their ways. This is why the support of the Southern states is so important to me. I have decided to send a formal request for help to this conference Edgar is holding. As for the Empire, I sent instructions for each duke to raise his army.' Baldwin smiled grimly at this, as if he had just made a sour jest.

'Well,' he continued, 'each duke has raised his forces. At the moment, however, Ellard's is the only one within range of Trevenza and Grienna.'

'Under the control of my sons,' Ellard added proudly.

'Walter has my forces prepared, but we are wary of moving into Rotelegen for fear of leaving Kelland undefended against Emeric's army. Arne, to be fair, should be moving his forces today. But the rest…'

Belwynn didn't quite know where to look. The Emperor was criticising the dukes of Brasingia in front of them. Perhaps he found it easier to unload his problems onto strangers. It was a brutally frank analysis of the situation. She felt a little disappointed by it all the same. It seemed that emperors were just men with their own problems, like any other.

'Anyway,' resumed Baldwin, 'I won't go on any more, but you see my dilemma. Perhaps if you return to Magnia, you could help explain the situation to people there.'

'That would no doubt be of value,' said Gustav, 'but we must not overlook this dagger in their possession. Simply returning it to Magnia may not now be the right thing to do. I need to discuss this further with them.'

'I will leave you in the hands of Gustav regarding the weapon,' said Baldwin. 'You have agreed to write a letter to Edgar. Whatever else you and Gustav decide you should do, it has my blessing. Ellard is returning to Rotelegen tomorrow, and we need to plan our next move. Thank you for your help.'

With that, everyone was suddenly standing up, and before she really knew it, Belwynn was leaving Baldwin's hall. Gustav and Rainer followed them out into the courtyard.

'The Emperor sounded down in there,' said Rainer. 'He is not usually like that. He's had to listen to the ambassadors from Haskany and Barissia lying to him all morning, pretending he doesn't know what they're up to. Don't worry. Whatever else he is, Baldwin is a fighter.'

Gustav gave a cough. 'I would like to speak to you, Soren. About the dagger, and about your powers.'

'I would appreciate your guidance, Gustav.'

'Very well, we can go to my rooms,' said the Archmage.

'Would anyone be able to write that letter now?' asked Rainer.

'Sure, I can do it,' Belwynn agreed.

'Thank you. Follow me, please, if you will.'

As Rainer led Belwynn in one direction, she watched Soren and Gustav head off in another, wondering what kind of guidance Archmage Gustav was about to give her brother.

Soren and Belwynn looked out over the battlements of Essenberg Castle as the sun rose. Soren was staring down at the early morning streets of the city and gazing beyond the city walls, to the southern horizon, imagining briefly that he could see all the way to Magnia.

He turned to his sister.

'I spoke to Gustav for a while last night. I've slept on what he said and come to a decision on what I want to do now. I'm going to tell the others in a minute, but I wanted to talk to you first. I don't mind what the others do now, but I want you to agree—to come with me.'

'Soren,' Belwynn said, her voice showing a trace of dry humour, 'you haven't said where you want to go yet.'

'The Blood Caladri.'

Belwynn said nothing, waiting for an explanation.

'I have two good reasons. First, the selfish one. Gustav had some knowledge of overextension, which I didn't. You know that overextension breaks the bonds, the bonds that you build up between yourself and the magic you try to control?'

'Yes, you've explained that.'

'Gustav has heard of a method which can repair the bonds. A second wizard can charge their power into you and repair the bonds. Gustav has never done it himself—he says it is a highly dangerous piece of magic. It would be too risky for him to try. But he said the Caladri wizards would know more of the technique. He has spent some time with the Blood Caladri himself.'

Soren produced the insignia Gustav had given him. It was a delicately-crafted silver hawk with runes inscribed upon it. Soren had recognised the runes as Caladri, but could not completely decipher it, though it was clear that the first line read *Gustav the Hawk*. He handed it to his sister.

'He says they would recognise his symbol and grant us passage.'

Belwynn stood for a while, absent-mindedly looking at the silver emblem. Soren knew what his sister was thinking. They were close, and not just because they were twins. They had lost both their parents when young and struggled to keep their family's estates. They had struggled, also, with Soren's gift. It had marked him out as different from a young age, and Belwynn had often had to act as an older sister or a parent, protecting him and hiding his secret.

Soren had needed help with controlling his magic powers. He had been lucky, in the end, to have found Ealdnoth. Wizards were a rare species. To have another living close by was one thing. For Ealdnoth to be open about his magic, to be friendly towards Soren, to be prepared to teach him—that was another; and Soren sometimes wondered what would have happened to him without Ealdnoth.

In the end their master and pupil relationship had come to an end. Ealdnoth had taught him everything he knew. Meanwhile, Edgar had befriended the older man through Soren, and invited him to his court. Soren knew that to improve, to enhance his powers, he had to learn from other wizards, who could teach him new skills and knowledge. He was ambitious. The desire to master magic burned through him. That ambition had led him to go to Delyth, the marsh witch. It had been the right choice as far as his development was concerned. But the experience had changed him, and his relationship with Belwynn had suffered.

Belwynn's voice interrupted Soren's train of thought.

'What is the other reason?'

Soren knew that Belwynn didn't understand his ambition, that she even resented it. Part of her would prefer it if he never tried to get his powers back. She certainly believed that it wasn't worth risking his life over, that he should be happy just to have his health. But Soren also knew that Belwynn would do what he wanted.

'The dagger. Gustav studied it, for a long time. I think he was hoping for a reaction when he touched it a second time, but there was none. He even looked it up in some of his books, but found nothing. But he still feels that it is important, and I agree. He suggested I take it to the Caladri and see what they know of it. They have texts which go back hundreds of years, learned men who could examine it. Once we know what it is, why Ishari would want it, then we can make sensible decisions about what to do with it.'

Soren knew that Gustav had made sense on this. He also knew that Belwynn wouldn't want to walk away after all they had been through. She was as curious about the dagger as he was.

'So be it, Soren. I will come,' she said. 'Let's explain this to the others.'

The conversation with the rest of the group was shorter than Soren had expected. He began by putting forward the case for taking the dagger to the Blood Caladri. Herin and Clarin nodded, as if there was nothing unusual in Soren's suggestion. Elana, in that mysterious way of hers, agreed immediately. She and Dirk would go with them. Gyrmund was not so sure.

'Our task was to take the thing back to Magnia, and its resting place in the Temple of Toric. I don't see where this is all going.'

Belwynn answered him. 'Look, we've completed that task of recovery. I have told Edgar this in my letter. If anyone chooses to go back to South Magnia now, I am sure that Edgar will pay the reward in full. You've done what was asked.

196

No one is asking you to do any more. It's just that some of us need to know what this dagger is.'

Gyrmund looked over at Moneva.

'We need to discuss this,' she said.

Gyrmund and Moneva walked out of the room. Until now, Soren had not really noticed those two becoming so close.

'Soren,' said Rabigar, leaning against the wall, his new eye patch a reminder of the terrible injury inflicted on him in Coldeberg. 'I've made a good physical recovery, thanks to Elana. I can walk and ride fine. I don't know how much use I'll be with my sword any more. I've decided that I would like to see this thing through to the end. It would make things...' The Krykker struggled—to find the right words, perhaps. To control his emotions. 'It would make things seem like there was a purpose. But if you feel I wouldn't be of any help, you only need to say so. I will understand.'

'No,' said Soren immediately. 'I would like you to come.'

'Then I will,' replied Rabigar.

Gyrmund and Moneva re-entered the room.

'We'll go with you to the Caladri,' Moneva said, flashing a quick smile.

Soren felt himself smiling, a bit foolishly, at the show of solidarity from this group, many of whom had been strangers to each other only a week before.

'Well then...' he began, but didn't really know what he was going to say.

'I think everyone should get ready immediately,' began Belwynn, jumping into the silence in her slightly officious way. 'I'm going to see if I can find Rainer and add something to the end of that letter, if Baldwin's ambassador hasn't left yet. Edgar should know what we're up to.'

Belwynn found Rainer in time, and got much more from him besides. Their mounts were sent for from the Imps, and he arranged for supplies and equipment to be provided, including the weaponry of their choice. He also explained that they would have an escort. Duke Ellard and twenty of his retainers were leaving Essenberg at the same time, heading back to Guslar, the capital of his duchy.

It was still morning when Soren, his sister, their friends, and the men of Rotelegen set off north along the Great Road.

XIX

THE ROAD TO WAR

SHIRA WALKED SLOWLY ALONG the stone corridor, her footsteps echoing around the cold, seemingly empty fortress.

She was feeling queasy. She was tired, for one. Yesterday she had led her Haskan troops through Trevenza and Grienna. She smiled to herself. *Like a hot knife through butter.* The Griennese were good talkers, and maybe they had brought the Empire into the fight. But that was all they could do: they barely had an army, and what they had soon melted away when faced with the numbers at Shira's disposal.

She made a left turn, becoming more apprehensive as she went. When she had been given the news that Erkindrix demanded her presence here the next morning, she had actually laughed. How was she supposed to get to Samir Durg within a matter of hours? Now she knew better. Shira mistrusted magic. When the Isharite magi who accompanied her army had explained that they would teleport her to the meeting, she had told them where to go. Empty words, of course. Everyone knew she would do it, for who would refuse the demands of Erkindrix of Ishari?

The magi had worked together on the spell and sent her off. It had lasted hours—hours upon hours of stomach-churning movement. As soon as it began, her vision had left her. When she'd opened her eyes, they would not work, unable to focus on anything as strange lights shot past. She felt the wind on her face, the same sensation as when galloping a horse. Her sense of balance had gone, too. She had the sensation of travelling, but whether she was lying down, upside down, or some other position, she had no idea. When it stopped, Shira found herself lying in a crumpled heap, outside the walls of the fortress. She had retched on the ground. She had retched again, until there was nothing left to bring up. It was morning, and she had travelled all night without sleep.

But Shira was a soldier. She stood up and walked to her meeting.

At the end of the corridor the huge iron gates of the throne room loomed large. Shira made out a figure waiting in the shadows. It was Arioc. So, he had been summoned too. After their successful invasion of Persala, Arioc had been ordered to complete the occupation of the country, destroying any remaining opposition. Shira had been given the task of completing the conquest by taking Trevenza and Grienna. Although only briefly, it had been the first time that she had been put in sole charge of a campaign. She was gradually moving out of Arioc's shadow.

Shira had first met Arioc in her home country of Haskany. She had been attracted to him from the beginning. She was attracted to powerful men, and he was the most powerful she had ever met. Arioc was a great warrior and war leader. Well over six feet tall, he stood above most men in height, but stood above all in sheer presence. Only a few did not succumb totally to his authority. And there was Arioc's Isharite heritage. His legend said he was the son of Erkindrix. If so, he had inherited his father's magical abilities. Shira knew little of magic, but she knew that Arioc had few peers as far as that went.

When she had first met him, nothing had happened. But soon, Arioc's ambitions and those of her family united. Shira's uncle became a close ally, plotting with him to secure the throne upon the death of King Harel. It had been Uncle Koren who had first suggested their marriage, to lend legitimacy to Arioc's seizure of the throne. But playing the part of the good wife had little appeal. When the fighting started, Shira played her part as a soldier. It was only once they had fought together that Arioc and Shira became true lovers.

Shira knew that becoming Arioc's wife and lover might bring her power, but she was unprepared for what followed. Arioc proposed to Erkindrix that she become the new member of the Council of Seven. He had a good argument. The people of Haskany respected, or feared, Arioc. But they could love Shira like they could never love him. Having no magical powers, she posed no real threat to anyone in Ishari either. For Arioc, of course, it would strengthen his position on the Council.

Since becoming King of Haskany, Arioc was increasingly establishing himself as second in command in Ishari. He got his way and Shira—a human, a woman, with no magic—joined the Council of Seven. In a formal meeting of the Council, she was appointed by Erkindrix himself. It was the only time she had met with the leader of Ishari before today. Shira had never felt true fear before that day.

Shira was feeling queasy, but not just from her journey. From dread at what lay beyond the doors.

'I hear congratulations are in order,' said Arioc drily, as Shira approached the doors. 'I've heard about Trevenza and Grienna. You look like shit, by the way.'

'Yes,' replied Shira, barely taking in what he was saying. 'What are we here for? Is it a meeting of the Council?'

Arioc shrugged. 'I don't know why we're here. It's not a Council meeting, though. Just you and me.'

Arioc smiled, appreciating the look on Shira's face as she realised that meant an even closer, more intimate meeting with Erkindrix. She felt angry at his pleasure in her weakness.

She asked Arioc a question she had not dared to ask before.

'You are his son, aren't you?'

The question hung in the air for a while. Eventually, Arioc shrugged again, his face showing little emotion.

'I don't know,' Arioc paused. 'I've never asked.'

An unbelievable answer, but Shira believed it all the same. For a second time, Arioc smiled at the reaction on her face.

'Time to go in,' he said.

Before Shira could say anything, something which might delay proceedings for a few seconds more, Arioc pushed open the doors and walked in.

***

Edgar was feeling pleased with the day's proceedings so far.

The response from his neighbours had been good. Prince Cerdda had come himself. Lord Rosmont, the Cordentine ambassador, was here to represent King Glanna. From the Midder Steppe, two chiefs, Brock and Frayne, had come. Emperor Baldwin's ambassador, Lord Kass, had arrived this morning. He was a heavy-set man with a large stomach and a handlebar moustache that gained a life of its own whenever his mouth moved.

Guivergne had also sent a representative. Bastien, Duke of Morbaine, was brother to King Nicolas. He had attended Edgar's coronation, and they had got on well. Bastien himself was not here, but he had sent a rather brusque, red-headed man named Russell. Edgar had, at first, not taken to Russell, who seemed to be a soldier by trade rather than an ambassador. After a while, however, he began to take his presence as a compliment. Russell was not here to play with words or waste time. He was here to tell Edgar and the others the truth, then report back to the Duke.

Edgar had wanted the numbers at the Conference to be kept down to a minimum, and this had been achieved. He himself had excluded all the nobles of South Magnia, such as Otha and Wulfgar, who had both requested a seat at the table. Ealdnoth and Wilchard were his only advisers.

His guests had followed Edgar's lead. Rosmont and Kass sat alone. Altogether, twelve men sat around a table in Edgar's castle at Granstow, on the border between South and North Magnia. It was a good location for the Conference, but also it made Edgar feel good to be here—the castle which, until recently, had been held by Harbyrt the Fat.

Edgar had sent out invitations for the Conference on the same day he had Harbyrt beheaded.

Edgar was also pleased because Lord Kass had passed on a letter from his cousin, Belwynn. It was the first communication he had received from the group since they had set off over a week ago.

He had not fully digested the contents of the letter. Parts of Belwynn's story sounded strange, and he did not fully understand why she and Soren had decided to head further north rather than bring Toric's Dagger back to Magnia. But the central facts: they had the dagger; they were safe. This was good news.

Lord Kass began the proceedings with a formal request for help from Emperor Baldwin. He then outlined the position the Emperor faced: an enemy much larger in size, a divided Empire, and little prospect of help coming from anywhere else. The Magnians and the Steppe chiefs were eager for all the information from around Dalriya they could get. Lord Kass and Lord Rosmont were often the better informed and therefore did more of the talking.

'In the margins, Ishari has been flexing its muscles for some time now,' Rosmont was saying. 'In the east, the Barbarians have gradually been subjugated by Ardashir, a member of the Council of Seven. He is now pushing into the territory of the Bearmen. The Shadow Caladri have allied with Ishari and are waging war against the Blood Caladri.'

'We believe that King Dorjan of the Shadow Caladri is another member of the Council of Seven,' added Kass, his moustache bouncing about.

'In Halvia, Drobax are raiding the kingdom of Vismar,' continued Rosmont. 'The Vismarians have already lost Alta island to the Kharovians, who now have mastery of the western sea. In the north, King Jonas of Kalinth has all but handed his realm over to Erkindrix. But now Erkindrix and Arioc are putting their cards on the table. The conquest of Persala has drawn Baldwin to the brink of war. The intentions of Ishari are becoming all too clear. They want the whole of Dalriya.'

'The trouble,' began Kass, 'is that the rest of Dalriya is not ready. The Empire is perhaps as much to blame as anyone. The danger from Ishari had become a thing of history. We have become obsessed with our own petty quarrels. Brasingia has warred with Guivergne and the Confederacy. Magnia has fought itself. The Caladri and the Krykkers have left the humans to themselves and become insular. Now that the threat has returned, there is no alliance to withstand it. My Emperor, Baldwin, has realised this. He hopes it is not too late.'

Edgar nodded. 'As do I, Lord Kass. I want to ask: you refer to the previous threat Ishari posed this land. For me, this is a story passed down from so long ago it has more the feel of legend than history. But I feel that we should now learn all we can from it.'

Kass chuckled. 'I agree, Prince Edgar, but the legends I was told round the fire of an evening are likely to be no more illuminating than yours. If anyone here can teach us, perhaps it would be Lord Ealdnoth?'

Ealdnoth nodded. 'It is history, not legend. But it is a history from hundreds and hundreds of years ago. A time before humankind recorded events through writing—or at least such writing has not survived. If written accounts do survive, they were written by the Caladri.'

Ealdnoth took a breath, pausing before recounting his knowledge.

'This was a time before the humans had spread throughout Dalriya as they have now. Before the Persaleian Empire was created—perhaps before Persala itself. The Caladri held lands that stretched from north to south. The Krykkers built their kingdoms in the north and west. The Lippers cultivated much of the south, including modern-day Magnia. And, of course, Dalriya was much larger than now, for she and Halvia were one.

'The Isharites invaded. The humans had arrived in Dalriya by sea. The Isharites arrived from another world, transporting themselves here by magic. A terrible war of survival followed, when the Isharites aimed to take Dalriya for themselves. The people of Dalriya united together. If I were to stick to true history, then I know nothing else for sure except the end of this war. A great battle between the two sides was fought in the centre of the continent. Incredible magic forces were released. The cracking of the world was the result. In the stories, we are victorious. But what does history really tell us? This great conflict seemed to end the war, but it was not decisive. We survived, but so did Ishari.

Not a victory, then. More like a bitter truce. That truce has lasted hundreds of years, but the Isharites, it seems, have not forgotten. They have been waiting. The truce is over. I don't know why it has happened now. But we should know that Ishari wants total victory—Dalriya for themselves only.'

The formal meeting lasted until the end of lunch. It was then agreed that they would hold a series of breakout meetings, where small groups could discuss their goals in the hope that they would all be able to forge a deal that everyone could sign up to by the end of the day. After talking with Cerdda and Russell at first, Edgar found himself alone with Ealdnoth, waiting for news from others.

'No one has really needed persuading that Ishari represents a threat to all of us,' Ealdnoth commented.

'Yes,' agreed Edgar. 'But does that mean they'll do anything about it? I want them to commit troops. Russell has already said that Bastien will not send troops without the agreement of King Nicolas.'

'That was always likely, Edgar,' said Ealdnoth. 'Guivergne were never going to give any of its soldiers to Baldwin. To be fair, Nicolas will doubtless be concerned about his own borders.'

Wilchard entered the room. Edgar noted at once that he was trying to conceal a grin.

'Well?' he demanded.

'I've just spoken to Prince Cerdda. Seems like he's been testing out Lord Kass. He's drawn a commitment from Kass—Baldwin will pay half the wages of any troops we send once they arrive in Brasingia. Cerdda says he'll discuss precise numbers with us, but he is prepared to match ours, within reason.'

'Great,' said Edgar. 'A fair enough demand, since Baldwin will in reality have command over any soldiers we send. Go back; see if he'll agree to two thousand each. What about the others?'

Wilchard frowned. 'Well, I'm not sure yet. Brock and Frayne are in a private meeting with Rosmont. I tried to find out what was going on. Rosmont was polite enough, but beneath all of his pleasantries he basically told me to get lost. I don't know what they're up to.'

'Speak to Cerdda. Ask him whether he has a leader for his forces in mind. Do your best to find anything else out.'

The North Magnians were on board. But Edgar wanted more. He waited for an hour. Wilchard came back and forth, but there was no more news from

Rosmont and the Middians. Edgar wanted them to commit. If King Glanna were to send troops to fight for the Empire, it would effectively be a declaration of war against Ishari and Haskany. Edgar wanted as many rulers as possible to join with the Empire now. It would encourage the other powers in Dalriya to do the same.

But Edgar waited, and no news came. Wilchard would enter the room and shrug. Lord Rosmont would not be disturbed. And then Wilchard arrived a final time. His shoulders did not shrug this time, and his mouth was twitching into a smile.

'Lords Rosmont, Brock and Frayne send news,' he began. 'They are making us privy to a private agreement between Cordence and the two tribes. It amounts to this. The Middians match our commitment and provide a total of two thousand mounted fighters, which Brock will lead himself. Cordence has agreed to pay for all expenses incurred.' Wilchard smiled sardonically. 'The sum involved was not disclosed.'

Edgar nodded. 'I shouldn't be surprised. The Cordentines have managed to get on board without actually sending any troops. The Middian chiefs are making a profit out of it. So be it—the result is a substantial number of well-trained fighters. Wilchard, can you organise a final meeting with everyone present? We need to sort out logistics.' Edgar smiled grimly at Ealdnoth and Wilchard. 'The second army I will raise in the space of two weeks. And unlike the first, this one is going to see action.'

***

The vaulted ceiling of the throne room rose so high above them that Shira almost felt herself losing her balance when she looked upwards. At the top, it was finished with a gold dome, that could be seen from virtually anywhere in the fortress of Samir Durg. She turned her attention to the throne itself.

Situated in the centre of the room, the carved red crystal shone uninvitingly, drawing the eye nonetheless. Shira felt her feet move in that direction, alongside Arioc. Her eyes flickered on to the small, crumpled figure occupying the throne before she forced them to look at the second figure present, standing to one side. Siavash, High Priest of Ishari and fellow council member to Shira and Arioc, was wearing the hooded black cloak of his order. The Order of Diis was a powerful but secretive sect in Ishari. Shira knew little of their ways, but understood that they had a special relationship to Erkindrix, making Siavash a commanding figure. Even Arioc treated him with care.

Before she knew it, Shira and Arioc were standing before the throne. The fetid smell of decay assaulted her nostrils, and it was all she could do to stop herself from gagging. Someone had scented the throne, or Erkindrix himself, with a sweet, cloying perfume, but it did nothing to hide the smell.

Erkindrix was living in a dying body. It had been rotting away for years, kept alive only by his immense magical powers. It was clear to Shira, however, that even such magic could not hold back time forever.

Erkindrix turned to look at Shira full in the face. Shira now had to look back, without revealing her disgust. His flesh was not lined and wrinkly like the elderly she knew in Haskany. For the most part it was grey and waxy, but frequently interrupted by red and black sores. Shira could see a sore on his neck oozing with yellowish-green pus. This was unpleasant, but Shira had seen much worse after a battle.

The eyes, which looked at hers, were grey and watery, almost lifeless. But once Shira looked into those eyes, she could see the second pair of eyes, staring back. Like burning black coals, they fired alive once they realised that they had been seen.

Shira felt them boring into her, feasting on her, as her chest tightened. The black eyes would know everything about her.

Hard and bruising, they interrogated her. Her body, her private parts, her private thoughts—nothing could be hidden from them.

The eyes abruptly withdrew. Shira controlled a little convulsion. She wanted to scream out, turn around, and run. Now she could see more of the second face, moving and rippling beneath the pallid grey surface of Erkindrix's skin.

Shira experienced what true fear was. A fear that no human could ever cause or recreate, deep and primeval, spirit-sapping. Shira's being knew instinctively that this was a creature she should never have met.

But Shira stood still, looking at Erkindrix.

'You have my congratulations, Shira,' said Erkindrix, his voice stronger and harder than should have been possible when one saw his weak and crumpled form. He dribbled as he spoke, as if he had too much moisture in his mouth.

'Thank you, My Lord,' Shira responded. 'Trevenza and Grienna are secure. We need to fortify our position on the Brasingian border.'

Erkindrix turned away, as if he had not heard her. He fixed his gaze on Arioc. Shira turned to look at Arioc and wondered at his ability to remain composed and nonchalant in front of such a sight.

'You have not found King Mark.'

'No,' replied Arioc. 'Persala is secure but Mark has not been found. I don't know if he's alive or dead.'

'Persala is not secure if King Mark is alive,' retorted Erkindrix sharply.

Arioc said nothing.

'Our enemies are becoming aware of our power and may try to unite against us,' began Erkindrix. 'The time for secrecy is now over. We must finish the process quickly. I have decided to move against our two greatest enemies simultaneously. Arioc, you will leave Persala and plan the destruction of the Grand Caladri. The magi of Ishari and one third of the Drobax will be at your disposal.'

Shira could not help but take a sharp intake of breath. The Grand Caladri were the greatest of their race, heirs of a civilisation which had stood in Dalriya for centuries, a place of great learning and magic. Erkindrix had dismissed them to oblivion in a sentence. Even Arioc showed surprise, his expression changed to pleasure as he considered the enormity of the task given him.

The leader of Ishari turned back to Shira herself.

'Shira, you will continue south and occupy the Brasingian Empire.'

A thrill coursed down Shira's body. What an honour! This was better than Persala. Persala had been an overripe fruit, easy to pluck. Its greatness was in the past. The Empire would be a different, far worthier opponent. And in Persala she had been Arioc's number two. This time Shira, a girl from Haskany, would be the one to bring the Empire to its knees.

She trembled again at the thought. This was too good!

'You will command the Haskan army. I will also divert one third of the Drobax to your command.'

Shira reacted instantly. Her disgust at the thought of commanding those creatures prompting her to challenge the dread Erkindrix.

'I don't need the Drobax. They are not soldiers. I can take the Empire with the Haskan forces.'

'You misunderstand me. The time for human warfare, for pitched battles and sieges—that time is over. This is Ishari's war. You will use both the Haskans and the Drobax. The fall of the Empire must be quick, decisive, and inevitable. The humans' defiance must be totally crushed.'

Shira nodded her acquiescence, not quite believing that she had dared to argue in the first place. Her excitement at the charge given her had been dulled slightly by the knowledge of how it would be done. One thing was certain, however.

The Brasingian Empire would fall.

XX

SECRET PATHS

G YRMUND'S EXCITEMENT MOUNTED as they left behind the last traces of human habitation and moved ever closer towards the alien lands of the Caladri.

It had been a tiring two day of travelling. On the first day Duke Ellard of Rotelegen had led them at a hard pace, northwards along the Great Road. He was a tough old boot of a soldier and had a clear schedule which he always kept to when travelling between Essenberg and Guslar. At midday they stopped at the town of Appen, where he had his own stables. He had enough spares to swap everyone's mount before they headed off again. By the end of the day they had reached Herdorf, not far from Ellard's duchy.

The next morning, they set off at the same pace, leaving Kelland for Rotelegen. To the west they could see the formidable, brooding presence of Burkhard Castle. As the castle retreated into the distance, they were met by a small group of Rotelegen soldiers, bearing weighty news for their duke.

The Haskan army had invaded Trevenza and Grienna and the vanguard was stationed on Ellard's northern border. Given that the two provinces had recently been incorporated into the Empire, the two states were now at war. If the Haskans continued further south, Rotelegen was clearly the next target.

It was at this point that Ellard curtly made his farewell and his force galloped off at an even faster pace. The threat from Ishari and Haskany suddenly seemed very real to Gyrmund. Although he and the others went their separate way, Gyrmund at least felt that what they were doing was part of the same fight that Ellard was involved in.

Gyrmund took his group at a slower pace than the Duke had led them. There was no point pushing them to reach the land of the Blood Caladri that evening. It was better to give them one last night in a decent bed before stepping into the unknown.

They headed east, entering Luderia by midday. The roads turned into paths as they pushed into the sparsely populated northern part of the duchy. Gyrmund was familiar with this part of the Empire and knew it to be different from the farming regions of Barissia and Kelland. The Luderian Forest covered the land—miles upon miles of pine trees, inhabited by only a few woodsmen. To the east, the run-off from the Karnica mountain range had created wetlands. Here lived the Sparewaldi tribe, largely independent from the rest of the duchy. Gyrmund had spent half a year living with the tribe. They lived a good life from river and lake fishing and burned peat for fuel. The quiet, slow pace of life had done him good, and he still felt a sense of regret for having left.

It was evening when they reached the village of Guben. The White Boar Inn had been recommended by a couple of travellers as one of the last places big enough to sleep and feed them all with comfort.

The White Boar served a simple vegetable pottage with huge chunks of dark bread. They were so famished that they wolfed it all down. Gyrmund could see that Elana could barely stay awake long enough to eat. She went to bed immediately after the meal, as did Rabigar and Dirk. The others stayed up awhile to talk with the innkeeper and his guests.

It was only natural for them to ask Gyrmund and the others where they were going. When Herin confidently replied that they were headed to the Blood Caladri, a lively conversation followed, with much advice given.

The innkeeper seemed worried for them. 'You're not invited? If you're not invited, you won't be coming back. The Caladri don't let strangers come and go in their lands—you must know that. They want to protect their secret paths, don't they? To their cities.'

'He's right,' joined in one of the regulars, who seemed to be glued to a stool at the bar. 'There's a few in these parts disappear each year. They get too far into the forest and aren't heard of again.'

'Some say they don't kill 'em. They just don't let them leave. Have to live amongst the Caladri 'til they die.'

'Well, anyone who gets caught by the Caladri is plain stupid,' said an old man, nestled by the fire. 'They've got poles up in the forest, marking their territory. There's writing on 'em, in their own language sure enough, but the message is plain and simple. Don't go any farther. If you go farther, you're invading their territory. Shouldn't expect to come back alive.'

'Whose side are you taking, Trevor?' countered an angry woman. 'We want Duke Arne to show his face round here with an army at his back. That would sort the Caladri out.'

'You ignorant woman,' responded Trevor. 'We've had peace here for generations. It works because we respect them and leave them alone, and they do the same. You all know what happened to my brother. Now there was a stupid man. We was out hunting in the forest and he got himself too close to a boar. Nearly sliced him in two. I couldn't move him. He was dying on me. Then three Caladri came along and dressed up his wounds. Used these special medicines on him. I seen them do it with my own eyes. They're an old, wise people.' The old man turned to face Gyrmund and the others. 'They don't need folk barging into their lands for no good reason.'

'We've got good reasons,' Gyrmund heard himself say, almost before he realised he was speaking. 'You know that the Empire is under threat. We may need the help of the Caladri.'

'Hmm…' pondered the old man. 'I can understand that. I just don't see why they should stir themselves to help us out.'

***

Farred turned in the saddle to look behind him. Over a thousand mounted troops waited there. His army.

He had burst with pride when Prince Edgar had first asked him to lead the South Magnian troops. It was a sign of how close they had become since the attack on the Temple of Toric ten days ago. Edgar had turned down a number of other noblemen who had demanded the position. He had insisted on Farred being the right man for the job. The good relationship Farred had built with Cerdda was also important, given that troops from both countries would have to work together. His Middian heritage was another quality in his favour. It was the chance he had been waiting for, to rise above his position as a middling lord on the outskirts of the realm.

After a while, other thoughts had crept in to Farred's thinking. His prince had given him a difficult mission. The Empire was in serious danger from Haskany and Ishari. Farred and his men would soon be in the middle of that. What would happen when Farred and his men reached the Empire? How would Emperor Baldwin treat them once they were there? There were uncertainties ahead. But there was doubtless action as well. And Farred was ready for it. He thought of Gyrmund, journeying around Dalriya on his adventures. Now it was his turn.

210

In recent hours he had enjoyed little time for further reflection. Farred wanted as large a proportion of the South Magnian troops to be as personally loyal to him as possible. He travelled to his homeland on the border between Magnia and the Midder Steppe. The fighting men from his own estate formed the nucleus of his force. He then recruited from his friends and neighbours, men who could be vouched for and who knew him. Edgar was offering excellent wages for recruits, but insisted that each supply their own mount, armour and weaponry. This reduced the pool of potential soldiers, but did ensure that only those with a decent level of training were likely to sign up.

When Farred returned to Bidcote, Edgar had also managed to raise around five hundred mounted soldiers. They were mostly young sons of noblemen, eager for glory. This made them naïve but well equipped and, in the main, well trained. This combined force was now ready to head north. Wilchard, Edgar's steward, had ridden north immediately after the Southern Conference. He had been given the task of raising around another thousand soldiers. This was to be done by gathering the only permanent army in the kingdom: those men who were stationed as guards in the castles on the border with North Magnia. These men would be career soldiers, though perhaps, thought Farred, less than keen to leave their easy existence for the obvious dangers in the Empire. Since Edgar already paid their wages, however, they had to go where he asked. Cerdda of North Magnia was using his border soldiers for the same purpose, leaving both sides of the border undefended.

This would become the full contribution of troops from South Magnia. The Conference had agreed that all troops raised should be mounted, since it would be a long journey north. Farred would lead his force to the north-east corner of the kingdom. Here the forces of South and North Magnia and the Steppe would combine to make six thousand. Prince Cerdda's own brother, Ashere, was leading the North Magnians, and Brock was leading the fighters from his tribe. It was hoped that Bastien of Morbaine could arrange safe passage for the force to travel through Guivergne on its way to Kelland. This would help them to avoid trouble from the rebellious Duke Emeric.

The moment to leave had arrived fast. Farred trotted forwards. Ahead, a scaffold had been erected. The flag of Magnia, the Sun in Glory, had been draped around it to create a kind of rostrum. It was an image rarely used in recent years, since it represented the whole of Magnia; neither Edgar nor Cerdda had been willing to use it very often. But Edgar had requested it for this occasion, since troops from both countries would be fighting together in one army.

He waited on top of the scaffold with other notable persons of the realm, ready to give his blessing to Farred's army. Underneath it stood the more ordinary folk of Magnia, seeing off their loved ones. Farred nodded to the noblemen and churchmen atop the scaffold, some of whom solemnly nodded back; others gave an encouraging welcome; yet others studiously ignored him. Succeed in this venture, thought Farred, and they could not afford to ignore him in the future.

Edgar moved forwards and they clasped hands.

'Are you ready, Farred?' asked the Prince.

Farred nodded. 'Ready.'

'You will meet up with Prince Ashere soon. You must make sure to give him every courtesy as befits his rank. Defer to him when possible, but control over my troops ultimately rests with you. In the Empire, the same applies in your dealings with Baldwin. Is that clear?'

'It is clear, Your Highness.'

Edgar grasped his shoulder. 'Good luck.'

Farred nodded. He walked his horse a few feet away from the rostrum. He drew his sword and held it in the air. A cheer rose up. Farred's army began to move.

$$***$$

'This is as far as we go,' said Trevor.

Belwynn and the others looked over to the old man they had met last night in the inn. They had been travelling for about three hours. He and a couple of younger men from the inn had taken them along a route which they had said would get them to the lands of the Caladri quickly. They had passed by the odd cottage at first, where woodsmen eked out a lonely existence. The countryside north of the inn was not suitable for arable farming, but Belwynn observed that most people kept pigs, who were left to their own devices to forage and root amongst the trees. As they moved further into the forest, human habitation ended and any pigs they saw were wild ones. The going got slower and slower as their horses were forced to pick their way through denser and denser cover.

He nodded ahead.

'Up there, you can make out one of the Caladri poles.'

Belwynn looked ahead and could just make out a light brown wooden pole which had previously blended in with the trees around it. She looked at Soren and he nodded back.

They all dismounted and took what they needed from the saddlebags of their mounts. They were leaving yet another set of horses behind. Trevor had agreed to take the horses in return for guiding them here. He had also promised to sell them back at a reasonable price if they came back, but he didn't seem very convinced that was likely to happen, and Belwynn had the same feeling.

Trevor and his two colleagues gathered the nine mounts. 'Good luck,' he murmured, the others nodding silently in their direction. With that they turned around, looking relieved to be heading back in the direction they had come.

Belwynn watched them leave until they were no longer visible before turning around to the others. They stood around looking at each other, less than eager to press on. To Belwynn they looked like nine little children who had got lost in the woods.

'Let's take a look at this pole, then,' suggested Herin.

He marched off in that direction.

One by one, they followed him.

As Belwynn approached the pole, she could see that it stood in a small cleared circle within the forest, suggesting that it was maintained fairly regularly. It stood approximately two-thirds the height of the biggest trees around it. Gyrmund was talking to Clarin and pointing to his left. Belwynn followed his finger and could just make out a second, similarly-designed pole in the distance. Curious, she looked in the other direction and saw yet another.

Soren was studying the inscriptions on the pole, carved in and coloured in with inks. There were a series of pictures running down it. At the top of the series was the largest image—a three-dimensional face. Belwynn was struck by it, for in many respects it resembled a human face, and yet clearly it was not. She knew she was looking at the carved face of a Caladri.

She took a while to study it and identify what made it different. The face was tilted upwards slightly. It began with a pointed chin and thin lips. The nose was hooked and the eyes full circles. Belwynn felt that she could stare at this alien face for hours and remain fascinated, but she made herself look at the other carvings on the pole.

Beneath the face were three smaller and less detailed pictures: a skull; a knife dripping with blood; another face, neither human nor Caladri, but some kind of devil with glaring red eyes. Clearly these were designed to scare off or warn people who came across them.

Beneath the pictures was a short piece of carved writing, but the characters were undecipherable to Belwynn. Soren was studying it.

'Do you know what it says?' she asked him.

Moneva and Dirk looked up at the question and moved closer. Belwynn felt a certain amount of pride in her brother, since both held expressions of surprise at the idea that Soren might be able to understand the strange looking characters.

'Just about…it is mostly straightforward. The first line says *Turn around, walk away, do not look back and you will live*. The second is *Or face ahead, walk on and you will…* I don't know what the last word means.'

Dirk shrugged. '*You will die* seems to fit.'

Soren smiled. 'Yes, that's possible…but it's not a word for death that I've come across.'

'Well,' said Moneva, 'seems to me a bit of a waste of time to carve a message in characters which no one will understand.'

Moneva had a point and, growing bored with the pole, the group pressed on into the lands of the Blood Caladri. Gyrmund, as usual, led from the front, though Belwynn wondered why; he had already admitted that this was one part of Dalriya he had not visited before. Rabigar walked next to him. Soren had suggested that the Blood Caladri might be curious if they saw a Krykker in the party and be more likely to refrain from killing them on the spot. Rabigar had looked at him sceptically, but took his position at the front willingly enough.

They walked into the forest for three hours. There were no paths, since humans did not enter the lands of the Caladri and, according to the folk at the inn last night, they did not leave either. Gyrmund took care to follow the easiest route, but the going was difficult. The forest itself was pleasant enough, having nothing like the oppressive quality of the Wilderness. After travelling so far so fast on horseback, however, Belwynn found the current pace frustrating. The knowledge that they did not actually know where they were going made things worse. The others were getting equally fed up and Belwynn asked for a rest.

'This is hard work,' she commented. 'This may turn into a long journey before we reach the inhabited part of the forest.'

'This was a stupid idea,' said Herin, less constructively. 'We've only gone a mile or two in all this time. We're bumbling around like a bunch of idiots.'

'If you have a better idea where we're going, feel free to take the lead,' said Gyrmund defensively.

'That's the point, isn't it?' replied Herin irritably. 'None of us know where the hell we're going. We don't know of a town or city. Finding a settlement in this forest is like finding a needle in a haystack. We could spend the next month here walking around and not find one stinking Caladri.'

'True,' said Gyrmund. 'We're going to have to wait for them to come to us.'

'And if they don't?' asked Clarin.

Gyrmund shrugged.

'They'll have to find us first,' Belwynn considered, thinking that they might have to do something to draw attention to themselves.

'They already know we're here,' said Gyrmund.

'What do you mean?' said Belwynn.

'What are you talking about?' demanded Herin.

'I think they've been following us for a while now,' explained Gyrmund.

'Why didn't you bloody say so?' shouted Herin, getting increasingly angry.

'You didn't ask,' Gyrmund responded calmly.

Herin drew his sword.

'Oh Toric, not more hysterics, Herin,' complained Belwynn.

Gyrmund backed away, his hand on his sword hilt.

'I haven't seen anyone, and my eyesight's as good as yours,' said Clarin.

'Perhaps, but do you know what you're looking for?' asked Gyrmund.

'This idiot is pushing us too far,' growled Herin, pacing forwards as Gyrmund walked backwards. 'How do we know he's seen anyone?'

There was sudden movement about them.

A form appeared out of the forest behind Gyrmund, and before Belwynn could shout out, Gyrmund had a knife at his neck.

There were about a dozen other figures surrounding them, with bows drawn and arrows aimed at them. The Blood Caladri had found them.

'Now do you believe we're here?' asked the Caladri who had his knife pressed against Gyrmund's neck.

Belwynn looked about her, fearful that with one word the arrows pointed at them would be loosed to find their targets. She was still able, however, to take some pleasure in the look of total surprise on Gyrmund's face.

Soren fumbled about in his cloak; two Caladri were training their arrows on him should he try something.

He produced Gustav's signet, the silver hawk with runic inscriptions, and handed it to the nearest Caladri. The Caladri soldier studied it briefly and showed it to his leader, who still had his knife at Gyrmund's throat. The leader had a look himself before turning back to Soren.

'What are you doing here?' he demanded.

'We are representatives of Emperor Baldwin of Brasingia and of Prince Edgar of Magnia. The primary purpose of our visit here is to discuss with King Tibor the shared threat from Ishari, and how our peoples can help each other.'

The head Caladri stared at Soren for a few seconds, as if doing so would tell him whether Soren was lying or not.

'It seems as though you have important business,' he decided. 'King Tibor is a long way from here. His son, Prince Lorant, is close by. We will escort you to *him*.'

With that, and with no other introductions, the Caladri leader released Gyrmund.

'We require that you give your weapons to us.'

After a confusing few seconds, Rabigar acted first, and handed his sword to the nearest Caladri soldier, who decided it was easiest to sling his bow over one shoulder and carry the sword in his hands. Belwynn and the others followed his lead.

Satisfied, the Caladri turned around and headed in a north-westerly direction. They spread out in a fan shape, not bothering to give Belwynn's group a second look.

'Right,' said Soren, seemingly to himself as much as to anyone else, 'We'll just follow them. Be careful. I think that little argument between Herin and Gyrmund was ...*encouraged*. They have at least one wizard amongst them.'

Herin and Gyrmund glared at each other, but the anger seemed to have gone.

So, Belwynn thought to herself, we're walking through the forest again. At least they were now being led by the Caladri, to a specific location. Despite carrying two sets of weapons, while Belwynn and her friends carried none, they set a quick pace.

As she settled in to her walking again, Belwynn took the time to study the first real-life Caladri she had seen.

The carved face on the pole she had examined was a very accurate representation. Indeed, she could see that, compared to humans, their faces were sort of tilted at a slight angle, giving the impression that they were always looking down their noses at people. To them, she guessed, humans might appear to have rather flat faces. Their hair, like humans, could be blonde or dark or red, but the fashion among these male Caladri was to grow it long to their shoulders. Most of them tied it up or braided it to keep it out of their faces.

The body structure of the Caladri was also different. Most noticeable was the feet: four long digits ending in claws. They walked barefoot and put their weight on these four toes rather than on the rest of the foot. It gave them a more broken, bird-like gait than the smoother walking motion of Belwynn's group, but it seemed to allow them to travel at a quick pace. They were, on average, a couple of inches smaller than humans, and had noticeably thinner frames. Their arms and legs looked so thin to Belwynn that they might snap if pressed too hard, yet clearly, they were strong enough. One of them was carrying Clarin's huge sword, resting the flat end on his shoulder as he navigated his way through the forest.

The Caladri did not stop for rest or food, and Belwynn and the others ate their lunch as they walked. The interest Belwynn had in the Caladri eventually began to wane and the journey once more became a drain. The Caladri, clearly forest dwellers, were used to the dense foliage and seemed able to find obstruction free pathways without even looking for them. The others, save perhaps for Gyrmund, were not doing so well. Although they were, in theory, simply following the path the Caladri at the front were taking, they tripped on snags and undergrowth, slipped in the permanently-damp forest floor, and jammed their feet in holes in the ground, which the forest seemed to have deliberately covered over with leaves. Belwynn noticed that Moneva, in particular, was increasingly swearing under her breath. When Gyrmund reached over a hand to guide her along, she snatched her arm away from him and continued to run through the long list of expletives she knew.

Then, sometime around mid-afternoon, Belwynn found that the Caladri had led them onto a stone path. It was more than a path worn into the forest floor by feet; it had the look of something deliberately created, being wide enough for five people to walk side by side. Belwynn supposed that it was the equivalent of a road.

None of the Caladri made any comment on the introduction of a new surface to their guests. They didn't talk amongst themselves, either.

The journey continued on foot on the Caladri path, in silence. The Caladri still walked in a kind of triangular formation, so that while the leaders at the front walked on the road, most of the Caladri were scattered to either side, seemingly happy enough to keep walking on the forest floor.

After thirty minutes they reached a way station. A large timber building had been constructed a few feet from the road, along with several smaller ones. In the yard between the road and the building there waited a couple of huge carriages. Four powerful-looking male gaur were connected to the front carriage, which in turn was attached to the rear one; both of them large-wheeled, roofed, and luxurious looking.

The group approached and then stopped on the road while the leader of the Caladri soldiers walked over and entered the building. Three minutes passed in silence. The remaining Caladri soldiers seemed disinterested in the proceedings and in their human guests. Belwynn found this surprising, since she and the others could not stop themselves from staring at the strangeness of them.

After three minutes the leader returned. He uttered a few commands to his soldiers; each of them walked over and handed back the weapons they had been carrying to their rightful owners. The Caladri who approached Belwynn held up her sword, balanced on his palms.

'Thank you,' she said, taking the handle and lifting the weapon.

The Caladri inclined his head in recognition, but said nothing.

'We are leaving you here now,' the leader said to everyone. 'Good day.'

With that, the troop of Caladri soldiers turned around and walked back in the direction they had come. Belwynn turned around again to look in the direction of the building, anticipating that they were a responsibility which had now been passed on to someone else. Sure enough, there was another Caladri now waiting to greet them. He stood by the gaur, where steps on the carriage led up to the driver's platform.

'Greetings,' he began. This Caladri was not dressed as a soldier, but wore leather leggings and top. 'My name is Gyuri. I will now transport you to the camp of Prince Lorant. You are most welcome in the lands of the Caladri. I may apologise if, so far, you have not been treated as honourable guests.' Gyuri waved in the direction of the departing soldiers. 'They are soldiers, yes? Not diplomats.'

Gyuri smiled.

'We will load up this carriage and then depart. If there is anything you want, please ask us. We have toilets inside, if you wish.'

As Gyuri finished speaking, six more Caladri arrived by the carriage: three men and three women. Belwynn was approached by one of the women and ushered over to the second carriage.

'Hello, my name is Marika. The ladies will be travelling in this coach.'

Moneva and Elana had joined Belwynn, each of them gathered by the other two female Caladri.

'Toilet?' asked one of the women.

Moneva rolled her eyes. 'Yes,' she said bluntly.

Moneva and Elana were taken towards the timber building, while Belwynn and Marika stood outside the carriage. Belwynn looked over to the second carriage, where the men were being organised in the same manner. She turned her attention to the gaur. Gyuri was patting their heads and talking to them, seemingly in preparation for the journey.

'You like?' asked Marika, smiling sweetly. 'Come.'

Marika took Belwynn's hand in hers and walked her over to them. Belwynn was taken aback by the physical contact, especially since the Caladri soldiers had been so aloof. She allowed herself to be led, however. Marika stroked the neck of the nearest gaur, on the rear right side, whispering into its ear. They had big, strong shoulders and curved horns on their heads, and Belwynn approached with care. Their tails whipped constantly, and they breathed heavily. Encouraged by Marika, she stroked the neck of the same animal. It turned its head to look at her and she felt its breath. As she made eye contact Belwynn felt that she sensed a greater intelligence there than in human-bred cattle.

Once everyone was ready, they entered the two carriages—men in the front and women in the rear. The six Caladri accompanied them, while Gyuri clambered up into the driver's seat and led them off.

The wooden interior of the carriage was painted in a floral design. It was designed to hold perhaps ten or twelve passengers and was therefore very roomy, allowing everyone to relax on the upholstered benches and cushions. It had been perfumed with an exotic smell that Belwynn had never come across before. Belwynn sat with Moneva and Elana on one bench, facing the three Caladri women.

The Caladri introduced themselves. Beside Marika sat Dora and Emese. They explained that they were all young women who worked on the transport system. This involved looking after the animals, supplies, and the needs of travellers.

'How old you are?' asked Moneva in her direct manner.

'We are all in our thirties,' answered Dora.

'But,' added Marika, 'Caladri live longer lives than humans, don't they?' Her two friends nodded.

'How long?' demanded Moneva.

'On average, perhaps one hundred and fifty years,' replied Dora.

Belwynn took a sharp breath. 'That's more than twice as long as humans,' she said.

The three Caladri looked sad for the human women. Marika leaned over and stroked Belwynn's hair, seemingly to make her feel better. It was the second time the Caladri had been a bit overly familiar. Belwynn looked over at Moneva and Elana, who held the same quizzical expressions on their faces as she did.

'It may be that Caladri mature more slowly than humans?' suggested Elana.

'Then you are the equivalent of human teenagers?' Belwynn asked Marika.

She shrugged. 'Perhaps so.'

The Caladri provided them with drinks and food. There was water and fruit juice, which the Caladri mixed together. To eat there was more fruit, as well as nuts and seeds. As the carriage gathered pace they ate and drank and grew more comfortable with each other, the conversation becoming more relaxed and wide ranging. Unlike the male soldiers, Belwynn saw that these women were at least as curious about Belwynn and the others as she was about them. They asked about their families, about the human cities and kingdoms and their way of life. They were curious about their looks and not shy about it. More than once one of the Caladri would reach across and touch someone's hand, hair, or face with an almost childlike curiosity. They giggled a lot, confirming Elana's perception that they were in some ways younger than their thirty years.

Marika asked which of the men were theirs. It was an interesting question. In the event, Moneva answered that none of the men were 'theirs' in the sense of being a partner. The Caladri were confused by this, wondering aloud why three women were travelling with five men who were not their spouses or relations. Belwynn confirmed that this was unusual in human society as well. It became clear that the three Caladri men in the next carriage were the partners of the three Caladri women, but not yet, they made clear, married husbands. They would wait awhile for that ceremony which, as with humans, meant that they were committed to that person for life and would have children.

Belwynn wondered idly, to herself, about Marika's question. The answer to it was more complicated than Moneva's answer had admitted. If she were to pick a partner for Moneva, she would have immediately answered Gyrmund, for it was clear to Belwynn and to most of the others that the two had formed a special friendship of some kind. For Elana, perhaps it would be Dirk, since he was an attentive follower of hers and, Belwynn sometimes wondered, perhaps had deeper feelings for the priestess. And her man? It could be Clarin. He had made it clear, in his own way, that he was interested in her. He had not, though, done anything in particular about it. Belwynn, she admitted to herself, was confused about what she wanted. Their relationship, therefore, was one of perpetual, albeit buried, tension.

As the conversation in the carriage died down, and Belwynn found herself getting drowsier, she was content to gaze at the three Caladri women. All three were beautiful creatures, slim and delicate in body and features, and she wondered if they would be attractive to most human men. The clawed feet were surely a bit of a turn off. The Caladri men certainly held no appeal to her. Their thin yet powerful bodies, their pronounced features, while arresting, could hardly be considered physically attractive. She wondered what the Caladri made of them.

It was in this cosy and contented frame of mind that the last part of the day's journey passed. Before Belwynn knew it, they had stopped, and Marika was helping her down from the carriage.

Outside the light was fading. They found themselves in a part of the forest which, to Belwynn, looked exactly the same as that which they had left. In the distance they could see triangular tents, presumably the camp of Prince Lorant. Marika and the others said goodbye, but promised that they would try to visit with them again tomorrow. They, and their three men, stayed behind to sort out the carriage and gaur. Gyuri led them off towards the camp.

Belwynn fell in stride next to Soren.

'Did you have a good journey?' she asked.

Soren smiled. 'Yes, thanks, very comfortable.'

'And your hosts?' Belwynn asked.

Soren's mouth twisted to one side. 'They were very friendly, just…maybe a bit too friendly.'

Herin, walking in front, turned around. 'One of them tried to give my legs a massage!' he exclaimed, his face a mixture of anger and concern as he recalled the encounter.

Soren and the others chuckled at the incident.

Belwynn smiled. It sounded like the men had enjoyed a similar experience to theirs.

They approached the Caladri tents. They consisted of long strips of timber formed into a circular shape at the base. At the top they leaned into each other to form a roof and were tied off with rope to keep secure. Finally, a large strip of canvas had been placed over the top, with a hole which fitted over the pointed roof. Each was individual, being a different height, width and colour from its neighbour. Many of the Caladri were sitting outside their tents in small numbers, with individual fires burning. They talked quietly or listened as others played music and sang.

Gyuri passed without comment, leading them towards the centre of the camp. Many of the Caladri stopped what they were doing as they passed, staring at the Krykker and the humans and whispering to one another.

They approached a large tent, guarded by soldiers. Gyuri and one of the soldiers went into the tent, presumably to fetch the prince.

Instead, he returned with a female Caladri. She approached the group.

'Greetings, visitors,' she said. 'My name is Hajna. I am the wife of Prince Lorant.'

She was blonde and blue-eyed, older, and carrying more authority than Marika and the others. Belwynn found it difficult to guess her age, but felt sure that she was the most captivating looking woman she had ever seen. Hajna smiled and nodded politely as she waited for Belwynn and the others to introduce themselves in turn. Finally, she said:

'Prince Lorant is not here tonight. He is further west, on the borders of our lands. He will be here tomorrow morning, when he will devote himself to speaking with you. Is there anything you need to tell me about immediately?'

Belwynn and the others looked at each other, tired and sleepy after their journey. Soren responded for them.

'We can wait until tomorrow, Your Highness,' he assured the princess.

Hajna smiled again. 'Very well. Night is falling,' she said, gesturing towards the sky. Everyone followed her gesture and looked upwards, as if it was the first time they had realised this was the case. 'We will find food and shelter for you here tonight.'

Hajna busied herself in organising the appropriate accommodation for her guests. This was achieved in a matter of minutes. As before, Belwynn, Moneva and Elana were accommodated together, separate from the men, in a small tent. Belwynn quite liked the arrangement—having some time away from the men. They spent a few minutes chatting idly about the Caladri, laughing at the thought of the tactile Caladri men in the carriage with Herin and the others, wondering together at the beauty of Princess Hajna of the Blood Caladri.

Very soon, though, they became too tired to speak. The food provided by the Princess lay largely untouched in the corner, and they went to sleep.

XXI

A HISTORY LESSON

S OREN WOKE AS THE EARLY morning light filtered into the tent he was sharing with Clarin and Herin. He was wet with sweat. He knew that his dreams had been troubled.

One had been about his mother. She was being attacked by vossi-like creatures, and when he had gone to help her with his magic, he had been powerless. The whole tent was damp from the three of them sharing such a confined space, and as the other two men slumbered on, Soren clambered out of the cloth doorway.

Outside, a sea of Caladri tents dominated the view. The early morning forest air was chilly on his damp skin and he rubbed himself before stretching out his back and legs. Today, thought Soren. Maybe today. He hoped so. It had been about ten days since he had woken in Vitugia without his powers. But it felt like a lifetime. If, somehow, the Blood Caladri could restore them, it would feel like a new start. Like a rebirth. Soren looked out over the forest, eager for what the new day would bring.

He had to wait a while until Joska, one of the carriage attendants from yesterday, came to collect them.

'Prince Lorant is ready to meet with you,' he said simply, and led them back to the large tent in the centre of the camp.

On the way they met up with Belwynn, Elana and Moneva, who were being led in the same direction. Once there, Joska held open a flap in the tent and gestured for them to enter. Soren ducked his head and walked in.

Rabigar, Gyrmund and Dirk were already seated in the middle of the tent on one side of a small fire. Opposite them sat Princess Hajna and two other men, one seemingly much older than the other. Soren found a space by the fire and sat down. As he waited for the others to sit, he pushed his hands to the fire, rubbing them together. The smoke drifted upwards towards the hole in the roof.

'Hello again, friends,' welcomed Princess Hajna, once everyone was settled.

'Greetings,' said the younger man. 'I am Prince Lorant, son of King Tibor of the Blood Caladri. You have all met my wife,' he gestured to his right. 'This is my chief adviser, Szabolcs,' Lorant continued, now gesturing to his left. 'He is a learned man, much wiser than I. I trust these two to hear all that you have to say. You may trust me to tell my father your news. He is currently in the north of our country, waging war against the Shadow Caladri.'

Everyone began to introduce themselves. Prince Lorant had a more formal manner compared to his wife, but Soren supposed that he was naturally wary of them. He had blonde hair, tightly plaited to his head, sea blue eyes and an athletic build.

'How long have you been at war with the Shadow Caladri?' asked Soren.

'This war began two years ago and has been fought with varying intensity ever since. Recently, King Dorjan has increased the severity of his raids. It feels like a preparation for an invasion. He is working closely with Erkindrix of Ishari. We had feared that the army of Haskany which has invaded Grienna and Trevenza might turn against us. That is why my forces are currently based in this region. It seems, however, that the army is meant for the Empire.'

'That does seem to be the case,' agreed Soren. 'And that is one of the reasons we are here.'

'I see. Now that the humans are under threat, they want our help, when they have given us none for two years?'

Soren let the question hang in the air for a while. He could not afford to offend the Prince. The Blood Caladri may well have just cause to be bitter if they had been fighting alone for two years.

Elana spoke up. 'The peoples of Dalriya must unite to stop Ishari. Some have been slow to see this, but we must look forward not behind us.'

Lorant made a motion with one arm towards Elana, which Soren read as an acceptance of the point she had made.

'Very well,' replied the Prince. 'I do not intend to blame any of you directly for diplomatic failures. Let me hear what Baldwin of Brasingia and Edgar of Magnia have to say.'

'Well,' said Soren, warily re-joining the conversation. 'I think it best for us to start with the events of two weeks ago. This way you will better understand who we are and what we have to ask.'

Soren explained the events surrounding Toric's Dagger and recounted their experiences in Coldeberg and Essenberg. Half way through, Szabolcs, the old Caladri, stood up and shuffled over to the corner of the room, where he began rummaging through some books. Picking up three, he returned to the fire and began flicking through the pages while Soren spoke. Soren finished by passing Lorant the insignia that Gustav had given him.

'Gustav is a friend of the Blood Caladri,' said Lorant. 'I understand that Baldwin needs allies. He cannot stand up to Ishari and Haskany alone. The truth is, however, that the Blood Caladri make poor allies now. Erkindrix has made sure that we are tied down in war with the Shadow Caladri. We cannot spare troops to help him; he cannot spare troops to help us. We must work together in some other way.'

'Can we see the weapon?' asked Hajna.

Dirk produced the dagger from inside his cloak. The princess examined it.

'Beautiful,' she commented, before passing it over to Szabolcs.

The old man studied it intently for a long time, saying nothing.

If Caladri live to a hundred and fifty, Belwynn said to Soren, *he must be nearly there.*

Szabolcs did indeed seem to be a man of great age. His skin was wrinkled; the hands that held the stone were gnarled and gently shook. Soren, however, could tell that this was a wizard of significant power. Despite the current topic of conversation, he could not help thinking of his own magical powers and holding onto hope that this man could restore them.

'I think I know what this is,' Szabolcs said slowly.

He looked up at the others, as if waking from a dream and readjusting to the waking world.

'This is an old story. I don't know it all. But it goes back to the Cracking of the World. This occurred hundreds of years ago when the Isharites first arrived in Dalriya. They came from another world, sent by a dread demon to take ours.

Our Lady Onella created seven weapons with which to defend the land. To the Caladri she gave a staff with magical properties. Each other race of Dalriya was given a weapon. I believe that this is one of them. But the demon did the same, and poured his own magical power into seven weapons, granting them to his servants. The war culminated in a great battle. The two sides met in the middle of Dalriya. The champions of the gods met in combat, armed with the weapons. A great magical energy was released when the two sides clashed. The continent collapsed into two. The soldiers of each army were drowned in the flood.'

'Who is this Lady Onella you talk about?' asked Elana quietly.

'Onella is Dalriya's goddess, who protects all of us,' answered Hajna simply.

'I...,' Elana started, and Soren detected emotion in her voice, which was usually so controlled. 'I believe I serve this Onella, though she calls herself Madria to me.'

'Our Lady is known by many names,' said Hajna. 'In the Brasingian lands she is known as the Lady Alexia.'

'And these seven weapons are hers?' Elana asked Szabolcs.

'Yes.'

'Madria wants us to find all of them,' said Elana firmly. 'We need them to defend against Ishari.'

'Why didn't you mention this before?' asked Herin sceptically.

'I cannot speak to Madria in a normal conversation,' Elana answered him. 'I cannot ask her every question I have and get an answer. But she guides me. These weapons are vitally important; I am sure of it.'

'Szabolcs,' said Soren, 'do you know where the other six are?'

'No, I don't know where they are; I don't even know *what* they are. With one exception. Onella's Staff is a precious treasure, kept by the Grand Caladri in Edeleny. I don't know what happened to the others after the Cracking of the World. But we may have the story in our histories.'

Szabolcs opened one of the books he had been flicking through before.

'There is a chance that I can get answers in here. *Zoltan's History* was written when the Caladri were still united.'

Szabolcs began reading. Some time passed in silence.

'While we wait,' began Belwynn.

Soren smiled, knowing that watching someone read would not hold his sister's attention for long.

'May I ask about the Caladri?' she continued. 'They were once united? Why did that come to an end?'

Lorant and Hajna looked at each other. The prince smiled and gestured that she should answer.

'Our history in Dalriya,' Hajna began, 'goes back much further than humans'. When they first arrived, we were the strongest people in the land, and lived across the continent. Our strength lay in our magic. A great number of our children are blessed by Onella with magic. For humans, this is very rare. For Krykkers—' the Princess smiled at Rabigar— 'never?'

Rabigar solemnly nodded his agreement.

'We like to think that we taught many of our skills to the humans who arrived. We gave them our language,' Hajna continued, with a slight shrug; 'maybe they would have described it differently. Either way, the power of the Caladri began to fade as the humans grew stronger and more numerous and the Isharites pressed us from the north. There appeared a faction within the Caladri who argued that we should fight against this decline with magical forces which we had never touched before. They believed that we should tread the same path as the Isharites and gain extra power by contacting demons from beyond our world; that this was the only way to save our civilisation. This faction is the group you call the Shadow Caladri. An opposition faction emerged, who believed that this dangerous practice should be forbidden, that it threatened the power of Lady Onella. This was our faction, the Blood Caladri. We pressed the elites of our society to put a stop to the Shadow Caladri, but they did not intervene. Civil war between the Shadow Caladri and the Blood Caladri erupted. Both groups were condemned and exiled by these elites, who are known as the Grand Caladri. A fourth faction eventually came to settle in the far corner of Dalriya, becoming the Sea Caladri. As time went by, human kingdoms took away lands from all four realms. The Persaleian Empire became the dominant force in Dalriya, driving us into the forest. By that time our divisions were too entrenched to unite together and we each, in our own ways, accepted our new place.'

'Thank you,' said Belwynn. 'So, the Shadow Caladri and Blood Caladri have been at war ever since?'

'No,' answered Lorant. 'Initially we fought long and hard, but neither side won, and meanwhile we had weakened ourselves against outside enemies. So, many years of truce followed—necessary to ensure our own existence. But there can never be true peace when each side opposes every principle the other stands for. The current war is a very recent reopening of ancient hostilities.'

Szabolcs cleared his throat. 'It may take me some time to find the information I am looking for.'

'Yes,' agreed Lorant, 'there is no point in us all sitting here wasting time.'

'I suggest we meet up here again at midday,' added Hajna. 'There are a number of things we can offer our guests in that time. However, if Rabigar would agree, I would like to spend some time with him. I have experience in helping soldiers recover from injuries. I know certain exercises that help to improve strength and coordination after the loss of an eye. I could teach them to you this morning, for you to use in the future.'

228

'I would be much obliged of such help,' answered Rabigar.

Hajna then began assigning activities to the other members of the group. Soren decided to get in his request early.

'I should like to stay with you, Szabolcs, unless you feel I would disturb your concentration. I have some questions I would like to ask of you…' Soren found his sentence trailing off.

Szabolcs nodded his agreement, hiding any curiosity or irritation he might have felt, and continued to flick through his book.

Everyone began to leave the tent in twos and threes, as Princess Hajna allocated them to a Caladri guide who would see to their needs.

Eventually, Soren and Szabolcs were left alone.

***

Belwynn emerged from the tent and drew a deep breath of the forest air, gazing up to the canopy of trees, where sunlight dappled down through the gaps to reach the floor. She turned around to find out what was in store for her this morning.

Soren had stayed behind in the tent with Szabolcs, and Belwynn knew that he would be asking the old wizard about his own magic powers. Elana stood talking to Prince Lorant, with faithful Dirk a couple of yards apart from them, seemingly content to stand close by rather than join in the conversation. Princess Hajna was talking to a group of Caladri, whom Belwynn recognised as Marika and the other attendants who had travelled with them on the carriage. Hajna sent them over in the direction of Belwynn and the others, while the Princess herself walked over to Rabigar and, with a quick word and gesture, led him away from the tent. Meanwhile, Lorant, Elana and Dirk began strolling away in the opposite direction.

The six Caladri attendants approached the entrance to the tent where Belwynn and the others stood, waiting.

'Princess Hajna has asked us to show you something of our home,' said Marika, a pleasant smile on her face. 'Do any of you have any requests?'

'The Blood Caladri are known for their archery,' Herin said. 'Do any of you use a bow?'

'Elek is the best archer here,' said one of the men.

'I will teach you what I know,' agreed Elek. 'You come too, Joska.'

'Since our men are leaving us,' said one of the girls, whom Belwynn remembered from the carriage ride as Dora, 'Emese and I shall show you two a lovely walk.' Dora reached out and took Moneva's hand. Emese then linked elbows with Gyrmund and began to walk off.

Belwynn found herself left with Clarin. Remaining with them were Marika and another male Caladri.

Marika introduced herself to Clarin.

'I am Vida,' said the man to Belwynn.

Clarin and Belwynn, looking at each other a little uncertainly, exchanged introductions.

'I can think of a nice walk, too, if you would like to come?' asked Marika.

Belwynn and Clarin accepted the invitation. Marika led the way and Belwynn stepped in next to her. She explained that to the east of the camp Prince Lorant had established a temporary exercise camp, for physical training. That is where Rabigar and Herin had been taken. To the west was a garden, which the local inhabitants had created and maintained. It seemed that Gyrmund and Moneva had been taken in that direction.

'We are going south, though,' said Marika, an ever-present twinkle in her eye. 'This is a beautiful walk, but made by nature, not ourselves.'

They walked past the tents of Lorant's people; occasional stares and whisperings directed at Belwynn and Clarin by those who were working there. Some cooked food; others mended tools or weapons.

'Is this an army?' Belwynn asked Marika.

'Yes. Not everyone is a fighter — some people are here to support, looking after food or animals. But most of them will do battle if Prince Lorant orders it.'

'There are a lot of women.'

'Human women do not fight?'

'Some do, but not many.'

'Hmm,' considered Marika. 'Perhaps that is because there are fewer Caladri than humans, and the women need to fight. A number of these people fight with magic.'

'How many Caladri have magic in them?'

Marika breathed out heavily as she thought about this question. 'Perhaps...one in every few hundred are born with the gift. For humans, this is much less?'

'Yes,' agreed Belwynn.

Behind them, Clarin had struck up a conversation with Vida about military tactics. It was not a subject that particularly interested Belwynn, but she heard the Caladri man explaining the value of every soldier being armed with a bow and arrows. Clarin, meanwhile, defended the human custom to fight in heavy, metal armour.

They left the camp behind them and entered the thick forest. A footpath carried them in a winding, uphill direction. The conversation petered out as Belwynn looked about her and used her breath to help her legs make the climb.

After an hour's walk, the path emerged at the top of a ridge.

Belwynn gasped as she looked out over the ridge. The position gave her a 180-degree view down over miles of the Caladri lands. Most of it was forest—what Belwynn knew to be great trees looking like tiny little models of the real thing. But she could see that the forest was occasionally broken up by areas of grassland or scrub. Rocky outcrops dotted the ground, rising and falling in gentle waves. Belwynn could also make out tiny settlements. She could see half a dozen of them, the wooden buildings clinging to the edges of the tree line.

Clarin arrived to take in the view.

'Those are your villages?' Belwynn asked Marika, pointing below her.

'Yes. Most are very small, with only a few families. At times of war like this, the youngest and oldest are left behind in the safety of the forest. Our settlements are safe from invaders. They are very difficult to find.'

Vida joined Marika and they walked on ahead, hand in hand. The path continued along the ridge, enabling walkers to keep the view below to their right. After a while, Belwynn and Clarin followed after them, some distance behind.

'I never imagined that I would ever visit the lands of the Caladri,' Belwynn said as they idly walked along.

Clarin smiled ruefully. 'This is turning into our biggest adventure yet. Magic weapons, meetings with kings and emperors…'

'It's the most serious, Clarin. If Ishari wins, then this place will be destroyed. Magnia will fall eventually. Our whole way of life…it will all be gone.'

Clarin shrugged and then patted the sword strapped to his waist. 'We won't let that happen.'

Sometimes Belwynn found Clarin's confidence and unlimited, misplaced optimism infuriating. Now, though, she found it reassuring.

She reached for his hand. He looked down in surprise, but then smiled, and took her hand in his. They walked on in silence.

***

Gyrmund could not help himself smiling foolishly at the young Caladri women, Dora and Emese. They had brought Moneva and himself to a garden, about a mile to the west of the camp. A stony path snaked its way through plants, lined by trees and flowers on either side. Further on, cut stone steps took them higher, until they reached a small, trickling waterfall, which emptied into a large pool where a number of fish swam. Dora and Emese began to dip their hands over the side of the wall into the pool and splash water at each other, cackling and giggling as they did so.

A month ago, Gyrmund thought to himself, he would have found such a sight alluring. He had been a single man for a long time, but he had never found it difficult to make women like him. The two young Caladri women were attractive, in their own way. But now he had eyes for only one woman.

She was next to him. Sitting on the wall at the edge of the pool, Moneva had placed her hands palm down either side of her and looked out over the gardens. Gyrmund liked the fact that they could now relax in each other's company. After an eventful two weeks, they were both content to be still and silent.

The wind gently lifted Moneva's dark hair, which was usually kept rigidly straight to her neck. Gyrmund found himself looking into her dark eyes as she turned her head to look back at him; her raised eyebrow was her only comment on finding him gazing at her. Gyrmund felt like a teenager caught staring too long at the source of his infatuation, but he enjoyed the feeling.

The moment was then broken as Gyrmund received a splash of cold water on the back of his neck. He stared at Moneva for a moment, who shook her head in mock despair, as if indicating there was nothing she could do about the situation.

Gyrmund turned to his attacker, Dora, and began to launch handfuls of water in her direction. Overwhelmed by the volume of water Gyrmund was splashing at her, she screamed, turned, and ran away. Gyrmund gave chase, as she darted away from the pool and behind the rise of rocks from which the waterfall coursed. Gyrmund followed and quickly caught her, which only made the screams grow louder.

Eventually, Dora controlled herself. Gyrmund let her lead him further round the corner. An archway had been created in the stone, so that Dora and

Gyrmund could walk underneath the waterfall. The drumming sound of the water could be heard above.

'Under here,' began Dora, 'all questions have to be answered truthfully.'

Gyrmund nodded cautiously, deciding to go along with the premise, though he considered it highly likely that the girl had just made it up.

'Do you love Moneva?' she asked, her face a sudden picture of seriousness.

Gyrmund felt his face growing hot at the personal nature of the question. Whether it was the location, or the apparent innocence of the questioner, he was not sure, but he found himself answering honestly.

'Yes, I…have fallen in love with her.'

Dora nodded encouragingly before her next question. 'Are you going to make her yours?'

Gyrmund was not entirely sure what was meant by the question. He decided on a vague answer.

'We cannot marry…we are very busy. We are both independent. We have not known each other long.'

Dora nodded slowly, as if digesting each word. She crooked a finger at Gyrmund to follow. They walked through to the other side of the arch. Dora then abruptly stopped.

By the rocks was a patch of plants Gyrmund did not recognise. The plants were thin, ending in small white flowers, and the tallest reached as high as his knee. They had bright green leaves with a shiny texture. Dora knelt down and, one by one, carefully picked about a dozen leaves from the plants. She stood up and offered them to Gyrmund, who dubiously accepted them.

'Joska and I cannot yet join together as husband and wife. This means that we are not yet ready to bring children into the world,' Dora paused, to make sure that Gyrmund was following what she was getting at. 'We still wish to be together as man and woman, though.'

Gyrmund felt even more embarrassed at the turn of the conversation, but allowed her to continue.

'You must take two of these leaves and crush them. Then add hot water to it and make it into a drink. When a woman drinks this, she cannot produce children.'

Gyrmund understood what she was saying. 'Thank you, Dora,' he said, stuffing the leaves into a pocket.

'You are welcome.'

Jamie Edmundson

Dora led Gyrmund back round to the pool, where Moneva and Emese were talking quietly. As they approached, Moneva looked up at Gyrmund and blushed. He had more than a suspicion about what they had been talking about.

***

For some time, Soren and Szabolcs sat in silence, the Caladri wizard intent on finding any relevant information he could. While he spent most time on *Zoltan's History*, he would occasionally cross-reference something from one of the other books. Soren would have offered to read something, but while he might have been able to decipher the characters, he would have been slow and unsure, little real help.

After a while, Szabolcs looked up at him.

'I have found a relevant passage. Not as complete as I would have hoped, but it tells us something. Before that,' he continued, focusing more intently on Soren, 'you have a question?'

'Yes,' said Soren. 'I'll get straight to it. On our journey through the Wilderness, we were attacked by vossi. I used too much magic in the encounter and overextended. I haven't been able to do anything since, not the slightest thing,' Soren took a breath as he heard the despair in his own voice.

'I spoke to Gustav. He said that wizards amongst the Caladri might be able to help me. He said that he had heard of powerful users being able to channel their power into another, in order to repair the broken bonds.'

'I see,' said Szabolcs, a look of pity slowly crossing his face. 'I believe that I have spoken to Gustav about such a practice myself. I have to tell you; I have only known one such case in my lifetime. This is because it is rare for enchanters to survive overextension. About thirty years ago, a young male enchanter, while warring with the Shadow Caladri, overextended, and somehow survived. No one knew how to treat him. In the end, he travelled to the lands of the Grand Caladri. An enchanter there knew how to perform the healing you describe. It worked, and he returned. This enchanter is still alive; he is part of King Tibor's retinue. That does not mean he could perform the task himself — I doubt whether he could. No other enchanter amongst the Blood Caladri has been involved in such a healing to my knowledge.'

Szabolcs paused.

234

'I know what it is to be blessed with magic. I also know that it can be a curse. The desire for knowledge can become all consuming. I have lived a long — some would say useful—life. But I have never had a wife, or a family.'

Soren knew that Szabolcs' words were true. If not for the determination of his sister, and the link they shared as twins, he would likely be a very lonely man already. Szabolcs looked him in the eye.

'As I say, I know what it is to have the hunger for magic. If you are desperate to regain your powers, I suggest travelling to the Grand Caladri. If there is an enchanter who has the skill, you will likely find them there.'

Soren's stomach lurched. He had hoped to find a cure in these lands. Indeed, he had hoped that Szabolcs might be his saviour. Now he had to make another journey, with little certainty that he would find anyone to help at the end of it. It was a desperate move, but one he knew he would take.

Soren had done worse for his magic. When Soren had requested to study with Delyth, the marsh witch, it was to develop his skills after his apprenticeship with Ealdnoth had come to its natural end. Her magic was totally different to Ealdnoth's, and he was quickly learning new things. But Belwynn had come with him. Soren had begun to realise that Delyth resented his sister's presence. She wanted Soren all to herself. She was a dark and dangerous character, totally different to Ealdnoth. Soren had been naive to think otherwise. Belwynn hadn't seen the threat at all.

Soren had told Belwynn to leave, for her own safety. It had hurt her, he knew, but she couldn't have stayed any longer. When Belwynn left, Soren gave Delyth what she wanted, and they had become lovers. The sex had repulsed him, yet he knew he was learning more about his craft, faster than he ever had. All the time he knew that Delyth would never let him leave, that she wanted him to stay with her forever. He went along with it. When it became clear that she had nothing left to teach him, he only had one option.

She was taken by complete surprise. He turned on her before she had a chance to defend herself. Under the cover of night, he had dumped her body in a bog and fled, returning to Magnia.

He couldn't explain any of this to his sister. She was the same Belwynn when they met up again, only too pleased to see him. He had changed, however. Their year apart had created a distance between them that hadn't been there before.

'There is another reason for you to go there, too,' said Szabolcs slowly, bringing Soren's thoughts back to the present.

'What is that?' asked Soren calmly.

Szabolcs located the passage he wanted in his history book, placing a finger under the words as he began to read.

'Zoltan says the great battle of which I spoke took place in the high mountains of the Krykker kingdoms.'

Szabolcs traced the lettering with his finger.

'He says that both sides had seven champions, armed with a weapon each.' Szabolcs looked up at Soren. 'I wonder if Erkindrix's Council of Seven is more than coincidence? It could be that as well as looking for Lady Onella's weapons, Erkindrix has been looking for his own.'

Szabolcs bent his head down to his book again. 'This is where Zoltan is vague. He says that the seven allies who fought at the great battle each returned to their homeland, to guard their weapons and to make sure that they would not fall into the hands of any one person unless needed again.'

Though vague, this was an interesting piece of information to Soren. 'That makes sense. Our legends say that Toric's Dagger was taken by King Osbert of Magnia from the Lippers. So they may have been one of the allies in the battle.'

Szabolcs nodded. 'That would make sense. Unfortunately, Zoltan does not specify any more. Apart from to say that the Caladri took their staff home and kept it in a place of honour in Onella's Temple.'

'I guess,' said Soren dryly, 'that Onella's Temple is in the lands of the Grand Caladri?'

'Yes. There are other histories I can read which may say more, but I don't carry them with me.'

'Still,' replied Soren, 'that tells us quite a lot. If Elana is right, we need to find all seven of them. We already have one. We know the location of a second. The battle was fought in the lands of the Krykkers, so presumably they had a champion and a weapon themselves.'

'Yes,' agreed Szabolcs. 'The humans were present in Dalriya at this time. It is likely that they were one of the seven allies, too. As for the other three, I would only be guessing.'

'Well,' said Soren, as the information Szabolcs had given him began to sink in, 'it looks like you have given me two good reasons to go the Grand Caladri.'

***

As he walked a discreet distance behind Elana and the Prince, Dirk peered closely at the flora of the Blood Caladri kingdom. In truth, he admitted to himself, he had never had much interest in such things. He was, in fact, listening intently to the conversation ahead of him. Listening. Gathering information. That was what he had always been good at.

Lorant had led them through the gardens to the west of the camp. The conversation there had been limited. The Caladri Prince would occasionally stop to comment on a flower or plant of some kind as they walked past. Elana would make some appreciative noise. Dirk, following a few feet behind them both, wondered whether she was as bored by it as he was.

After they left the gardens, where no other ears could hear, Lorant turned the conversation to weightier matters.

'I believe you entirely, Elana,' Lorant was saying. 'Onella, or Madria, does appear to be communicating with you.'

Dirk noticed how Elana relaxed and, turning slightly to her left, gently smiled at the reassuring words.

'But you must understand,' Lorant continued, 'that you are the first person I have heard of who can communicate, in such a direct way, with the Goddess. No one in our lands has been gifted in such a way. I want to know what she has told you to do.'

'As I said earlier, I don't have a direct conversation with Madria. But I now know that it is my duty to find and collect her weapons. They must be used to defend Dalriya, just as they were before.'

'But that will never happen.'

The words rang out, cold and hard and loud, and floated in the air around them.

Ahead, a tall, black figure emerged and walked on until he stood facing them.

It was Nexodore, the wizard who had attacked them on the Great Road. A feeling of dread and panic rose in Dirk. He forced himself to control his roiling stomach.

'Nexodore?' asked Prince Lorant, with disbelief in his voice. 'How have you invaded our realm?' he demanded.

'With ease, Prince,' replied the sorcerer dismissively. The voice leaving the death mask sounded like rock grinding on granite. Nexodore turned to look at Elana.

Jamie Edmundson

'My master gave me the task of watching the other lands, to find the whereabouts of the lost weapons and to discover who She has chosen as his enemy.' The sorcerer made an unpleasant noise, which Dirk surmised was laughter, but it was so devoid of emotion it could hardly be called that. 'A clever choice by your goddess,' he said grudgingly, 'to choose a nobody. It has made it more difficult for me to find you. However,' he continued, and drew his sword, a cruel scrape of noise as it left the scabbard, 'now I have.'

The drawing of the sword seemed to prompt Lorant into action. Drawing his own, he launched himself at Nexodore, shouting spells as he went. Two vines thrust themselves out of the ground and clasped themselves around the legs of the sorcerer.

'Run!' shouted the Caladri.

Dirk rushed forwards to grab Elana and escape with her back to the camp. However, by the time he reached her Nexodore had responded to Lorant's attack. One scream of a word and the vines securing him withered and died. In the same breath he hurled his own sword at Lorant's approach.

The prince had made up half the distance between them when the hurtling sword came straight for him. He blocked the weapon with his own just in time, sending it flying into the grass by the side. There was no time to react further, however, as Nexodore slammed an open palm towards him and sent a powerful blast of magic in his direction. Dirk could feel the force of it as a tremor in the ground and a blast of warm air on his face. Lorant just had time to surround himself with a glowing, light blue shield. But this defence was to no avail. The magic blast was too strong for him and he hurtled through the air until his body slammed into a tree.

Nexodore wasted no time and marched towards Elana, his mask of death implacable. Elana shivered. She seemed unable to move.

Nexodore's march ate up the space between them in seconds. Dirk found himself releasing his grip on Elana and backing away, to one side. Elana began to pray to Madria.

Nexodore stopped in front of her. He stretched out his hand in a grasping movement and his sword, which Lorant had knocked aside, came flying back into his grip. Through his fear and shock, Dirk was surprised to see the sword was not made of steel, but some kind of black crystal. Almost subconsciously, Dirk found himself pulling out the dagger from inside his cloak.

'Your goddess cannot help you.'

238

Elana looked up into the mask as Nexodore raised his black sword behind his head.

This was the moment to act. Dirk forced his body to follow his orders. He hurled himself at the sorcerer and planted Toric's Dagger into his groin.

Nexodore screamed out in pain, and his sword fell out of his hands. For whatever reason, he had not seen Dirk's attack coming. Dirk looked up to see the mask staring down at him. He twisted the dagger further into his enemy in defiance. Nexodore had made a mistake, and Dirk intended to punish him for it.

Nexodore's gauntleted hand smashed into Dirk's face. He fell flat onto his back, the impact knocking his senses out of him. Dirk struggled to sit up. He saw Nexodore rip the dagger from his body, toss it aside, and then pause with his hand over his groin area, looking in Dirk's direction.

Dirk struggled to make himself stand up, swaying on his feet as he did. Nexodore advanced quickly and grabbed Dirk by the wrist. Dirk yanked and punched and kicked, but Nexodore's grip was like a vice.

Pain shot through Dirk, from his wrist, down his arm and into his body. He could no longer struggle or move, except to scream in agony. It felt like the sorcerer was burning him alive, sending fire through his body. Within seconds he could no longer even scream—his mouth held rigid in a rictus grin, his vocal chords frozen in place; but Nexodore's grip still held him.

Dirk felt like his insides were slowly being cooked. Then, just out of the corner of his eye, he could see Elana pick up the knife that Nexodore had discarded. She ran at the sorcerer, but he was aware of her approach. He turned towards her and, with his free hand, slammed a fist into her head.

Elana collapsed and crumpled to the floor. It was a horrible sight; Dirk hoped that the blow had killed her, that she would avoid any further suffering.

Nexodore turned his full attention back to Dirk. The burning sensation increased and Dirk could feel himself dying. He kept his eyes fixed on Elana's body, but his own could no longer cope with the pain he was experiencing. His body spasmed and a shower of blood spurted from his mouth onto the sorcerer.

Dirk looked up to see the death mask's expression remain fixed as Dirk's blood trickled down its face.

Then, suddenly, something seemed to erupt from the Isharite's right eye. The energy entering Dirk's body stopped. Nexodore's grip loosened and Dirk fell to the ground.

Dirk tried to concentrate on breathing, but his insides seemed burned away, leaving a crumpled husk of skin and bones. His breathing rattled around in his head. Dirk forced himself to look up.

Nexodore had his back to him, and poking out of the back of his head was the point of an arrow. Beyond him came Lorant, bow in hand, and a second arrow nocked and ready to be released.

'A nice trick,' came the grinding voice from behind the mask. 'But I've survived the fires of the underworld. Your bow and arrow and petty magic can't do me harm.'

The Dagger, thought Dirk. *The Dagger harmed him.*

'Maybe I can take your other eye,' said Lorant viciously, and fired his second arrow, chanting more magic as he did. The bolt flew towards its target but Nexodore casually waved a hand, and it disintegrated.

Dirk made himself sit up, pain wracking his body so that he had to bite down on his tongue to keep from screaming out. Lying next to him was Elana: out cold, but breathing. He grabbed the Dagger that she had dropped. He forced himself to stand up, his legs threatening to give way. If he didn't act now, Elana was doomed.

Nexodore fired a blast of magic at Lorant, forcing him to dive to the side to escape, dropping his bow as he did. Nexodore followed his target, winding up another assault. Dirk launched himself at the sorcerer, holding the dagger in both hands and driving its thin point into the back of his neck.

Then Dirk's vision blurred, and all was dark.

XXII

GOOD NEWS

BALDWIN HAD SEEN HIS SCOUTS riding up to the front of the column. A halt had now been called. Clearly, something was happening.

'I'm going up to see what's going on,' he said to Rainer, who was riding next to him.

'Very well, Your Majesty,' replied his chamberlain.

They detached themselves from the line and made their way to the front, a hundred yards ahead, in no particular hurry. An army needed a good organiser, and Baldwin had therefore decided to bring Rainer with him to oversee logistics. He had some reservations about this decision. He had a great fondness for his Queen, Hannelore. She was a loyal wife, but not a politician. Rainer would have been useful back in the capital. He hoped that Archbishop Decker would keep his wife safe in Essenberg while he was away.

Baldwin had decided that he had to head north with his forces, even though most of his dukes had not. He could not expect Ellard of Rotelegen to hold the border by himself. He had to be seen to be defending his Empire. But he was uneasy about leaving his own duchy of Kelland virtually undefended with the treacherous Duke Emeric and his army waiting to pounce. He hoped that he could rely on Coen of Thesse to keep Emeric pinned down. He hoped that his other dukes would heed his orders and bring their armies north.

Baldwin looked up, not for the first time that day, at the towering presence of Burkhard Castle, only a mile away now, to the north-west. It was the key to the Empire's defence against invasion; legendarily never taken by an enemy force. Despite this history, a shiver ran down Baldwin's spine at the thought of it all. The idea of being trapped in there by the superior forces of Ishari and Haskany; of it becoming his grave. These thoughts were bad enough. But the prospect of being the first emperor to lose the castle, and the lasting shame that such a loss would bring to his name—such thoughts were far worse.

'What's going on?' he said abruptly when he and Rainer reached the front.

'Riders approaching ahead, Your Majesty,' quickly replied one of his scouts, sitting straight to attention.

'Numbers?'

'About thirty, sire,'

Baldwin peered ahead. He could make out a group approaching, but the sun was in his eyes.

'Banner?'

'The tree of Luderia, sire.'

'Luderia, eh? Then maybe Duke Arne has beaten us to the castle. I hope my brother has made him welcome.'

Baldwin had sent Walter up to the castle a few days before to speed up preparations. Parts of it needed repair, and large amounts of supplies had to be brought in to feed the size of the force he intended to keep there.

Baldwin waited for a few minutes. Sure enough, his father-in-law, Arne, rode at the head of around thirty Luderian noblemen. Arne was not getting any younger, mused Baldwin; nor was he getting thinner. Baldwin knew himself that as the years went by, iron discipline was needed to keep in the same physical shape as a young man. His father-in-law had let his discipline slide for a few years now; the size of the gut resting on the saddle was testament to that.

When they arrived, there was much shouting, hugging and shaking of hands as Baldwin went out of his way to thank every man for being there, and each nobleman made sure that they clasped hands and were acknowledged by their Emperor.

'And how is my daughter?' Arne bellowed, perhaps to remind anyone who had forgotten that he was father to the Queen.

'She gets more beautiful every day,' Baldwin answered, with the expected charm. 'It was a wrench to leave her back in Essenberg.'

'Quite, quite,' replied Arne. Baldwin could almost detect a tear in the older man's eye.

'But I've got news to cheer you up, my son,' said the Duke, a term of address that Arne always used and that Baldwin had never got used to. 'When you were spotted on the road, I insisted that I ride out and be the first to tell you. Our cousin Duke Ellard has been busy since he left you at Essenberg. When he arrived in Guslar, he wasted no time in raising a force of his own men and headed north yesterday. The Haskan forces were camped out in Grienna, idly waiting for orders from Ishari. They weren't expecting us to take the fight to them! But that's exactly what Ellard did, riding his force in and engaging the bastards. The Haskans put up a fight for a while, but then turned and ran! I don't want to build

242

this into something more than it is: they were routed, but they'll be back. Still, a victory is a victory!'

By this point Baldwin himself had a genuine, beaming smile on his face at the news. This was exactly what his nervous Empire needed. Bless Ellard!

'It certainly is,' he replied. 'Rejoice!' he shouted, 'and spread the word down the lines!'

A cheer rose up, and his soldiers did as they were told, retelling the story of how their fellow Brasingians had given the army of Haskany a bloody nose. Baldwin fell in next to Arne and the army continued towards Castle Burkhard.

Looking up, Baldwin could no longer think why the sight of his mighty stronghold should have made him feel grim at all.

***

Waking up was a gradual process and took a number of minutes.

Dirk was first aware of a sickening, pounding headache. He focused on his surroundings. He was lying in a bed, his head propped up by pillows. He was inside one of the canvas Caladri tents. Sitting at the foot of the bed was Elana. Her head was resting on a hand. He couldn't tell whether she was asleep or not. He looked at her awhile. He became aware of a great pressure in his bladder, but Dirk supposed that he would have to wait a bit to relieve himself.

'Elana.'

His voice croaked out the name, practically giving up on the final syllable.

He saw Elana raise her head and look at him.

'Dirk?'

Her concerned face caused him to remember, with a jolt, his last waking memory. Nexodore had attacked them. He had forced a burning magic into Dirk's body, and then…

'What happened?' he asked.

'He was holding you and…damaging you in some way,' Elana said. 'I tried to stop him…'

Dirk remembered Nexodore's fist crunching into Elana's head, and how he had wondered if the blow had killed her.

'…but I couldn't. I blanked out myself after that. But Prince Lorant survived the blast from Nexodore. He blacked out for a couple of minutes but woke up to see Nexodore attacking us. He fired an arrow…luckily for us it hit the mark.

When Nexodore's attention was turned to the Prince, you used Madria's Dagger to kill him.'

Dirk had no memory of the last bit; his head felt foggy. 'What about your injury?' he asked.

'I had a headache for the rest of the day,' Elana smiled, 'but I am fine now.'

A thought occurred to Dirk. 'How long have I been here?'

'Two nights have passed. It is now about six in the morning. The Caladri, including Princess Hajna herself, helped me to tend you. We all thought it likely you would die at first. You have still sustained serious injuries, though. You will never be fully healed, Dirk.'

Dirk nodded briefly to acknowledge the information. He certainly felt like he had been seriously damaged. He remembered the burning sensation of his insides. At the time he had assumed Nexodore had killed him. Elana had saved his life for a second time. He hoped that his actions had gone some way to repaying the debt.

Elana walked over to the bed and picked up a jug from the table in the corner. She carefully poured some of the contents into a mug.

'The Caladri have prepared this for you. It will help with recovery and with the pain.'

She reached over to let him drink it, but Dirk insisted on reaching out to take it himself. He gave it a brief smell, but his stomach roiled in protest, so he decided to quickly take a gulp. As soon as the liquid hit his stomach he received a piercing, shuddering pain. It was as if the acids in his stomach were attacking his organs. He cried out in pain and doubled over as his stomach cramped, spilling the rest of the drink onto the bed. Gritting his teeth, Dirk controlled himself and sat back up, red faced.

'Are you alright?' asked Elana. Her voice did not sound unduly concerned, and that helped Dirk to calm down.

He nodded, 'Yes.'

'You will have that kind of reaction to anything for a while. This drink will help to heal your insides. But I think you have permanent damage there. You must eat and drink only the blandest of foods. And drink water instead of beer or wine.'

'Very well,' agreed Dirk. What else could he say? 'What's been going on while I've been asleep, then?' he asked, hoping that a change of subject would make him feel better.

'Szabolcs, Prince Lorant's adviser, has identified the location of another of Madria's weapons. It is in the hands of the Grand Caladri. I…asked Soren to wait until you had regained consciousness, which he agreed to. But now that you have, we will make our way there immediately. Nexodore's comments were worrying. If Ishari knows of the existence of Madria's weapons too, we are in a race to collect them all.'

'I am going with you,' said Dirk, worried that Elana was implying that he was to stay put and recover. He knew he was in no physical shape to continue the journey at the pace they travelled. But he was desperate not to be left behind here with the Caladri.

Elana frowned, as if she was about to deny his request. However, something seemed to make her change her mind and her face relaxed.

'Very well,' she said, giving a nod in acceptance. 'I will go to see Soren about it. You need to get ready immediately, then.'

Dirk nodded. *First, though,* he thought to himself, *I need to empty my bladder.*

***

It was night-time. The sun had set about an hour ago. Farred sat at his table in his tent. A couple of candles shed a bit of light about him and cast some flickering shadows, but the rest of his tent was shrouded in darkness. The united army of North Magnians, South Magnians and Middians were camped in the relative safety of Kelland. Farred and his men had made speedy progress since leaving home, successfully meeting up with the forces controlled by Prince Ashere and Brock, the Middian chieftain, at the agreed location.

Things had become more difficult since then. Firstly, Bastien, Duke of Morbaine, had been unable to persuade his brother, King Nicolas of Guivergne, to allow their force passage across Guivergnais territory. Wary that they should respect this, Farred and the other leaders had agreed to march from the Steppe to Kelland across the northern part of the duchy of Barissia. This meant moving across what was effectively enemy territory, since it was now well known that Duke Emeric had declared his duchy to be an independent kingdom from the Empire. Emeric had raised a large army which, although based in Coldeberg, could destroy their force of six thousand if they encountered it. They had decided that today they should ride across the duchy in one day. This was a tall order, but they were a highly mobile force, since most soldiers had their own mount.

Those without shared mounts. They had been successful, though it had been a long and tense day.

Secondly, relations between the soldiers were not good. Many had, a week before, literally been enemies. Soldiers amongst the North and South Magnians had been stationed on either side of a hostile border. They were now expected to be comrades in arms. The tensions of the day had perhaps added to the problem: a fight had broken out this evening. A soldier of North Magnia had been stabbed. Luckily, the injury was not fatal, but Farred needed to restore order now or it would be lost forever.

The tent flap, facing Farred, was pulled aside. Burstan walked in.

'You wanted to see me?' he grunted.

Burstan was the captain of the troops who had been stationed on the Magnian border, about one thousand in all. This was about one half of all the troops under Farred's command. Although Burstan had not directly disobeyed an order, he had made it quite plain that this experienced core of the army were *his* soldiers, challenging Farred to act otherwise. Since it was clear that he did command the loyalty of his men, Farred had avoided a confrontation over the issue. Until now. Burstan had been present at the confrontation earlier this evening and, according to accounts, had done nothing to stop it from taking place.

'Yes, I sent someone for you about a half hour ago,' Farred replied to the captain's question. 'Take a seat,' he suggested, offering the chair opposite him.

Burstan sat down, a nonchalant air about him.

'I'll get straight to the point,' said Farred. 'As you know, there was a stabbing a couple of hours ago. By one of your men. Apparently, you were there. I've heard mention that you did more to stir up the antagonism than stop it. I shouldn't have to remind you that we need to maintain unity amongst our forces so that we are an effective fighting force against the Haskans.'

'Anyone who says I was stirring up trouble is a liar. I want a name,' demanded Burstan angrily.

Farred remained quiet. With no name forthcoming, Burstan continued.

'What you don't understand is that for my men, most of whom 'ave served their country for years, it's the North Magnians who are our real enemies, who are responsible for spilling South Magnian blood. Haskany poses no threat to us. That's the way my men see it, and then they see you licking the arse of their Prince.'

The insult was meant to provoke, but Farred kept cool.

'That sounds like treason to me. It's Prince Edgar who decides who our enemy is, not you.'

Burstan's face reddened. 'I'm passing on to you what my men are thinking, that's all. And my men,' he continued, 'make up half of our army, so I suggest you start listening to 'em. Cos they won't tolerate you accusing me of treachery.'

The gauntlet was being thrown down, much more obviously than before.

'What you fail to appreciate, Burstan,' Farred replied, keeping his voice neutral, 'is the fact that there are four thousand other soldiers in this army in addition to ours. One of ours has stabbed one of theirs. Prince Ashere is outraged; Brock supports him. They came to see me about one hour ago. It's all around the camp that you were there at the time. They're asking for your head, since you were the officer in charge. And while you may have the support of your thousand men, that's not enough to fight off four thousand.'

'They want my head? What for?' demanded Burstan. 'I don't believe you.'

Farred could see in the man's eyes, however, that he almost did.

'How did you expect them to react?' asked Farred simply, almost gently.

Burstan thought about that for a while. 'Look, I didn't do the stabbing. It was Vanig. I didn't encourage him, neither. I'm not that stupid.'

'I believe you, Burstan. That's what I said to Prince Ashere.'

Burstan looked at Farred gratefully. Farred almost felt sorry for him.

'You're a good soldier with a fine record. Prince Edgar told me as much himself. But we're in a situation here. This attack can't go unpunished. You know what has to happen.'

Burstan breathed out slowly. 'Vanig's not a child. He knows that something like this can get you killed. But he'd been drinking and he was provoked...he didn't kill the other lad after all, did he?'

'No, but what's the message, Burstan? Stab a comrade and get away with it if you're a bit tipsy? I'm not going to stand for that; neither are Prince Ashere and his troops.'

'Alright, discipline is discipline,' responded Burstan gruffly. 'Death it is.'

'There's one more thing, Burstan. I told you that Ashere and Brock wanted you punished as well. I told them no, that you believe in discipline. But you're going to have to prove it.'

Burstan didn't understand at first. He frowned, then shrugged, as if to say that he kept discipline amongst his soldiers anyway. Then his face went pale as he realised what Farred was saying.

'You mean—you want me to…do Vanig in myself?'

'You have to. You're his commanding officer. You need to show that you're in charge.'

Burstan said nothing for a while, his mouth open as he thought about his situation.

'So be it,' he said finally, his voice thick. 'I'll do it.' There was a pause. 'May I be dismissed now?' Burstan asked, not looking Farred in the eye.

'Of course.'

Burstan stood up and made his way out of the tent withoutlooking back. Farred was left in darkness. He turned around to look at the far corner of the tent. Prince Ashere was sitting in the shadows.

'You handled that well,' he commented, his voice a soft whisper.

Farred sighed. 'We've maintained a united front for now, that's the main thing. I'm thoroughly sick of this day.'

'This is the hardest part: controlling the troops when there's no fighting to be done. I tell you, it will be a relief when we reach Castle Burkhard and meet with the enemy. Things will be easier then.'

Farred gave a brief smile, for in the darkness he could not tell whether the Prince was making a joke or not.

XXIII

DARK TIDINGS

D IRK HAD BEEN GIVEN a few minutes to prepare himself, and then they had set off. Prince Lorant, still recovering from his own encounter with Nexodore, had given them fresh mounts and loaned them the use of a couple of Caladri soldiers to make their journey out of his lands speedier. The soldiers knew the route, so the group could concentrate on setting a good pace.

For Dirk, the journey was intolerable. The physical pressure on his battered body made his head pound like someone was smacking it with a hammer. He felt nauseous and faint. Princess Hajna had bestowed on him plenty of herbs and medicines which might help his condition before he had left. She had been very gracious, calling him a hero. Dirk had never been called a hero before, and it had made him feel better for a while. There was plenty of the drink which Elana had introduced him to this morning. He took an occasional swig of it as they rode. His stomach protested at having to digest it, but it did keep the direct pain from his injuries down to a minimum. The bitter after-taste he could live with. He found that chewing on some herbs, from a pouch which Hajna had provided, eased his nausea. Not, he thought grimly, that he had anything left inside him to expel.

After days of sunshine, rain clouds had rolled in, depositing a steady drizzle onto their heads, making Dirk's mood even worse. The forest glistened wetly and the water soaked into his clothes, making them stick to his skin. They stopped briefly for a rest at lunchtime. Dirk immediately swung down from his horse, hoping that someone else would see to its needs. He staggered off into the trees. By this time his limbs were shaking from his exertions. Dirk gritted his teeth and insisted his body do what he told it to for a while longer.

After he had gone a distance which he thought was far enough to avoid people overhearing, he allowed his body to take over. His insides convulsed sharply, and he doubled over in pain. He then faced a wracking series of coughs which resulted in dark coloured blood coming up, spattering the leaves and grass on the floor. Another bout of coughing followed and more came up.

He wiped his sleeve over his mouth and headed back to the others. He knew that Elana would be keeping an eye on him, and he didn't want her to see. He was enough of a liability as it was. If Soren and the others knew how ill he was, they would doubtless have left him behind; for his own good as much as anything else, he knew. But he couldn't leave Elana on her own when he was her only disciple. He had to deal with his injuries.

As he returned to camp he met eyes with Elana, who was nervously looking out for him. He nodded in her direction in a neutral way. She would think he had gone into the trees to relieve himself. He had been doing enough of that, lately.

Dirk went over to the saddlebag and rummaged around until he found a Caladri bread roll, dark brown and savoury to the taste. He took a bite and chewed thoroughly, making sure he didn't swallow any of it until he had turned it into a watery paste. He swallowed, feeling the food go all the way down. His insides protested at the arrival of solid foods. It was the first thing he had eaten for two days. He kept it down. That was important, and he was hopeful that it would get better over time. He couldn't face eating anything else, however, and returned the roll to his bag.

Before long they were travelling again. The two Caladri soldiers led them onwards, as efficient and as serious as they would be on any military mission. After a couple of hours, they informed everybody that they had moved into that indistinct part of the forest where the lands of the Blood Caladri ended and those of the humans of Grienna began. They had to be more on their guard from this point onwards.

They carried on into the evening, deliberately skirting around any signs of human habitation. It would be easier if they were not seen by the local inhabitants at all. Eventually, and to Dirk's relief, the two soldiers stopped them in a suitable clearing.

'Half a mile in that direction and you will find yourselves on the brow of a small hill,' one of the soldiers told them. 'If you look down from there tomorrow morning, you will see the Great Road and a number of settlements. The Road is only about three miles from here. You can work out your favoured route then. I suggest you try to head due west as much as possible, while avoiding settlements. Be careful of the Road. We know that large armies have passed south along it. But it is still being used to carry supplies south to the Haskans.'

The two soldiers did not hang around. It seemed that their orders were to head straight back that night. After they left, taking the horses that Lorant had loaned them, Herin said that he had suspected Lorant's army was ready to move out. He added, in his typically dark manner, that Lorant wouldn't have shared such information in case any of them were captured and revealed the destination under torture.

That night Dirk retreated into the trees again and coughed up more blood. This time it only happened the once. He was too tired to worry about it and went straight to sleep, as everyone else around him busied themselves with making camp and dinner.

The next morning Dirk was one of the first to wake. Gyrmund and the others had constructed a basic shelter from the branches they had found in the forest which had kept them all dry. Outside the shelter it looked like it had rained all night. The ground had become soggy and muddy.

Hunger pangs afflicted him, preventing him from resting further. Dirk collected his bread roll from yesterday and a flask of water. He sat down and began to eat. He took one bite from the roll and a sip of water to go with it, to help him work on the hard bread. Like a child or an old man with no teeth, Dirk thought to himself. But he persevered, forcing himself to complete his breakfast. It was a long process and by the time he had finished, the others were up and preparing to go.

Gyrmund had followed the advice of the Caladri soldiers and surveyed the plain below them. He led them along a route he had planned out from the viewpoint. They headed west, for the woodland and rugged terrain which lay between the settlements of the Griennese dotted around the countryside. Dirk could tell that these settlements they skirted around were getting progressively larger the farther they went.

As it turned out, they smelled the Great Road before they saw it. At first it was an unpleasant odour on the wind which one or two of them would catch before it disappeared. But as they walked onwards it became a consistent stench. Dirk's nausea returned. He tried chewing on the herbs he still carried, but the smell in the air mingled with the taste in his mouth and he had to spit them out. In the end, he resorted to holding a piece of cloth over his nose and mouth.

The countryside had now become flatter, the trees replaced by grassland. This was man-made scenery. The woodlands had been cut back from the Great Road to prevent robbers from waiting in ambush. The Great Road appeared on the horizon up ahead. There was no traffic on it, but the smell in the air made the group wary.

'Smells like shit and rotting meat,' Herin suggested. The comment didn't make Dirk feel any better.

As they approached the road they found that Herin's identification of the smell was accurate. The road itself, and the trampled grass to each side, was dotted with faeces.

'It's not animal droppings,' said Clarin, screwing his nose up at the smell.

'I don't think it's even human,' added Rabigar, his one good eye studying the ground carefully.

Dirk waited a few yards away as the others strode over to the road to inspect it more closely. He feared losing his breakfast if he were to do the same.

'I would say Drobax,' Gyrmund added, confirming Rabigar's thought.

'How do you know? You've travelled that far north?' asked Moneva.

'I have, very briefly. Look around us. What else would have left a trail like this? But the sheer numbers of them that must have passed through...I can't believe it.'

'Has anyone else seen Drobax before?' asked Soren, trying to establish the facts.

A few heads were shaken, but Rabigar spoke up. 'I have, many years ago now. If this is what it looks like, countless thousands have been marched through here.'

'Look at this,' said Herin, who had walked down the road a few feet.

Dirk looked at what he was pointing at. At first it was an indistinct blob by the side of the road. Curious, he followed the others to take a look.

Suddenly, he realised what it was. A dead baby. But not human. It was a greyish colour, with a sharp, grotesque looking face. It looked like it had been trampled on repeatedly, lying flat to the ground.

Dirk couldn't look any more. He turned away, but it was too late; the sight of the baby and the smell combined to make his damaged body spew out the contents of his breakfast on to the ground. Elana edged over towards him, but Dirk waved her away.

Belwynn made an upset noise as she, too, recognised what it was. 'What is it doing here?' she demanded.

Nobody seemed to have an answer for her. Then Rabigar spoke up.

'The Drobax are unlike any other race in Dalriya. They are so numerous and yet so despised by their masters in Ishari that, when they march to war, everyone goes. Not just male adults, but everyone—even infants. If a few thousand die on the way, no one cares. So many have marched through here, if you were to follow in their path you would find many bodies along the way.'

'Thousands of them,' said Gyrmund. 'What can the Empire do to stop that?' No one answered him.

'It can't,' said Herin finally.

'Do all the Drobax…look like that?' asked Moneva, gesturing towards the baby, though keeping her eyes fixed away from it.

'Their skin is grey in complexion. Adults are often hairy. The strongest will wear armour they have taken from somewhere, but many wear nothing. They can reach five feet in height, thin-looking, but that hides their strength. They are a created race,' Rabigar continued, 'by the wizards of Ishari. They bred them for their own purposes. Stupidity and base instincts make them easy to control. But they can be cunning and cruel. They have as strong an instinct for self-preservation as any living thing. That makes them dangerous. But they are a blunt, imprecise weapon. If Erkindrix has sent them to take the Empire, it means he has decided on a speedy destruction. Nothing much will be left surviving afterwards. These are new tactics from him.'

'New tactics?' asked Belwynn.

'Up to now Erkindrix has used the people he has conquered. Arioc was made King of Haskany, and their soldiers now fight for Ishari. The Drobax have hardly been used. Their use now suggests that Erkindrix isn't that interested in the Empire as a rich resource to be exploited. He wants total victory, whatever the cost, and soon.'

Soren nodded. 'What you say makes sense, Rabigar. I wonder if anything has prompted this change in approach.'

Nobody seemed to have any suggestions, so Soren's question was left unanswered.

'I'm going to bury that baby,' said Belwynn suddenly.

'Belwynn—' began Soren.

'I know, it may be stupid,' said Belwynn, interrupting him, 'but I'm not leaving it like that.'

She walked over to the body. Clarin followed her and offered his help.

Everyone waited in uncomfortable silence but the big man dug out a shallow grave quickly enough.

Gyrmund wordlessly led them off away from the Road. Everyone followed in silence. A sombre mood had fallen on the group, and everyone seemed lost in their own private thoughts. As he struggled on at the back of the group, Dirk tried to imagine a horde of these Drobax descending on his homeland. *Maybe I hadn't fully realised,* he admitted to himself, *what was at stake. I have to force this broken body to help Elana as much as possible. Only she can save us.*

***

Farred felt a sense of foreboding as the combined forces of Magnian and Middian soldiers arrived at their destination: Castle Burkhard. It had been a looming presence in the distance for the last few hours, and the closer they had got to it, the more formidable it seemed.

Two giant rocks shot upwards from the ground, dwarfing the countryside around. Brock fancied that they looked like the bent knees of some immense sleeping giant. The slightly smaller rock, where they were now heading, was thinner and irregular in shape, while the larger rock was shaped like a pyramid. Both had stone-built structures on top of them, and Farred had noticed a bridge connecting the two about three quarters of the way up. Coming to it from the east, which most people would do, would make it even more formidable-looking, he considered. The land to the east, including the Great Road, was relatively flat and featureless. Castle Burkhard dominated this territory. To the west, from where Farred and his soldiers had come, the land was rocky, tough, barren and virtually unsettled by humans. They had, in fact, seen more impressive slabs of rock on their journey. None of which, of course, had a stone castle built on top of them.

At the base of the castle they were met by Rainer, the imperial chamberlain. There was a small village here which must have found itself suddenly overwhelmed with soldiers. The road which ran through the village and approached the castle was a muddy mess after the comings and goings of so many soldiers. Their force had been allocated a temporary barracks to the south of the village, which was adequate enough. There was no time to rest, however. Rainer led the way up to the castle, followed by Prince Ashere, who was flanked by Farred and Brock.

They followed the path and reached the base of the first rock. Farred was keen to study the defences of the famous fortress, which they might have to help to defend. This first rock, even more so than the other, was a virtually vertical climb upwards, and so the path, which had been hewn into it, wound its way upwards around the rock. Any defenders were automatically given a height advantage on the path itself, but more than that were able to hurl down onto the attackers all manner of unpleasant objects. Rock, thought Farred, being the most obvious.

Half way up, a massive boulder was positioned just off the path, kept in place by a wooden buttress. When released, it would roll down the path, squashing anything in its way. They stopped for a brief rest.

'The castle atop this crag is known as the Duke's Keep, traditionally occupied by the dukes of Kelland,' said Rainer, breathing hard from the steep climb. 'It's linked by the bridge to the Emperor's Keep. Duke Burkhard built both structures here as a defence against the Persaleian army, which couldn't be beaten in a pitched battle. How times change, eh?' he said wryly. 'Baldwin has garrisoned the Emperor's Keep; his father-in-law Duke Arne has his forces in the Duke's Keep.'

'Are you expecting the other duchies to send forces here?' asked Ashere.

'Yes...' Rainer replied, though he sounded unsure of himself. A look of worry crossed his face. 'I'll let the Emperor explain all that to you.'

They walked on, and Farred began to feel the effects of the upward climb in his thighs, especially after all the riding they had done. 'This is one hell of a thing to climb up when you've got people trying to kill you every step of the way,' he commented.

Brock chuckled and slapped him on the back. 'Good job we picked to fight with the defenders, my friend!'

'We're here...Your Highness,' said the chamberlain, stopping to catch his breath.

It must have taken them close to an hour to reach the summit, and all four men were perspiring freely after the steep upwards climb. To attack such a place, thought Farred, must surely be madness. At this point the path divided into three ahead of them, while, in-between and to the side of each path, sheer rock walls loomed above. Even now the Brasingians had stationed some men here on guard duty, but in a real attack these defences would be bristling with soldiers.

Rainer began towards the left path.

'Does it matter which path is taken?' asked Ashere.

'Only the left path takes you to the top,' said the chamberlain, turning around and resuming the last ascent.

They followed behind and reached the top. Although it was a mild day, the wind whipped about them at this exposed height and soon cooled off Farred's sweat. To their right lay a stone-built fortress which perched close to the far edge of the summit: the Duke's Keep. Farred counted five towers, the farthest one being the tallest, soaring above the walls as if trying to reach the sky. To their left was the bridge, which Farred had noticed from the ground. Rainer took them in this direction. As he approached, Farred let out a whistle.

'It's made of stone!' he marvelled.

The bridge arched across the divide between the two rocks as if held there by magic. On the other side of the bridge, and slightly higher up, stood a larger fortress which took up the whole of the opposing summit. Below was a sheer drop of several hundred feet. Farred had only seen a handful of stone built bridges in his life. To see one here, spanning these huge crags, was stunning.

'How did they—' he began.

'I've got no idea how they built it,' Rainer interrupted, obviously expecting the question. 'Marshall Walter, the Emperor's brother, might know. He seems to have studied this place as much as anyone. My job is to lead you across. Emperor Baldwin's hall is in the Emperor's Keep opposite. I advise you not to look down.'

With that, Rainer placed his first foot on the bridge. He began to walk steadily, if carefully, across it. Farred and his companions exchanged worried glances.

'I'm staying here,' announced Brock, folding his arms.

'If you do,' replied Ashere, placing one foot and then the next onto the bridge, 'I'll have to tell your men that you were too scared to cross.'

Farred held his breath and joined Ashere on the bridge. The bridge did not, as he had half expected it to, suddenly collapse.

'Oh, shit,' swore Brock, and, after a moment's hesitation, followed on.

Emperor Baldwin had invited only Ashere to the Royal Council, but the Prince had insisted that Farred and Brock attend as well, since he could not speak alone for all of the soldiers in their force. Rainer had assented, but was clearly in a rush.

'This is the main hall,' he said breathlessly, before barging open the double doors and entering what must be the largest room in the fortress. Like everything else, it was designed with functionality rather than elegance in mind, but it impressed with its size. No doubt it would have looked larger, but most parts of the hall were being used for temporary storage. Pieces of armour, for every part of the body, had been unceremoniously dumped in one corner. In another, barrels of food and drink had been stacked. It was at the far end of the hall that the meeting was taking place.

Rainer led them over to the small group of men sitting about a plain wooden table. As they approached, the men stood up to greet them.

'Your Majesty, I present His Highness Prince Ashere of North Magnia and the lords Farred and Brock.'

Farred looked to see who Rainer directed the introduction to.

Emperor Baldwin looked confident and physically fit, his hair dark but studded with grey. This was the man responsible for the deployment of Farred's troops and the defence of the lands of the South. On first sight, Farred could not be disappointed. He detected a slight look of anger in his eyes and jaw, presumably at the fact that Farred and Brock were attending as well. It was a small war council, and no doubt Baldwin would rather have had men around him that he knew he could trust. Still, the Emperor hid his annoyance. Farred didn't mind the anger. It showed a man used to having his orders followed.

'His Imperial Majesty, Emperor Baldwin; His Grace Arne, Duke of Luderia; Lord Walter, Marshall of the Empire; Lord Gustav, Archmage of the Empire.'

Baldwin moved and shook Ashere by the hand, thanking him for coming. Everyone then made sure they shook a hand or nodded an acknowledgement before they were quickly seated.

'I hope you will excuse our grim faces and lack of hospitality this day,' began Baldwin, 'but we have bad news and difficult decisions to make.'

'We expected such a situation, Your Majesty,' replied Ashere. 'That is why we are here.'

Baldwin nodded. He let out a breath of air, as if deciding which bad news he should relate first.

'Two days ago Duke Ellard of Rotelegen made a second raid on the Haskan forces positioned just over the border in Grienna. It seems that the first time he caught them by surprise. But on the second, the tables were turned. They were waiting for him—probably lured him into a trap. He was killed.'

Baldwin paused a few moments to let that news settle in. Farred felt a tingling along his spine. This was important news of war, but it was magnified in that it had happened only miles away from where they were now.

'Most of his army was slaughtered, including his three eldest sons. A few escaped to bring back the news. His youngest and only remaining son, Jeremias, was left back in Guslar. He is now duke. Only sixteen, we think.'

Walter, Baldwin's brother, nodded grimly in confirmation.

'So, in most ways that matter, we have lost the army of Rotelegen. The duchy is indefensible...' Baldwin's voice trailed off a little.

Indefensible. Farred wondered what that meant, what decisions had already been made.

Baldwin gathered his thoughts together. 'Gustav had just begun to tell us his news. If you could go over that again, Gustav.'

The other three men were dressed in the leather armour of soldiers, as if ready to ride and fight at a moment's notice. The brothers, Baldwin and Walter, looked the part. Duke Arne of Luderia didn't. In fact, the man looked ill, his face pale and his eyes baggy. They seemed to wander around, as if he were not really involved in the conversation. The fourth man, Gustav the Archmage, was wearing knee-high black leather boots and a yellow robe with a patterned hem, belted at the waist. He began to speak.

'On hearing the news of the battle yesterday, I went to Grienna to see for myself. To check on the facts of the battle as they were reported to us. The facts are true, I am afraid. However, once there, I discovered yet worse news. The Haskan army has now been joined by a force of Drobax from the north. The size of this force is beyond imagination. It sits like a plague on the edge of our lands. Perhaps less than half of these Drobax are fighters, as we would call them. For Ishari has sent all of these creatures, be they male or female, old or young, healthy or ill. As for numbers, I could guess, but it would be meaningless. Millions. When it is in those numbers, you cannot count or assess size.'

'Millions?' Brock let out, his voice incredulous.

Gustav simply nodded. 'It is not a military force as we would understand it. They are not trained fighters, but beasts who would do Ishari's bidding. They are not even being provisioned. Supplies come in for the Haskan soldiers, but hardly any for the Drobax. They steal what they can from any Griennese stupid enough to get caught. But mostly they eat each other.'

Farred gasped, an involuntary sound.

'To me, it seemed a practice the Drobax were familiar with. The smallest and weakest are killed and eaten. And yet at the same time, more are produced. I could see them fornicating; I could see pregnant Drobax females walking around. In one sense, it is the ultimate army, capable of feeding itself. The commanders seem not to worry about logistics or keeping them alive. Each day they are there, many thousand will perish. But that is something hardly worth caring about, since such mortality hardly takes away from the overall number. Soon, they must unleash this force on the Empire. When one combines it with the large and well-organised army of Haskany and the Ishari sorcerers they have gathered there, I am afraid it is unstoppable. To put an army against it in the field would be laughable. A fly attacking a horse.'

'So,' said Ashere, speaking slowly, as if still absorbing this terrifying information, 'Rotelegen is virtually defenceless, while there is such a force on its border ready to invade. Have you any ideas about how to respond?'

Baldwin gave a pained smile, as if the question were a cruel joke. 'I know how I will respond. Unfortunately, it is not a response which holds out any real hope. That, I am afraid, is beyond me.'

Baldwin paused. Farred wondered whether he hoped that someone would interrupt, and demand that there was cause for such hope. But how could there be?

'I have already sent word to Jeremias and his advisers in Guslar. Rotelegen is to be evacuated. The whole duchy. Everyone there is at the mercy of Ishari. I'm not going to waste what force I have left on making a vain gesture. I'm going to make it as hard as possible for the fuckers.'

Farred liked what he heard. Ashere seemed to agree.

'Yes. Give them the hardest fight you can. That is all you can do.'

Baldwin seemed to take some encouragement from those words.

'What forces Jeremias has left he will have to use to make their people leave. Arne's troops will help. Those who can fight will be sent here. Those who can't will go south to Essenberg. Any source of food or water for the invaders will have to be destroyed or poisoned. We're not giving them one free meal. Walter will finish the defences here. I pray to Gerhold and any other god who will listen that the other duchies of the Empire send their troops in time. And then we hole ourselves up in here and last as long as possible.'

Ashere nodded. Farred wondered how he could, since Baldwin of Brasingia had just spelled out a nightmarish end to his Empire: its army holed up in this castle, its people scattered to the south, utterly defenceless against Ishari's armies.

'May I ask,' said Ashere, 'whether you have found a role for our small force?'

Baldwin smiled. 'Thank you for coming to help us,' he said, making sure that he met eyes with both Farred and Brock as well as with Ashere. 'You have arrived sooner than most of my dukes. I would like to think I would have done the same for your countries, but...anyway, I owe your people a debt of gratitude. To answer your question, Your Highness: yes. I do have a role for you. You are to check the advance of the enemy while my people escape.'

XXIV

SWIFT MAGIC

B ELWYNN DID HER BEST to put the sights of the Great Road behind
her as the group continued on their journey westwards. Everyone was
quiet, however, and that did not make it easy. The whole experience had
been very unsettling. The Drobax were a disturbing intrusion into the world she
thought she knew.

Grienna was not a large state, and it did not take them long to travel the width
of it. The major settlements were clustered around the Great Road, which fed
their economies. But travel a few miles either way and the ancient forests of
Dalriya reclaimed their dominance of the landscape. It was not long after midday
that they found the terrain getting more difficult and the signs of human
habitation disappearing.

They pressed on. As was usual by now, Gyrmund led the way. He was taking
them in a north-westerly direction, hoping to cut into the centre of the lands of
the Grand Caladri and find the inhabitants. The forests of the Grand Caladri
were larger than those of the Blood Caladri. That meant they would be even
more sparsely settled. Soren pointed out that finding the Caladri would be almost
impossible. They would have to hope that, instead, the Caladri would find them.

As time went by, Gyrmund began muttering to himself. Then he abruptly
stopped.

'We've been past here already,' he exclaimed angrily.

'Are you sure?' asked Belwynn.

'Yes. I've had the feeling awhile. At first I thought I was going mad. So I
snapped a twig.'

Gyrmund pointed to a low hanging branch of a tree a few feet in front of
him. A twig lay hanging down from it at head height, snapped but still attached.

'Well, stop taking us the wrong way,' suggested Herin.

'I'm not!' shouted Gyrmund.

'Calm it,' said Soren. 'This is the work of the Grand Caladri. They are stronger
magic users than the Blood Caladri. They have always used magic to defend their

boundaries rather than weapons. They obviously confuse anyone who tries to get too far.'

'Then how can you stop it?' asked Gyrmund.

'I can't!' snapped Soren.

Now he seemed to be losing his temper. He held his hands up in an apology and took a deep breath.

'Sorry. It's happening again. They are casting a subtle sort of magic which encourages people to fight with each other. I suspect that most unwanted intruders end up killing each other so that the Grand Caladri don't have to bother. Anyway, we'll have to control ourselves and be careful. Especially you two,' he said, gesturing at Herin and Gyrmund.

Herin and Gyrmund stood sour-faced, but said nothing.

'So, Soren,' began Belwynn carefully, 'any ideas what we should do?'

'Not really. There's no point carrying on. I guess we just wait here and hope they come to us. That's the trouble with shutting yourself away from the world. You cut off potential friends as well as enemies.'

'Why should they come to us?' asked Moneva.

Soren shrugged. 'Perhaps we look more interesting than the usual visitor?'

'Well I would think so,' said Herin. 'A one-eyed Krykker for a start…'

Herin realised what he had done in mid-speech and clapped a hand over his own mouth.

'Sorry,' he said to Rabigar.

Rabigar shrugged the insult away.

'I think I'll go for a walk and cool down,' Herin said.

'I wouldn't,' said Soren. 'You might never find us again. I think we should all rest up here for a while. Gyrmund, maybe you could start a fire?'

The group sat down around Gyrmund's fire. There was an uneasy feeling amongst them, and most people took the chance to eat their midday meal in relative silence.

Perhaps an hour went by before the Caladri arrived. Where the Blood Caladri had intercepted them with an armed group of soldiers, the Grand Caladri had apparently sent only one person.

He was dressed in loose tunic and trousers and carried no weapons that Belwynn could see. Belwynn knew that didn't necessarily make him any less dangerous.

Wizard, said Soren, confirming her suspicions.

262

The Caladri wizard approached from the direction they had been heading in. He walked slowly, but with the same jerky motion Belwynn had noticed amongst the Blood Caladri. He had a long, grey beard that covered his facial features and went down to his chest. It was difficult to place an age on the Caladri they had met, since they had longer life spans than humans. But Belwynn guessed that this man was of the generation between Szabolcs and Prince Lorant.

The group hastily stood up as he approached. He stopped a few feet from them and stood still for a while, observing. Did Belwynn feel a feather-light touch on her mind? She couldn't be sure.

No one said anything. The group had become accustomed to taking the lead from Soren in these situations. He seemed content to wait for the Grand Caladri to speak, and so everyone waited.

'You are not from Ishari.'

It sounded like a statement rather than a question, but Soren nodded to confirm it.

'You bring news of the invasion?'

The invasion? Does he mean that Ishari has invaded the Empire? Belwynn asked her brother.

I don't know what he means.

'We bring news from Prince Lorant of the Blood Caladri and from Emperor Baldwin of Brasingia,' said Soren. 'This news is about the threat from Ishari. However, we have been travelling, and have not heard from the south for a while. Has the Empire been attacked?'

'Quite possibly, but I have no news of that myself. I speak of the Ishari attack on our lands. They are mounting their challenge now. The news you bring us is perhaps redundant now?'

'I don't think so,' replied Soren, 'I think it's vitally important.'

'You must understand,' said the wizard. 'Time is short and all enchanters are needed for the defence. Why should I expend my energies on bringing you into our lands when they are needed to defend them? You must give me an acceptable answer.'

Soren thought about it. Before he came up with a reply, Elana answered for him.

'We bring tidings from Lady Onella. She has told us how to defend Dalriya from Ishari.'

The wizard's eyes widened a little at the answer to his question. He stood looking intently at Elana for a while. Again, Belwynn wondered whether he was using magic to search within her, checking on the truth of what she said.

'Very well,' he said eventually. 'Your presence may be important. We have no time to go by foot. I must transport you inside. I will get little help to do that, and it is costly. The more people I transport, the more difficult it is. Must you all enter our lands?'

They all looked about at each other. How could they decide who was important and who wasn't?

'I think we all should go,' said Belwynn honestly.

The wizard nodded his acceptance of this.

'My name is Ignac. Please follow me.'

Ignac led them back in the direction that he had appeared from, past Gyrmund's broken twig. Except this time, instead of more forest, they came upon a wooden pole. It was just like the one they had found when they had entered the lands of the Blood Caladri, with similar markings on it.

'Place at least one hand on the pole,' instructed Ignac.

'It's a form of transport?' asked Soren wonderingly.

'Yes. They help us to guide a transportation from one location to the next.'

They all crowded around it. Belwynn sat down on her haunches so that she could grab a lower section of the pole and leave room for everyone else.

Ignac recited some words under his breath, and Belwynn felt her stomach lurching. Lights swirled around them and her vision receded, until all she could see was her friends clasping the pole. Then she could see nothing.

She gripped the pole tightly as she experienced the sensation of moving. She thought she could hear some of the others speaking or shouting, but they seemed like faraway sounds. Her stomach roiled as she moved, cut off from most of her senses. Then she stopped. She saw her knuckles, white from clinging on to the pole. Her vision expanded. Soren and the others were there. She took a deep breath and tried not to vomit. Clarin didn't manage it, staggering off to the side and hurling against a tree. Dirk had a coughing fit that brought up blood and mucus.

Belwynn used the pole to lift herself to her feet. She realised that this pole must be a different one, because they were now in a new location, but at no point had she let go of the original.

Ignac had taken them to the outskirts of what looked like a sizeable settlement, by Caladri standards.

'Are we ready?' he asked.

The group gathered themselves together.

Are you alright? asked Soren.

Yes, why?

Nothing. You just look very pale.

Looking around, she saw that she wasn't the only one. Dirk looked dreadful, but Elana was tending to him, and he gave a weak thumb up to indicate that he was ready to move on. After hearing how he had killed Nexodore three days ago, Belwynn found that she had a completely different opinion of the man, and she admired his bravery in continuing their journey despite his obvious physical frailty.

Ignac led them towards the settlement. The Caladri did not appear to engage in arable farming at all, so there were no fields or such signs of habitation, as Belwynn would expect to see in human lands. There was a Caladri road, however, and on each side of it sat timber buildings, nestling in amongst the trees of the forest. The settlement was designed, it seemed to Belwynn, to blend in to the natural surroundings as much as possible.

She worried, however. There were no signs of defences here. The bigger towns of the Empire and even of Magnia all had some kind of walled defence, of timber if not of stone. The Caladri, it seemed, did not feel the need for such defences. Yet Ignac had told them that Ishari was about to invade their lands.

He began to lead them along the road towards the settlement. Coming in the opposite direction were about a score of Caladri, a mixture of males and females. As the two groups approached each other, they slowed down and stopped. One of the male Caladri left his group to approach them. Belwynn thought he looked about the same age as Ignac. Ignac fell to one knee.

'Lord Kelemen,' he began.

The man he addressed made a wristy movement with one hand. Ignac stood up again. Kelemen looked Belwynn's group over.

'This is a delegation, apparently from Prince Lorant and Emperor Baldwin,' explained Ignac.

'With what purpose?' asked Kelemen.

'We bring news of a threat from Ishari,' explained Soren.

'Ha,' Kelemen laughed bitterly. 'A little late.' He looked them over. 'Rather a strange group to be representing the Blood Caladri and Kellish. May I ask what you are doing in this company?' he said, directing the question at Rabigar.

'I am…exiled from my homeland. I do not represent the Krykkers.'

'I see,' said Kelemen. 'I will be frank with you all, since you arrive at a serious time, when our presence is needed elsewhere. We are the ablest enchanters of this region. We go to our capital, Edeleny, to defend the borders of our realm. The forces of Ishari are preparing to attack them. An army is poised to invade from the north should our defences be breached. As a leader of this region, it is my duty to bring my enchanters to Edeleny as soon as possible. Ignac says you have news of the threat we face. I must hear this news quickly.'

Soren began to speak for the group, going as quickly as he could. He told Kelemen what they had learned of the weapons of Madria from Szabolcs of the Blood Caladri. He explained how they had come to be in possession of one of them. Finally, he told Kelemen that they believed Ishari posed a threat to the whole of Dalriya.

'So,' he concluded, 'this attack on the Grand Caladri is part of a greater scheme that Ishari has. I believe that to defeat Ishari we need these weapons. And I fear that Ishari has grown in power. How sure are you that your magic defences will hold against them?'

'They have never been breached,' replied Kelemen simply. 'May I see the weapon you have?'

Dirk fumbled in his cloak for a while before producing Toric's Dagger. He looked nervously at Elana, who nodded at him, before he passed it over to Kelemen. The Caladri studied it closely, tracing a finger along its edge.

'Of course, you are interested in Lady Onella's Staff, in the temple at Edeleny. That is partly why you are here,' he said, making it a statement rather than a question.

Soren nodded.

'You intend to take the staff from us just like you have taken this dagger?' the Caladri said, in accusing tones.

'The Lady Onella, or Madria, as she names herself to me, needs the weapons to fight Ishari,' interjected Elana. 'We do her work.'

'Onella speaks to you?' demanded Kelemen.

'Yes,' replied Elana simply.

Kelemen looked at Elana for a good while. He thought carefully.

'You may come with us to Edeleny. Perhaps your words should be passed on to the elders of the Caladri. Any decision is for them to make. But Edeleny is under attack. I cannot guarantee your safety if you come with us.'

He gave the dagger in his hands another look. Belwynn saw the look in his eyes.

He wants to keep it, she warned Soren.

A few moments passed before Kelemen offered the weapon back to Dirk. He had obviously decided to return it. For now.

Soren looked around the group. 'Not everyone has to come,' he advised them.

Indeed, not everyone looked sure that they wanted to go. But the alternative, stuck in an unknown part of the Grand Caladri forest, didn't seem too appealing, either. Belwynn knew that everyone had made their decision back in Essenberg, for good or ill. No-one was about to change their mind now.

'Are you still strong enough to help us?' Kelemen asked Ignac.

'Yes, My Lord,' Ignac replied.

Kelemen pointed towards the pole they had arrived at. 'Then we will all go on to Edeleny at once.'

With a gesture towards the other Caladri, Kelemen led them on towards the pole. They were now about thirty in number. Kelemen decided that they would travel in two groups. He asked Belwynn's group to split into two, so that there would be sufficient magic users in each group.

Kelemen and half of the other Caladri placed their hands on the pole. Belwynn joined them, along with Soren, Rabigar, Elana and Dirk.

As before, Belwynn felt a strange lurching sensation in her belly first, then the rest of her senses began to be affected as the teleportation began. She felt a kind of itchiness inside her head, then her vision left her and the feeling of nausea kicked in. They were travelling faster than before, and she felt the sensation of speed on her body. They were also travelling further this time, and the longer it went on, the more tiring and difficult it became. Then, without warning, they had stopped. Belwynn felt like the world was spinning around her. She was physically sick. She actually felt a bit better for it. A hand brushed her hair back.

'Belwynn? Are you alright?'

It was Soren. She opened her eyes. She could see, but they were unable to focus on anything properly. Soren helped her pull herself up. The spinning sensation returned as she stood up, but she gradually began to recover. Rabigar had put Elana into a sitting position and was talking quietly to her. It looked like she, too, had been sick.

Then Belwynn saw Dirk. He was still lying in a prone position, seemingly unconscious. He had also been sick, but it was stained red with his blood.

'The teleportation must have affected him badly,' said Soren. 'He has not recovered from the injuries Nexodore gave him. Not nearly recovered.'

A female Caladri was crouching over Dirk, while feeling his forehead and the pulse in his neck. When Elana saw him she gave a little cry and crawled over to check him herself.

'Will he be alright?' asked Belwynn.

'I'm not sure,' said Elana. 'He's breathing…'

The female Caladri crouching next to her reached up to receive an item passed down to her. Belwynn could see that it was a small vial. The Caladri worked away a stopper at the top. She then delicately passed the vial under Dirk's nose.

Nothing happened for two seconds, then Dirk suddenly jerked awake. He gave a horrible, rasping cough, and more drops of blood were expelled. He fought to breathe in air for a while, looking like a fish that had been pulled out of the water. Elana whispered quietly to him and slowly his breathing steadied and he opened his eyes. Dirk was helped to his feet, and everyone moved a few feet away from the pole to make space for the arrival of the second group.

Belwynn looked about her. They were in another forest clearing, but close by she made out a Caladri road. Following its path, she could see what must be Edeleny in the distance. The peaks of tall buildings rose up as high as the trees, and she thought she could faintly hear the noise and bustle which always emanates from large settlements.

The second group arrived at the pole. The arrival was fast, but Belwynn's eyes detected a degree of movement, as if they had arrived *from* somewhere, to the east, rather than appearing from nowhere. The Caladri seemed immune from the side effects of the teleportation, but Herin, Clarin, Gyrmund and Moneva were all affected in the same way she had been. They lay in a confused state, clutching their disturbed stomachs, before they slowly began to recover.

It was another few minutes before everyone was ready to walk the short distance to Edeleny. Dirk said he felt better, but he was still pale and fragile-looking. They connected to the road, and as they walked, Belwynn began to get a better view of the capital.

It was smaller by far than human cities such as Essenberg or Coldeberg, but Edeleny did stretch out over a reasonably large area. The buildings were bigger and more substantial-looking than she had seen elsewhere in the lands of the Caladri. They began to walk past small, one-storey houses, made from timber with thatched roofs. They all had the same conical shape and were virtually identical in size. Kelemen had intimated that wizards would arrive here from all over the lands of the Grand Caladri to work together in its defence. Belwynn wondered whether some of the accommodation they passed was built to house visitors to the capital, rather than serving as people's permanent homes.

Belwynn regularly caught glimpses of the taller buildings of the settlement, which all had a central location. These were white in colour, looking as if they had been made of marble. It gave them a delicate, ethereal look. As they neared, Belwynn found that many had been constructed in and around trees. Tree trunks and branches somehow mingled with the white walls of the buildings. It looked as if the Caladri had used the trunks as central pillars for construction. The wide, strong branches were used to build the floors of the buildings. The largest had many floors, each with wide windows that allowed Belwynn to see through and get a look at the interior.

There was little sign of habitation. Some looked like industrial buildings, with spinning machines inside. Gyrmund brushed his hand along one of the white walls, then gave it a knock.

'Wooden,' he said, when he noticed Belwynn taking an interest. 'It looks like it's been treated with some substance that turns it white and reinforces it.' He gave it another slap. 'It feels as strong as stone.'

They began to pass other Caladri, all of whom seemed busy on some errand. Some were guiding others to various locations; others carried food, or wooden boxes.

None of them carry weapons, or wear armour, Belwynn said to Soren.

They seem totally confident in their magical defences, he replied. *I fear it is over-confidence.*

The main road they were walking on now joined into a central square, which had three other roads running off it at parallel points. The square surrounded by the roads seemed to be a gathering place, mostly covered in grass; wooden seats and a garden were located in the middle. At its centre, a fountain sprayed water into the air in beautiful, frothy arcs. But no one talked by the fountain or walked through the gardens now.

Kelemen pointed to a large, one-storey building roughly opposite them.

'That is Onella's Temple,' he said. 'Her staff lies there.'

Built of the white wood material, the temple consisted of a number of wings connected to each other at right angles, so that it took up a large amount of space on the ground.

'We are going to the Temenos,' continued Kelemen, this time pointing to a building sited on the left hand side of the square. This had been constructed around one huge tree, which rose up through the centre and was the tallest building in the complex, presumably consisting of many floors. It was cylindrical in shape, the white wood punctured in various places to allow certain branches of the tree to continue out of the structure. The tree, and quite possibly the building, must have been hundreds of years old. The building gave off an aura, almost as if the presence of the tree meant that the whole building was alive.

Outside, eight Caladri soldiers stood guard. They wore brightly-polished armour and carried impossibly long pikes, at least twenty feet in length, all held at the same angle. They looked straight ahead and were perfectly still, as if they were not living creatures but statues. The spikes and blades on the end of the pikes looked viciously sharp. They were the first soldiers Belwynn had seen in the lands of the Grand Caladri, but their presence seemed as much ceremonial as practical.

The large wooden doors of the circular building were open, and as Kelemen approached them another Caladri came out to meet them. He wore a plain white outfit and had white hair which was tied up in a ponytail.

'Hurry!' he said, jerking his arm vigorously to get them into the building. He then stopped short as he noticed the strangers in his capital.

'What are they doing here?' he demanded, sounding almost hysterical.

'They are messengers from Baldwin of Kelland,' explained Kelemen, not looking happy at how he was being addressed. 'Lorant of the Blood Caladri sent them here.'

'Who is he?' Belwynn asked Ignac in a whisper.

'That is Agoston, one of our elders,' replied the Caladri.

'...haven't got time,' Agoston was saying, lecturing Kelemen. 'Whatever Baldwin and Lorant have to say isn't going to change anything.'

'I have spoken to these people myself,' replied Kelemen, standing his ground. 'I believe that Lady Onella has directed them here.'

In the end Kelemen got his way. The white-haired Caladri elder waved all of them in.

XXV

THE TEMENOS

THE TEMENOS WAS UNLIKE ANYTHING Belwynn had ever seen. The whole of the ground floor was taken up by one large circular room, while a flight of stairs twisted around the wall to the next level. The great trunk of the tree rose up in the middle of the floor and carried on through a massive hole in the ceiling. Around the circumference of the trunk, a large circular table had been constructed. Nearly a hundred Caladri sat at chairs around the table. All the chairs seemed to be filled. There was a mixture of Caladri: old and young, male and female; all sat calmly, as if in meditation. Some had their eyes closed; others had their eyes fixed on the giant tree in front of them. Agoston led them around the table and took them upstairs to the next floor.

As they ascended, Belwynn noted that two great branches of the tree stretched along the full length of the ceiling. She surmised that the Caladri must have shaped the growth of this giant tree over the years to suit the design of their building.

'Well, this is peculiar,' Belwynn heard Clarin mutter ahead as he reached the next floor. When Belwynn got sight of the room, she had to agree. It was set up in an identical fashion to the room below. Most of the chairs around the table were filled with Caladri sitting quietly at the table.

Are they all wizards? she asked Soren.

There was no answer. She looked behind her. Soren was staring at the room. She sighed. Sometimes he would nod or shake his head in answer to a question without realising that she couldn't see it.

Are you going to answer me? she demanded testily.

Sorry. Yes, all of them are wizards. Some will be very powerful, some less so. I'm just wondering how many floors there are. I've never imagined this many wizards present all in one place.

It looked like Soren would find out. Up they went, past the third to the fourth floor, each room identical, except that the trunk of the tree became gradually narrower and the rooms therefore slightly less cramped. On the fourth floor there was a group of empty chairs, and here Kelemen's group of wizards, including Ignac, took their seats.

Agoston led the rest of them all the way up to the seventh and final floor. Kelemen turned to them.

'The Grand Caladri are unlike most other peoples. We have no kings or emperors to rule over us. We make our own decisions. But we do have three elders in our society: the wisest of our people who reside in Edeleny to guide our affairs. These are the people who wear the white. They must hear what you have learned about the weapons of Onella.'

The last step brought them into the highest room in the Temenos. The tree was thinner at this height, which meant that there was a bit more space around the edges of the room. This was taken up by shelves, mostly containing books and scrolls of parchment. There were only about thirty Caladri here.

Two of them stood away from the table, wearing the same white garments as Agoston. They were facing the direction of the stairs, as if waiting for their arrival.

Agoston spoke with his comrades. 'Kelemen intercepted this group on his way here. He insists we need to listen to them.'

One of them, a brown-haired man with fierce eyebrows, riled at the suggestion.

'The attack has begun. We need to respond now.'

'They should go,' said the second, a woman who held her chin so high it gave her an arrogant demeanour. 'They could interfere.'

'I wouldn't have brought them here if I didn't think it was important,' said Kelemen, holding his ground.

'Very well, Kelemen,' the first man responded. He turned to face them. 'We still have our manners, even on a day like this. My name is Odon. This is Dorottya. We will hear your news.'

Elana spoke to them, explaining her relationship to Madria as clearly as she could. The three elders seemed to listen to what she said. Dirk produced the dagger, and it was briefly passed around.

'Clearly this information is important,' said Odon when Elana had finished. 'Our current situation makes it clear that we are as guilty as anyone else of underestimating the threat from Ishari. We have been deceived, or deceived ourselves. The other weapons should be found and brought together again.'

'We can discuss this further after the attack,' Agoston added.

'No,' said Elana, surprising Belwynn with her defiance. 'There is no time to lose. We must take the Staff now, before it is lost to Ishari.'

'Don't worry about that,' said Odon reassuringly. 'They have an army out there, but it won't be able to get into our lands. If they try to invade, we will ensure that they wander in our forest, lost, until they drop from exhaustion.'

'You are missing the point,' interrupted Soren. 'Erkindrix can call on far more wizards from Ishari than even you can muster on your own. I fear that your defences will not hold against a committed attack. You need to prepare your military forces as well.'

'This is nonsense,' said Dorottya. 'Our defences have never been broken. If Ishari attacked us with all their wizards, they would suffer as well. Wizards from both sides would perish. What would they have to gain from that? They are testing our defences, that is all. But they will find them as robust as ever.'

'We have not threatened them,' Agoston added. 'We have remained uninvolved in their affairs for centuries.'

'But,' argued Kelemen, 'the objective of Erkindrix has now changed. He wants all of Dalriya. Including our lands. He may well be prepared to lose some of his forces to defeat us. What if he did? Our people in the north would be totally defenceless. We must act now. Give the order to raise an army to meet the invaders.'

'Listen, Kelemen,' said Odon. 'Our magic is our only hope. Do you know what waits for us on the northern border? Drobax. Thousands upon thousands upon thousands. If you raised an army, you couldn't stop them anyway. When was the last time the Grand Caladri fought in a war? We must rely on our magic. It has ever been thus, because we cannot hope to match them any other way.'

'Then evacuate,' said Rabigar. 'Tell your people in the north to move south now. Get a message to the Krykkers. They will take your people in. But you must do something. It is your duty to protect your people.'

'Don't tell us how to protect our people, Krykker,' said Agoston angrily. 'You do not understand magic and so cannot understand how strong our defences are.'

'This is getting us nowhere,' insisted Kelemen. 'Authorise me to raise an army and begin evacuations. If you can stop the invasion here, well and good. But let me put a contingency plan into operation.'

'If you wish to leave we cannot stop you, Kelemen,' said Odon. 'Though we could do with your help here. And that of your wizards.'

Kelemen nodded. 'I will give them a free choice. They may stay here or come with me.'

Odon spread open his hands, as if there was nothing more he could do or say.

'You are free to go, Kelemen. But these visitors and their weapon must remain. We cannot afford to let it leave. It must be properly examined.'

'You can't keep us here!' shouted Herin, his hand moving to his sword hilt.

Odon turned to him. 'This is the safest place in Dalriya. Until we decide what should be done about the dagger you have, here it stays. You are guests here, not prisoners.'

Belwynn and the others looked to Soren for a lead. He shrugged. 'Very well, we stay.'

Herin didn't like it; nor did Gyrmund and Moneva. But they trusted Soren enough to follow his lead.

Soren turned to Kelemen and held out his hand. 'Good luck.'

Kelemen took his hand. He nodded to the others. 'I wish it hadn't turned out this way. But if the worst should happen and Ishari breaks through, know that your coming here will have helped to save some lives.'

With that, Kelemen turned away and left. Belwynn watched him go, a sinking feeling in her stomach. She then turned back to the Caladri elders. Agoston was instructing a couple of Caladri to fetch something from a corner of the room.

'I am sorry,' he said, 'that this room is not very comfortable for you. But it is the best place for you to stay for now. We do have some refreshments, however.'

A couple of Caladri men brought over some trays containing biscuits, fruit and jugs of water.

'We must resume our places at the table for now,' Odon explained.

Soren sat down on the floor. Reluctantly, Belwynn and the others did the same, though Herin muttered darkly about their predicament. Belwynn herself was worried about the turn of events, though curious about what they would see take place in this room. She knew that Soren's curiosity would be tenfold. She also knew that he still hoped for a magical healing of his overextension. He would never get a better chance than this, in the presence of hundreds of Caladri wizards. Soren was clearly happy enough to stay here for now, but the threat from Ishari hung heavy in the air.

Others weren't so happy to stay.

'This building might become the site of a battle,' Gyrmund whispered to the group, 'and the fact that it would be a magical one doesn't make me feel any better, since Toric only knows what that will involve.'

'Let's see what happens,' Belwynn whispered back. 'We can always try to escape if we need to.'

They sat in silence, watching the wizards on the top floor prepare the defences of their realm. Belwynn wondered whether this group somehow channelled the power of everyone else in the building and sent it out to hold up the barrier around the forest.

After a short period, perhaps only half an hour, the Caladri around the table began murmuring to themselves. Belwynn sensed an intensification in the atmosphere throughout the building.

'It's started,' said Soren quietly, but so that the whole group could hear. 'The forces of Ishari must have decided to try to break open the barrier and let their soldiers in. I suspect that they have gathered a large group of their own wizards together somewhere in order to do so.'

The Caladri were now in full concentration on their purpose. Odon sat still, palms flat on the table and eyes open, staring forward at the tree in front of him. Other magicians held a different pose. Some had eyes closed, some leaned forward, and some muttered chains of words under their breath. Belwynn felt goose pimples on her skin as the magic being deployed in the building rose to new heights. Her companions sensed it, too. Their expressions ranged from disapproval on Rabigar's face to exhilaration on the face of her brother.

Somebody began shouting on one of the floors below. It didn't stop, a lone Caladri voice wailing and crying out.

'What's going on?' demanded Herin, his voice on edge.

'They will soon start to suffer,' said Soren. 'The longer this goes on, the more casualties will be taken on each side. Clarin, have a look below, will you?'

Clarin stomped off down the stairs. Belwynn studied the faces of the Caladri magicians around the table and could see the strain starting to show. Sweat began to run down the side of Agoston's head. Others frowned in concentration or clenched their teeth. A number looked like they were in pain. As the minutes went by other noises from below added to the wailing. Shouts of pain, muffled grunts, and bangs. The magic battle did not seem to relent, however.

There was a sudden bang on their floor. Belwynn looked for the source of the noise and saw that it was the head of one of the wizards, cracking onto the table. He now sat there, not moving at all.

'What happened to him?' asked Moneva, fear plain in her voice.

'Most likely dead,' said Soren, a strange tone to his voice. 'They're starting to get drained of all they have. I think they should stop. I'm not sure that they can keep Ishari out.'

Clarin re-emerged from downstairs. 'It's worse down there.'

Soren stood up. 'Stop!' he shouted in Odon's direction. 'You are taking too many casualties.'

For a few seconds it seemed that the Caladri elder was too involved to reply. But then his voice rasped out, 'Then so are they!'

It was impossible for Belwynn to know whether Odon was right about the Isharites, but she could tell that the pressure on the Caladri did not seem to relent. Individual wizards continued to fall, now on the top floor as well as below. One of them suddenly started screaming, her hands gripping the sides of her head and her eyes bulging out. Another jerked backwards as if physically pushed. He fell back in his chair to collapse in a heap on the floor. Yet another simply crumpled down, head resting on arms as if he had suddenly gone to sleep.

Belwynn and the others were now standing up, the deaths around them becoming unbearable.

'Let's get out of here now,' advised Gyrmund. 'They're losing and there's nothing we can do to help.'

Belwynn felt that he was right. Up to a quarter of the Caladri magicians on their floor were either dead or broken. She sensed that the situation was even worse on the floors below. As each magician fell, their ability to resist Ishari must surely be diminishing.

Then there was a sudden burst of power. The whole building was rocked by it. Some of the Caladri were thrown backwards from the table. Others shouted at each other or screamed in terror. Agoston, the white-haired elder who had led them upstairs, stood up.

Bolts of magic shot out from his outstretched hands, striking the ceiling and the walls of the room. His face was stuck in a grimace as he began to stagger around the room, with no control over his movements. Those Caladri who could were standing up and moving away from the table.

It looked like they had lost. Ishari had broken through the defences and had killed about half of the Grand Caladri's best wizards in the process.

Then Soren leapt forward. Agoston's magic was still draining out of him in an uncontrolled way, fortunately not striking anyone since his hands were in the air. Soren rushed over and seized his hands.

Belwynn looked on in dread. Soren cried out in pain as the magic entered his body. His body began to shake. But after a moment, his expression gradually changed, until it was one of exultation.

'Yes!' he cried out, 'oh, yes!'

Agoston's magic continued to pump into him. Soren must have been able, somehow, to control and direct the magic into restoring his own powers.

He shouted out again, a wordless cry of delight as his eyes shone with ecstasy. Belwynn was a swirl of emotions, deeply disturbed by what she was witnessing and only too aware that the others were watching it too. She felt like she no longer recognised her own brother: his facial expression, his voice, were somehow different. At the same time, she knew how much this meant to Soren and a part of her was able to be happy for him.

Agoston's body fell to the floor, a discarded husk that her brother had sucked dry.

Belwynn looked around. The others were staring at her brother, fear and even loathing in their faces at what they had seen. Even Clarin looked at Soren with something approaching disgust.

Elsewhere, those Caladri magicians who had kept their sanity and their lives were rushing down the stairs to evacuate the building. Others lay dead, or twitching, or still sat in their chairs, screaming out their madness.

'Let's go,' Belwynn shouted desperately.

The others reacted to her voice, and they all made their way to the stairs. Belwynn went over to grab Soren and pulled him along.

The defeat of the Grand Caladri had engendered a sense of panic in the building. Surviving wizards scrambled down the stairs in a hurry, tripping over each other to leave. The feeling spread to Belwynn and her companions as well. Herin and Clarin barged ahead at the front, while Belwynn and Soren brought up the rear. It was silly, really, thought Belwynn. The defences had been broken and the Ishari army of Drobax could now invade. But that army was miles to the north. On the fourth floor she looked for Ignac, but couldn't see him. Perhaps he had left with Kelemen. Then a thought struck her.

Soren, she said.

Yes, he replied. His mind still seemed foggy with euphoria.

The forces of Ishari can now enter the forest. Does that mean that they can teleport into Edeleny like we did?

Soren paused while he thought about it. When he replied, the fogginess had left his thoughts, as if he had been suddenly sobered up from too much drink.

Yes. They have more magic users than the Grand Caladri. Although the battle will have been draining, some of them may still be strong enough to teleport. They may even have kept a fresh force of them ready for such a purpose.

Nexodore knew we had the dagger, said Belwynn. *They might know that the staff is here.*

You're right, said Soren. *We need to get it and get out of here as soon as possible.*

They reached the ground floor of the Temenos and ran for the exit. Caladri wizards lay dead or broken on the floor.

They rushed through the front doors of the building, still guarded by the eight Caladri pikemen, before nearly crashing into the others who had come to an abrupt stop.

Belwynn's worst fears were already realised. In the distance, on the far side of the city square, a small force from Ishari was gathering. Perhaps forty of them. They had already arrived and would soon be heading their way. The Grand Caladri wizards were running in the opposite direction. Their clawed feet allowed them to sprint away at an incredible speed. All of them had decided to run, except for Odon the elder, who faced the invaders alone.

He turned around to look at them. 'Flee. Everyone must flee. We cannot win this battle now. You cannot be captured with the dagger in your possession.'

'Onella's Staff,' said Soren. 'It must be made safe.'

Odon nodded. 'Dorottya has gone to get it. She will take it away from here.'

Only Odon and the eight pikemen remained to defend Edeleny. Those who still could were running into the forest. These survivors would be needed to defend their people. But Belwynn was in no doubt that the forces of Ishari would hunt them down and the Drobax would come. Whatever makeshift army Kelemen could raise wouldn't be able to stop them.

'To the Temple,' Soren said to the group.

For a moment, they hesitated. Soren's performance in the Temenos had lost him the unquestioning trust of the group. But Belwynn followed her brother, as did Elana and Dirk, until the whole group began to follow the path around to the left, where the Temple stood.

Soren looked across the square behind them and took a sharp inhale of breath.

'It's Arioc himself,' he said.

XXVI

ONELLA'S TEMPLE

EVERYONE STOPPED IN THEIR TRACKS and looked in the same direction. Striding ahead of the group of Isharites who had been transported into Edeleny was Arioc: King of Haskany, member of the Council of Seven, second in command to Erkindrix himself. Tall and powerful, he wore gleaming black armour. Black shoulder-length hair framed his features. Even at this distance, he exuded power like no one Belwynn had seen before. More even than Pentas or Nexodore. It was an alien power, as if he did not truly belong among mortals, and it struck Belwynn with fear.

Arioc was marching his troop directly towards Odon. The sword he carried did not have the glint of metal but was black like his armour. He reached the path which took a route around the central square of Edeleny. The grassed recreation area in the middle was desolate, save for the solitary figure of Odon.

But then Belwynn felt something stir from behind her. She spun around. The eight Caladri soldiers. They stood so much like statues that Belwynn had forgotten about them. The presence of the Isharites on the path had seemed to trigger a reaction. Moving in perfect unison, the eight soldiers lifted up their pikes and marched to join Odon in the defence of their city.

'Come on,' said Soren, as the pikemen crossed past them. 'We don't have much time. We can expect a number of them to be wizards, not just Arioc.'

Soren sprinted towards the Temple, and everyone else followed at the same pace. Clarin and Herin barged open the white wooden doors.

A scream echoed around the square behind them. Belwynn turned back to look. Odon was hanging in the sky, suspended four feet from the ground with an orange light surrounding him. Belwynn traced the light back in a line to Arioc's outstretched hand. Another burst of power, and Odon's body turned black and the screaming stopped. Arioc withdrew his hand and the body fell to the ground.

A number of the Isharites looked in their direction. The Caladri pikemen had formed a line on the grass of the central square and were taking most of their attention. Their long pikes whirled around them, making a ghostly whirring noise as they cut through the air. The main group of Isharites looked at the pikes warily, unsure how to tackle them. A small group of Isharites detached itself and headed towards the Temple.

'What do we do?' asked Belwynn. She wanted to run.

'Some of us are going to go inside and get the staff,' said Soren. 'Some of us are going to hold out here for as long as possible. I am staying here. Belwynn, you go in so that I can communicate with you. Dirk, you go in because you have the dagger. Everyone else, do what you think is best.'

Separate? Belwynn didn't want that. 'But…'

'Hurry up, now. Just do it, Belwynn. And take this. Just in case.'

Soren reached into his cloak and handed her Edgar's bag of money.

Belwynn knew she shouldn't argue. She entered the building. Dirk and Elana went with her. Everyone else drew a weapon and waited with Soren.

'Rabigar,' said Soren. 'Will you go with them? They might need protection.'

Rabigar looked at Soren for a moment. Belwynn thought he might argue, but he nodded and followed them in.

The entrance chamber to the Temple was large but poorly lit. Before Belwynn had time to look around, Elana had opened a door at the far end of the room and was beckoning everybody through.

Belwynn took one last look behind her. Moneva and Gyrmund were talking to each other hurriedly. They kissed once. Gyrmund and Herin knocked arrows to their bows. Soren and Clarin turned to look at her. Soren looked at peace. Clarin lifted a hand in farewell.

Belwynn turned around and left them behind.

***

There were four of them. Gyrmund noticed their swords. They weren't made of metal, but he couldn't put his finger on what they *were* made of. In fact, they were different colours. Two of them had swords which looked more like clear glass. Another was yellowish, another light blue. Crystal. They were made out of some kind of crystal.

The Isharites advanced further.

'Now!' shouted Herin.

They drew back their strings and let fire. Both hit their mark. One of them went down and did not get up. The three that remained ran at them. Gyrmund discarded his bow and drew his sword.

Clarin charged at them, supported by Moneva. Gyrmund and Herin followed close behind. They backed away from Clarin's lunge, but two then moved in on him, lashing in simultaneous blows. He blocked them both, on sword and shield, but was forced to back away.

The third took on Moneva. He avoided her first blow and met her second with his yellow crystal sword. He smashed her sword out of her hand and moved in for the kill. Gyrmund arrived just in time. The Isharite had to back off, and now faced both Gyrmund and Moneva, still grasping her second sword. He feinted towards Moneva and then launched a savage blow at Gyrmund. Gyrmund blocked it and they held for a while. The Isharite seemed stronger. He suddenly raked his sword down the length of Gyrmund's towards his hands. Gyrmund pulled away. Moneva lashed in with her sword held in both hands, but her blow was sidestepped. The Isharite moved straight into the path of a blow from Clarin. It was too late for him to change his momentum, and Clarin's sword entered his chest and came out the other side. The big man yanked his weapon free. He and Herin had dealt with the other two. They backed up towards the door of the Temple.

Gyrmund looked up at the fight in the central square. There were only three Caladri soldiers left. They were being pressed backwards and were moving towards the Temenos, backing up one pace at a time while trying to keep in touch with each other.

The pikes were swung wickedly around their heads. The length of the pole and speed and power they generated kept the Isharites at a distance. One of the Isharite attackers got too close and the passing blade opened up his neck. Gyrmund saw him stagger back and grab his neck, but the wound was far too big, and he collapsed to the ground.

Ultimately, however, the fight was not even. One of the Isharites blocked a swinging pike and three others pounced in, making quick work of the soldier once inside the pike's arc. Another Isharite launched a blast of magic at a soldier's feet at the same moment he swung his pike. He toppled over forwards and was quickly finished. One soldier remained. He backed up closer and closer towards the Temenos. Arioc and his men drew closer, crystal swords in hand. Gyrmund dropped his sword to the floor and picked up his bow. Moneva handed him an arrow. He notched it onto the string.

***

Belwynn and the others put their faith in Elana, hoping that she knew where she was going. She raced along the corridor from the entrance chamber. The Temple was deserted and eerily quiet. When they got to the end of the corridor they passed through another door. They found themselves in what must have been the central place of worship. It was a circular room with seats, capable of holding about two hundred people, facing the centre. Here there was a dais, from where ceremonies could be conducted. The treated wood with which the Caladri had built the Temple shimmered brightly, illuminated by the sun shining in through glass skylights in the roof.

They stopped. Elana stood by the dais, still and silent. Belwynn wanted to ask her how she knew where she was going, but the priestess seemed to be concentrating. She swung to her right and moved to the far end of the chamber. Another door was opened, and Belwynn found herself chasing Elana down a second corridor.

The end of the corridor opened up into a small circular antechamber. Inside, a woman's body lay face down on the floor. Rabigar knelt down and gently rolled it onto its back. It was Dorottya, the elder who had greeted them at the Temenos. There were no obvious signs of physical injury. Rabigar put a hand to her neck, checking for a pulse.

'She's dead.'

Belwynn looked around nervously. Wooden shelves, from floor to ceiling, lined the wall. Most were filled with objects: metal chalices stood next to wooden bowls; jewelled rings and decorated knives shone out in greeting.

'It's here somewhere?' hissed Belwynn.

Elana nodded, but seemed unsure.

'Looking for something?'

A voice behind them.

Belwynn whirled round. Standing in the corridor was Pentas, the wizard who had joined them on the Great Road and who had fought with Nexodore.

In one hand he held a staff.

His red eyes surveyed them, inscrutable.

Belwynn looked from Pentas to the body of Dorottya on the floor.

'We had an argument,' he explained. 'Unfortunate,' he added.

Rabigar took a step to stand between Pentas and the others, sword in hand. Pentas took a step back and held out one hand.

'I'm not here to kill you or take the dagger you have in your possession. You must know I could if I wanted to,' he added, studying them again with a light smile. 'I am wondering, in fact, whether I owe any of you a word of gratitude. Last time we met, you will recall, I ended up in a fight with the dread Nexodore. I came off second best in the end, found myself trapped underground by one of his spells. Thought I might live out my days buried alive. Then, all of a sudden, I was able to break free. I assumed, at first, that I would be too late, that Nexodore would have found you and killed you. But he didn't?'

'Dirk killed him,' said Elana after a pause.

'Then thank you for saving my life. I will now return the favour. Arioc is outside. We can't let him get his hands on either of these weapons. I'm going to teleport you away. If you help me rather than resist, the easier it will be for all of us.'

A riot of thoughts swirled around Belwynn's head all at once. Could they trust this wizard? Did they have a choice? Who was he? But one thought shone through clearest of all.

'Soren and the others. They are at the Temple entrance. They need your help.'

'Very well. I will do what needs to be done. The quicker we do this, the sooner I can get to the others. Here,' he said, passing Belwynn the staff, which she reluctantly took. It was an ordinary enough piece of wood to her, with some runes carved into the side that were similar to those on Toric's Dagger. 'You can look after this for now.'

Belwynn nodded in compliance.

We've found it, she said to Soren.

Good. Don't come back this way, came her brother's quick reply. *Find another way out.*

Pentas got them to link hands. Then it happened again. A swirling feeling in the pit of her stomach, the senses dissolving away, and Belwynn was moving.

***

Gyrmund witnessed the fall of the last Caladri defender of Edeleny, surrounded and brought down by the Isharite attackers. Herin told everyone to retreat into the Temple. If they took their stand inside, the Isharites couldn't surround them and would have to force their way in through the small opening.

Of course, that was without adding magic into the equation. The Isharites approached. Gyrmund could see them gather outside. Then one of the wizards sent a blast of magic towards the door. Gyrmund grabbed at Moneva to shield her, but a sudden burst of white light in front of the door blocked the attack.

Soren. Gyrmund had no idea what had happened up in the Temenos. He hadn't liked it one bit. But obviously the result was that Soren had his powers back.

Soren put a shield up in front of the door, made up of the same bright white light.

'Get into the Temple and find the others,' he said. 'They've got the staff. I'll hold this for as long as I can.'

But it was no longer. The white shield was exploded away. Then Soren buckled over, crying out in pain. He seemed to be gripped by some magic. He whined in pain and sank to his knees, head on the floor. A couple of figures approached the doorway. A wizard was concentrating on Soren, holding him down. Next to him stood Arioc, sword in hand. He peered in.

'Well, well,' he said, looking from the dead bodies of his soldiers lying on the floor to the group huddled in the doorway. 'I didn't expect to find this. I have strict instructions from Lord Erkindrix to kill every Caladri I find. But he didn't say anything about humans.'

He put on a puzzled face, in mock consideration of the situation. Herin was standing on one side of the door. Gyrmund saw him gripping the hilt tight as if ready to take a swing. If he did, Gyrmund was sure they would all be dead in seconds.

'I'll tell you what,' said Arioc, apparently enjoying the confrontation so much that he gave a smile. 'You surrender now, lay down your arms and I will spare your lives. And his,' he said, gesturing towards Soren who was still pinned to the floor.

They weren't going to win this fight. But did they really want to be captured? Gyrmund's thoughts went back to Coldeberg, the cell in the dungeon, the feeling of helplessness. He looked at Herin, who was no doubt thinking the same way.

Arioc looked around at them, a smile still playing on his face. His eyes finally rested on Herin's.

'Well? What's it to be?'

Herin stood, still gripping his sword. *My life is in his hands*, thought Gyrmund. *There's a very good chance I'm about to die.*

He felt strangely calm.

Herin dropped the sword onto the floor with a clang. Clarin and Moneva followed his lead.

'Surrender,' said Herin.

Two weapons found, five still to go.

The Weapon Takers return in Book Two, *Bolivar's Sword*.

Many thanks to my family for their encouragement over the years—this book has been a long time in the making. Thank you to everyone who has read it and given feedback. Thank you to Anne Casey of Invisible Ink Editing.

CONNECT WITH THE AUTHOR

Visit Jamie's website to claim your free digital copy of the prequel to The Weapon Takers Saga, *Striking Out*

Website:

jamieedmundson.com

Twitter:

@jamie_edmundson

'The best way to thank an author is to write a review.'

Please consider writing a review for this book.

Turn over for a sneak preview of the sequel to
Toric's Dagger...

BOLIVAR'S SWORD

Prologue

SIAVASH PAUSED OUTSIDE THE PRIVATE chambers of Lord Erkindrix, a thrill of anticipation coursing through his body.

To be invited here was a rare honour, even for him. Ordinarily, Erkindrix only held meetings in his Throne Room, or the Council Chamber. The private chambers were only accessed by those servants who tended to his physical needs. They were nameless, nugatory creatures, who no doubt saw him at his most vulnerable and repulsive. Siavash didn't dwell on that.

No. Siavash, High Priest of the Order of Diis, member of the Council of Seven, didn't thrill at the thought of sharing an enclosed space with Erkindrix and his decaying, putrid body. He craved proximity with a God. For Diis himself, the mightiest deity of all, inhabited the body of Erkindrix. His eyes rolled beneath the Lord of Ishari's. His words could, at times, be heard through the reedy voice of his vessel.

Siavash entered the room. The stink of Erkindrix knifed through the cloying perfumes which were used to mask it. The Lord of Ishari lay prone on his bed. He had yet to regain strength enough to stand since the attack on Edeleny. Ishari had won a great victory against the Grand Caladri, but at a price. Scores of their magi lay dead, scores more had been pushed into madness by the confrontation.

'What news?' asked Erkindrix through a gargle of saliva.

Siavash approached the bed. He felt the presence of Diis—powerful, malevolent. It was as if his God, crushed inside the tiny, wizened frame of an old man, cast a shadow the size of a mountain. Siavash felt the primeval fear of encountering such a being; he felt the ecstasy of proximity to such power. Instinctively, he dropped to his knees.

'I can report that most of the lands of the Caladri are being taken with no resistance. The only exception is to the south, where a faction has organised a military defence, supported by some surviving magi. It is not a significant threat, but they are able to use the terrain to their advantage.'

'Good.'

Siavash prepared to deliver the bad news. He would enjoy the telling, but he had to be careful not to let Erkindrix see it. The Lord of Ishari's relationship with Arioc was a close one, and Siavash knew that he always had to tread carefully on such territory.

'Unfortunately, when our forces reached Onella's Temple, Her Staff was missing.'

'Missing?' Erkindrix spluttered.

'I should say, taken. It is unclear by whom, or where. But King Arioc has captured some prisoners whom he believes can reveal that information.'

'Inept,' Erkindrix barked, 'to allow such a thing.'

Siavash smiled inwardly.

'What other news?'

'Queen Shira's force has crossed into the Empire. Given her victory over the Rotelegen army, she should not take long to complete the conquest.'

Calling Arioc's bitch a Queen never fails to stick in my throat, he added to himself.

Erkindrix grunted. With what looked like some effort, he pushed himself up into a sitting position. 'The weapons,' he hissed. 'The threat from these weapons should not be underestimated. Nexodore has failed to deliver them, now Arioc fails me.'

Siavash almost volunteered then. To gain these weapons would be a trifling task, and yet give him success where the dread Nexodore and Arioc had both failed. But to leave Samir Durg, to leave his Master and his God, when he enjoyed such unrivalled proximity; that could be a dangerous mistake.

'Send Pentas,' said Erkindrix. 'He must retrieve them.'

Siavash's lip curled up into a sneer at the mention of the name.

'What?' demanded Erkindrix.

'A human? He can't be trusted with such a task,' he replied with distaste.

'Then who?'

Me? No. I must play a cautious game. My place is here, at the centre; at the very heart of power.

'You are right, My Lord. I will instruct Pentas. I will make sure that he understands the importance of these weapons.'

BOLIVAR'S
SWORD

War comes to Dalriya in the next instalment of
The Weapon Takers Saga.

Lightning Source UK Ltd.
Milton Keynes UK
UKHW011102301220
376033UK00001B/158